TRIAL

by Don M. Mankiewicz

TRIAL

HARPER & BROTHERS

PUBLISHERS

NEW YORK

for H.J.M.

and

J.K.

to whom

special debts

are acknowledged

TRIAL

1

On the west coast of the United States, there is no twilight. It is as if the sun were a nervous sea bather and chose to plunge into the ocean, hoping thereby to shorten the discomfort of entering the icy water.

Angel Chavez watched the sun drop behind the watery horizon, saw the daylight fade quickly, so quickly that where, an instant before, it seemed, he could see the smoke from the campfires on the beach below him, now only the flickering light of the fires themselves and the wandering trails of light that were flashlights being carried from place to place as their owners searched for wood came to his eyes.

Angel Chavez sat in silence, hugging his knees, on the landing halfway down the staircase that led from the top of the cliff down the face of the cliff itself, then out across an archway to the beach. With the coming of night, his presence on that landing—where he had no right to be—ceased to be a lark and became, in his own view, something terribly dangerous and fearsome. Angel shivered.

The beach below was called San Juno Village Beach, and that beach itself, and the stairway leading down to it, and the archway that carried the stairway over the highway and down onto the sand, everything, in fact, from the top of the cliff to the water's edge (except for the highway itself, which was the property of the State) was, as a sign at the top of the cliff stated, village property for the exclusive use of village residents.

Angel Chavez was seventeen years old, a slim, rather serious young man, a senior at San Juno High School, shortstop and leading hitter on that school's baseball team; but he was not a resident of the village, but of an area just outside its limits called Juno Flats.

Actually—though Angel did not know this—there was no law that barred him from becoming a resident of the village, and the State—which, having had two successive progressive administrations, had both a "little FEPC" and an antidiscrimination act—stood ready to enforce his right to live wherever he chose. He had only to enter the office of any real-estate broker who handled village property, obtain proof that the broker had property inside the village line listed for sale, deposit the price of the property, and then prove that the broker's refusal to sell to him was motivated solely by Angel's Mexican descent.

In the meantime, however, Angel Chavez was a trespasser, and, as the darkness swiftly became complete, the fear of discovery mounted in him. As if to prove that he was master of that fear, he moved down the stairway to a landing nearer the beach, and there, because he was not really master of his fear but only trying to prove he was, he moved to the edge, out of the path that would be taken by anyone going up or down the steps, and looked down at the beach.

The campfires were thick, thicker than Angel had ever seen them on other occasions when he had looked down on them from the safety of the path along the top of the cliff, and Angel knew that this was partly because this was the first fine night of June, 1947, and also because it was the night of the season's first grunion run.

The grunion is a sort of smelt with spawning habits not unlike the salmon. It is a tourist attraction because, incredibly, it comes ashore to lay its eggs on the wet sand left behind a wave. The newspapers, when announcing the dates at which the weather bureau, by abstruse calculation, predicts a grunion run, invariably explain the process. The female grunion congregate by the thousands at the crest of a shore-bound wave. When the wave breaks on the beach, the females remain behind to lay their eggs. This mission accomplished, they retreat on the following wave, which brings in the males, who quickly fertilize the eggs (dancing almost erect on their tails in the process) and then are washed out to sea on the next wave.

The grunion run is the occasion for beach parties at which men and women make an orderly attempt to interfere with the grunion's reproductive schemes. The rules restricting this interference are more than social usages: they are laws. One may grab the grunion with one's bare hands; that is all. Hooks and nets are equally forbidden, the only permissible equipment being a bucket.

It is not surprising, then, that most hunters return empty-handed from the chase. There are even some Easterners who maintain—half in jest—that the entire event is a fraud, like a snipe hunt, the grunion being a fictitious fish and the hunt a massive joke played by the natives on gullible visitors.

There is no truth in this charge, but it is true that the success of most grunion parties, as social events, has nothing to do with the appearance or nonappearance of the fish.

The voice of a Texan discussing this point came crisply to Angel's ears. "The grunion doesn't matter at all," the Texan declared. "The whole thing's just an excuse to get out under the moon with a gal and a blanket and a bottle of something."

"Could be, Harry," another voice put in. The voice pronounced the name as *Hairy*, thus stamping its owner as a native son. "But every now and then—"

"You ever see a guy at one of these things alone?"

"No."

"Or with another guy? Pansies excepted, that is?"

The native son laughed.

"Never see a man of sixty at a grunion run, do you?" the Texan asked. "You don't, and I'll tell you why. When a man's pencil runs out of lead, he loses interest in grunion, because there's nothing in it for him but a fish that maybe doesn't even exist."

"What about the Governor?" the native demanded. "You see his picture in the paper every year with a grunion in his hand."

"That," the Texan said loudly, "is nothing but a smelt, probably a rubber one at that. The Governor poses with it because it's good for business. A tourist attraction. The State'd get a black eye if the idea got around that all people at a grunion run were only there for a little n——!"

"Red!" This was a girl's voice.

"I'm sorry," the Texan drawled. "Forgive me, honey. I forgot you weren't supposed to *say* it."

"Well—"

The voice faded into mumbling and then into nothingness. Angel leaned back against the corner of the parapet. He was very tired.

Angel did not understand exactly what it was that, in the Texan's words, you weren't supposed to say. That lack of knowledge, he felt, was somehow responsible for his presence just a few feet from Village Beach, in a place he had no right to be.

The day had been the last day of the school term, and it had been given over, in accordance with a long-standing custom, to class parties and to the collection of autographs in yearbooks, except for the final hour. This period was devoted to a lecture so delicate in subject matter that the boys and girls, in the normally coeducational classes, were separated to receive it.

The lecturer was an earnest young man who waved his arms when he spoke. His subject, as he often stated, was "bodily corruption and venality," by which, he explained carefully, he meant any use of the sexual act other than as a procreative tool by married people. He did not describe the act itself, saying that he

4

was sure "we all know what I'm talking about"; and he touched but lightly on the moral consequence of its wrongful use, because to do more would be to impinge on the separation of church and state. For the greater part of an hour, he spoke at length and in colorful detail on the physical penalties of incontinence, illustrating his remarks with vibrantly tinted lantern slides.

When the purple hues of the final soft chancre had faded from sight, the lecturer turned on the lights and spoke firmly.

"I have only two more things to tell you boys," he said. "The first is that if any of you have indulged in the shameful practices I've discussed—either through ignorance, or because some older person led you to think it was 'smart'—then I'll ask you to remain after class and see me. I won't preach to you; I don't believe in it; I only want to help."

The clock on the wall behind the speaker's head clicked from 3:06 to 3:07, and the dismissal bell in the hall rang. "Just a moment," the lecturer said sharply as his audience started to rise. "One more thing. These lectures are required by law. I'm required to give them, and you're required to attend *and* to understand. If there's any part of my lecture that isn't clear to you, you must come forward now and give me your name, and I'll make an appointment with you to go into it further. Dismissed."

Angel knew that this final admonition applied to him, for, while he understood fully the penalties of which the man had spoken so graphically, he did not understand, except in the vaguest way, just what it was that he was to avoid doing so as not to undergo the penalties. "Carnal knowledge," the lecturer had called it, when speaking of what he called its illegitimate use, and "whole love," in speaking of its proper use between married people, but neither term seemed to Angel fully descriptive of the act itself.

Still, Angel did not go forward, partly because to do so would have been embarrassing, partly because the idea of putting his name down for further instruction was repugnant to him, but most of all because he saw that Stretch Wiltse did not go forward.

Stretch was Angel's friend. He played second base on the baseball team. And, if the lecturer's final point applied to Angel, as it did, Angel knew that his next to last point applied equally squarely to Stretch.

After school, as they walked together toward Stretch's home, which was just inside the village line on the way to Juno Flats, Angel asked Stretch why he had not gone forward.

Stretch laughed. "Why the hell should I, greaser?" he asked.

There was affection even in the appellation, understood by both. Ordinarily, Angel bridled and sulked when called such a name even in joke. But Stretch was his friend.

"Well," Angel said uncertainly, for he was speaking of something he could not describe, "didn't you and Annie—"

"Damn well told," Stretch said easily. "She'll do it in the back seat of a Chevvy and hand you a dollar for gas."

"Aren't you afraid?"

"Of what? Of what Holy Joe said? The disease?"

Angel nodded.

"I'll tell you something," Stretch said, conspiratorially. "Nobody's afraid. They talk like they were, but they're not. If you get it, you get it. It's not a punishment, just something that happens, like a sore arm, or a cold in the head. If it was a punishment, married people would never get it, would they?"

"Do they?" Angel had wondered about this.

"You heard the man," Stretch snorted. "Didn't he say if you get it you might give it to your wife later on? If it's a punishment, nature's discipline, like he said, how come some pure sweet girl can get it if she marries a guy that's had it around?"

Angel did not answer, because he could not.

"There's a lot of things like that, Angel," Stretch said, as they came to the driveway that led to the Wiltse house. "You say one thing, and you do another. Everybody does."

Angel could have gone with Stretch into the house, but he did not do so. Stretch's mother always made him nervous by talking to him about Mexican cooking and Mexican pottery, two subjects of which Angel was as thoroughly ignorant as Stretch was of their American equivalents.

He walked instead on into Juno Flats, which the village people called Mex Town, and through it, and along the road on top of the palisade that divided the beach from the plateau on which Mex Town and the village stood. And finally, just before dark, he came to the sign: NO ADMITTANCE. RESERVED FOR RESIDENTS. VILLAGE OF SAN JUNO. And, seeing no one, he went quickly past the sign and down the steps toward the beach.

Now, thinking back on it, he decided that it had, perhaps, been because of what Stretch had told him—you say one thing, and you do another—that he had gone down the steps. Perhaps he had felt, without reducing the thought to words, that it was time he broke some rule as Stretch and the others did, and that this rule was the only one conveniently at hand for the breaking. None of that mattered. It was now late at night, nearly midnight Angel guessed, and he was a trespasser, near the bottom of the stairway leading to Village Beach.

Behind him, on the staircase, Angel heard footsteps and laughter, and, panicky at the thought of discovery, he ran down across the archway and down the steps to the beach itself and cast himself down in the sand next to the sea wall several feet from the point at which the steps from the archway gave on the sand. There he lay, motionless, hearing his heart pound in his chest, as the man and woman whose footsteps and laughter he had heard came down the steps and across the archway and down onto the sand, passing not ten feet from where he lay.

The fact of the matter is that Angel's terror was largely unjustified. Mexicans were frequently found on the beach. Usually they were migrant workers from California to the south; often they could not read at all, and were genuinely bewildered when challenged. Sometimes they could read the sign but were naïvely unaware that their presence on the sand was precisely the sort of trespassing those who erected the sign were seeking to forbid. The worst that might befall a Mexican caught on Village Beach, in cold fact, was that while he was being ejected, chivvied back to the sea wall, and up the steps to the road, he might overhear an occasional insult.

But Angel did not know this, and would not have believed it. It was an article of faith in Juno Flats that a Mexican boy caught on Village Beach would be, if caught by day, tossed into the sea with his pockets full of stones, or, if caught by night, roasted alive over a bonfire.

Angel lay on the dry sand and felt the dampness of the ocean's spray as a wave broke on the beach nearby.

"We'll have to put that bonfire someplace else." It was the Texan's voice. "Or maybe we should just say the hell with it and go home."

"Aw, Harry," a girl's voice protested. "It's early."

"That's right," a man said. "It's only twelve-thirty. The paper said they'd run anytime before two."

"I don't aim to sit here and shiver," the Texan announced. "How about putting it back in the corner next to the sea wall?"

For a moment, Angel did not sense the full significance of what was said. Only as the two men and the two girls arose and began to search with flashlights for missing bottles, a comb, and other items whose absence they loudly proclaimed, did he realize that "the corner next to the sea wall" meant either the spot where he lay or a point so close to it that he was certain to be discovered in the search for firewood.

Momentarily, he considered going out onto the beach, walking quickly and cautiously, avoiding the many campfires, to the point where a high wire fence marked the limit of Village Beach. Passing the fence would not be impossible. If the area adjacent to it were deserted, he could climb it. Otherwise, Angel, who was an excellent swimmer, might slip into the surf, swim out to the end of the fence, and return to the public beach on the other side.

It took less than a second for Angel to reject this method of escape as too risky. Not everyone on the beach, he knew, had a campfire, and the consequences of stepping on someone who did not were, in his view, too dire to contemplate. Between the time of the finding of the Texan's bottle and that of the finding of his girl's comb, Angel turned, and went back up the steps, over the archway above the highway, and started up the staircase leading up the face of the cliff. If he met anyone coming down, an unlikely event, he thought, he would step aside and remain silent and trust that the passing might be accomplished without incident. That was a risk he had to take.

He climbed swiftly through the darkness. Once his foot came down on a beer can, and he would have fallen except that, knowing that such objects might be underfoot, he stepped carefully, and sensed what he was about to step on in time to shift the downward thrust.

He was on the second landing from the top, four flights, one landing, three turns from safety, when he heard noises from above. An instant later he heard a girl, stumbling, gasp, and a man swear, and a flashlight blinked on above him and made a cone of light on the staircase, widening toward his feet.

"Take it easy," the man said. "I'll keep the light ahead of you."

"How about you?" the girl's voice asked.

"I'm sure-footed," the man replied. "A big cat."

Angel backed to the edge of the landing, to that portion extending beyond the staircase, obviously designed as a resting place for those making the ascent, and remained there as the girl, with the shadow of light wavering about her feet, came past him. The man was coaching her, telling her to slow down, to wait until the light showed each step before moving. Then the girl started down from the landing, and a second later the man followed.

Angel started to move out of his corner. Before he could take his second step, a hand touched his elbow and held his sleeve loosely.

"What's your hurry?" a girl's voice asked. The voice was low, the question a half whisper.

Later Angel realized that he might have pulled away and run on up the stairs, that no girl could have stopped him from doing this. But, in that instant, he was paralyzed.

"You don't belong here, do you?" the girl asked. "Well, neither do I."

Angel gasped in relief, and spoke in Spanish, asking the girl her name, almost laughing as he spoke. She did not reply. He asked again.

"It's not that," she said. "Here. Look."

She struck a match and held it in her cupped hand, so that the glow lit her face. Her hair glinted blond in the matchlight, and Angel thought she was blond, then decided she was not. It didn't matter though. Whatever the color of her hair, she was not Mexican, nor half Mexican, nor one-eighth Mexican.

Angel stared dumbly and tried to pull away, but the girl still held his sleeve. "Don't go," she said. "I'm Marie Wiltse." She paused, and then added: "Angel Chavez."

Angel remember suddenly that Stretch Wiltse had a younger sister, that her name was Marie; he even remembered that Stretch had her picture on the dressing table in his room; but he had not looked at the picture, merely noticing that it was there.

"Where do you go to school, Marie?" Angel asked, mechanically, ridiculously.

Marie threw the match away. "Miss Daitch's," she said. Then she added, in explanation, she thought, and irrelevantly, in Angel's view: "I've been sick."

Marie Wiltse had indeed been sick. She had suffered, at the age of three, and again the previous summer at the age of fourteen, severe attacks of rheumatic fever. They had damaged her heart, and it was as a result of this that she had been sent, in the fall of the previous year, not to San Juno High School as she had always planned, but to Miss Daitch's School, an exclusive finishing school fifteen miles away, which had, in her parents' opinion, two important advantages. It was a boarding school, so her entire life could be carefully supervised there, and it was all on one floor.

Marie had cried for a week before entering Miss Daitch's School, and she had only stopped crying when her mother had promised her, vaguely, that if she "co-operated" she might, the following summer, have, as reward for that co-operation, certain "privileges" for which she might otherwise have had to wait until she was sixteen or even seventeen. "Like what?" Marie had asked, brightening. "Like going out on dates," her mother had said.

This evening had been, for Marie, the first of these privileges. The grunion run, her mother had explained, was out, because it involved the climbing of steps, which was strongly prohibited by Dr. Schacter. "An adult," her mother explained, "doesn't risk her life to see some fish burrow in the sand."

"But I can go out that night?" Marie counter-proposed.

Having just conceded her daughter adult status, Mrs. Wiltse realized she could hardly reassign her the role of a child by confessing that every moment Marie was absent from the house on the night of the grunion run her mother would picture her gasping up the steps between Village Beach and the highway. "Won't everybody else be on the beach?" Mrs. Wiltse asked brightly. "I mean: can you get a date that night if you can't go with the gang?"

Marie smiled. "If I can't," she conceded, "I can't. But if I can, can I?"

"May I?" her mother corrected. She detested pedantry, but *can* made a snarl too complicated for untangling.

"May I?"

"I suppose so."

At the time, Marie knew there was a great deal of truth in what her mother said, and she made an issue of that particular night mainly because, if she failed to get a date, she felt she could use her not having gone out then as a basis for extracting some compensatory future concession.

But as things worked out, Marie did go out that night, and with Greg, a tall boy from down the street whom Marie had idolized ever since it had occurred to her, at the age of eight, that it might be nice to idolize a boy. What made it even more perfect was that Greg was, so the talk at the coke shop had it, the property of Carol Beale, who lived next door to Marie. Carol and Marie had been Best Friends in grammar school, but the friendship had foundered in recriminations when Marie entered Miss Daitch's School and Carol (in fact, perforce; allegedly, by choice) had entered S.J.H.S.

Marie did not know that Greg, before responding to her rather transparent statement that "nobody wants to go out with a girl on grunion run night if they can't go to the beach" with an offer to take her to the movies, had been refused a date for that same evening by Carol Beale on the grounds that she had to visit a cousin, nor that Greg had discovered that the cousin was really only a third cousin, eighteen years old, and that the visit was to consist of a prom date at Capitol City Junior College. Nor did she know that, before leaving his house to pick her up, his father had taken him aside and warned him of Marie's physical delicacy. "Sam Wiltse's a close friend of mine," Greg's father had said, "so take it easy. That's a sick girl."

Greg had protested that he knew this, and his father had gone on to explain that Marie was sicker than even she knew. "It's her heart," Greg's father said. "She can go any time. Like that. I know," he went on, "that when you're out late with a girl, you're probably giving her a little loving. But no rassling with this one. It wouldn't be any fun to have her—well, pass out on you."

Greg did not know whether it was the fact that, despite Carol's defection, he felt somehow disloyal to be out with Marie, or his father's parting warning, that caused him, when they parked after the movies beside the cliff overlooking the ocean, to remain on his own side of the car seat, instead of edging toward the middle and Marie. Marie, who knew neither of these facts, assumed that his behavior was a reflection on her, and she grew angry and surly, and Greg became angry and surly too. And so it is not surprising that, ten minutes after Greg parked the car on top of the cliff, Marie opened the door on her side, thanked Greg icily for his company at the movies, and walked away. She half expected that he would follow, but he did not, calling after her instead. She did not turn and, as she walked, she heard the squeal of rubber as Greg backed the Model-A onto the road, and a second squeal as he set off toward town.

She stopped then, and leaned her elbows on the little wall, and stared down at the beach, dotted with campfires, and the moonlit sea beyond, finding a perverse romantic satisfaction in being alone on such a lovely night. As the minutes went by, self-pity mounted in her. She fancied herself, not without cause, the only one within range of her eyes (though not within sight because of the darkness) for whom this night would have no romantic significance.

Marie had spent the early evening with Greg, watching a movie in which Bette Davis had disobeyed her doctor to seek love, in which Bette Davis had all but courted death in a search for the one man who could make her happy. Because of this, and because she was fifteen years old, she started down the stairs toward the beach. Because, though fifteen, she was basically sensible, adult, as her mother had said, she stopped on a landing, part way down the stairs, and waited there for some minutes. And then Angel Chavez came and stood beside her, not seeing her in the dark. Unfortunately, this was almost the way Bette Davis had met her lover in the picture; the romantic coincidence was too great for Marie. When Angel started to leave, she stopped him.

There is more to this, Marie thought, than there was even in the movie, for we are both outcasts, both forbidden to be where we are.

"I know your brother," Angel said, knowing that she probably already knew this, saying it for want of anything else to say.

"He's often spoken of you," Marie said.

"I'd better be going."

Angel tried again to break away, but Marie, still holding his sleeve, sat down on a wooden bench in the corner of the landing. Angel sat beside her. He dared not, he reasoned, incur this girl's ill will. She had only to scream, he reasoned, or even to tell someone the following day of their meeting, and he would be as good as roasted on a bonfire or drowned in the sea.

"I want to talk to you," Marie said.

"What about?"

"Nothing much," she replied. Then, feeling a great surge of pity for Angel because he was, like herself, barred from the joys that were other people's, that belonged to insensitive people like Greg (she had decided, somehow, that Angel was not insensitive), she let go of his sleeve and reached out to touch his hand.

Startled by this totally unexpected touch in the dark, Angel drew back his hand. Marie's hand followed his, pulling her off balance. Her skirt, which adhered to the wooden bench better than to her body, rode up above her knees and, because this was instinct with her, even in the dark, she reached with both hands to pull it down. Angel let his hand ride with hers, and his finger tips came to touch her leg just above the knee.

Marie brushed half-heartedly at the hand, but Angel let it remain where it was. "Stretch," she murmured, "said I should never let a boy do that."

"Well?"

Above them the moon, which had gone behind a patch of coastal mist, emerged. Angel could see Marie's half-wistful, half-playful smile before she answered.

"Stretch isn't here," she said, her voice shaking. As she spoke, she tipped her face toward his, and the moonlight—as she knew it would—drained across her, putting half her face in silver light,

14

half in blue shadow. The face she saw, six inches from her own, was not that of Angel Chavez but of the young man who had made love to Bette Davis in the early part of the picture, before she came to know the meaning of love as applied to herself and her husband, who was a surgeon.

Marie Wiltse was a pretty girl, though later press references to her as a "San Juno beauty" were somewhat exaggerated. But her prettiness did not matter to Angel Chavez. What mattered was that she was white and female and that he, Angel Chavez, might make love to her here on the landing that was really a part of Village Beach.

The kiss was fumbling and inexpert. It was Angel's first. In the beginning, he contented himself with a light touch of his lips to hers, fearful each second that she would recoil from him. As second followed second, and she did not, he increased the pressure, driving forward and downward until he could feel the shape of Marie's teeth through their lips. Slowly, cautiously, alert to reverse the motion if she objected, he inched his hand upward from its position just above her knee, the hand pushing the skirt before it as it passed over her thigh, over the smooth cloth of her underpants, and came to rest on the strangely soft flesh of her stomach.

Marie stirred and tried to draw her head back, not wishing to end the kiss, driven not to end it by a new and frightening sensation, and yet vaguely, unhappily aware that she ought to end it, that this was not the way it had happened to Bette Davis in the picture. As her head went back, Angel followed it hungrily with his own.

His free hand, partly in response to primitive instinct, and partly because of a half memory of something Stretch Wiltse had said, went to the top of Marie's dress and fumbled with the topmost of three buttons there. Unable to unfasten the button, he thrust his hand between the dress and Marie's neck. The space was too small for even a small hand, and Angel's was not small.

It was the pop of the buttons and the clicks as they fell against the brick floor and the ugly sound of the tearing cloth that caused Marie suddenly to pit her strength against Angel's in a frantic effort to raise herself from half supinity in his lap, and, failing in the attempt, to rake her hand against his face. Her short fingernails scratched but did not draw blood. Angel, frightened and surprised, took his lips from hers. In the same motion, he took his hand from her bosom and, so doing, ripped the cloth of her dress again.

It was hearing that ugly tearing rasp a second time that drove Marie to force herself erect and to break away, to run across the landing to the steps. She cried aloud, and the tears and the terror caused her to catch the first step with her instep and to plunge forward onto the staircase. She thrust herself erect by straightening her arms, and started on.

When she fell for the second time, with her feet on the third step and her hands flung out above her, Angel thought she had tripped again. He ran to her and put a hand on her shoulder. When she did not move, he turned her over and put his hand on her chest where the dress was ripped away. He felt no motion, put his ear to her body, and heard nothing.

Later Angel was to ask himself why he did not, at that time, continue up the remaining steps and onto the road and on into Juno Flats. He owed this girl nothing, and, in any event, she was dead and he could not help her.

Instead he turned and shouted, in the direction of the beach, the word: "Help!" He shouted it many times, and finally a man came and struck a match, and, when he saw what was on the staircase, put a hand on Angel's shoulder and held him. Soon another man came with a flashlight, and then another, and suddenly there were dozens of men on the landing, shouting excitedly to one another, and below, on the stairs leading to the landing, more people milled, jostled, swore, and threatened. And one man called loudly for a rope, but he was drunk and tripped and pitched forward down the stairs, the people below breaking his fall.

In the end, it was a man from the Fish and Game Commission, on the beach to see that no grunion were taken by net, seine, or hook, or lured ashore by bright lights, who took Angel into custody. He was uncertain of his authority, but he felt justified in acting as he did, because, having uniform, badge, and gun, he was the only one in a position to uphold the authority of the State. That authority was plainly needed, he explained later to his superiors, to prevent a lynching which, had it occurred, would have been the first in the State in three decades, and the first since the era of "Chinese cheap labor" if a lynching is considered to include a racial factor.

2

David Blake finished shaving, dipped a washcloth in icy water and rubbed it across his face. He stared hard into the mirror and ascertained that he was indeed clean-shaven. It was nearly four in the afternoon, and David, who was thirty years old, and whose beard was not a heavy one, tried to remember when he had last shaved in the middle of the afternoon and decided it must have been when he was in the Army, just before his appearance before the O.C.S. selection board.

This, he thought as he finished dressing, is also a special occasion. It will not do for an assistant professor of criminal law to keep an appointment with the Dean of the School of Law even faintly bearded. Not even, he added bitterly to the thought, buckling his wrist watch, if the appointment is merely so the Dean can serve formal notice that the professor's contract is not to be renewed.

David walked from his room out onto the campus, and across the trimly bordered walk, up the hill toward the Dean's house. There will be other jobs, he told himself. And if there are not I can always practice law. But even as these thoughts came to him David knew they were untrue. The number of assistant professors of criminal law is a limited one; ordinarily the supply far exceeds the demand. And David knew that he would never practice criminal law, nor any other kind of law, because he simply was not cut out for it. David had, he knew, a neat and orderly mind, admirably designed for dealing with the geometric puzzle that is the law on the campus of the School of Laws, and utterly unadaptable to the lush tangled jungle that is the law in practice.

Terry Bliss had told him this ten years before, when David was a first-year student and Bliss an assistant professor, lecturing on torts. And at that time David had not believed him. But three years later, when Bliss had risen to the rank of full professor, and David was on the point of graduation, David came to understand that Bliss was right. And when Bliss had offered him a job as lecturer David had grasped at it gratefully, and he had remained on the campus ever since, seven years in all, except for two miserable years in the Judge Advocate General's Division of the Army, compared to which the civilian practice of law is an orderly Chinese puzzle. Now David was, after receiving the Dean's formal notice of the fact, to leave the campus and to begin—what? David shook his head as he walked, as if he had asked himself the question aloud and was confessing that he did not know the answer. He might, he decided, become a clerk for some large law firm, with the possibility of emerging from the firm's library some day to do trial work, become an associate, and then a partner, and suddenly he knew this was what he would do, and, as suddenly, that the trial work and the partnership would be forever mere prospects, something always to be considered as in the future, but that that future would not, could not, could never arrive.

The Dean's outer door was open. David went in. Terry Bliss, smiling, heavy-set, prematurely gray, sat on a bench in the anteroom. The Dean's inner door was closed.

"It may be several moments, David," Terry Bliss said, "before we can enter into the Presence."

David sat on the bench beside Bliss, grateful that the instant at which he would be notified officially that his contract was not to be renewed was to be postponed if only for a few minutes.

"Don't look so glum," Bliss said. "You've still got a chance."

"You really think so?" David brightened.

"Not a good one," Bliss admitted. "He's a stubborn cuss when he gets hold of one of his rare ideas. I think I've been on the wrong tack with him."

David mumbled his thanks to Bliss for having taken up his cause with the Dean at all.

"I've been trying to argue him out of his idea," Bliss went on. "That's impossible, even though the idea happens to be one hundred per cent wrong. But he gets hold of words like 'practical experience' that have a nice sound to them, and it's no use telling him that to demand practical legal experience of a law teacher will be to bar pedants, like you, their natural habitat, the campus. He just repeats, 'A man shouldn't teach what he can't do'—which I suppose he picked up at some convention of deans—it's the kind of nonsense you'd expect one dean to tell another, at any rate—and he thinks he's won the argument."

"He has won it," David corrected. "He's the judge."

"Maybe," Bliss conceded. "But there's another way to get at it. You wouldn't know this, having no trial experience, but there's an old lawyers' maxim: if you can't find a case to fit the facts, look for some new facts to fit the case."

David stared at Bliss in bewilderment. There were no new facts that could possibly be adduced to fit his case. The Dean had decided that no man could teach criminal law who had not practiced it, and David had never practiced it, and no juggling, no restatement—

Suddenly the door to the Dean's inner office flew open, and the Dean himself beckoned them inside, and moments later they were inside, sitting in deep leather chairs, and the Dean, behind his desk, was launching himself into his discourse.

He was, the Dean said, deeply regretful of what he was required to do. David was not, he assured him, to take the action personally, or to assume that he had failed in any way in his professorial duties.

"On the contrary," the Dean said, "your work has been highly satisfactory. But you will recall that you were hired when classes were large and teachers scarce. You must admit that. No reflection on you, of course. But it's true, isn't it?"

David admitted that it was true.

"I have decided," the Dean went on, "that when contracts like yours come up for renewal, they shall be considered as if the matter were arising *de novo*. You will appreciate, I am sure, that today your experience would not justify me in hiring you."

"I can't see it," Bliss said. "What more satisfactory evidence that a man would make a qualified teacher than the fact that he has been one could there be?"

"You miss the point," the Dean said. "His academic qualifications are excellent. It is his total lack of actual experience in the field, as it were, that causes me, unhappily, to conclude that his services—"

"Only that?" Bliss demanded.

"It is a serious flaw," the Dean replied. "The student has a right to expect that the man who teaches him has demonstrated his own—"

"But is that all?" Bliss said. "Is that the only reason David isn't going to be rehired?"

The Dean thought for a moment. "Yes," he said at last. "That is all."

"Now," Bliss went on, "do I understand correctly that David's contract does not actually come up for renewal until the fall?"

"All contracts," the Dean said, "expire on October first, just before the opening of the school term. Notifying a man now, in June, that his contract is not to be renewed is purely a courtesy, designed to give him time to make a new connection."

"Technically, then, the issue of whether he is to be rehired does not arise until the end of September."

David stared at Terry Bliss, trying unsuccessfully to guess where the older man's argument was leading.

"Quite so," the Dean agreed. "He will remain on salary through the summer; but, of course, he will have no duties. This will give him an ample opportunity to—"

"Suppose," Bliss cut in, "he uses that time to acquire some practical experience."

"Impossible," the Dean said flatly. "In three months, we can hardly expect that a man who has never practiced law—"

"Nearly four months," Bliss corrected. "In which time he could acquire nearly four months of actual practical experience."

"No," the Dean said with finality. "That would not be the sort of experience I had in mind. A man's first few months at the bar . . ."

The Dean left his thought uncompleted. David, who had felt a surge of hope a moment before, felt the hope ebb away, not so much because of the Dean's attitude, but because the Dean was so plainly right, because Bliss was merely attempting to find a way for David to comply with the letter of the Dean's edict while evading its spirit.

"I think you forget," Bliss said, with the air of a man making a telling point, "that we are not speaking of an ordinary graduate fresh out of school, but of an assistant professor of criminal law at the State University."

"I fail to see—"

"Suppose he had a letter of introduction," Bliss proposed, "signed by you, as Dean. It would be to the effect that David Blake, the bearer, is a member of the faculty, and so on. It would state that, in line with the school's constant efforts to maintain and improve the quality of instruction offered, certain faculty members, of whom Blake is one, are voluntarily devoting their summers to surveying the law in practice, working with attorneys in the field, making available to such attorneys as choose to co-

22

operate their own knowledge of the law as taught, and gaining for themselves and for the school a more intimate knowledge of the law *in vitro*."

David brightened. Put this way, Bliss's proposal seemed to him to have some merit.

"I think many graduates would co-operate," Bliss said. "I think they'd give David interesting and valuable work, perhaps even courtroom—"

"Nine out of ten," the Dean said firmly, "would push him right out of the office. Politely, but quickly. The tenth, I suppose, might use him as a sort of unpaid clerk."

"You may be right," Bliss conceded. "But," he added, "we'll never know if we don't try."

"How will we know then?" the Dean asked.

"I beg your pardon?"

"What sort of experience he will have had?" the Dean explained.

"Ask him, then," Bliss suggested.

"Not good enough," the Dean declared. "I don't mean to question his veracity, but surely you can see the temptation—"

"His journal!" Bliss said suddenly. "That'll tell us. He can use it as the basis for a written report when he gets back."

The Dean smiled and studied David narrowly. The fact that David kept a journal—that he spent the latter part of every evening recording what had happened to him during the day, whom he had seen, and what he had done, and where he had gone, and, above all, what he had thought—was, David knew, already known to the Dean. In a college town, faculty members come quickly to know one another's habits, peculiarities, and eccentricities; and jokes were made about David's journal as regularly as about another professor's weather-map keeping, or the habit of another of making elaborate "paper investments" in which no money ever changed hands.

"He doesn't have to limit himself to one summer," Bliss pointed out. "If you're satisfied that he's making progress, he can do it again next year."

"I'm not promising anything, Mr. Blake," the Dean said. "But if you want to try, I'll be glad to help."

"I really don't have anything to lose, sir," David said. "Do I?"

"You have the summer to lose," the Dean declared. "If you spend it on the kind of field trip Bliss proposes, you may wind up wasting those months when you could have been looking for another job. It's your gamble, and your decision."

David looked from the Dean to Bliss. Suddenly he knew that it didn't matter how slim the chances of success were for Bliss's plan, that it was his only chance to remain in the one world where he could survive, and that, accordingly, he had to take it.

"I'll draw up the letter," Bliss volunteered to the Dean, "and bring it back to you to sign."

In saying that, Bliss made it possible for David to consent in silence. This David did.

from the Journal of David Blake
Thursday, June 5, 1947

. . . after some argument, Dean Paley yielded to Bliss's proposal, and he is to provide me with a letter of introduction for use on what he calls "Bliss's field trip." So, in a sense, I won, but whether I won something of value or only a reprieve remains to be seen. Terry is quite sure his plan will work. . . .

I think I must face now, as I have known before but never faced, certainly never wrote down, that I am fit only for the academic life. Just why a man who is so limited should be an object of scorn is something I have never understood. If a man is a plumber, or a United States Senator, or a maker of artificial

24

3

David stood in the hallway of the second floor of the San Juno Professional Building, in front of the office door on which was lettered: LAW OFFICES, BERNARD CASTLE. Castle's name was the third of five on the page of Terry Bliss's list headed: San Juno. David thought of the polite evasions he had received from the first man whose name was on that list ("Call me back in a couple of weeks; I'm terribly busy right now") and the rude refusal of the second ("Jesus Christ, this is a law office! I'm not running any god damn earn-while-you-learn program!"), and the temptation to turn and go back down, out of the building, and into his car, and away from San Juno mounted in him, and only the fact that he did not know where he would go after that, or what he might do when he got there, prevented him from yielding to it.

Somewhere a bell tinkled as David entered. He waited a moment for someone to answer the bell, then seated himself on a worn mohair divan, picked up a folded newspaper someone had left there, and opened it. A banner headline proclaimed: RAPE-MURDER ON VILLAGE BEACH. Below it were pictures, one of an attractive "victim of savage assault," the other of a dark young Mexican boy "held by police." David glanced quickly through the accompanying story and turned to the sports section. The Dodgers had lost, but Jackie Robinson had stolen a base and hit a home run. David had never seen a major league game, never lived in Brook-

flowers, to say that he would be a total loss in any other occupation, that he could not survive in another field, is not a cogent criticism of him, nor would to grant the truth of such an accusation be to plead him guilty to being less than a man. But to say of a man that he can *only teach*, that he could never do successfully what he teaches others (successfully) to do, is to condemn him, and, in cases such as mine, even to cast doubt on his ability to teach and thus to force him into the very thing which your major premise asserts he cannot do.

. . . In any event, tomorrow I must begin. The nearest city of any size would appear to be San Juno. Ought I to start there? Or should I begin in Capitol City? My inclination is to start in San Juno. But is this because Capitol City, being larger, really offers more opportunities for me, and, by starting elsewhere, I leave myself Capitol City to fall back on? Isn't this really merely postponing the decision? (Ask Bliss about this. He will have lists of Law School graduates practicing in both places.)

lyn, and knew nothing of Robinson save the color of his skin, but he took satisfaction in Robinson's hit and his stolen base and did not regard that satisfaction as inspired by any racial bias.

"Yes"

David looked up. It was the first time he had ever seen Abbe Klein. Later he was to try, without success, to recall her appearance at that moment. But, because she was not Abbe to him then, but only someone who had come out of the inner office, he saw her without seeing.

"I'd like to see Mr. Castle," David said.

Abbe frowned. "He's rather busy. Could you tell me what it's about?"

"It's personal. " David offered his card. "But not urgent. I'll wait."

"It might be a while," she said, and, when David did not reply, she took his card, went out, leaving the door open behind her. Now, through the open door, David could hear the murmur of voices, hers, and a man's. Then, following the ringing of a phone, there was silence, broken occasionally by the man's voice. David picked up the paper again. In the Senate, opponents of the Taft-Hartley bill were filibustering to delay what the paper called "the inevitable overriding of Truman's veto." Russia, France, and England were about to engage in a conference to discuss the rebuilding of Europe with the help of U. S. aid as had been suggested by Secretary of State Marshall. A New Jersey city had traded in its old prowl cars and bought new ones, turning a small profit on the deal due to the whimsical operation of the price control laws.

"Jesus Christ!" the man's voice said. "What makes you so sure there'll be another bus?" There was a pause, and then the voice said: "I'll take the responsibility." David heard the phone being slammed down into its cradle, and Abbe reappeared at the door.

"Mr. Castle will see you now," she said. David followed her into the inner office.

Barney Castle, a big man in his fifties, sat with his feet on a battered desk, the sun streaming through the window down across him, detailing the lines in his face. He looked relaxed almost to the point of sloppiness, but there was about him, even in repose, a suggestion of vigor and power. He swung his feet down and spun his chair to face David. "What'll it be, Mr. Blake?" he asked. "I'll tell you right now I've got all the books I need."

"It's not that," David said smiling. "I'm from the University."

"All I want from the University," Barney said, not unpleasantly, "is they should please let me alone and not fill my mailbox with sad stories about how the library's going to hell if I don't come up with an extra contribution this year."

"It's not that either." David produced the letter of introduction that Terry Bliss had written for the Dean's signature and handed it over. Barney read it silently.

"The polite thing for me to do," he said when he had finished, "is tell you I'll call you this afternoon, and then not call. Then, when you call tomorrow, I'd be out of town. But why waste time? I can't work with people looking over my shoulder. That's all."

"It's your decision to make," David admitted. "But I don't think of what I'm trying to do as looking over anybody's shoulder."

"What then?" Barney demanded.

David hesitated. "Observation would be part of it," he conceded. "But not all. I'd help out with the work, too. But—" David shrugged, got up, and started toward the door. "Thanks just the same."

"Hold it." David turned at Barney's command. "You really mean that?" Barney asked. "About helping out? You really want to work?"

"That's right," David said. "Of course, I don't claim—"

Barney waved his hand and David was silent. "I may be able to help you," Barney said. "How long can you stay?"

"A few days, maybe a week," David said. "I've got a lot of territory to cover."

"What do you want to do most?" Barney asked. "Cover all your territory, or learn something about the practice of law?"

David did not reply.

" 'To familiarize himself with the actual practices of criminal law,' " he read from the letter, " 'and to learn how the principles taught in the classroom are brought to practical application in the field.' Does that mean what I think it means, or is this just some kind of boondoggle?"

"I want to learn," David said.

Barney stared at him. "I believe you," he said finally. "But to do what you're trying to do, you've got to take a case and stick with it. From the beginning to the end. Don't you see that?"

He sat back and smiled. David knew he was right, that the only way to see how something operated was to observe a complete operation. "You go on with your scenic tour of the law if you want," Barney said. "On the other hand, I've got something that you could work on right here, I think. Until you've learned something, or until you're sure you're not going to learn anything."

David found himself smiling back. "You said I'd need to follow a case from the beginning," he pointed out. "Are you beginning one?"

"My client's in stir," Barney declared. "And he doesn't even know he's my client. Signing him up is the first part of the case. I don't suppose they teach that at law school. Well, you coming along?"

"You're sure I won't be in the way?"

"I expect you to make yourself useful."

"I'll do my best, Mr. Castle."

"Call me Barney," Barney said. He turned to the receptionist who sat at a smaller desk. "This pretty girl," he said—and David noticed that she was pretty, in a sternly efficient way—"is Miss

Abbe Klein. I call her Miss Klein by day, and Abbe by night. Miss Klein, Mr. David Blake."

"How do you do, Miss Klein," David said.

She grinned at him. "You're not really a member of the firm," she said. "You can call me Abbe all the time, David."

"You two can get acquainted later," Barney pointed out. "Right now, we've got a client who doesn't even know he's to have that good fortune rotting in the local jail. Let's get moving." He got up and headed for the door. David followed him.

In the anteroom, Barney picked up the paper David had left on the divan. "Our guy got an extensive press," he said, indicating the picture of Angel Chavez and the three columns of copy about the case. "Not a good one. But extensive."

"That your client?"

"If he's got any sense. If not, the M.A.A.'ll get him." Barney signaled to Abbe to come along, and tested the office door to be sure it was locked after she had followed him out.

In Barney's unobtrusive black car, en route to the jail, Barney explained that the Mexican Advancement Association would almost certainly offer to defend the Chavez boy. "A bunch of handkerchief heads," Barney growled, answering David's inquiry into his reason for not wanting them to have the case before David could even ask it. "They'll tell you themselves that all they want is to see the boy get a fair trial. That's their policy. If he's guilty, they'll want him found guilty. If he's innocent, they want an acquittal. That's not enough. Not for a kid in the spot he's in."

"Why not?" David asked innocently.

"Why not?" Barney swung the car out onto the left side of the road to pass a slower one, then ducked back barely in time to avoid colliding with an oncoming bus. David braced his hands against the dashboard. Abbe grinned at him. "Fairmindedness is the judge's job," Barney said. "Maybe he sticks to it, maybe he doesn't. The prosecutor's job is to get his conviction. And, chances are, he has plenty of help." As he spoke, Barney cut sharply to the right to ease past a line of cars waiting for a traffic light to change. As he came abreast of the lead car, the light changed. Barney double-shifted and gunned across the intersection. "Look here," he was saying. "Here's the poor Mexican. Here's the prosecutor, straining his gut for a conviction. Up above it all is a fairminded judge, keeping order. Doesn't it need something else to give that boy a chance? You bet it does," he replied quickly to his own question. "It needs somebody working the other side of the fence, somebody who doesn't care about fairness any more than the prosecutor, somebody who wants to get the boy off just as badly as the prosecutor wants his conviction. And that's just what the M.A.A. won't provide." Barney thrust out his arm, and, almost in the same movement, turned left into a parking lot past a sign marked: OFFICIAL BUSINESS ONLY.

The San Juno jail, architecturally speaking, belonged to the village's middle, or Hispano-Moorish period. It was built in the early twenties. Had it been built twenty years later, it would have taken the lines of the "new jail," a building that existed only on the drawing boards of the city engineer's office, neo-native modern, of redwood, fieldstone, and glass, none of which is widely found in the West, save in Western-style homes and public building. All this David noted as he followed Barney up the steps, through the open gate, and into the courtyard. The general dinginess of the pink stucco, topped by the curved roof of bent orange tiles, was broken only by the sunlight glinting off the polished steel bars in the second-floor windows.

"Out of towners." Barney waved a hand at a group of people milling about a door at ground level marked: SUPERINTENDENT. "People around here," he explained, "know the superintendent's just the Mayor's brother. The guy to see is the jailer, Fats Sanders." He led the way up a short flight of steps and through an unmarked door into the building. David held the door open for Abbe, then let it swing back with a click that shut out the sound of the people milling about in the courtyard.

Fats Sanders' considerable bulk was balanced precariously on a folding chair which was tipped back to let his feet rest on top of his desk. "He never falls," Abbe whispered to David.

"You'll pardon me for not rising, Miss Klein," Sanders rumbled. "Do something for you, counselor?"

"Angel Chavez," Barney said.

"No can do," Sanders replied.

"I know," Barney said. "He shot himself in his cell. Let's skip the jokes today. I'm in a hurry."

"You can be in as much of a hurry as you want," Sanders said. "But you don't see that Mex."

"Why not?"

"You saw them out there." Fats Sanders gestured as broadly as he dared toward the door through which his visitors had come. "That changes things."

"Changes what?" Barney snorted. "A man's right to have a lawyer?"

The jailer's feet came clattering to the floor. "You know me, Barney," he said. "Ordinarily, I don't care who visits a prisoner. A lawyer, a dame he's sleeping with, the landlord to holler for the rent. Anybody. What can happen with a guard in there?"

"But today's different?" David asked.

Sanders stared at him, as though tempted to ask by what right he was taking part in the conversation.

"This is Mr. Blake," Barney said. "He may be doing some work for me."

Sanders nodded. "Today," he said, "somebody just might try to knock off my prisoner."

"Nonsense—"

Sanders ignored David as he turned to face Barney. "I don't give a damn for the Mex, Barney," he explained. "Not after what he did. But he's my prisoner." Sanders snatched a piece of paper from his desk and waved it in the air. "That's my copy of the receipt I signed for him. I'll get another receipt when I turn him over to somebody else—in good condition. Until then, that grease-ball is my property, and I figure to take good care of him."

"So much," Barney remarked, "for the philosophy of a guardian of law and order. Now why can't I see the boy?"

"Because," Fats Sanders said with an elaborate show of patience, "we've got to follow one of two policies. We let everybody in to see him. Or nobody. If we let people in, somebody's going to kick the living crap out of *my* prisoner. So?" He spread his hands helplessly.

"If you're so scared," David asked, "why don't you clear the courtyard?"

"There's a class of guys," Sanders said, staring at David, "who, the minute they get in a strange town, before they even send their laundry out, they got to run down to the jail and straighten out the jailer. Jesus Christ!" For the first time there was a note of anger in the big man's speech. "If I start pushing people around, it's going to be force against force. I got four cops here, and I can get hold of maybe twenty in the next fifteen minutes. How the hell long you think I can defend my jail?"

"You asking him how to run your business?" Barney demanded. "Well, I'm asking you. Do I get to see Chavez, or do I go over to the courthouse for an order?"

"On what grounds?" Fats was all innocence.

"On the grounds that you're denying a lawyer reasonable access to his client."

"Oh." Fats seemed surprised. "You didn't say you were his lawyer."

"I'm not," Barney conceded. "But I'm *a* lawyer. I want to talk to him about representing him."

"Not much of a fee in it," Sanders said.

"I don't have to take that from you." Barney wheeled and started to the door, signaling to David and Abbe to follow. "We'll be back with a court order," he remarked over his shoulder. "And the next time the city council meets—"

"Hold it," Fats said. Barney, in the doorway, stopped and turned. Fats was grinning now like a man about to deliver the punch line of an elaborate joke. "There's one thing you should know."

"Yes?"

"That Mex has already got a lawyer."

"What?"

"That's right."

Barney scratched his head. "You know him?"

"Uh uh. Showed me a card, so I let him in."

"Jiminez?"

"I don't remember, Barney."

"A Mexican?"

"I don't have to tell you—"

"Is he a Mexican?"

"Yes," Sanders said wearily. "He's a Mexican."

"All right," Barney said. "I want to send a note in. It's important. You going to fight me on this?"

Sanders smiled. "If you need the business that bad, go ahead."

Barney scribbled a note, using paper and pencil supplied by Abbe. Fats Sanders called a guard, who took the note and went out through a door in the back of the office. In a few minutes, the guard returned. The short man with him wore a dark, too formal double-breasted suit. His horn-rimmed glasses and round beardless face made him look almost Japanese. He did not seem happy to see Barney.

"This is your lucky day, Vince," Barney said, as they shook hands. "You won't get stuck with this one."

"If you don't mind, Barney," Jiminez said uncertainly, "I really feel—"

"Forget it," Barney commanded. "We'll take it over."

"We?" Jiminez looked at the others as if noticing them for the first time.

34

"Miss Klein you know," Barney said. "And this is my associate, David Blake."

David was puzzled by Barney's designation of him as an associate, but no harm seemed to be done by it. He accepted Jiminez's limp handshake.

"I promised the boy's mother I'd handle the case personally," Jiminez argued. "She's going to be upset."

"She in there?" Barney asked.

"That's right. A nice lady. Barney, I wish—"

"We'll explain it to her," Barney said.

"If she'd rather have the Association—"

"We'll let you know."

"Gentlemen," Fats Sanders put in, "I don't like to intrude, but when you get it straight which one of you boys is doing the job, I'd like my office back."

"I'm taking it," Barney said. "Right, Vince?"

Jiminez nodded his assent. Barney half waved to him as he left. "Let's go," Barney said to the guard. David and Abbe started to follow him through the door by which Jiminez had entered.

"Just a second," Sanders bawled. "How many people you need in there?"

"This is my associate," Barney said, jerking his thumb toward David.

"Since when?"

"Since right now."

Fats seemed satisfied. "How about her?" he asked, indicating Abbe. "I suppose she's your junior partner?"

"Look," Barney said. "Trust me, Fats. I won't let you down." His right hand went to his pocket. "I give you my word it's all right," Barney went on, withdrawing the hand and thrusting it toward Fats as if to shake hands and seal a bargain.

Fats took Barney's handshake, removing what was in the hand, and spoke quietly to the guard. "That was twenty," Barney muttered a few moments later, as the guard let the three of them through the doorway and past a bank of empty cells. "Good thing I'm not paying."

"Who is?" David asked, but Barney did not reply. They had rounded a corner in front of a cell. From inside, David could hear a woman's slow, purposeful weeping. The guard slid the cell door back, waved them in, and closed it behind them, stationing himself outside, next to the grilled door.

The weeping woman sat on a camp chair, next to a bed on which the boy whose picture David had seen in the paper sat. She looked up, and David could see that hers was a classical Mexican face, thick, sturdy, the skin somewhat darker than her son's.

"You're his mother?" Barney asked. "Consuela Chavez?" She nodded. For a moment, David wondered how Barney knew the name; then he decided he must have seen it in the newspaper story. "My name is Castle. This is Mr. Blake. We're here to help you."

"The other man?" The woman's voice was low, but strangely impressive. She had only a trace of an accent. "Señor Jiminez?"

"We're taking over for him," Barney said easily.

"I don't know—"

Barney put his hand on the woman's arm. "He's from the M.A.A. You knew that?"

"Yes. They are good, the M.A.A."

"Of course they are," Barney agreed. "But we're better. To them, your boy's case would be one of many. To us, it will be our entire concern."

"Why?" she asked. "We cannot pay."

Barney grinned. "Maybe we're crazy," he said. "We both like money, but we like other things, too."

David wondered how that remark fitted in with Barney's mumbled implication that someone else would bear the cost of the twenty-dollar bill he slipped into Fats Sanders' hand. But this was no time to ask. Barney, taking Consuela Chavez's indecision to signify at least conditional consent, eased himself onto the bed beside the serious-faced boy who, until this point, had said nothing. "Angel," Barney said. "My name is Barney Castle. My friend's name is David Blake. We can help you if you'll let us."

"I'll help," Angel said. "Any way you want. Just tell me how." His voice, like his mother's, was low, but he lacked accent entirely, speaking in the flat, nasal tones he had learned from his schoolmates, who had learned it from their parents, who had learned it back in Iowa, which they called, rather proudly, Ioway. He told his story under Barney's patient questioning, exactly as he remembered it, answering "I don't remember" when he did not remember, as when Barney asked him why he had gone onto the stairway in the first place, and "I don't know" when he didn't know, as when Barney asked where Marie had come from. Watching the boy give his answers, not quickly like something memorized, nor slowly like something he was making up, with an occasional hesitation that was too genuine to be acting, David felt strongly that he was hearing the plain truth.

"You're sure," Barney was saying, "that you met this girl by accident?"

"I am sure."

"You didn't make an appointment to meet her there?"

"No."

"Accidentally on purpose?"

"No."

"Stop." Consuela had dropped her head to her hands. She straightened up suddenly. "He's a good boy," she declared.

"No, Mom—" Angel began, but Barney cut him off.

"Good boy? I don't care if he's a saint. I just want to find out how that girl died."

"Yes."

"Well?"

"I don't know."

"What don't you know?"

"How the girl died."

"You were with her. You must know."

"I don't. I told you!" For the first time, Angel's voice was raised. "We were—well, making love—and then she ran, and she was dead."

Barney stood up with surprising speed, grabbed Angel by the collar and pulled him erect. "Don't ever say that again!" he stormed. "Don't say that about 'making love.' That means—" He glanced at Consuela. "You know what it means. You weren't doing that! Were you?"

"No." Angel made the admission almost grudgingly.

"What were you doing then?" Barney let go of Angel's shirt, and the boy dropped to his former position on the bed.

"I kissed her."

"And? Did you feel her here? Here?" Barney indicated the points on Angel's body.

Consuela's racking sobs were becoming louder. "Please, Mrs. Chavez," Abbe said. "They're trying to help." Consuela Chavez did not reply, but the sobbing subsided.

"I touched her here," Angel said, drawing a hand across his chest. "I put my hand on her leg. Then she ran—"

"No more than that?" Barney asked. "God help you if you lie to me, boy."

"I swear by my mother," Angel said. "It is true."

"I believe him." Abbe had her hand on Consuela's shoulder.

"Good." Barney nodded in mock satisfaction. "We'll get you on the jury. That'll make it eleven to one."

"Were you drinking?" David asked, sensing that an open break between Barney and Abbe would be purposeless, and there was no time for purposeless things.

"I don't drink," Angel said.

"Might be better if he'd been looped," Barney said, throwing up his hands despairingly.

"You wanted the truth." Angel was becoming confused and a bit petulant.

"I wanted something that makes sense," Barney said angrily. "He kissed her, pawed at her a little, she got scared, she ran. That makes sense. But she died. That doesn't. There's got to be more to it."

"There isn't," Angel said. "I've told you everything."

"You didn't put your hands on her throat? Could you have accidentally cut off her wind?"

"No."

"Barney." Abbe took her hand from Consuela Chavez's shoulder. "I can help, I think."

Barney stared at her, almost as if resenting the interruption. "All right," he said, after a moment. "Help."

"You didn't know this girl, Angel?" Abbe began, speaking no lower than Barney had, but more casually. "How is that?"

"I don't understand."

"She was your age. Wasn't she in your class at school?"

"She didn't go to San Juno. Some girl's school, I think."

"But you knew her brother?"

"Stretch? Sure. We were on the ball team."

"Did you ever meet her mother?"

"Yes," Angel said. "A few times."

"Do you know her name? The mother, I mean?"

Angel's face wrinkled with the effort of remembering. "I don't think so," he said. "Stretch called her 'My mother, Mrs. Wiltse.' "

"According to the *Standard*," Barney said impatiently, "her name was Gail. G-A-I-L. I see no reason to question the *Standard*'s accuracy in that respect. I also don't see any god damn point—"

"The name mean anything to you?" Abbe asked.

"I don't think so."

"Come, come." Abbe gave the impression that she was enjoying herself. "You can do better than that. You remember the Committee for Decency?"

"I remember a thousand of them. Sacco, Haywood, the MacNamara boys, Tom—"

"More recent than that. Right here in San Juno. About a year ago. A committee formed to investigate racial zoning in the village. It broke up after one meeting."

Barney grinned sheepishly. "I should remember, I guess," he admitted. "I presided at the meeting."

"Why?"

"Somebody was sick, I think. The chairman." He snapped his fingers. "Gail Wiltse!"

"That was her name, all right," Abbe said. "And it was sickness that caused her to miss the meeting. There's a letter about it in your files. Only she wasn't sick."

"Her daughter." Barney shouted. "I remember now."

"Rheumatic fever," Abbe said, quickly and without triumph. "The girl—Marie—had it as a little child. They thought she was over it, but she had another attack about a year ago. That's why they sent her to Miss Daitch's School, where she could be watched."

"It begins to make sense then," Barney said. "The running might have done it."

"Any sudden spurt of activity," Abbe added.

"He's a good boy," Consuela said suddenly. "He speaks only truth."

"It helps, doesn't it?" Abbe asked.

"It does and it doesn't," Barney replied. "It helps because it gives us a theory to go on that doesn't involve figuring the kid for a liar. But it doesn't give us a theory that gets him off."

"Why not?" David asked. "You argue it was an accident. Suppose—"

"Suppose nothing," Barney said heatedly. "Take his story as fact. He was fooling around, and she got frightened and started to run. Her heart couldn't stand it."

"Accidental death," David argued. "He didn't intend to—"

"Felony murder," Barney said firmly. "You're making a getaway after a bank robbery, and a drunk steps in front of your car.

His death is accidental. It may even be due to his own negligence. But it's murder just the same, because—"

"Because," David finished, rather testily, "death was a result of an event growing out of a felony."

"All right," Barney snorted. "I'll give you a passing grade on that. In this case, we have a girl under age, therefore incapable of consent. Ergo, a rape was in progress. Her death was one of a series of events set in motion by the rape."

"Why rape?" David argued. "A little harmless necking—"

"He felt her breast. Probably put his hand under her dress. Did you?"

"On her leg," Angel said. "I think I put my hand on her leg."

"You messed up her clothes, didn't you?"

Angel made no reply.

"What if he did?" David asked.

"Evidence of intent to rape. Maybe he didn't really plan any such thing, but—"

"No, no!" Angel shouted. "She was willing! I wouldn't force her—"

Barney's hand was a blur as, lashing out, it found Angel's cheek and knocked the boy back across the bed, his head striking against the far wall of the cell with a heavy *plop*. "Damn!" Barney shouted. "Say that at the right time and you've talked your way to the gallows!" Angel began to cry.

"Why did you hit my boy?" Consuela Chavez started toward Barney. Abbe stepped between them, brushing the older woman back. "He's trying to help," Abbe said.

"He shouldn't hit my boy."

Barney continued to talk to David, ignoring his own violent gesture and Consuela's reaction to it. "If he intended rape, the death, however accidental, must be murder."

"But—"

"What he did creates a *presumption* of intent to rape," Barney went on. "The presumption, of course, is rebuttable. All we have to do is prove he didn't intend to rape her—and remember, all intercourse with a girl under age is rape—and presto, the death is an accident, the jury is dismissed with thanks, and everybody goes home."

"How do you prove—"

"Easy," Barney said. "You take off the top of his head and show the jury just what his state of mind was at the time. And that's all that can be done, once his story goes to the jury."

"But this *was* an accident," David argued.

"I may have to clip you one, too." Barney smiled at Angel who, surprisingly, smiled back. "Accident growing out of felony, or attempted felony, is murder. M-U-R-D-E-R. Consent is no defense here. By God, you could come into court with a notarized invitation from Marie Wiltse inviting the pleasure of the company of Mr. Angel Chavez for a sexual act on the landing of the staircase at the time it happened, and all you'd get is a directed verdict of guilty."

David stared at the cement floor, ashamed of his own stupidity.

"Don't feel bad," Barney said. "You're an academic chap. You're doing pretty well for your first day out of the tower."

"Thanks." David tried to keep his tone light, to hide his humiliation.

"Let's adjourn the meeting," Barney suggested. "Preferably to some place where they serve food. Can we drop you anywhere?" This last was addressed to Consuela.

"I stay with Angel," she said.

"All right. But listen. This is important." Barney paused. Consuela and Angel looked at him. "Angel," he said, "your case is *State against Chavez.* You know what that means? It means everybody in the State—a million and a half people—against you. I want both of you to remember that. You talk to no one. Reporters, police, other lawyers, no one. Only me, and the people I tell you to talk to. You both understand that? The others—everybody—they're the State. Got it?"

"I understand," Consuela said. Angel nodded.

"Good." Barney's grin was infectious. David felt an incomprehensible impulse to laugh. "Not one word." Barney clapped Angel lightly between the shoulder blades. "Remember that, and you've got a chance," he said.

Throughout the long walk back to Fats Sanders' office, and from there through the courtyard, where the crowd of idlers seemed neither to have increased nor diminished, and across the street to the Courthouse Rest, a chrome-and-glass cafeteria, David thought about Barney's last words. Were they, he wondered, part of some bedside manner, merely a means of buoying Angel through his next few days, which might be the worst he would ever experience, worse even than the last two days in the death house, if it came to that? Or did the words have real meaning? Did Angel Chavez really have a chance?

In the cafeteria, after they had taken their food from the counter and carried it to a table, after the trays had been disposed of, after Abbe had been sent for forgotten items of silverware, and had returned, David put his wonderment into words.

Barney shrugged. "What do you think?"

"Why me?"

Barney crumbled a cracker in his hand, dropped it into his soup, and very carefully transported a spoonful of the resulting mixture to his mouth. He swallowed it slowly, as if doing so required concentration. "Because," he said, "if you'll take the case into court, I think we may get the boy off."

"Me?" David looked about him wildly, as if he had been struck and was looking for the author of the blow.

"You want to find out how the practice of law compares with its teaching. At least you say you do. Well, what better way could there be?"

"But I'm not qualified. I've never practiced—"

"But you've taught. And now they're questioning how you teach. I tell you, David, you couldn't do more for yourself than by taking this case and winning it. And incidentally, if this means anything to you, you'd be saving a man's life."

David sat silent for a few moments, stunned by the enormity of what Barney was proposing. "How will it help the boy for me to come in?" he asked finally. "What can I do that you couldn't do?"

"Don't be so modest," Barney said. "I have the feeling you'll make a hell of a trial lawyer. But even if you only do what I might do in court, you'll be freeing me to do the things that have to be done to give Angel his chance."

"Like what?" David challenged.

"How much money do you suppose the prosecution can spend to get their conviction?" Barney asked.

"I don't know. As much as they need."

"Exactly," Barney agreed. "And the defense?" David was silent. "As much as I can raise," Barney said, answering his own question. "If I have to handle the case myself, that isn't going to give me much chance to raise money. That would be too bad. Because there are plenty of people who'll give money for a case like this. People who like to see even a Mexican kid—especially a Mexican kid—get a fair shake. But they have to be asked. Sometimes they have to be asked twice. It takes more than a letter from a lawyer, who's busy running the case, to get the kind of money this case needs. The kind of money I can raise, if I'm not tied down. Come on, David, what do you say?"

"I don't know." David stirred his coffee, forgetting that he had not yet put sugar in it. "You said yourself it's a hopeless case."

"I said the facts as we heard them back there in the cell would send him to the gallows."

"Well, then?" David knew that he was asking Barney to tell him the theory under which a defense was possible, that, in so doing, he was implying that, if such a theory existed, he would do what Barney had asked. But, he reasoned, he could never be held to so tenuous a promise.

"Maybe," Barney said slowly, "maybe the defense just sits back and does nothing, and lets the State try to prove Angel did what he told us he did. And maybe—just maybe—they can't do it."

"But the evidence—"

"What evidence?"

"He shouted for help. Didn't it say that in the paper?"

"It did," Barney admitted. "But only Chavez can say that in court. Other people can only say they heard a shout."

"But he was with the girl. There were witnesses."

"Let me tell you something about the witnesses," Barney said. "I think you're going to be amazed at how few witnesses turn up and how thin and unconvincing their stories will be."

"I don't see—"

"David, for Christ's sake, this happened at night, on a dark landing, fifty feet from the beach."

"But afterward—"

Barney went along smoothly. "You want to know the best place to commit a murder?" he asked. "In a whorehouse," he said. "The very best. Second best: a stag movie. Why?"

David mumbled uncertainly.

"Because nobody wants to admit he was there," Barney thundered.

"Maybe I'm stupid."

"Maybe. Look. I've been on grunion runs. And I've been on them when I was married. *But not with my wife.*"

"Oh." David began to see where Barney was heading. "I suppose there will be some people who won't be happy to come forward," he conceded. "But not all of them. Not everybody goes to a grunion run with somebody else's wife."

"But I'll bet you damn near every party on that beach had at least one person in it who shouldn't have been there," Barney declared. "Give the first witness a good cross-examination; make an example out of him; the rest of them'll get the idea."

"But you can't do that," David said. "The questions you'd have to ask—they just wouldn't be relevant."

Barney sipped his coffee. "Let me give you a rule of law you won't find in the books. Castle's maxim, I call it. In cross-examination, you can ask any question you want, and get an answer, if you ask it correctly."

"Maybe," David said. "I wouldn't know. But even so, you can't build your whole defense on embarrassing a few prosecution witnesses."

"You don't build a case at all," Barney snapped. "It's just straight defense. They've got a body, and a theory about how that body got to be dead. Let them try to prove their theory. You fight them every inch of the way. You never concede a thing. Make them find testimony to put that boy on the landing. Let them produce all the guesses they want as to what happened there. Then pile on your own medical evidence—" He stopped suddenly, seeing someone over David's shoulder. "The man who just entered," he said quickly, "is John J. Armstrong. He's on his way from being captain of baseball, football, and debating at the local high school to the United States Senate. Right now, he's District Attorney here. Also Chairman of the Community Chest, President of the State University Letterman's Club, Vice-Chairman of the Republican County Committee, and Membership Director of the State Association of Young Republican Clubs. I leave anything out, Abbe?"

David turned in his seat. From the faint outcropping of gray in his crew haircut to the bright polish on his dark brown shoes, the young man who stood, hands in pockets, surveying the room, was the epitome of the rising young politician Barney had described. "You left out Director of the State Association of Methodist Youth Groups," Abbe said.

"O.K.," Barney said. "Here he comes. All ashore that's going ashore." David knew that that last was for his benefit, that if he wanted to decline Barney's bid to take part in the case, now was the time to speak up, but, though he was not convinced that he ought to accept, he did not speak, because he was not sure he ought to decline.

"May I?" Armstrong stood by the table and gestured toward an empty chair.

"By all means." Barney made a small ceremony of pulling the chair out. "This," he said, "is David Blake, my associate. David, I want you to meet Jack Armstrong, the All-American boy."

"John Armstrong," the District Attorney corrected. "You've got to remember, Barney, it's not my fault that I'm a native-born white Protestant. In my heart, I'm as good an American as if I'd just stepped off the boat."

Abbe laughed. "You asked for that, Barney," she said.

Barney did not laugh. "If you want something, Mr. Armstrong," he said, laying a heavy, unpleasant emphasis on the title, "speak up. If you just came here to eat and make bad jokes, go right ahead."

Armstrong sat down and looked around unhappily. "You representing Chavez?" he asked after a moment.

"In a way," Barney said. "David'll appear at the trial. I'm going to be the outside man."

"That so?" Armstrong's reply was automatic and not intended to question the accuracy of what Barney had said. But David knew that he could treat it as a genuine question, that he could reply to it in the negative, and that, by allowing the statement that he would be the trial counsel for the defense to be made in the presence of the District Attorney without denial, he was making it a fact, and the sudden acceptance of it as fact made him shiver. He gulped at his coffee to stop the shivering and swung his chair around so that he faced Armstrong, so that, by looking at him directly, he might be able to stop thinking of Angel Chavez.

Armstrong favored David with a grin that would, David decided, be a great asset to him when, assuming Barney's prediction to be accurate, he made his race for the Senate. "All right," Armstrong said. "Let's put it on the table. How do you want to plead the boy?"

"What have you got in mind?" Barney asked.

Armstrong considered this a moment, "A fair question," he admitted. "Actually, I'm prepared to go quite far to avoid—well, an unpleasant trial."

"How far?" Barney demanded.

"I'm coming to that." Armstrong's face assumed the expression of a man revealing a proposition so disadvantageous to himself as to make the offer of it a little shameful. "Actually," he said, "we'd be willing to take a plea of guilty to manslaughter."

"What sentence?" It was the first time David had spoken in his capacity as attorney for the defense. The moment the words were out, he knew he had spoken wrongly.

"That," Armstrong said flatly, "would be up to the judge."

"What would be your recommendation?" David amended.

"Ten to twenty." Armstrong's manner was no longer that of a man making an overgenerous offer against his own better judgment. He was prepared to bargain, David realized, willing to come down a little. With that realization came a partial lifting of the heavy responsibility that had descended on David when, by his silence, he had accepted Barney's identification of him as the defense attorney. Armstrong, David decided, was going to be reasonable; his reasonableness might well lead him to propose a sentence of five to ten years, which would mean freedom for Chavez in about three years. "You'd give your word, informally of course, that that's what he'd get?" David asked.

"Because if you did," Barney snapped, "I'd have you up on charges so quick it'd make your head swim."

Armstrong looked suddenly sick, bewildered, unbelieving, the way McKinley must have looked, David thought, when he thrust out his hand in a gesture of friendship and received the assassin's bullet. David was astounded at Barney's flat refusal to begin bargaining on most advantageous terms; but he carefully kept all evidence of astonishment out of his expression.

"All right," Armstrong said helplessly. "Let's hear your idea."

"If the charge is manslaughter," Barney said, "the plea is not guilty."

"If he's going to plead not guilty," Armstrong countered, "he does it to a murder charge."

David opened his mouth to speak, but Barney was already speaking. "That's up to you," he said. "I'm just listing the alternatives. He pleads not guilty to anything—"

"Anything?" Armstrong was visibly upset.

"Anything except—" Barney's hesitation was plainly deliberate.

"Except what?"

"Just between us," Barney said, "I have a pretty good idea that kid was somewhere around that landing."

"Don't strain yourself. He was on the landing. So what?"

"The landing is part of the beach. The beach is for the use of village residents only."

"So?"

Barney leaned back in his chair and stared at the ceiling. "Not wishing to defeat the ends of justice," he said, "I'd be willing to recommend to Mr. Blake that he suggest to Chavez that he plead guilty to trespassing."

"Trespassing?" For the first time, the District Attorney raised his voice. "A girl is dead, and you think the guy's going to do thirty days on the farm? What would people do to me if I went for that kind of deal?"

"I really don't know," Barney said, "and I honestly don't give a god damn. Actually, I've done you a favor. The State is supposed to make the charge, and *then* the defense decides how to plead."

"Don't teach me law," Armstrong snapped.

Barney ignored him. "I've given you free information," he went on, "because I'm a nice guy. I tell you right now: make the charge more serious than trespassing, and you're going to have to sell it to a jury."

Armstrong turned, red-faced, to David, and steadied himself with a visible effort. "How do you feel, Mr. Blake?" he asked, almost plaintively. "I think we might manage five to ten on a manslaughter plea."

David looked uncertainly at Barney. This, he assumed, had been Barney's objective, but, having achieved it so easily, Barney might still wish to sit tight hoping to gain a further concession. "Don't look at him," Armstrong snapped. "You're the one that has to go into court with the boy. How about it?"

"Of course," Barney drawled, "you're ready to guarantee that the boy will get no more than five to ten?"

"Oh, for Christ's sweet sake!" Armstrong was near the exploding point. "If you want to take the poor kid to trial, say so. I'll be happy to accommodate you. But don't talk to me like we were all second-year men in some two-bit law school kicking *State v. Doe* around for some moot court." He stood up, pushed his chair back from the table, turned smartly on his heel like a soldier executing a facing movement, and walked rapidly away from the table and through the swinging doors at the end of the cafeteria.

Barney clucked regretfully. "Too bad," he said. "He might have paid for lunch."

"Weren't you a little rough on him?" David asked. "Isn't it best all around if we don't go to trial?" It was the first time David had spoken of the defense as *we*. He was surprised that the word came easily.

"I'm not interested in what's best all around," Barney said. "Only in what's best for Angel Chavez."

"That's what I meant," David said.

"It isn't what you said. Now Armstrong," Barney went on. "He doesn't care what's best all around either. All he cares about is that he's got to be a Senator in fifteen years so he can serve two terms and still be young enough to be a possible President. He's

50

right on schedule now. A *cause célèbre* might hurt him. It might help too, but why should he gamble?"

"How?"

"How what?" Barney asked.

"How could it hurt him?"

"Suppose he loses the case," Barney replied. "And suppose six months from now, or six years, Angel commits another rape; or even commits some minor crime; or even gets accused of a crime. That's possibility one. Possibility two: he wins the case, but it's upset on appeal. People get impatient with a prosecutor who needs two shots at a murder case. Possibility three." Barney began counting the choices on his fingers. "He gets his conviction. Later on, a similar case comes up in the county, only this time it's a white boy and a Mexican girl. So if he prosecutes and wins, he makes some important enemies. If he doesn't prosecute, or if he prosecutes and loses—which is the most likely, by the way—then he's helped make one law for whites and another for Mexicans. The State is about fifty-fifty, Republicans and Democrats. A Republican doesn't need Mexican support, but he can't risk a Mexican blackball. Possibility four— No. This is a certainty. The prosecutor of Angel Chavez becomes a controversial figure. Armstrong's whole career is built on avoiding controversy. He's the man everybody loves."

"All right," David argued. "So we use all this as a bargaining lever. He lets us off the hook, we let him off the hook."

"Balls," Barney exclaimed, not angrily.

"Really." Abbe sounded more hurt than shocked.

"If you've heard it before," Barney said, "you can't complain. If you haven't—"

"If I haven't," Abbe said wearily, not smiling, "how do I know what it means?"

"That's it." Barney leaned forward. "He's not letting us off any hook," he said. "His proposition is for us to trade away our guy's freedom for his own political advantage."

"But we'll be saving his life."

"By giving him a five-year bit."

"If we don't—"

"Are you presuming him guilty?" Barney demanded. For the first time, he sounded almost angry. "He's innocent, by God. Innocent until a jury finds him guilty and a court upholds the verdict. The only bargain we can make is to bargain an innocent man into jail!"

"That's theory," David objected. "We're dealing with facts."

"Like love thy neighbor."

"Huh?"

" 'Love thy neighbor.' That's another theory. Like the presumption of innocence. But when your neighbor's dog digs in your shrubs, then you say 'that's just theory,' and you bring yourself to face facts."

"Do you love your neighbor, Barney?" Abbe asked suddenly. David found himself resenting her intervention, reading into it an implication that he was somehow unable to defend himself.

"No," Barney replied. "I love some and hate others and some I'm just indifferent to. But I don't espouse the rule. If I did, I'd treat it as fact, and not throw it overboard every time it forced a tough choice on me."

"You're gambling with the boy's life," David pointed out. "Why don't you find out what theory he believes in?"

"Theory hell!" Barney blurted out. "Don't call the presumption of innocence a theory! Don't handle it like company chinaware that you put away when there's real eating to be done. And especially, don't do it when you're handling the defense of a case I'm in on." He smiled suddenly and slapped David's shoulder so sharply that David's hand swung against a coffee cup, nearly upsetting it. "Let's get going," Barney said, standing up, "before we run up a cleaning bill."

David's punched counter check lay on the table. He reached for it, but Barney snatched it away. "Defense expenses," Barney explained. "Yours too," he told Abbe, and she obediently handed over her check. Barney paid the checks from a crumpled bundle of bills he produced from a pants pocket, dropped the change back into the pocket, and made a brief notation in his scratch pad.

"As long as the case lasts," Barney said when they reached the sidewalk, "you do that too. Write down every dime you spend. Not personal stuff, but on the case."

"Lunches?" David asked.

"That," Barney explained, "was a conference. Between you and me and the District Attorney."

"Where is all the money coming from?" David asked.

"You remember why I said I wanted you doing the courtroom work?" Barney replied. "So I'd be free to concentrate on raising money. Well, that works both ways. You concentrate on the case. Don't worry about the money. Abbe," he went on, as if it were all one subject, "you know Mrs. Wiltse, don't you?"

"I met her," Abbe replied. "When we were setting up the Committee for Decency."

"Would it make sense for us to go out and see her, do you think?"

Abbe considered the question for a moment, "What about?" she asked.

"I mean would she see us?"

"I think so," Abbe said. "She seemed like a very reasonable woman."

"What do you think, David?" Barney asked. "Is there anything else we have to do right now?"

David shrugged. "You're the boss," he said, not willing actually to take part in the making of the decision, but pleased that he had been consulted.

Barney's driving, as they passed through the city, through the open stretch of land that was called the "fringe," that lay between the city and the village, and on into the residential village itself, was more restrained, less savage than formerly, a circumstance

David attributed to the fact that he was forced to rely on Abbe for directions, and that Abbe seemed almost deliberately hesitant in providing them.

A battered open Ford was parked in front of the large, well-kept Wiltse house. Barney identified it as the property of the *Standard* and the man half-asleep over the wheel as Pete Wells, who had once been a foreign correspondent of some standing but was now, for reasons of health (the disease in question being chronic alcoholism), a member of the city staff of the paper. As Barney led the way along the sidewalk toward the break in the hedge that gave access to the front door, Wells roused himself to wave and call his name.

"You'll never get in there, Barney," Wells said. "Madam is not seeing the press. So I doubt if madam is seeing the ambulance chasers."

"She'll see us," Barney said.

"Maybe. If you do get in," Wells asked plaintively, "find out about the funeral arrangement for me."

"Sure," Barney said.

"I filed the name of the Pope," Wells said, almost to himself, "before they burned the ballots. Now I need pull to find out when they're planting a rape victim."

"Things are tough all over."

They moved on, up the walk, up the stone steps, and onto the porch. Barney rang the bell.

"Might be a good idea," David said, as they waited for the door to be opened, "to give that reporter the word. We might need a break ourselves later on."

"Uh uh," Barney said.

"Why not?"

"We want this funeral quiet and private, if there has to be one at all," Barney explained. "That's why we're here."

David started to say that he had thought their call had to do with what Abbe had said about the dead girl's health, but, before he could speak, the door opened. David realized with a certain shock that the boy confronting them, blinking in the sunlight, must be Stretch, the dead girl's brother, of whom Angel had spoken.

"No reporters," the boy declared. Then, seeing Abbe: "Oh, it's you, Miss Klein."

"Could we see your mother, Stretch?" Abbe asked. "It's important."

"I don't know. She said nobody. Who's 'we'?"

"I'm Barney Castle," Barney said. "This is Mr. Blake, my associate. Would you tell your mother we're here, please?"

Stretch turned and walked quickly into the house, leaving the door half open. "A public funeral would be murder," Barney went on. "It'd personalize the crime, make the girl real to people who never knew her. Also, a funeral means a public assemblage, and every one of those is dangerous from our point of view."

"If Gail Wiltse made the arrangements—if we helped—"

"The best we can get," Barney said, "is 'don't nail his ears to the post.' Every sanctimonious—"

Stretch appeared in the doorway. Barney stopped short. "Come on," Stretch said. "She's in the library." He started to lead them through the hallway.

"I'm sorry about your sister," Abbe said. "Terribly sorry."

"Yeah," Stretch mumbled, turning to face them. "That crazy Mex." He ran his hand through his hair nervously and said it again. "That crazy Mex." There was no rancor in his words.

Gail Wiltse rose mechanically to greet Abbe as they entered. She smiled, but with great effort. That her eyes were red was, to David, only to be expected, but he was surprised that the redness had spread to the rest of her face. He had never, he decided, seen anyone who had cried that much.

A small drab man got up from a footstool in a dark corner of the room and came forward. "My husband," Gail Wiltse said. Abbe completed the introductions, and the five of them, Stretch having gone out without speaking, sat in a semicircle of easy chairs facing the empty fireplace.

"How do I do?" Gail Wiltse echoed Barney's meaningless question. "My hair's a mess," she said, brushing the gray strands back from her forehead. "I keep thinking of something Ralph Castillo said years ago. You know Ralph?"

"I do," Barney said. "But Mr. Blake here is a stranger in town. You know the type, David," he went on. "The aristocratic-type bigot, gentle variety. Full of concern and compassion for his inferiors as long as they keep their place."

"I've even forgotten what the meeting was about," Gail Wiltse continued. "I think maybe it was that we thought it was wrong to send the Mexican kids outside the district to school. I remember that I was chairman, and, about halfway through the meeting, Ralph Castillo got up and said he was leaving, but, before he went, he'd like the floor on a point of personal privilege. Of course, nobody objected to that. 'I just wanted to say, madam chairman,' he said, 'that you'll feel differently about all this when some Mex rapes your daughter.' Well, we all sat there, too stunned to speak, and after he was gone somebody moved to strike out his remark, and that was that. I used to think about what he said, and wonder whether, maybe, he wasn't right, and now I just don't know. I just don't know if I feel differently or not. But maybe that's because I haven't really come to believe in what happened. I just can't bring myself to accept that last night Marie—"

"You don't have to talk about it," her hubsand said gently. His words seemed to calm her.

"I do, Sam," she said. "It's important how I feel. I was brought up to regard hate as a sin. If I hate, then my bringing up was wrong—"

"Not necessarily," David said. "There are times—"

"Hypocrisy," Gail Wiltse said flatly. "But, if I don't hate now, then no one else has a right to. I wish," she added, her voice dropping very low, "that I hadn't taken the Nembutal."

56

"You shouldn't talk now," Barney said. "We'll come back."
He started to get up.

"No, please," Gail Wiltse said. "You're defending the Chavez
boy, aren't you?"

"That's right," Barney said. "Mr. Blake and myself."

"I'm glad. That is," she amended, "intellectually, I know I
should be worried about the boy, and I should be glad he'll be
well represented. But, really, isn't it enough that I don't hate him?
Do I have to worry about him too?"

David found himself studying Sam Wiltse's face, wondering
whether Sam shared his wife's principles, whether he could escape
feeling that these principles, in some way at least, caused what
had happened to happen.

"There is one thing we could discuss," Barney said. "The
funeral."

"If it was my own decision, there wouldn't be any. I don't hold
with funerals generally. And I won't have my daughter's death
used as the occasion for a know-nothing rally. I'd like to get an
undertaker to get the body out of the—" she hesitated, then
forced the word out, and the following words came quicker, as if
carried along by that effort—"morgue, burn it, and dispose of the
ashes. No urn. No ceremony."

"Would a local man do that?" Barney asked.

"I doubt it. I'd be prepared to fly the body somewhere where
we could have it done."

"She hadn't much of a life," Sam Wiltse said. "I'd like her to
end up as more than ashes in some dump."

"*She's* got nothing to do with it," his wife said wearily. "I was
speaking of a corpse."

"That's all that's left. I want it put in the ground. Someplace
permanent." For the first time, there was urgency, even insistence
in Sam Wiltse's voice. David sensed that he could not be moved
from this demand, and a glance at Gail Wiltse told him that she
knew this too.

"So I've agreed to that," Gail said. "That's as far as we've gone."

"To what?"

"To putting her in the ground. Someplace permanent."

"Mr. Wiltse," Barney asked, "do you care what sort of rites she receives?"

"Call me Sam," Wiltse said with an effort. "No. I don't care. All I want is for her to be put in the ground somewhere, with a marker, so I'll know where to go in case I'd like to visit with her, and maybe a tree. I mean, I could plant a tree, and when it bloomed, I could think she was a part of it, so to speak."

"Scientifically—" Gail began.

"I'm not talking science." Again Sam Wiltse's manner turned hard. "I'm talking how I feel. Maybe it makes no sense. But I've got a right to feel. You can't take that away from me, Gail."

"The reason I asked," Barney said, "is that if the funeral is held quickly, it might be quiet and dignified. Otherwise—"

"I understand," Gail Wiltse said.

"I'll ask Donaldson, if you like. He might be able to do it tomorrow morning. If that would be all right with you."

"Donaldson? He was on one of the committees, wasn't he?"

"All of them," Barney corrected. "Would that be all right?"

"I don't care." Sam Wiltse spoke as if each word had to be lifted, carried some distance, and then dropped into place.

Barney stood up. "Sunrise?"

"It would be nice, at that," Mrs. Wiltse said.

"Hell," her husband remarked. "Why waste half the day waiting around? How about four in the morning? I got a flashlight."

It was surprising, David thought, that this not old, but old-seeming, man was capable of the most angry of angers, the one that expresses itself not in a sarcasm of inflection, but in ironic words delivered with apparent, almost negligent, sincerity.

"The graveyard back of the Unitarian Church then," Barney

said. "I'll call if it *can't* be there. The less we talk about this," he added, "the better."

from the Journal of David Blake
Friday, June 6, 1947

. . . but whether it was that Barney said what he said with such an easy, certain authority, or whether it was that what he said made sense, no longer matters. In any event, I did not contest his position with Armstrong, and, as a result, it is more or less certain that the boy, Chavez, will stand trial. And, if Barney means what he said earlier—and I have somehow the impression that he is a man who does mean what he says—I will be his attorney.

So it would seem that Bliss's position has been vindicated as against Dean Paley's. The conduct of a murder case can hardly be called routine, or compared with free clerking.

But in a sense, too, today's events have given some support to the Dean's demand for practical experience. At least in this sense: that there is a wide gap between the law as taught and the law as practiced. Bargaining with the District Attorney is not likely to be covered in a course in Criminal Law, yet it is frequently an important part of the defense. From the way in which Barney and Armstrong conducted it, it appeared to be a purely routine procedure. That is, while this particular bargaining session may have been conducted in an unusual manner, it was certainly routine that there should have been one.

And what would happen to the author of a text on C.L. if he undertook to cover such subjects as obtaining access to a prospective client by greasing the jailer? Or to the examiner if he included among the questions to be answered: Your client is accused of a sensational murder. The victim's mother is willing to hear your advice on the question of a funeral. What advice do you give? (1000 words.)

I begin to believe that the principal difference between taught law and practiced law, however, is not the theoretical nature of the one as against the practical nature of the other. It is that taught law is static. The situation is frozen, and the possibilities of various acts are explored. But in reality the situation constantly changes, and to choose one of several possible acts alters the situation in such a way that the other choices become meaningless. And no comparisons are ever possible. Thus, when Barney induced Jiminez to withdraw, all the choices which Jiminez might have made became impossible. Specifically, we can never ask how Jiminez might have conducted the trial because, had it been Jiminez and not Barney who sat at the table when Armstrong made his proposition, there might never have been a trial.

Not only does the client's position change constantly, but the personal position of the lawyer, and his relationship to other people, is likewise volatile. This morning, when I waited in the anteroom, Abbe Klein was only a device who took my message to the inner office, and Bernard Castle was just a voice asking someone how he knew there would be another bus. And now Barney and I are to be partners in a venture of high importance. (It would be theatrical to say that a human life is at stake, but that is the simple truth.)

The relationship between Barney and Abbe is an interesting one. She seems to have very little to say, but that little is likely to be important. She . . .

4

The sun was invisible in the early morning mist, but its light made half the mist that overhung San Juno white and the rest gray. The mourners stood to the west of the open grave, facing across the grave into the pallid sun. Between them and the sunlight stood the naked girders that, with the low bulk of the cellar, constituted the First Unitarian Church of San Juno. In that cellar the congregation had met and grown and prospered and raised a sum sufficient to begin (though not to complete) the building.

David shivered and crossed his arms. On his right, Stretch Wiltse gasped convulsively. Because he was aware that the boy's pain was from his unwillingness to display unmanly emotion under the scrutiny of a stranger, David considerately turned and looked at Abbe. A tear wandered from her right eye, under the shell frame of her glasses, and down her cheek. The night before, Abbe had sat with David in Barney's office as he searched through a mountain of books for cases of felony murder. From time to time, finding something of possible value, he would dictate to her in rambling fashion. Her notes, when she read them back to him, were more orderly than what he had dictated.

"Ashes to ashes," the Reverend Donaldson intoned, raising his voice a trifle to say the words, then letting his speech lapse back into the murmur with which, after speaking a few words of personal regret for the deceased, he had entered into the familiar litany.

David looked beyond Abbe, beyond Barney, at Gail and Sam Wiltse. Mrs. Wiltse's gray hair, he noticed, was no longer disarrayed; he hoped she had received the consolation which women are supposed to gain from the familiar motions of arranging the hair. The redness in her face had receded somewhat, but remained around her eyes and across the bridge of her nose, so that her face was like a white mask decorated with a red horizontal dumbbell. Her husband stood with his thumbs hooked into his belt, staring straight ahead.

"And to the earth we then commit her." The Reverend Donaldson raised his voice to a normal speaking level; after the mumbling that had preceded, it had the effect of an outrageous shout in a quiet room. Saying the words, he bent stiffly, picked up a handful of dirt from the heap at the end of the grave, tossed it down into the cavity so it clattered, drumlike on the coffin, and gestured to Mrs. Wiltse to do the same. Unsteadily, but submissively, like a dentist's patient opening wider at his command, she crouched, picked up a smaller clod than the minister had thrown, and tossed it onto the coffin.

The Reverend Donaldson turned away and gestured to two laborers, who had been standing nearby, to proceed to replace the mound of earth in the cavity its absence had made.

"Uh oh." David looked up at Barney's grunt. Beyond the gates that divided the graveyard from the street, he could see perhaps twenty people, standing silent, respectful, and expectant, the men in drab topcoats, each with a black band, garter fashion, around his sleeve, and a girl, a blonde teen-ager, in a light tan school uniform.

As the Reverend Donaldson, leading the funeral party, stepped forward to open the gates, the crowd came closer. A slim, black-hatted man, apparently the leader of the group, signaled the rest to stand back, and came forward himself, opened the gates to create a man-width gap, and stationed himself there, holding the gates in position with his outstretched arms. "Ralph Castillo," Barney muttered. David remember Barney's description of him as an "aristocratic-type bigot." He looked like a remarkably well-dressed scarecrow.

"Reverend," Castillo said overpolitely, "some of us would like to pay our last respects."

"Stand back from the gate," the preacher commanded. "Have the decency to allow the funeral party to leave in peace."

"Are you ordering us not to come in?"

"I'm asking you to have the courtesy to let these sorely tried people leave their daughter's grave."

"Is the funeral over, then?"

"It is."

"Are we, her friends, forbidden to offer our respects?" Castillo asked in shocked accents.

"Call yourself a Christian?" a voice from the crowd demanded. "Call this Christian burial?"

"Quiet, Cap." Castillo returned his gaze to the face of the Reverend Donaldson. "Mr. Grant is a little excited," he explained. "His granddaughter was a friend of Marie's over at Miss Daitch's. He doesn't see—"

The Reverend Donaldson held up his hand. "Entry in this churchyard," he proclaimed, "is free to any man who feels God in his heart. The gate is never locked. When we have gone, you may enter, if you choose."

"Thank you, Padre." Ralph Castillo said. "Only—"

"Yes?"

"Would you stay? It doesn't seem right—"

"You need no minister if the Holy Spirit is in you," the Reverend Donaldson declared.

"We'd feel better if you were there."

Donaldson turned to Mrs. Wiltse. "My place is with her," he said. "But if she wishes me to remain . . ."

Gail nodded. "You stay," she said, so quietly her voice did not carry to the gate. "Maybe that'll make it less of a pep rally."

The Reverend said something under his breath to Castillo and then led the three Wiltses through the gates and away, the crowd parting before them, surrounding them with low murmurs mixed of sympathy and the excitement always shown in the presence of celebrities. Barney remained, as did Abbe, and David took this for a cue that he should remain too.

For a few moments the two groups stood at opposite sides of the high iron fence, the townspeople staring through at Barney, big and unflustered and the only person present wearing an overcoat warm enough to withstand the matutinal chill, at Abbe, trim, pretty, red-cheeked, and somehow vivacious and sad at once, and at David. Then, in the distance, a starter engine turned over once, twice, and caught hold.

"He'll be back shortly," Ralph Castillo announced. "Said he just wanted to go with them to the car."

"You reckon?" It was the voice that had questioned the Reverend's Christianity.

"He's an honorable man," Castillo declared.

Abbe pointed out the questioner, a spry gent of great age. "He's the only old-time racist in town," she said. "Talks about white supremacy, mongrels, contamination, while Castillo talks about real-estate values, neighborhood identity, integration, racial respect."

Donaldson upheld Castillo's announced estimate of his worth by returning. "Before we go in," he said, "I want to remind you that this is a place of God, not a circus ground."

"You're upset, Padre," Castillo replied. "I'll disregard the insult. Let's go."

The Reverend Donaldson walked with Castillo through the gates. The others followed along, David, Barney, and Abbe attaching themselves to the tail of the cortege as it passed.

When the group had arranged itself in a rough semicircle around one end of the half-filled grave, and the laborers had retired at a word from Donaldson, Castillo spoke to the preacher. "Might we begin," he asked, "with a short prayer."

"Oh Lord," Donaldson declaimed, "send forth Thy grace, Thy love, and Thy infinite mercy upon this gathering. Amen." Ralph Castillo withdrew a paper from his pocket and began to read in a loud clear voice.

What he read was a long poem, the work of the State poet laureate, a hymn to the scenic beauties of the commonwealth and the joy of living there. It expressed thanks for the author's good fortune in having been "here born," in having been permitted "here to live" and "nature's glory see and beauty know." Its final stanza expressed a hope appropriate to the event:

> And when my Maker calls me,
> The last great rendezvous to keep,
> May He address me here,
> For it's here that I will sleep.

In the silence that followed, Cap Grant cleared his throat. The teen-age girl sniffled audibly. Castillo stared at the ground, then at the sky. "We will now hear," he declared firmly, "from Miss Lulu Belle Fremont, who was president of Marie Wiltse's class in school. Lulu Belle."

The girl choked back her sniffles and stepped forward as Castillo went back into the crowd. She touched her hand to her heart and, looking down at the mound under which Marie was buried, called her by name.

"This is Lulu Belle, Marie," she said. "I came to tell you that we all miss you, even though you've been gone *such* a little while."

"Send your girl to an Eastern school," Barney muttered. David bit his cheek to keep from laughing.

"We will never forget you, Marie," Lulu Belle went on. "Your name will be ever green in our hearts, like the green hills that surround you now." The metaphor was unsound. The gentle slopes around the graveyard were still green, but they would turn brown with the coming of summer. Marie's name, though, David thought, might well be remembered for a long time. If—as now seemed certain—Chavez went to trial, it would be a case of some importance. The Marie Wiltse Case. Or would it be the Angel Chavez Case? He tried to decide, but the comparable cases he could call to mind divided evenly between those named after the victim (Gedeon, Titterton) and after the murderer (Judd, Borden).

"You loved the flowers, Marie," the girl said. "I'm leaving these here with you. They are a gift from your friends at Miss Daitch's. Each year, we hope, the girls who follow you there will bring fresh ones."

A large woman waddled forward out of the crowd and handed Lulu Belle a wreath. "That's her mother," Barney explained. "She wrote the speech. A Past President of the United Daughters of Pacific America." Lulu Belle placed the wreath at one end of the half-filled grave, took her mother's hand, and retreated as Ralph Castillo came forward.

"That was beautiful, Lulu Belle," Castillo said, facing the group. "And, Marie," here he turned and faced the grave, "she spoke for all of us. Though perhaps we couldn't have said it as well."

He turned slowly, dramatically, to face the crowd which indicated with its suddenly vibrant, rapt attention that this was what it had come for. Donaldson, sensing something of what was to come, moved from his side, passed through the crowd, and stood a little distance behind it, as if to dissociate himself from what Castillo was saying even before he spoke.

"A tragic thing has happened," Castillo declared in loud, flat tones. "The deepest tragedy is that it was totally needless. We saw it coming, all of us, and we share the guilt of it. Because we were timid, afraid of being called names, we kept still when we had a holy duty to speak up."

"That's the truth!" Cap Grant's shout brought murmured assent and an anonymous "Amen." Ralph Castillo waited for the noise to die down, doing nothing to stop it, but nothing to further it, either. "We were afraid," he went on, "of being called 'un-American.' My family farmed the land our city hall stands on, and I was afraid of being called *that*. Oh, I have a full share in the guilt. I allowed myself to be intimidated, the same as the rest of you did."

"Is anybody scared now?" Cap Grant asked, and there was a roar of denial.

"I'm glad to hear that," Castillo said. "Because we've got a job to do" There was a shout of agreement. "And we're going to do it!" Castillo yelled into the din, and the din rose to match his yell. "We're going to see justice done. And that's not all." He half turned toward the grave. "We're going to see that this girl didn't die for nothing. Marie, we're going to see that no other family in town ever goes through what your family is going through now."

"How? How are you going to do that?" Incredibly, it was Abbe who asked the question, her shrill voice cutting through the hubbub sharply and distinctly.

"I'll tell you how." Ralph Castillo seemed to welcome the question. "We're going to see to it that people live with their own kind, the way it used to be. You call that discrimination, I suppose. But how is it discriminating to keep the races apart? Suppose we drew a line, and the Mexicans lived on this side and the whites over here. Who's being discriminated against?"

David could see Abbe's lips move as she replied, but the words were lost in the patter of resentment. Cap Grant moved toward her menacingly; Ralph Castillo stepped between them. "Quiet down, Cap," he said firmly, pushing him back, not gently, so that Cap had to take two quick backward steps to avoid falling. "That's what they want," he said. "They want us to lose our heads and make fools of ourselves."

"Who's *they*?" Abbe demanded.

"The Jews." Cap spoke so quickly the words were out before

Ralph Castillo's elbow thudded into his ribs. "You're mistaken, Cap," Castillo said sadly. "This isn't race against race. This is the peacelovers against the troublemakers."

"Peacelover?" Abbe hurried to speak before the crowd noise could boil up to hide her words. "You're hollering for blood!"

"Because I want to see justice done?"

The Reverend Donaldson came forward. "I will not have this place defamed by ugly wrangling," he declared. "If you've finished your—ah, memorial, I suggest that you leave quietly."

"He's right," Castillo said. "Nothing of this sort would have happened except for . . ." He let his voice trail off as he looked at Abbe. "So, if you'll make a short prayer, Padre, we'll all leave."

"The Lord make his countenance to shine upon you," the Reverend Donaldson said, overgently, "and give you peace. Amen."

"The mob's in business," Barney said gloomily as the three of them stood with the Reverend Donaldson watching the crowd file through the gates. "They won't break up when they leave. They'll go downtown, and there'll be more to join them, and they'll hold a meeting. 'Let the law take its course,' Castillo'll say, and everybody'll nod. Then somebody'll say it would give the town a black eye if they lynched the Mex. And everybody'll agree with that. Then Castillo'll say: 'He'll hang anyhow, so let it be a gallows instead of a tree.' And they'll agree to that, too. But all the time they're agreeing, they'll be looking around for a likely tree."

"Surely not," the Reverend Donaldson argued. "Surely Mr. Castillo's too wise to let them get out of hand."

Barney sullied the hallowed soil by spitting on it. "You ever ask your parishioners please to stop putting buttons in the collection plate?" he asked.

"No."

"If you did, it would just give them ideas. You don't want buttons, so you don't talk about it. But every time Castillo says let

68

the law take its course, he's reminding half those yahoos how much fun it would be *not* to let the law take its course."

"I hope you're wrong," the preacher said.

"I hope your churchyard doesn't get flooded next spring."

"It always does," the Reverend Donaldson said. Barney was silent. "Oh," Donaldson said finally. "I see. Well, I hope you're wrong just the same." He shook Barney's hand, nodded to David and Abbe, and departed.

"You responsible for this?" Barney asked, withdrawing a folded newspaper page from his overcoat pocket and handing it to David. David opened it. It was that morning's *Standard*. The headline, in type somewhat larger than that which had announced the "rape-murder" read: SECRET RITES FOR 'MARIE'!! The lead paragraph of the story gave the time and place and the family's request for privacy.

"Of course not," David snapped angrily. "I—"

"Don't get your water hot," Barney replied. "You suggested giving the story to Wells. Abbe?"

"No."

"I didn't think it was either one of you," Barney said genially. "I got my own candidate."

"Sam Wiltse," Abbe said flatly.

"Sure," Barney said. "He was being cheated out of the center of the stage when, for the first time, he had a right to it. And don't forget, he was the one who insisted on a funeral."

"I guess so," David said. "I guess it has to be him."

They began to walk down the little hill toward the spot where Barney had left his car. "At least," Barney said, "we know who we can't trust. That's something you never learn cheap."

"And how much co-operation," Abbe asked of no one in particular, "does the defendant usually get from the victim's parents?"

"Let's get down to the jail," Barney said. "We've got to push old fat butt into calling the Governor for troops."

Sanders was not in his office. He had, a policeman sitting behind his desk informed them, set up shop in an empty second-floor cell. "This here," the policeman said, "is too close to the courtyard." At Barney's insistence, the policeman phoned Sanders, asking permission to send Barney, David, and Abbe up. "O.K.," he reported, putting the phone down. "Sanders said he didn't see any reason for it, but the Mayor's there, and he gave the O.K."

The policeman led them through a cell block, and up a flight of stone stairs. "The Mayor," Barney said quickly as they walked, "is an old fool. Used to be chairman of the Realty Board. They kicked him upstairs when he started to turn senile." David nodded.

The cell in which Fats Sanders was making his temporary office was somewhat smaller than the one in which David had met Angel. In addition to the cot and wooden chair, which seemed to be standard equipment, a board table had been brought in, and a telephone placed on it. The policeman opened the door to admit them, and Barney made the introductions.

"I'm glad you're here, Barney," Mayor Morgan said, smiling vaguely. "Maybe you can convince Sanders here that he ought to call for troops."

"When the time comes, I'll call," Sanders said.

"By that time," Barney objected mildly, "my boy Chavez—"

"*My* boy Chavez," Sanders corrected. "He's my responsibility. I'm in charge."

"Of course you are," the Mayor soothed. "And you'll be in charge of the troops, when the Governor sends them."

"Won't be any troops," Sanders snapped.

Morgan threw up his hands in a gesture that, like all his gestures, seemed exaggerated. "He suspects me, Barney," he said. "You tell him. Tell him what I want. You know me."

"What the Honorable John wants," Barney said, "is peace at any price."

"Don't fast talk me," Sanders shouted. "Don't think you can joggle me into a wrong move. This is my jail. I'll call for the troops when I need them. Not before."

"A little while before," Abbe added helpfully.

"Huh?"

"Where are the troops?"

"Capitol City." Sanders blinked. "Oh. Yeah. I'll call three hours ahead of time. So they'll be *here* when I need 'em."

"Then what the hell's the matter with you, Fats?" Morgan demanded. "You may not have three hours, even now."

"You relieving me from duty?" Sanders asked affably.

"You know I'm not."

"Damn good and well told I know it," Fats remarked. "You're where you are because the people that count like you, and I'm one of the people that count."

"I'm not arguing with you."

"Don't."

"But I'll tell you something, Fats." Morgan lowered his voice to give his remarks an air of the confidential, though his voice still filled the cell. "There are people in town—influential people —who want to make this a sort of artists' colony. Like that place in California."

"Carmel," Abbe supplied.

"So?"

"They've got some colleges interested in running summer sessions here. That'd start it off. Next thing you know, there'd be little shops, a theater, pottery stands, everything. Those people have money."

"Artists have money," Sanders reviewed, "so I should call the Governor. You'll have to make it a lot plainer. I never got past the sixth—"

"All that money could do a lot for this town," Morgan went on. "And we'll never see a dime of it if anything happens to that boy."

"How you figure that?" Sanders seemed almost interested.

"Those people—they just wouldn't go for that kind of town."

"That's right," Barney said. "Artists are intellectuals. They think one man's as good as another. Of course," he added, "we know different, you and I."

"Think of it." Morgan tried to press home the advantage. "A bigger population. Bigger assessments. A new jail. We'd need it, and we'd have the money to pay for it. We'd need more guards. A deputy, maybe."

"Those jobs would be mine?" Sanders was openly impressed.

Morgan nodded. David watched Fats Sanders and saw, or fancied he saw, the process whereby the big man weighed the conflicting factors, his own prestige, on the one hand, on the other, the patronage, if what the Mayor said was true. "I'll think it over," he said.

"The crowd's turning ugly," the Mayor remonstrated.

"I said I'll think about it." Sanders gestured toward the door. "Leave me alone," he commanded. "I got work to do."

The Mayor looked at Barney, who shrugged and stood up. "Remember, Fats," Barney said. "The worst move you could make would be to call for the troops too late. Worse than not calling at all."

Sanders stared at the phone on the table. "I got a fine sense of timing," he said. David, Barney, and Abbe followed the Mayor out.

"You think he'll call?" David asked Mayor Morgan as they stood in the hallway outside the cell.

"He will," Morgan said. "Thanks to Barney." Barney made a grunt of surprise. "He trusts you, Barney," the Mayor explained. "Not your motives. Your judgment. It may cost us a new jail, but your boy'll get hung by a professional."

"If some amateur doesn't grab him first," Barney added.

The Mayor frowned. "Let's go down to Chavez's cell," he proposed, "and see what things look like. I'll admit I'm nervous."

At the foot of the stairs a guard stood at the entry to the cell block. He carried, in addition to the usual side arms and billy, a cumbersome riot gun. Another guard stood outside the cell itself.

He also carried a riot gun. He recognized the Mayor, greeted him, and opened the door to admit the party, clanging it shut when Abbe, the last to enter, was inside.

Angel Chavez sat bolt upright on the bed. His mother knelt next to him, facing him, so that her face could not be seen. When the grille clanged shut, she started, grabbed at Angel's knees, and pressed herself close to him. Angel reached a hand down and patted her shoulder abstractedly.

"Angel," Barney said, "this is Mayor Morgan."

"How do you do?" Angel was stiff, formal.

"Someday," Barney said, with a joviality in which David could detect no false note, "you can tell your friends how the Mayor of San Juno came to call on you in your own apartment."

"My friends will be very surprised," Angel said gravely.

Consuela Chavez stood up suddenly and turned to face Barney, her thick face ugly and distorted with fear and rage. "He'll never see his friends!" she shrieked. "He'll never see tonight."

"You're wrong," Barney said firmly. "He won't die today."

"The people outside," she babbled. "So many. So angry. No one can stop so many. They do what they like."

"Mom, please!" Angel was visibly embarrassed.

"Mrs. Chavez," Barney said, saying the name so emphatically that Consuela stifled an oncoming sob and was still. "Are you sure they're going to lynch Angel?"

"They kill him. They said so. Who—"

"He's as good as dead, then?" The question was so cruelly put that Abbe gasped.

"Barney—" she began. He silenced her with a wave.

"How about it, Mrs. Chavez?" Barney asked. "Isn't your boy as good as dead?"

"Yes." She parroted his words as a victim of a third degree might repeat the question in answering. "He's as good as dead."

"I say no," Barney said slowly. "I say they will not kill him."

Consuela Chavez made a helpless gesture. "I want him to live," she said. "Even if it's only for a little time."

"Have you given up?" Barney demanded. "Do you think—"

"I think," she said wearily, "I think they will kill him today. But if not, he will die just the same."

"We will all die," Barney conceded. "If Angel watches his diet, I think he has another fifty-sixty years left."

"No." Consuela shook her head. "They will hang him today. Or they will hang him later."

"If you're wrong about one," Barney said, "couldn't you be wrong about the other?"

Consuela made a helpless gesture of non-comprehension.

"I want you to trust me," Barney said. "If you trust me, and your boy does not die today, will you trust me later? Will you do everything that I tell you to do until he is free?"

Consuela thought this over. "If he does not die today," she said at last, "I will do what you ask. I will trust you forever."

"That's all I ask." Barney smiled at her. She smiled in return, and the anger faded slowly from her face, so that the red lines of the tears could be seen.

"May I come in, Mr. Mayor?" It was District Attorney John Armstrong, standing in the corridor outside the cell, who asked. That he took the Mayor's assent for granted was evidenced by the fact that the guard, at Armstrong's signaled instruction, was sliding back the grilled door to admit him before the Mayor could mumble his permission.

"Sanders just called the Governor," Armstrong reported. "They had the troops equipped and ready to load in the trucks. Just waiting for the word. Good thing, too."

"What's your guess, John?" Barney asked. "How much time have we got?"

"Hard to say." The District Attorney leaned against the side wall, supporting himself with an elbow braced against the con-

74

crete. "Like guessing when water will boil. You know it will, but when?"

"You talk to the newspapermen?"

"Dozens of them."

"Where from?"

"All over. Wire service. Radio people. A guy from *Life*. We're really national news."

"God damn," Mayor Morgan said sadly.

In the silence that followed. David could hear, for the first time, the sound of the mob. There was cheering, and above it, dominating it, a sort of chant. It grew louder, and now the words were audible.

> Hang Angel Chavez [they sang],
> To a sour apple tree,
> Sour apple tree,
> Sour apple tree.
> Hang Angel Chavez
> To a sour apple tree,
> As we go marching on.

The tune was "John Brown's Body." The last line was senseless; many of the singers seemed merely to hum when they came to it. The weird effect was increased by the fact that the tune compelled false accents in the first line, which sounded as: Ha-ang Angel *Cha*vez. Gradually the crowd seemed to tire of those words, and the singing drifted into a confused phase in which half the singers seemed to stick with Ha-ang Angel *Cha*vez while the others sang different words. Finally the second set of lyrics prevailed, and they were singing in unison again, and the sound was very loud and very nearby. David decided the mob was inside the jail, in the courtyard, and he tried to remember what the entrance from the courtyard to the building was like, how it was protected; and all the while the crowd sang:

> We want the man we came for,
> With a rope around his neck,

Rope around his neck,
Rope around his neck.
We want the man we came for
With a rope around his neck,
We do, by God, we do.

"They're coming," Consuela screamed. "They're coming for him!"

Barney said something to her and she subsided. David decided that their relationship was essentially that of priest and parishioner; Consuela obeyed unreasoningly and unreasonably because Barney's promise was all the hope she had, and disbelief in him would be disbelief in that promise.

"They're in the courtyard," Barney said suddenly. "What's between them and here?"

"Steel gates," Armstrong said. "Are there police on those gates?" he asked the Mayor.

The Mayor did not seem to be listening. "Our brave boys," he said. There were tears in his eyes. "Our noble city . . . this place we call home . . ." (Between each distinct, audible phrase there was mumbling. The Mayor, David realized, was a little mad. He seemed to be reciting snatches from dozens of dreary political speeches.) "The principles for which I have stood all my adult life . . . Not merely a privilege, but an obligation, a sacred trust—"

Armstrong took two steps across the cell, grasped the Mayor by the shoulders and shook him violently. "Snap out of it," he yelled, shoving him down next to Angel on the bed. "You can go crazy later."

"What are you men doing in a court of law with ropes in your hands?" When Morgan said *you* his finger pointed, not at anyone in particular, but straight in front of him, and when he spoke of *hands* he raised his own.

"Why are you so upset?" Angel asked him. "What does it matter to you?"

It would have been a rude question had anyone else asked it, but a prospective lynch victim has special privileges. At any rate, it brought Mayor Morgan at least partially to his senses.

"I'm a black reactionary," he said, turning to face Angel. "One thing about us black reactionaries: we're sticklers for rules. We like our evil ends accomplished strictly according to the book. Isn't that right, Barney?"

Before Barney could reply, Fats Sanders was outside the cell. "Let's go," he shouted, sliding back the door and coming in. He put a hand on Angel. "They'll be in here in ten minutes," he said. "There's a side door. Maybe if we—"

The Mayor, his eyes suddenly bright, slowly came erect. To David's astonishment, he produced from his coat pocket a shiny nickel-plated .45, which he pointed at the jailer.

"Hey!" Sanders yelled in alarm. "What the hell?"

"That mob's going to watch every side door, and you damn well know it!" Mayor Morgan declared.

"What do you want us to do then?" Sanders demanded. "Sit here and wait? That's a mean mob. They may not settle for the Mex."

The Mayor turned away from them and faced the corridor beyond the cell door, a short man who looked even shorter against the background of vertical iron bars. "The first one in here," he proclaimed, "will need a lot of nerve."

"No," Armstrong said. "Once that mob gets this close, there'll be no stopping them. The ones in front'll have no choice. They'll be pushed along. They've got to be stalled in the courtyard until the troops get here."

"You're right, pal," Fats Sanders said affably. "So take the Mayor's pea shooter and go out on the balcony and stall them. You're the silver-tongued—"

"Not him." Morgan gestured suddenly with the pistol. "You."

"Me?"

"It might work," Armstrong said slowly. "They—"

"You're crazy," Sanders said. "All of you. You're looking to get me—"

"Shut up," the Mayor commanded. "Shut up, or I'll make a hole in you. John, you go."

"They'd never listen to me," the District Attorney declared. "But they just might listen to Fats. He's one of them."

The crowd was still singing. The song was louder than before, and the words had changed. They sang:

> When we get hold of Chavez, we
> Will treat him nice and kind.
> When we get hold of Chavez, we
> Will treat him nice and kind.
> *Oh!* When we get hold of Chavez, we
> Will treat him nice and kind.
> We will like *Hell* we will!

"They're not going to listen to me," Sanders declared. "Because I'm not going out on that balcony to talk to them!"

"You'd be a hero," Armstrong argued.

"A dead one."

"Why?" Armstrong asked. "If they don't listen to you, they just go on in. It's not like defending the cell. They don't have to go over you."

Sanders did not reply.

"Your name'll be in the papers, coast to coast. You'll go on the radio."

"Yeah?" Sanders was visibly impressed.

"It'll be tough," Armstrong said, "but you can do it. When you're done, Castillo, or somebody like that, will tell them you're right, and there'll be some pushing and hauling, and they'll go home."

"All right," Sanders said. "So how about you going—"

"He told you." The Mayor waved his .45 menacingly. "They won't take it from him. What's the matter? Haven't you got the guts to go out there?"

78

Sanders thought for a moment. "Maybe I will," he said.

"Good boy." Mayor Morgan lowered his pistol.

"I said 'maybe,'" Sanders snapped. "There's only one thing that might stop them," he went on. "That's if I give them my word, my personal word, that the law will hang the Mex."

"I assure you that the law will," Armstrong said in a quiet voice.

David glanced at Angel to see if he had heard this last. He apparently hadn't, since Barney stood between him and Armstrong.

"And somebody goes with me," Sanders went on. "I got enough to do without holding the gun."

"I'll go," the Mayor volunteered.

"No." The jailer's refusal was flat. "Someone steadier." He pointed at David.

"All right." The Mayor proffered his pistol to David. After a moment's hesitation, David took it.

Barney slapped David's shoulder but did not speak. David searched Barney's face for a show of emotion, not at his own departure, but at the District Attorney's promise, which surely made the making of any deal now impossible. Barney's face was impassive.

Beyond him, Abbe shook her head. Suddenly David knew why she did not want him to go, and that her not wanting it was important. All this crowding in on him, overwhelmed him like a wave crashing over an unwary bather. He moved past Barney and stood next to her.

"I'll be careful, Abbe," he said. She smiled and offered her cheek to be kissed, and he kissed it, and turned, and followed Fats Sanders out into the corridor.

A grilled door at the end of the corridor led to a small balcony, and beyond the door, below the balcony, David knew, was the courtyard and the mob. He was suddenly acutely conscious of the fact that the range of the pistol he held in his hand was measured in feet and that, if any one in the crowd had a gun, it was likely to be a rifle. "Here goes nothing," Sanders said. He walked up to the door, kicked it open, and stepped onto the balcony. David forced his feet to take him to the jailer's side.

In the bright sunlight, David's first reaction was one of anticlimax. The mob below did not see them, being intent on the problem of the gates which barred its way from the courtyard to the first floor of the building itself. There were two, one on each side of the yard. In front of each, a section of the mob had gathered. In one section five men prepared to use a telegraph pole as a battering ram.

"That's a waste of time, that pole," Sanders said, mildly as a spectator might criticize a football quarterback for a poor choice of plays. "That's an iron gate, anchored top and bottom in concrete. What it needs," he added, "is a good charge of nitro on the lock."

"They'll figure that out," David said.

"I kind of think they have. Probably sent somebody for it. Look." The five pole bearers raced their pole up to the gate and into it, relaxing their grip at the last possible split second so as to avoid sharing the impact. "Just fooling around," Sanders sneered. "I figure some kids said a pole would do it, and they went and got one, and it didn't do it. So then somebody with more sense said dynamite, and the kids are still trying with the pole while everybody is waiting for what to make the bang with. If they were serious with the pole," he added, "they'd all be fighting for a place on it, and those that were edged out'd be standing around cheering the others on."

As Sanders spoke, the pole bearers backed up for one more try. As they came forward the anchor man lost his footing momentarily, and, stumbling, took the full weight of the pole in the stomach as the gate was reached. He fell over on his back with his legs in the air. A few bystanders laughed, and then, when he did not get up, propped him up in a sitting position against a wall and slapped his face lightly until he waved his arms as evidence of returning consciousness.

"Start it off." Sanders indicated the pistol. "Up in the air," he explained. "Got to quiet them down."

David obeyed, reflecting that, since they had no extra clips, he was thereby expending one sixth of their firepower.

The cheering, shouting, and singing stopped, not instantly as the shot rang out, but in the following seconds, slowly, as a spring-driven phonograph stops when the spring breaks.

"Men," Fats Sanders sang out, putting his hands on the wooden balcony rail, "I'm not asking you to leave. I'm only asking you to listen to me."

"Who the hell wants to listen?" a voice demanded. There was a mild hubbub from those near the questioner. Sanders stood patiently and waited for it to die down. This, David decided, was a wise move on his part. Nothing he could say could bear an influence on whether he would be permitted to be heard.

Finally the hubbub died to a murmur, which Sanders silenced by raising his hands. "One thing I want you to know straight out," he said. "You don't have to do what I ask. You don't even have to listen. But don't get the idea you can pitch anything up here at me. My friend here is a pretty fair shot. He might not get the man that starts anything, but he'll sure get somebody."

Again the murmur arose, and again Fats raised his hands for silence and got it. "Men," he began again, and David noticed that there were no women present, "I'm no outsider. I can call most of you by your first names. You don't even know mine." There was a ripple of laughter as he put his hand on his big belly to signify the name by which he was known.

"Make your god damn pretty speech." David recognized Cap Grant's raspy voice. "We got work to do." Where Sanders' allusion to his nickname had drawn meaningless murmurs and mild laughter, Grant's interjection brought forth a roar of approval.

"What do you want then?" Fats shouted, and the crowd roared back, each saying what was wanted in his own words, and the words intermingled, and yet their sense distinguishable. Beyond the open gate to the street, David could see a photographer working with a Big Bertha on a tripod. If Fats succeeded in turning back the mob, David felt—quite correctly—the picture being taken would be *Life's* "Picture of the Week." GLORY COMES TO FATS SANDERS. A JAILKEEPER TURNS BACK A LYNCH MOB FROM THE INTERIOR COURT OF HIS JAIL.

"If you do that," Fats said, in allusion to the crowd's reply to his rhetorical question, "you'll be cheating the hangman. Probably got a wife and kids. We all got to live."

"Can't trust the hangman!" Cap Grant shouted. "Can't trust the State." After each phrase, the crowd cheered briefly, then quieted down so that Cap could go on. "Can't trust anybody!"

"How about me?" Sanders demanded. "Can't you trust me?"

"No!" Cap Grant shrieked. He waited for a cheer, but got none, only a mild, confused sort of mumble. "He's only stalling!" Cap shouted. "The troops are coming. They'll make it safe. Safe for the Mex and the high-class citizens."

Silently the crowd fell back, away from the balcony, so that Cap Grant stood alone, facing upward at Fats Sanders. It was as if, David decided, the crowd, knowing that the decision was its own to make, was allowing the two adversaries vantage points from which to fight for its favor. David realized unhappily that what Cap Grant had said was essentially true; he doubted that even Fats Sanders could make a lie stand up against it.

"That's right," Sanders declared, as if daring Cap Grant to make something of the admission. "The troops'll be here soon. Until they come, what happens is up to you."

Two men came in from the street. The crowd parted to let them through and watched them as they showed Cap Grant a paper bag and said something to him. "There's your nitro," Sanders remarked out of the side of his mouth. "I give you my word," he went on, raising his right hand like a witness taking the oath, "I give you my solemn oath that if you go home, go about your business, the man who killed Marie Wiltse will hang for it."

"And if he gets off," Cap Grant shouted, "then you'll say he isn't" (here he essayed an imitation of Sanders' professional fervor) "the man who killed Marie Wiltse. We won't take that!"

"You tell 'em, Cap!" The speaker was the man who had been injured in carrying the pole. His shout drew an appreciative roar of approval from the rest of the crowd.

"I'm surprised at you, Cap," Sanders said. "I'm surprised at all of you. Making me out a man who plays with words like that. I'm no lawyer. I'm a plain citizen of this town like all of you, and proud of it. And you all know for damn sure I never yet made a promise I didn't keep."

"Got to be a first time," Cap Grant pointed out.

Sanders inspected the crowd for a moment, then pointed his finger. "You there," he said. "Mr. Castillo. You tell them. Won't it be better for everybody if that Mex gets hung at State Prison with all the trimmings?"

"Of course it would," Castillo said. Those around him fell back to give him room. "That's what I've been saying," he went on. Then, turning from Fats to the crowd around him: "Men, I tell you to let the law take its course. It may take years, but it's better that way than to drag the Mex out of his cell, out of the law's protection, and hang him from the big tree across from City Hall."

"Very helpful," Fats Sanders muttered. Then, aloud, he proclaimed: "I'm going to make my promise once more, and I'm going to make it so everybody's got to understand. If that Mex don't hang, I swear to almighty God to quit my job and never run for office again. And," he added, shouting at the top of his lungs, "I been twenty-seven years on the public tit!"

The crowd laughed wholeheartedly at this public declaration of what all of them knew to be true. Ralph Castillo shrugged and said something to those around him that David could not hear, and turned and walked slowly toward the open gate that led to the street. A few others did likewise.

Sanders turned and looked at David and smiled like a man who has, by random experiment, finally pushed the button that causes a piece of machinery to operate. Then he turned to the crowd and shouted: "Cap. Cap Grant."

Grant still stood in the open space between the balcony and the now inattentive crowd. For a moment, he seemed about to shout at the others in the courtyard. Then he turned and looked up. "Yes?"

"If that nitro isn't back at the Amalgamated in twenty minutes," Fats said ominously, "somebody's going to get arrested for illegal possession."

Cap Grant took the package from the man who held it and started toward the open gate. Slowly at first, then in a rush so great that there was pushing and shoving, the rest did likewise.

Fats Sanders turned his back on the departing crowd and left the balcony. David followed him into the corridor.

"I've got to hand it to you, Sanders," David said, slipping Mayor Morgan's .45 into his pocket. "You going to call off the troops?"

"Like hell," Fats said. "Cap Grant had it taped. I was stalling them till the troops get here."

"But now—"

"They'll be back," Sanders said. "This is Saturday afternoon. Nothing to do but sit around in a saloon and look at the bottoms of glasses. After a while, they'll change their minds. But by then there'll be six hundred good reasons why it won't matter. Three companies of State Guard. Machine guns. Tear gas. Iron hats. Bayonets."

Fats Sanders, David reflected, had lived off the favors of the mob for a quarter of a century. He was, in the ordinary sense, an ignorant man, but he was conversant with the anatomy of the mob as a doctor—who might also be ignorant, in the ordinary sense—knew the anatomy of the human body.

84

The guard still stood outside the cell. "Christ, Fats," he asked worshipfully, "what did you tell them?"

"Last one out is a nigger baby," Fats grunted. The guard stared at him in surprise, and then slid the door back. Fats and David went back into the cell.

Angel stood by the doorway, having surrendered his bed to his mother, who lay prone on it, moaning into a pillow. "Congratulations," Mayor Morgan said. He sat in the straight-backed chair and waved at them as he spoke, as if to indicate that he knew he should rise but lacked the strength. David handed the gun back to the Mayor, and turned, and looked at Abbe, and smiled. When she smiled back, he, guiltily—because he knew he should have been thinking of other, more important matters—decided that she was pretty, almost beautiful.

Consuela Chavez's moans became louder and then stopped. "They're coming!" she shrieked. "They're coming for him!"

Abbe put a hand on the woman's arm, but the almost incoherent shrieks continued. Suddenly Barney, brushing Abbe aside, grabbed Consuela's shoulder. "Shut up!" he roared, flipping the big woman over onto her back. "I promised they wouldn't kill your boy. And they won't. They're gone. Listen."

There was silence.

"Gone?" For a moment, Consuela seemed confused. Then she laughed. "Gone?" She was still laughing.

"You trust me now?" Barney demanded.

"Sure." Consuela, who had seemed close to hysteria, was now laughing happily, as if someone had told her a funny joke. "Sure I trust you."

"From now on," Barney asked slowly, "you'll do exactly what I say?"

"I promised," Consuela said. "I promise again now."

"What was it like out there?" Abbe asked.

David glanced quickly at Fats Sanders, who was involved

in a hectic conversation conducted in undertones with John Armstrong.

"He's a hell of a guy with a crowd," David said. He took Abbe's hand. "I felt like I was in a lion cage with Frank Buck and a kitchen chair."

He stood next to the door, staring out into the hall, holding Abbe's hand in his, saying nothing. Finally a man came and stood in the corridor. He wore green fatigues with a captain's bars stenciled in white on his shoulders. He carried a pistol and wore a helmet with his name (QUIST) lettered on the front. Strapped to his belt were three oversized tear-gas grenades.

"Is that the prisoner?" Captain Quist asked. "I'm the C.O. of the task force."

"Yes," Mayor Morgan said. He identified himself. "I don't mind saying," he said as the guard admitted the captain, "that I'm damn glad you fellows got here."

"Well, pal," Captain Quist told Angel Chavez. "Your worries are over. This State guarantees you a fair trial and a humane hanging."

"Let's go," David said. He was still holding Abbe's hand. He felt a tremendous desire to get outside, to go for a walk somewhere.

from the Journal of David Blake
Saturday, June 7, 1947

. . . and the question then becomes: is there such a thing as experience being *too* practical? Thus, though a defense attorney may sometimes be called on to help in keeping his client alive until he can be brought to trial, it can hardly be argued that every defense attorney ought to be prepared and equipped to do so.

Monday, June 9, 1947

Barney left today on what he calls "a bush-beating, money-raising expedition to points east." The task of preparing the defense and conducting it will thus be mine exclusively. Of course, this is what he proposed from the first, and what I agreed to. But I don't think I really believed it would happen until he handed me the keys to his "shack"—a beach house, actually, which Abbe and I are to use as a sort of headquarters—loaded Consuela into his car, and left for the airport.

Tuesday, June 24, 1947

. . . In addition to this purely legal research, we must locate and interview witnesses. Also, in the two weeks remaining to us, we must read and understand and make digests of the reports on the prospective jurors which are only now beginning to come from the detective agency we hired to do this work. It is Abbe, of course, who makes it possible to think of all this in terms of what *we* must do. Without her, the defense would be, as I wrongly stated, "mine exclusively." If it were, it would be an impossible burden. Her help with the case is utterly invaluable. But, beyond that, she . . .

5

At first, David was conscious only of the voice—Abbe's voice—calling his name, and, half asleep, he reached out for her in the bed and found nothing. Then, opening his eyes, he became aware that she was shaking him.

"Let's go, counselor," she said. "Today's the day." He turned over and saw her standing by the bed, the sun streaming through the window behind her, making a scrim of the pale blue night-gown she wore. He was reminded that he had once cautioned her against wearing that gown in front of a strong light, and that she had laughed and said: "Only for you, David." The memory of what had followed moved him to grasp her wrist and pull her gently toward him, but she laughed and broke away. "Rise and shine," she said. "Your client goes on trial in three hours."

David shook his head and reached for her. She jumped back. "No more sleep," she said. "There's time for a swim if we hurry."

"I wasn't thinking of sleep," David said.

But she was firm. "A swim'll do both of us more good."

She was probably right, he decided, getting up. Abbe was nearly always right. It was she, he knew, who had contributed more than anything else to his feeling, during the weeks of pre-trial work on the Chavez case, that he was, for the first time in his life, fully alive, working to his full capabilities on something that justified their full use.

She kissed him lightly and skipped away when he tried to detain her. "Get your trunks on," she commanded. David watched her as she went into the other room of the beach shack. Then he stripped off his pajamas and put on the bathing trunks.

A minute later they raced, hand in hand, across the warm dry sand, across the cool damp sand, and the cold wet sand, and into the green Pacific. This they had done together a score of times, and always David had felt an unreasonable impulse to yell *eeYAH*, as, when a child, he had shouted from pure unthinking joy when the street lights went up. Today, the impulse being stronger than usual, he gave way to it. Abbe laughed, took her hand from his, and dived under an incoming wave. David followed.

She swam ahead of him outside the surf with an easy efficient crawl. David knew Abbe could outswim him and that she forbore to do so because she sensed that this would somehow break the joyous mood in which he found himself.

There was never another like her, David thought, criticizing himself for the triteness of the thought, but telling himself that, trite or not, it was true. Abbe's charm and her beauty were important to him, but by no means all-important. Her lightning competence was important too. Because of it he could dictate to her in rambling, casual fashion, developing points of law as they came to him, supporting as he found support, striking out as diversions were found to be such, and yet be certain that when (an impossibly few minutes later) Abbe would hand him the neatly typed product, it would consist only of the final thought and the argument and documentation supporting it. Her infallible sense of timing was likewise important; it enabled her, when the work dragged on, to sense whether a stop for food, or for rest, or for the unbearable ecstasy they seemed able to create on demand would compensate for the time lost at it in time gained from the increased strength with which he could return to work, or whether, contrariwise, such a stopping would be a breaking of a thread, a destructive act for which no renewal of energy could compensate.

Suddenly Abbe turned in the water and swam rapidly toward the beach. David dog-paddled, watching her overtake a wave in the act of breaking, then seeing only her upraised right foot as she rode the wave, Hawaiian fashion, onto the beach. He tried, as he always did, to do likewise, and ended, as usual, in a confused tangle as the wave upended him and then rolled over him. He got up and splashed through the shallow water while Abbe laughed.

With mock rage he chased her back across the beach to the house. Then, as they stood outside the house, under the spigot that, secured to the eaves, served for an outdoor shower, he took her in his arms, marveling at the warmth of her body as the icy water sprayed over them, making them gasp.

"Barney wanted to run the hot water out there," she said, as they stood a few moments later, toweling themselves and dripping water onto the kitchen floor. "I told him not to."

"You were right," David said. "The cold's more stimulating." He frowned. The remark had reminded him that this was Barney's beach shack, and that, in turn, reminded him that the Chavez case was Barney's case, and the bed in which he slept Barney's bed; and Abbe—

"Undo me," she said, turning her back to him, and gesturing toward the knot which secured the top of her bathing suit. And, as his suddenly trembling fingers fought with the knot and forced it apart, as Abbe, letting the halter drop to the floor, turned to face him, he forgot Barney, forgot Angel Chavez, forgot everything in seeing, as for the first time, the pink dots set proudly in the white, untanned band, against the sundarkened body, then feeling the tingling of her against him, the joy in her and in him as she twisted in his arms.

"Umm," she said, as she struggled, but not hard, to break away.

"There's time," he murmured, and they might have made time by forgoing breakfast had not the loud thump of the morning paper, thrown hard against the front door, first startled them, and then, in that single startled instant, reminded them of what was scarcely more than two hours away, and of what had to be done during those two hours.

David shaved and dressed and, when he emerged, found Abbe already dressed and breakfast on the kitchen table. They ate in silence, because David had, as he ate, to read that morning's *Standard* and consider what it might mean in terms of the state of mind of the the prospective jurors, most of whom would also be reading it. PICK CHAVEZ JURY TODAY, the headline on page one read, and the editorial reminded the prospective jurors—as well as every other resident of San Juno—of the importance of the trial, of the fact that "the nation's eyes" would be focused on San Juno to see how justice was administered "and the guilty punished in accordance with Constitutional procedures." There was, David noticed, no reference to "the innocent set free." He pointed this out to Abbe.

"You're thinking," she said, "of asking for a change of venue?" She gave her question the inflection of a statement of fact, but David nodded in useless agreement. "We've been through all that," she said.

"I know," David said. "With Barney." Before leaving with Consuela, Barney had cautioned David not to yield to the temptation to ask to have the trial moved out of San Juno. "I just don't see," he went on, "why we have to put Angel's life in the hands of a jury made up of people who—"

"Because Barney's right," Abbe said. "If you ask for it, you'll be turned down. Then you'll get the same panel to pick from you would have had anyhow. Only now they'll be people the defense has called incompetent to sit in judgment. People don't like to be told that their prejudices are stronger than their thinking powers. And the more prejudiced they are, the less they like it."

David gulped down his coffee. "Still—" he argued—"there's always a chance—"

"Not to do any good there isn't," Abbe said firmly. "Suppose they give you the change of venue," she went on. "They won't, but suppose. Then you go somewhere else before a jury that knows your boy is guilty because you were afraid to let him be tried by his own neighbors."

"All right," David said. His tone indicated that it was not all right, but that he was consenting because further argument was useless, the decision not really being his to make, and having already been made past any possibility of his remaking it.

"Besides," Abbe said, correctly disregarding his expressed consent, "you've got an investment in these jurors." She reached behind her and took from a sideboard, where it had been placed the previous night, a thick manila envelope, bearing the imprint: PINE & PINE, CONFIDENTIAL INVESTIGATORS.

"Oh God!" David said, guiltily aware that the envelope contained dossiers on the hundred jurors who constituted the panel from which the twelve to try Angel Chavez would be chosen, and that he should have been devoting what spare time he had to rereading those dossiers, and transferring pertinent bits of information to his notebook, because he would need the information in questioning potential jurors, in challenging them, or in letting them pass unchallenged, and he preferred not to refer to the thick, professional-looking reports of the detective agency in open court.

Abbe passed the envelope over the table. David opened it, took out the dossiers and his notes of the evening before, and went to work completing the task of putting—on the typewritten sheet that showed only the names of the panel members—a check mark next to those who were in no event to be accepted as jurors, and a circle next to those deemed favorable to the defense and therefore to be subjected to a mere cursory examination sufficient so that the attention of the prosecution would not be called to the defense's desire to have them serve. As he worked half of his mind seemed to detach itself from his purely clerical labors to dwell on the fact that a dossier of prospective jurors was nearly always made available, where a case was of any importance, to the State, but was available to the defense only if the defense were sufficiently well heeled to pay for it. For its availability in this case he had Barney to thank, and the thought made him regret having, even momentarily, questioned Barney's decision in the matter of asking for a change of venue.

It was because of Barney, because of the checks Barney had sent back, which totaled nearly $3,000 with a promise (from Barney) of "much more to come," that it was possible to hire private detectives to make these dossiers (100 dossiers @7.50, $750.00), and to find and interrogate missing witnesses (including one in Houston, $375.00). Barney's checks, too, paid the salaries of the two young men who had been hired to help interview the dozens of local people deemed likely to be subpoenaed by the State, as well as to aid David in the research into the strictly legal aspects of the case, and the salary of the stenotypist hired to aid them in the making of their reports, and the secretary hired to aid Abbe in the final typing of the collated documents, and the rental of typewriters and stenotype equipment, and of file cabinets and a place to put them.

There were still many things left undone that might have been done. David had considered having exhaustive psychiatric tests run on Angel, against the possibility that it might seem desirable to make his sanity an issue, but this, like the other things David had left undone, had been deliberately omitted, not because there was no money to pay for it, but because it had seemed likely to do more harm than good. The defense, in a criminal case, is hamstrung by many limiting factors, of which time, though prominent, is only one. But the one great limiting factor the Chavez defense had been spared, David knew, was poverty, and of all the limiting factors, poverty is by far the cruelest.

W. W. Younger, the last juror on the list, was, according to the information supplied by the detectives, married to a woman whose brother had formerly been married to the daughter of a senior partner in Ralph Castillo's insurance firm. David worked the tangled relationship out in his own mind, decided that it *was* likely that Younger and Castillo moved in the same circles and might, therefore, have the same prejudices, and put a check next to the name. The doubtful cases were already covered by David's notes, abstracts from the dossiers indicating matters that might be inquired into. He slipped the notes, the dossiers, and the typed list of names into a plain envelope.

"This might interest you." Abbe had abstracted the *Standard* while David was at work on his list. Now, she slid it across the table to him, folded in such a way that, when he picked it up, he was looking at a syndicated column. It was not a column David habitually read, being ordinarily composed 50 per cent of planted items ascribing old jokes to the clients of the press agents who rewrote them and made them topical, 40 per cent of bad guesses at the future private life of public figures, and 10 per cent of items recounted merely to provide a medium for the use of words coined by the ex-juggler who wrote the column. For the convenience of readers interested only in the proper names, all such were customarily set in boldface type. David's eye ran down the names until he came to Consuela's, "**Consuela Chavez,** whose boy will be tried out there for murderrape," the item ran, "will script her life-yarn for *Struggle,* a race organ which is having one to break even. Heavy sugar paid her will go to boy's defense fund, itsezzere."

"*Struggle,*" David said. "That would be—"

"What Pegler calls a butcher-paper magazine," Abbe replied.

"But why should she—"

"You read it," Abbe said. "For money."

"But she can't write," David protested. "Can she?"

"She can endorse the checks," Abbe said. "She's literate."

"That's not what I meant," David said, angry with Abbe because he knew she knew that was not what he meant, and angry with himself because he *was* angry with her, and still more because his anger was showing in his tone. "Can she write her life story? Write it so people will want to read it?"

"Of course not," Abbe said sharply. "Neither can the ball players who write the inside story of the World Series. She's a celebrity. Celebrities don't write their life stories. They tell them to bright young men with horn-rimmed glasses, and the bright young men turn in the stories, and bright old men fix them up. What's the matter with that?"

"Nothing," David admitted, feeling, deep inside him, a nameless sense that there was something wrong with what Abbe was describing. "But why *Struggle*?"

"What's the matter with it?"

"It's—well, call it its political orientation."

"No, don't," Abbe snapped. "Don't pussyfoot. Say what you mean. Come on, spit it out. It's a Communist sheet. Is that what bothers you? Because it is," she went on, giving him no time to say that that was what was bothering him. "Copy goes down to Fourteenth Street to get the Party chop before they print it. The Party provides the circulation and the distribution machinery. The Party buys some of the advertising and sells most of the rest. What does all that have to do with Angel?"

David drummed with his fingers on the table and shifted uneasily in his place. "It's just that I don't see what their interest in it is," he said weakly.

"And you don't have to," Abbe said. "My grandfather was a stockbroker," she went on with seeming irrelevance. "He taught me a lot of things, mostly lies. But one of his sayings had a lot of truth to it: Money Has No Morals. He never asked his customers where they were getting the money to buy stocks, or what they proposed to do with it if they made a profit, or what it would mean to them if the stock went bust. He kept his head down and took care of his job."

"The law's a little different from the brokerage business," David pointed out.

"It's more complicated," Abbe said, agreeing. "You've got to know more, and you've got to use more of what you know. That only makes it more important for you to keep your mind on your job. To defend Angel. Barney's raising the money."

"But how he raises it—"

"Doesn't matter one god damn bit," Abbe said. "My God, you don't have to come to a complete understanding with someone to take his money? Do you?"

David shook his head. Nor to sleep with a girl, he thought. But couldn't there be more to it. When you took a contribution, didn't you make the contributor's cause your cause? Couldn't it be part of a pattern that led to a greater unity, just as the temporary unity he and Abbe had made, in Barney's bed—now why, he thought, was it important who held title to the mattress and sheets on which they had coupled? He broke the thought off abruptly. This was surely a diversion, a lifting of the head, as Abbe had put it, from the job at hand. And on that job a life depended.

"Let's go," he said, standing up and beginning to put the dossiers, his notes, and his keyed roster into the brief case leaning against the wall.

Setting out in the ancient convertible with the top down and the warm July sun beating pleasantly on him, seeing the road gleaming black, winding its way south, between the cliffs and the beach, toward San Juno, smelling the salt-tar elements of the onshore breeze, sensing Abbe's nearness to him as he drove, David felt the same bonhomie, the same sense of contentment, that he had felt on awakening. Not even the pedestrian bridges arching across the highway as they passed Village Beach had the power to depress him, and yet, above one of those bridges—

"That one," Abbe said, pointing. Answering his unspoken thoughts was something Abbe did often. "That's where they say it happened."

That was where Angel said it happened, too, David thought; it was, he knew, the place where it did happen. But, as Abbe's phrasing had suggested to him, he began to try to think of the bridge, now swiftly passing overhead, as the place where *they said* it had happened, because it was the State's task to prove what had happened and where it had happened. The defense's task was to prevent the State from performing its task; and to refuse to recognize, even in his own mind, any fact not actually proved by the State in open court would be an excellent policy for David to follow.

The bridge was behind them now, hidden by an outjutting of the cliff and corresponding turn in the road. David left the sea road and drove quickly—like a man with nothing to fear—up the incline, along the face of the cliff, to the top, and then, with the cliff and the sea at his back, through the park, and into the main street of San Juno.

A line of people—would-be spectators at the trial, he realized—stretched down the steps of the courthouse and along the sidewalk, across the little street that led to the tiny parking lot that divided the courthouse from the jail. David hesitated before turning into the little street, wondering if it was, perhaps, closed to traffic. It appeared that it was. But a policeman called David's name, and waved him through. At the officer's urging, the line of pedestrians bent and then broke to admit the car. David saw the people craning their necks to see who was being permitted thus to pass, and heard the murmurs as his identity became known.

At the end of the street, a uniformed parking-lot attendant scrutinized the car, recognized the occupants, and handed David a gummed sticker with the word OFFICIAL printed in green on the gummed side, and under the printed word the handwritten explanation: *Defense Attorney*. "Armstrong left this for you, Mr. Blake," the attendant said. "Said for you to put it on your windshield. That way you'll be able to park here during the trial."

David thanked him and made as if to drive on. "That's all right," the man said. "I'll park it for you."

"Good enough." David got out. The attendant, he noticed, had gone to Abbe's side of the car to help her make the eight-inch descent to the street.

"Armstrong said if you need more stickers, just see him," the attendant said.

"How about a wash and polish job while we're gone?" Abbe asked.

"Well, I don't know—" The attendant seemed genuinely puzzled. Then, hearing Abbe's laugh, he realized it was a joke and joined in her laugh. He was still laughing as he drove the car away.

"You better go over to the office," David said when he was gone. "Check through the mail. If there's anything you think is important, bring it to court with you."

"Check," Abbe said. "And good luck." Abbe grinned at him, and David realized with a sudden sinking sensation that it was likely that, when he next saw Abbe, the trial of *People v. Chavez* would have begun, at least in the formal sense that the preliminaries would be in motion.

"Thanks, darling." David returned her smile, turned on his heel, and walked quickly across the lot to the jail entrance. A guard, the same one who had been on duty when David had, on a dozen occasions, passed through this entrance en route to Angel's cell, greeted him by name and opened the door for him. The guard had never greeted him, by name or otherwise, before.

It was all part of a pattern. Armstrong's solicitude in arranging for the parking sticker, the attendant's offer to park the car for David, the guard's respectful greeting; none of this, David knew, was accidental. The editorial in the *Standard*, calling on all San Junians to conduct themselves as "honorable, adult citizens of the world's greatest republic"; this was likewise part of the pattern. It was not that the guard, the District Attorney, the parking-lot attendant, the editorial writer, or, for that matter, his twelve thousand readers, felt no hostility toward Angel Chavez or had suddenly resolved to reserve their decision until the evidence was in. It was rather that out of their hatred of Angel, out of their certainty that he was a murdering rapist, arose a resolve that when (not *if*) he was convicted, the verdict would not be susceptible to reversal, nor even to criticism, on the ground that it had been the result of animosity or bias. Tolerance and good will were therefore the order of the day; a tolerance founded in bias, David thought bitterly, and a good will that was only a mask for hate.

Only Cap Grant had resisted the new order, which had come into being and full acceptance on the day that Fats Sanders became a national hero by turning back the lynch mob. And the order, and those who issued it, had dealt with Cap Grant—who had continued for a few days to mouth threats against Angel Chavez in bars and on the streets, and whose mouthings had been reported by the press, and even recorded and broadcast by an enterprising radio man—by dispatching him six hundred miles to Santa Barbara, California, to represent the village at a month-long conference on Fire Prevention Education.

That David was no longer required to confer with Angel in his cell, but was given the use of a conference room with leather chairs, a fluorescent light, and an unbarred window was another manifestation of the new order. A custodian admitted David to the room and went to fetch Angel. While he was gone, David sank into a leather chair, considered using the phone at his elbow to call Abbe, and rejected the idea. Then the custodian returned with Angel, not holding him, just walking beside him. Angel sat in a chair facing David, and the custodian left, closing the door behind him.

"You look fine, Angel," David said. "How do you feel?"

The description was, perhaps, more accurate than David intended. Angel looked drawn, his face longer than when David had first met him, his eyes no longer fearful, but worn. His expression, which hardly ever seemed to change, was what David considered ideal for a defendant: sufficiently animated so that no one could suppose that he was depressed by a tormenting guilt, yet not bright enough to be called arrogant.

"I'm all right, Mr. Blake," Angel said. David had tried to get Angel to use his first name, but this was hard for Angel to do, and the idea had been abandoned.

"All right, boy," David said. "This is the day. You remember what I told you?"

"I remember." Angel's declaration was flat, revealing no doubts.

"Tell me."

Angel repeated the instructions as David had often given them to him, effortlessly, yet plainly speaking from comprehension, not from rote. He was to stand when told to stand, he said. At other times he was to sit erect. He was to pay attention to everything that was said in court, yet his concentration was not to lead him to stare at anyone. Under no conditions was he to speak unless David gave him permission to speak.

"That last is very important," David said. "The reporters may ask you questions. The guards may stop them, and they may not. But you have nothing to say."

"I have nothing to say."

"Right." David patted Angel's shoulder. "Any questions?"

If the positions were reversed, if David were the client and Angel were the attorney, David would surely have asked him what chance he thought he had. But he knew, somehow, that Angel would not ask such a question. Probably, David decided, he was afraid that it might be considered evidence of a lack of faith in his attorney.

"When will my mother be back?"

David was suddenly sickened by the realization the question brought to him that this defendant, though calm and reserved, was only an adolescent, that, given an adverse verdict, this adolescent would lose all the years of his life beyond his eighteenth, that he had, therefore, a greater stake in the trial than anyone else, greater than David's, or Barney's, greater even than John Armstrong's, though Armstrong's political future was certainly at issue, that, strong though the desires of the people of San Juno to obtain a conviction were, the desire of Angel for an acquittal was as strong, precisely, as Angel's wish for life itself.

"Pretty soon," David said. "She's helping Mr. Castle raise money for you."

The answer seemed to satisfy Angel. "Is it true," he asked, "that the judge will be a Negro?"

"That's right," David said. "Who told you?"

"One of the men at dinner last night," Angel said. "He told me that the reason it will be a colored man is because they can trust him to do his best to hang me—on account of his not being white either. Is that true?"

David hesitated before replying. In his judgment, Angel had stated rather precisely why Theodore Motley had been assigned to hear this case. It was David's view that the intent of those who gave him the assignment was that he should feel that he himself was, in part, on trial, that not merely the guilt or innocence of the defendant was to be tried, but also the question of whether a dark-skinned judge could dispense even justice to a slightly less dark-skinned defendant. Only a conviction could answer such a question in the affirmative. "It might be true," he admitted. "But it won't hurt your chances. You see," he explained, "the judge has to act according to the rules, and the rules don't give him much leeway. If he breaks the rules, then we can probably get a higher judge to give you a new trial."

"If I'm found guilty at this one," Angel added.

David was shocked to realize that his answer had, in part at least, presupposed Angel's conviction. "Sure," he said, smiling. "If they turn you loose, we don't care how many mistakes the judge makes. Any more questions?"

"Will you be with me in court?" For an instant, David thought he saw fear in Angel's face.

"All the time," David said. "But there'll be guards all around. If you want to tell me anything you don't want them to hear, write me a note."

"Sure." Angel stood up and opened the door. The custodian was outside.

"You want to take a shower before you get dressed for court?" the man asked.

"I guess so," Angel said. He turned to David and smiled. "Like a baseball game," he said. "You should look your best."

The door closed behind Angel. David sat for a moment in the chair, then rose, left the room and the building, walked along the sidewalk to the courthouse, and started up the courthouse steps.

The would-be spectators, David could now see, were formed into a double row that snaked its way up one side of the steps behind a barrier of saw horses. There was a mumble of interest as he walked by, and David reflected that this glimpse of the attorney for the defense might be the nearest any of them would come to seeing the trial that day.

The guard at the main entrance tipped his cap and held the door open for him. Inside, the double waiting line was isolated from the corridor by a rope, and the rope itself was held inviolate by three policemen spaced out along its seventy-foot length. It ended twenty feet from the entrance to Courtroom One, and two more policemen guarded the rope where it turned to mark the end of the line. David knew one; as he passed he made a joking reference to the usher's job to which the guardian of the law found himself assigned.

"Beats working, Mr. Blake," the cop said, more loudly than was entirely necessary. The cop enjoyed being in charge of the crowd, David decided, and trading banter with the defense attorney added spice to that enjoyment.

The courtroom was almost full when David entered. He felt an odd, momentary twinge of sympathy toward those in the queue outside. A third of the spectators' section was roped off for the use of the press, while most of the remainder was filled by the hundred men and women making up the first day's jury panel.

Fats Sanders sat with John Armstrong and two assistant district attorneys at the prosecution table. Three young ladies, whom David took to be clerks, sat at the far side of that table with their backs to the judge's bench.

By contrast, the defense table, with its three chairs, looked pitifully undermanned. When the trial began, David and Angel would occupy two of those chairs and, from time to time, Abbe would occupy the third. It was possible that a fourth chair would be added later, if David felt that a member of the office staff might be profitably employed in the courtroom. But there were advantages, psychologically at least, to keeping the number of people at the defense table at a minimum. The contrast with the overpopulated prosecution table might give the impression that the defense, having the better cause, had no need of great personnel, and the picture presented by this contrast illustrated a point which might be of value in establishing a friendly courtroom atmosphere in that it defined and personified Angel's position as the underdog.

David took his brief case to the table, set it down, and began to fumble with its snap lock. As he did so, Fats Sanders left the State table and came over. "Good luck, Blake," he said, standing behind David's chair. "You haven't got a chance. That's why I can afford to say that."

"Good luck to you," David said easily, twisting in his chair to face Fats. "You've got plenty to lose, too."

Sanders laughed and took his not inconsiderable bulk into the section reserved for the press, where he took a seat.

The door behind the bench opened, and the Judge came from his chamber. David was on his feet without having heard the bailiff's "All rise," without having consciously noticed the Judge's arrival, just as a soldier will sometimes find himself completing a salute he was not aware of beginning.

"This court is now in session," the bailiff said, "Judge Theodore Amos Motley presiding. *Be* seated." A few hundred feet slid noisily into comfortable positions, and then there was a rumbling, and David knew without turning his head that some of those who had been lined up outside were being admitted into the few vacant seats at the rear. Judge Motley raised his head and stared reprovingly at the source of the sound, like a preacher waiting for his congregation to quiet down before beginning his sermon. When it was quiet he glanced at the paper on his desk as if refreshing his recollection of just what case he was to try.

"People against Angel Chavez," Judge Motley said. Even in those few words, the Judge's clipped, vaguely Continental accent was apparent. The accent was because he had been educated abroad. This, David thought, was because it had been difficult for a would-be judge whose skin happened to be black to get his undergraduate education close to home. Yet now, David's thoughts raced on, people rose and were silent when this man came into the room; and his career was sure to take him far, unless, by some chance, Angel Chavez were to be acquitted.

"Ready for the State," Armstrong said, rising to say the words, then sinking back into his seat. The Judge swung around and looked at David.

"Ready for the defense," David said. Angel came through a side door and walked quickly to the defense table, accompanied by a guard. His entrance was made with such dispatch that the whispers of recognition did not begin until he was seated.

At Judge Motley's command, the clerk of the court reached into a butter-tub-size drum and began to pull out white cards and to read the names on the cards. Those whose names were called came forward and sat in the jury box. When the box was filled, the clerk took the cards, tore each of them in three parts along dotted lines, and hung the cards on three small boards, twelve to a board. One board he brought to David, another to the District Attorney. And from the third he read out, sing-song fashion, the names of those who had been selected.

Armstrong stood up. "The State," he announced, "objects to Juror Five."

"He is excused," Judge Motley said. A juror left the box. The clerk drew another card, called another name, divided his new card and substituted it for the old one on all three boards. David referred quickly to his notebook and found, to his regret but not to his surprise, that the excused juror was one Arthur Biegler, a labor organizer who had once attempted to organize the predominantly Mexican field hands. His name was one of the five of the hundred-member panel David had marked with a circle to indicate a probable pro-defense bias.

"Has the defense objection to any juror?" Judge Motley asked.

"If it please the court," David said, "we reserve our right to challenge peremptorily until we have finished challenging for cause."

This was routine. The rules allowed David twenty peremptory challenges, but his challenges for cause, where the court agreed that the cause was real, were unlimited. By using his peremptory challenges only where he could find no ground for a challenge for cause, or where the court disallowed his challenge for cause, he would have a wider latitude in the selection of jurors.

John Armstrong questioned the jurors, posing the routine questions that any prosecutor in a capital case might ask, inquiring into any religious scruples against invoking the death penalty, asking whether any juror was related to the defendant (a question which had a ludicrous ring when addressed to jurymen whose names had been drawn almost entirely from a list of real property holders, a list which, in the nature of things, could hardly contain the names of any of Angel's kin) and so on. When he was done, three of the twelve jurors had been dismissed and their places filled by three more. Armstrong indicated that the jury as then constituted was satisfactory to the State and took his seat. The courtroom buzzed. Judge Motley tapped firmly with his gavel. David approached the jury box.

The face of the juror at the left of the front row seemed vaguely familiar. Since the juror who finally filled that chair would automatically be chosen foreman, it was of some psychological importance that he, at least, be as free from prejudice, as fair-minded toward the defense, as possible. David stared at the man's lean face and tried to remember when, if ever, he had seen that face before. Somewhere someone coughed. David glanced at his notes and learned the man's name (Abbott), his religion (Presbyterian), his lineage (Scotch), his politics (Democratic), his occupation (salesman), and nothing more.

"Mr. Abbott," he asked gently, "do I know you?"

"I don't think so." Abbott did not look up when he spoke.

David yielded to an impulse and took a shot in the dark. "Were you a member of the mob that sought to lynch the defendant?"

"No. I was not." The answer came too quickly, almost as though Abbott had expected to be asked such a question.

"May this juror be put under oath?" David asked the question of Judge Motley, who seemed about to say something in reply, then thought better of it and signaled to the bailiff, who brought the Bible to the jury box and laid it on the rail. Abbott's response to the oath was mumbled.

"You are under oath," David said sternly. "Apart from the moral penalties, of which you must be aware, legally—"

"Please have the courtesy to ask the court to explain the law to witnesses if you feel such explanations are needed," Judge Motley said drily.

"I beg the court's pardon."

Judge Motley leaned forward and half rose as if to emphasize the importance of what he was to say. "Perjury, Mr. Abbott, consists of making a material statement which the maker knows to be false. It is a felony. The maximum penalty, under extreme circumstances, is five years' imprisonment."

"Thank you, your honor." David turned to Abbott, whose hands, on the rail beside the Bible, trembled noticeably. "Where were you on the morning of June sixth?" he asked.

"All right," Abbott blurted. "I was there. But I wasn't part of any mob."

"Why were you there, then?" David asked mildly.

"Just to see—to see—"

"To see the fun?"

"Objected to!" Armstrong shouted. "He's—"

"Quite so," Judge Motley said. "The juror is excused by the court. There is no need to pursue the questioning." He waited while Abbott left the box and the mechanics of replacing him were accomplished. "All jurors are cautioned to respond fully and truthfully to the questions of both counsel. Failure to do so is punishable as contempt, whether or not the oath has been administered. You may proceed, Mr. Blake."

As Abbott scurried down the aisle and out through the main door, as if afraid that he might be detained if he hesitated, David glanced at his list. The juror scheduled to replace Abbott as prospective foreman was one Charles Benedict, a truck farmer. He was a large man, red-faced, looking somehow out of place in a gray suit somewhat too small for him.

"Is any juror here," David asked loudly, "prejudiced against the defendant because of his race?"

The jurors sat impassively. "Mr. Benedict," David went on, "you're a farmer, aren't you?"

Benedict grunted assent.

"You employ migrant labor?"

"Yes."

"Any Mexicans?"

Benedict stirred in his seat. "Anybody that wants to work," he said belligerently, "can work for me."

"Do you pay all your workers at the same rate?"

"Huh?"

Benedict's expression of surprise came only a moment before John Armstrong's objection. "The jurors are not on trial here," Armstrong pointed out. "Their conduct of their own personal and business affairs cannot affect their competency to serve."

Judge Motley, who had swung his swivel chair about to face the District Attorney, swung it back and looked down on David, thus indicating that he found merit in the objection, but would hear David before ruling on it.

"This defendant," David began, "has a right to be tried by a jury without any racial bias against him."

"He's not asking that," Armstrong remarked with some heat.

"I'd like to go on without interruption."

"You may," Judge Motley said. Armstrong said: "I apologize," as if on cue.

"It is extremely difficult for a man to know whether or not he is prejudiced," David argued. "I think I have a right to inquire into any action which might reveal a prejudice, and, if such a prejudice exists, to move that the juror be excused for cause."

"I think you have a right to ask any question so long as it is not, in itself, prejudicial," the Judge conceded. "And," he added drily, "you have a right to make any motion whatsoever."

"Am I to understand," David asked, "that the court will not excuse for cause a juror whose past acts indicate a prejudice against the defendant's race?"

"You are to understand that the court will rule on motions when they are made and not before."

"Have you ruled on my objection?" Armstrong asked.

"It is overruled."

David returned his attention to Mr. Benedict. The clerk reread David's last question.

"The law says I have to pay the Mexicans the going wage," Benedict said.

"I know that," David snapped. "I asked what you pay."

"I never had trouble with the law," Benedict said.

"I didn't ask that either. Let me put it another way. Do you pay Mexicans the same wages you pay white workers?"

"They don't do the same jobs."

"What jobs do the Mexicans do?"

"Picking, mostly."

"All right." David spoke more slowly, as if to make his words easier for Benedict to understand. "The Mexicans who work as pickers—what do you pay them?"

"Fifty."

"Fifty cents a basket?"

"An hour. That's what everybody pays them."

"Do you have any white pickers?"

"Not *now*." Benedict smiled. "It's not the season."

Some of the spectators tittered appreciatively at the spectacle of the lawyer outwitted by the layman. Judge Motley raised his gavel, but the room quieted before he could let it fall.

"Have you ever used white pickers?" David asked evenly.

"Sure," Benedict declared. "Six, seven years ago."

"What did you pay them?"

"Fifty," Benedict said triumphantly. "Same as I paid the Mexicans last fall."

"Haven't wages gone up in the last six years?"

"I wouldn't know about that."

"Wouldn't you have to pay white men more today?"

"I don't know."

"What is the going wage for white pickers today?"

"I don't know."

"But it isn't less than fifty, is it?"

"No."

"How do you know that, if you don't know the wage?"

"I offered fifty and nobody wanted it," Benedict said. "So I brought in the Mexicans."

"Because they would work cheaper than the whites," David added.

"Because they'd work for fifty," Benedict corrected. "And that's all I can pay."

"All right," David said. "If you pay them less than you would have to pay white workers, don't you regard them as inferior? Aren't you prejudiced against them?"

"I can get Mexicans for fifty an hour," Benedict blurted. "Am I supposed to pay them more to prove it to you I love them?"

"Just answer the question please. Are you prejudiced against them?"

"No, I'm not," Benedict said with some heat. "I'm not prejudiced against anybody. I get my labor as cheap as I can. That's all."

"Thank you." David faced the bench. "I ask that this juror be removed for cause," he said.

Judge Motley spoke the single word: "Denied," clearly but without emphasis.

"Exception."

"Noted."

David hesitated. Despite what had been revealed, he was uncertain that Benedict's prejudice was so great as to justify a peremptory challenge. On the other hand, to accept Benedict as foreman would be to accept a defeat and would lower David's standing with the rest of the jurors.

"Do you know the defendant personally?" David asked, hoping to resolve his small dilemma by finding a more solid ground for a challenge for cause.

"No, sir."

"Or any member of the Wiltse family?"

"No, sir." Benedict smiled broadly. David weighed the smile with the other factors and challenged him peremptorily. Judge Motley directed Benedict to leave the box.

As David watched another juror come forward to replace

Benedict, he heard someone's fingers snap. He looked in the direction of the sound, and saw Abbe, standing beside the defense table. She set a brown manila envelope on the table and slid it significantly toward his empty chair.

David smiled vaguely at the jurors, in a sort of apology for momentarily deserting them, and walked to the table. The envelope bore the Pine & Pine imprint. Sprawled across the face was a message, block printed in red crayon:

PINE & PINE REPORT CITY DETECTIVES
CALLED ON JURORS LAST NIGHT

Beneath the message was a huge green exclamation point. David glanced at Abbe, who nodded, confirming his belief that the envelope contained documents to support the message.

"Are you through?" Judge Motley's tones were courteous. David, he implied, could take all the time he wanted, but the court would appreciate being notified when he was done, so that more important matters could be taken up.

"Not quite, your honor," David said. It was hard for him to restrain the intensity of his speech, but he knew that the dramatic impact of what he was to say would be greater if the manner of saying it was ordinary. "I now challenge this entire panel of jurors, and ask that it be dismissed by the court."

"On what grounds?" Armstrong shouted. Judge Motley glared at the District Attorney, who blushed in admission that the question was properly the Judge's to ask.

David forced himself to speak slowly. There was a tense, quiet expectancy in the courtroom. "On the grounds," he said, "that the panel has been tampered with by the State."

"That's a lie!" This time the Judge found it necessary to reprove Armstrong's outburst with a sharp rap of his gavel. A reporter knocked over a chair in trying, apparently, to retrieve a dropped pencil. The spectators laughed, partly at the spectacle of the overturned chair, and partly to relieve the tenseness of the moment.

"The District Attorney," David said, "is misinformed. I am prepared to support my charge with evidence."

Judge Motley linked his hands, propped his elbows on the bench, and leaned his head on his interlocked knuckles. The Judge had to choose, David knew, between two courses of action. To hear David's evidence in open court would have the merit, if the charges did not stick, of exposing their maker as a fraud. But if the evidence had any merit, even if it failed really to support the charge, its exposure in court might produce an expensive mistrial. On the other hand, to hear the evidence in chambers would be an indication that the Judge was taking seriously this complaint of the defense. He gestured first to David, then to Armstrong, beckoning them to approach the bench.

"You have made a serious charge, Mr. Blake," the Judge said, looking down at David and the District Attorney.

"I have, your honor."

"Do you know anything about this?" This to Armstrong.

There was no mistaking the sincerity of Armstrong's "I do not."

Judge Motley looked searchingly from one to the other. "We'll hear this out in chambers," he said. "Just a moment."

"Excuse me." David apologized for starting to leave before the Judge had given him leave.

"I want you to know," Judge Motley said, "that no one is going to play fast and loose with the dignity of this court. If I find your motion was made frivolously, for the purpose of impeding this proceeding, I shall take the sternest possible action."

"I understand." David hoped the gentleness of his reply would be taken as a tactful rebuke to the Judge for having called so obvious a point of law to his attention.

"You may," Judge Motley suggested, "withdraw your charge now. Without prejudice."

David returned Motley's blank gaze. The Judge lifted his head to address the court. "We will have a short recess," he announced, "while this matter is disposed of in chambers. The jurors will remain in the box." He lowered his voice and spoke only to David. "If you have any evidence, Mr. Blake, be kind enough to bring it with you." Gathering his robe about him, the Judge retired through the little door behind the bench.

Abbe hurried up with the manila envelope bearing the Pine & Pine imprint. "It's all there," she said. "And sworn to."

David fumbled with the clasp on the envelope. "By whom?"

"By the detectives who uncovered it."

David confirmed what Abbe had said in a quick leaf-through of the envelope's contents. "Have those detectives available," he ordered. "We just might need them."

"Check." Abbe turned and walked quickly away. David put the papers and the envelope under his arm and started toward the Judge's chambers. As he passed the bench, he saw John Armstrong talking earnestly to someone in the press section. As his angle of vision changed, he was able to make out, first that the District Attorney's face was dead white, and second that the man with whom he was talking was Fats Sanders.

The room beyond the door behind the bench was bare, minus the worn leather chairs and the walls of law books customary in a judge's chambers. But these, David explained to himself, were temporary quarters; Judge Motley did not ordinarily sit in San Juno, but in Capitol City where, it was to be presumed, he had more elaborate chambers.

"Sit, boy," Judge Motley exclaimed. He himself was seated in a straight-backed chair behind a card table. "I haven't got an ice-box in here yet," the Judge explained as David drew up another chair and sat down, "but if you'd like a drink, I can send out for something."

"No thanks, your honor." David watched the door for Armstrong's arrival.

"Court's not in session." Judge Motley grinned. "Forget that 'your honor' stuff."

"O.K."

"My name's Ted."

"Fine." David did not return the Judge's affable grin.

"What's the matter, boy?" Judge Motley demanded. "You sore at me for telling you frivolous motions are contemptuous?"

"A little," David admitted.

"All right. I shouldn't have. Well, like the navigator said when the bomber bumped into the mountain: 'So I made a mistake. What's a matter? You never made a mistake?' "

District Attorney Armstrong came through the door. He bore no resemblance to the All-American boy. His shoulders were slumped and his expression woebegone. He stood next to David's chair and opened his mouth twice before he could produce a sound. "I'm sorry," he said finally. David knew it was very hard for Armstrong to say these words; he found himself a little sorry for the District Attorney who, after all, was not really responsible for what had happened. "I wouldn't have had this happen for the world."

"You wouldn't have had what happen for the world?" Judge Motley asked.

Armstrong looked hopelessly at David. "Some jurors were visited by city detectives last night," David said. "The detectives asked them many questions, some quite personal. Would you call that a fair statement of the facts?"

"Yes." Armstrong looked as if he might shortly be sick to his stomach.

"Was this done with your knowledge?" Judge Motley asked Armstrong.

"No, sir."

"But you knew detectives were investigating prospective jurors?" In important trials, the practice is generally used by the State, and by the defense if there is money to pay for it. The

Judge's question, then, was not designed to learn the facts, but to test the District Attorney's veracity.

"We always do that in a murder case," Armstrong said. "The defense does it too."

"Investigate, that is," David added. "But not send detectives into juror's homes. Not frighten them, or intimidate them."

"I didn't intend that to be done," Armstrong said.

"Now *that*," the Judge put in, "goes only to the question of whether you have been guilty of contempt. The immediate problem is what to do with these jurors. Have they all been approached? Does either one of you know that?"

"I don't." David pushed his papers across the table toward the Judge. "These affidavits relate to *some* jurors we *know* were approached. We haven't checked them all."

Judge Motley glanced through the papers, and then passed them to Armstrong. "Do you know whether the charge is correct as to the jurors named in here?" he asked. "Have they all been approached?"

Armstrong did not look at the papers. "I have no way of knowing," he said. "But if Blake says the affidavits are reliable, I'd concede it."

"Don't rely on my information," David snapped. Armstrong seemed to be trying to associate himself with Judge Motley and the defense in correcting the situation; David was anxious to make their real roles clear. The defense was the aggrieved party; Armstrong was the culprit; and Judge Motley was charged with putting things right. "You concede whatever you like."

"Who was in charge of the detectives?" Judge Motley asked.

"I'd rather not say."

"I'd rather you did." The Judge spoke politely, but he was clearly prepared to insist on an answer.

"A. A. Sanders," Armstrong said.

"Who is?"

"The town jailer." Armstrong smiled the nervous smile

of a schoolboy giving a teacher an answer he knows to be wrong.

"Is that customary?" Judge Motley asked mildly. "I should think someone in the office of—"

"I wanted someone I could trust," Armstrong explained.

"And this man you could trust," the Judge went on, "exceeded his authority, and thereby impaired the defendant's right to a speedy trial by an impartial jury."

"It was a wrong trust," the District Attorney admitted.

"You're putting it rather charitably," Judge Motley said. "Your defense, then, is that you acted like a damn fool."

"I suppose so."

"You know so."

"Yes."

"You're a lucky man, Mr. Armstrong."

"I'm not sure I understand."

"Suppose the defense had not been able to employ detectives. We might have proceeded with a panel that had been most brazenly tampered with. Then suppose, as seems quite likely, these facts somehow became known to the court after the trial."

"I see." Armstrong said the words quickly, as if hoping to bring his reprimand to an end.

"The State," Judge Motley went on inexorably, "has been saved from a mistrial only by the alertness of the defense."

"I apologize to the court," Armstrong said. "I've made a terrible mistake. I take the full responsibility."

"Good." The Judge pushed his chair back and arose. "I warn you now—both of you—that I will hold counsel responsible for any acts by subordinates. Mr. Armstrong, don't get the idea that you will ever again escape so easily."

"Thank you," Armstrong said.

"As for you," the Judge told David, "it will no doubt cross your mind during the trial that, since the State has committed a malfeasance without punishment, you ought to be entitled to a similar 'one on the house.' I cannot punish you for entertaining such thoughts, but I will for acting on them. Understood?"

"Understood," David said.

The Judge sat down again. "You two can go now," he said. "Send this Sanders in, with his records, if he has any. I'll reconvene court after lunch."

Abbe was alone at the defense table when David re-entered the courtroom. "It's stuffy in here," she said. "How about eating outside on the lawn?" She indicated a brown paper bag in her hand.

"Fine," David said, thinking how much more pleasant lunch would be on the lawn than in the crowded courthouse restaurant, and how impossible it would have been had not Abbe brought the paper bag.

Lunch was indeed pleasant. David sat with his back against a tree and Abbe beside him, and enjoyed the nearness of her, and the respectful glances of the passers-by, while he told her what had gone on in Judge Motley's chambers. "We'll get rid of every juror that Sanders' people talked to," he concluded, "and Armstrong'll see there's no more of that kind of nonsense."

"But no mistrial," Abbe said almost wistfully.

For a moment David did not follow her. Then he brightened. "Oh. You're thinking of what Motley said."

"If you'd waited until after the trial—" she broke off the thought.

"Then if the verdict wasn't to my liking, I could bring in the affidavits and get a mistrial? Is that what you're thinking?"

Abbe nodded, and mentioned a California case in which the defense, after an adverse verdict, had secured a retrial by proving that some of the jurors had been favored with visits by members of the District Attorney's staff.

"In that case," David pointed out, "the defense found out about it after the trial."

"But—" Abbe struggled for words. "Who knew?" she asked. "Who knew that you knew?"

"You did," David said. "And so did Dick Pine, and the field-men who made the interviews, and the stenographers who took the affidavits, and maybe the notary who signed them."

"David—"

"If no one knew, that would only mean I'd have a chance to get away with perjury. It wouldn't make it right."

"Perjury? I don't see—"

"God damn it, Abbe, if you're going to practice law, you might as well find out what it is." David hoped that his near sarcastic reference to Abbe's "practicing law" would soften the nature of what he was saying, just as he knew it would not. "The legal system—judicial procedure—isn't a game. It's designed to protect your client's right, and you've got to use it that way. You can't allow those rights to be compromised without timely protest, and then come around later and bleed to the judge and try to have it all done over again—"

"It's over anyhow," Abbe said. "Isn't it?"

"I've made my move, if that's what you mean," David said. "In this business, they don't let you call those moves back."

"Then let's not argue about it." Abbe smiled at him, and reached out her hand toward him. He took the hand and held it, and was conscious again of the pleasant warmth of the sun and the good smell of the grass.

"Barney won't like it," Abbe said, resuming the expired conversation as if it were a wholly new matter.

"Barney," David began in reply, "can take a long running—"

"They're starting, Mr. Blake," a courtroom attendant said. David and Abbe, their fingers linked, rose and re-entered the courtroom.

Angel was already seated at the defense table. His posture, David noted with satisfaction, was erect, and his bearing alert but not aggressive. The spectators arose as Judge Motley entered, and then were seated. The Judge stared down at the jurors' section as though he somehow blamed them for what had happened.

118

"The clerk," Judge Motley announced, "will now read the names of certain jurors who are hereby excused from service at this trial. They are excused because the State, in an excess of zeal, caused its agents to make contact with them. All persons are cautioned against seeking to influence any juror, whether he has actually been selected or is merely one of a panel from which the actual jury will be selected."

The clerk began reading names. As each name was called, a juror arose from his place, either in the box, or in the spectator's section, and left the room. When the reading was done, there were nine potential jurors left in the room, including three in the jury box proper.

"Have any of you," Judge Motley asked the remaining jurors, "been approached in any way, by any person whatsoever, in connection with your service here?"

There was a pause, and then a man in the almost deserted section of seats arose. "Your honor," he quavered, "last night an officer—"

"That will do." Judge Motley cut him off sharply. "Give your name to the clerk as you go out. You are excused. Any others?"

There were none. Judge Motley counted those remaining and turned to the bailiff. "Are more jurors available?" he asked.

"Another hundred," the bailiff said, "but they don't report until tomorrow. Seemed sort of silly to make them wait around—"

"Yes, yes. No one's fault." Judge Motley turned to direct his remarks impartially at the empty space between the conflicting counsel tables. "It would seem useless to continue," he said. "Unless there are further motions to be made, I would be inclined to—"

David got quickly to his feet. "The juror Benedict, your honor?" he asked. "Had he not been challenged by the defense, would his name have been included among those dismissed by the court?"

"The point, I think, is moot. He will not serve."

"I submit, your honor, that if, in point of fact, he was ineligible to serve, then the defense ought not to be required to waste a challenge on him."

The Judge searched through the papers on his desk and then separated one sheet from the others.

"In the interest of fairness," Armstrong said, speaking rather more loudly than David had, "the State will challenge the juror Benedict."

At this grandstand gesture, David felt, for the first time, a real hatred of his adversary. "Surely, your honor," he protested, "there can be no challenge of him while he is not a juror. And if he is to be considered a juror," he went on, "I assume the court will dismiss him as it did the others."

"You ask to withdraw your challenge, then?"

"I do."

"A most unusual request."

"I submit that the State has brought about a most unusual situation. Ought the defense to suffer from the State's—" David searched his memory for the words the Judge had used— "excessive zeal?" David was beginning to regret having brought the point up at all. He was certain he was right, but, in bringing it up, he incurred the risk of a defeat which, coming at the end of the day's proceedings, would give the newspapers something to publish—and the prospective jurors, by extension, something to read and think about—other than the staggering defeat already suffered by the prosecution.

"Very well," Judge Motley said. David felt better. "The juror Benedict is reinstated." He hesitated; David felt again the twinge of fear of having made the wrong move. "We now note," the Judge resumed, and David knew then that he was right, "that a member of this jury is ineligible for the reason I previously stated. The juror Benedict is excused." He waited, as if for Benedict—who was not, of course, present for this brief reincarnation as a talesman—to depart. "Unless there are further motions . . ."

"Your honor." John Armstrong spoke slowly but firmly. "I apologize to the court for an action which might have prejudiced the rights of the defendant. Without in any way lessening my own guilt in connection with that act, I want to assure the court that it was done through inadvertence and without evil intent."

"Your apology is noted," Judge Motley replied. "I might add that the fact that you leave this courtroom a free man, and not under bond, is evidence that the court agrees that the disgraceful event was not maliciously caused. Neither ignorance, nor inadvertence, nor excessive zeal, however, will be considered in mitigation, Mr. Armstrong, if anything of this sort occurs again."

"Thank you, your honor."

"Court is adjourned until ten o'clock tomorrow morning."

On which happy—for David at least—note, the first day of *State v. Chavez* concluded.

from the Journal of David Blake
Thursday, July 10, 1947

. . . just when to follow the textbook rules and principles and when to throw the book away. Barney's objection to the M.A.A., for instance, would seem to be that they would stick too closely to the book where, if a genuinely fair trial is to be achieved, the defense must be prepared to go as far to excess as the State. Contrariwise, to have withheld from the court—as Abbe seemed to propose—the facts concerning the jurors, with a view toward using that information later on in order to obtain (in the event of an unfavorable verdict) a retrial, would have been wrong. It is hard to make a rule that will permit some *practical* (perhaps the wrong word?) acts, and yet forbid others. Is the rule simply that the defense attorney does whatever seems likely to aid his client, *so long as he can get away with it?* I think not. I would not have allowed the case to go to the original panel even if I had been sure of getting away with it. (And yet I made my argument to Abbe on the assumption that I would be caught. Why? Am I, for some reason, ashamed to admit to her that I am governed, to some extent at least, by considerations of morals and ethics?)

Yet Abbe could have prevented me from using the Pine & Pine reports, if she felt strongly about the matter, by failing to transmit them to me. Why did she not withhold them? Because I might have caught her at it? Hardly likely. Perhaps there was an ethical consideration in her case as well.

Tomorrow . . .

6

The second day of the trial was over, and a weekend lay ahead
David sat at Barney's desk, in Barney's office, watching the late
afternoon sun work its way past the window ledge, enjoying the
coolness of the early evening and the prospect of a weekend—
with Abbe, of course—at the beach house. From time to time,
reluctantly, as if answering to some call of duty, he shuffled the
stack of clippings on the desk, and glanced at some of them.

The clippings pertained to the first day of Angel's trial, and
they varied widely as to origin, placement within the paper, and
wording. Thus: GOON COPS THREATEN ANGEL JURY (Page 1, *The
People's World*); MASS JURY DISMISSALS IN CHAVEZ CASE (Page 19,
The New York Times); and DEFENSE MOTION STALLS TRIAL (Page
1, *The San Juno Standard*).

David pushed the clippings aside, and noticed that his hand, as
it rested on the desk, was shaking. He needed the weekend badly,
he decided. And yet, if he were to withstand the ordeal of the
trial itself, this pretrial period given over to the selection of the
jury ought not to be so exhausting, especially since, for the first
two days, at least, things had gone very well indeed. Of eighteen
jurors who had been excused at the request of the defense, only
one had been peremptorily challenged, seventeen having been
dismissed "for cause." This meant that David was, thanks to the
latitude Judge Motley was giving him, disposing of jurors he

believed to be biased at a good rate, without using his precious peremptory challenges. It also meant that he was presenting to the people in the courtroom, which group included some potential jurors, a series of small victories that lengthened every time he moved to excuse a juror for cause and Judge Motley granted the motion.

On the other hand, it was possible that in making these motions, even though Judge Motley consented to them, David was giving the impression that he was stalling, consuming time in petti-fogging to delay the dread moment when the merits of the case would be put to trial. Yet he owed it to his client to see that the issues, when finally put to trial, were decided by a jury as favorably constituted as could be managed.

The sun passed below the window ledge, and with its passing David realized that it had been in his eyes, that he felt better for its going. Abbe came in from the outer office, where she had been winnowing through the morning mail.

"Not a death threat in the lot," she reported cheerfully, dropping all but one of the envelopes in the wastebasket. "I thought you ought to see this. You'll have to sign the answer, anyhow." She tossed him the remaining envelope.

David slid the letter out of its container, spread it on the desk, and read it. It was on the stationery of the State Assembly Committee on Disloyalty and Subversion. The body of the letter was short and, to David, disturbing.

> Dear Mr. Blake:
> This Committee is informed that you have information which will be useful to it in fulfilling its aims as set forth in Assembly Resolution 12, Proceedings of 1946.
> Will you be kind enough, at your earliest convenience, to let me know when it will be possible for you to come to Capitol City in order that I may examine you informally, following which we may wish to take your testimony in public session?
> In the event that you wish to claim your traveling expenses,

please prepare vouchers covering them *in detail* and present such vouchers to the Clerk of the Committee on your arrival.

Very truly yours,

Carl Baron Battle
Chairman

"Jesus Christ!" David explained. "That's all it needed." Then he added, half to himself: "None but Americans!"

"None but Americans" was Carl Baron Battle's slogan. His most rabid partisans—who gave evidence of their partisanship by paying $1-a-year dues to None-But-Americans, Inc.—believed Battle had made the phrase up. Others, somewhat more sophisticated, were aware that the words came from the command: "Put none but Americans on guard," uttered by George Washington on Christmas Eve, just before his troops crossed the Delaware to ambush the British at Trenton. Still others—but these were mostly to be found in the ranks of Battle's opponents—disputed that Washington had ever said the words, and wrote learned treatises supporting their disputes.

But whether or not Washington had uttered the phrase, Battle had made good use of the three words. At the age of thirty, he was serving his third term in the State Assembly. It was at his insistence that the Assembly Committee on Subversion and Disloyalty had been created; he had been its first and only chairman, and, insofar as the public was concerned, the committee (which was usually called the Battle Committee) and its chairman were one and the same. Under his guidance, the Battle Committee had imposed on every teacher in the State, from nursery school through the graduate schools of the University, an oath not merely stating the teacher's fidelity to the Constitution of the United States, but to that of the State as well (including, a waggish journalist had pointed out, the State's barge canal, which was detailed in the Constitution) and to the Governor of the State, and affirming the affiant's devotion to the "principles of free enterprise" and his belief in "God or a supreme being." He had forced the discharge of one grammar school teacher who had been a member of the I.W.W. in his youth (the teacher was past seventy at the time of his discharge), and the suspension of eighteen others, of whom sixteen had been reinstated and two were awaiting a hearing. (As to the sixteen who were reinstated, Battle had announced his decision to subpoena and question the board which had reinstated them.)

All this David knew, and more. He knew of the immense political power of N.B.A.; in a state where the balance of power between the two major parties is uncertain, any sizable group, even a lunatic formation like N.B.A., can exercise a veto power. He regarded Carl Baron Battle as an evil man, a subverter of the democratic institutions of the State, and, worse, as an opportunist who played the part of the fanatic because, in an age of fanaticism, extremism offered attractive possibilities, mostly financial. He knew there were others in the State who regarded Battle as a savior, as the only man who could save the State (indeed, perhaps, the nation) from the alien "forces" which threatened to engulf it. And he knew that there was no middle position, unless you considered those who regarded Battle as a madman, and hence sincere, to represent a middle position between those who considered him a savior and those who considered him a cynical profiteer.

"I took his god damn oath," David said angrily. "What the hell does he want me to do now? Swear personal loyalty to him?"

"Well, don't take it out on me," Abbe snapped. "I'm sorry," she added. "We're both tired."

"I'm sorry too." Looking at Abbe, who seemed somehow cool, dry, and relaxed, in the hot, humid exhaustion of the summer afternoon, David felt his irritation at Battle's letter mount, seeing it as one last, unforecast impediment to be overcome before the weekend, before he could be close to her on the white, hot sand of the beach, and the cool, white sheets of Barney's bed—why did he always think of it as Barney's bed?—and regain some of the freshness and vigor with which he had begun the trial, was it only a day before? Perhaps, he suggested hopefully, they could forget about the letter until the following Monday.

Abbe shook her head regretfully. "That letter," she said, "is what Battle calls 'an invitation to appear voluntarily.' If you answer it on Monday, he'll get the answer Tuesday. But at nine o'clock Monday morning, he'll issue a subpoena for you, and at nine-thirty he'll call in the reporters and tell them he's issued it, and at the same time he'll tell them that he asked you to appear voluntarily and that you didn't reply."

"But—"

"Oh sure," Abbe said. "Then you'll get out a statement to the press pointing out that you only received the subpoena on Friday, and that you were planning to reply to it that day. And then Battle will graciously withdraw his subpoena. And as far as the public is concerned, he'll be courtesy itself, and you'll be the so-and-so that's stalling him in the performance of his duties."

"But after all—"

"I know how he operates," Abbe said. "And that's not all. You're not going to appear voluntarily, are you?"

"I'm trying a murder case," David said wearily. "I haven't the faintest idea what he wants from me, but whatever it is, he'll have to wait."

"And that's what you'll say in your letter?"

"More politely," David said. "But that's it."

"All right. Now," Abbe went on, "what happens if you wait until Monday night to write that letter? Remember, by Monday night, you're the guy who didn't reply to his invitation until he swore out a subpoena, and *then* you said you wanted to answer his invitation, and, on the strength of that, he withdrew the subpoena. Tuesday he gets your letter *declining* his invitation. Do I have to spell it out for you?"

"No," David admitted. "Only why—"

"Don't worry about why he wants to do it," Abbe advised. "Just stop him from doing it."

"You run up the letter," David said. "Address him as your excellency, or your highness, or however you address the chairman of a legislative committee. Say that I don't think I have any information that would be of use to the committee and that the press of my legal duties prevents me from going to Capitol City right now. Make it friendly, but not too friendly."

As Abbe inserted paper and carbon paper in a typewriter, one of the phones on David's desk rang. David picked up both phones, and experimented with the switch at his elbow until a voice from one of the phones inquired, in the artificial accents used exclusively by telephone operators, whether this was the office of Bernard Castle?

"That's right," David said. "But he's not here."

"Is Abbe Klein there?"

"Hell," a voice cut in. "I'll talk to anybody. That you, David?"

"Barney?"

Apparently David's surprise showed in his voice. "That's right," Barney replied. "You sound guilty, David. You doing anything you shouldn't?"

"Haven't had time," David said, looking at Abbe and wondering if his answer was entirely correct. "That all you wanted?"

"Not quite," Barney replied. "I want you."

"What?" David signaled to Abbe to stop typing so that he could hear better.

"It's a fact," Barney went on. "I need you for a meeting tomorrow night."

"Tomorrow?"

"It's important, David. Court doesn't sit on Saturday, does it?"

"No, but honest to God—"

"I'm sorry, David. You've just got to do it. I know how tough it is for you to lose your weekend, but I promised these people I'd get you for a big meeting—"

"I can't, Barney."

"If you can't, you can't," Barney conceded. "What's in the till?"

"A couple of hundred," David said. "I was counting on you—"

"That's the point. Can you get by for the rest of the trial with what you've got now?"

"I—"

"Because if you don't make that meeting, there won't be any more." It was no threat; Barney was merely stating a fact he obviously regretted but had to recognize as a fact just the same. "Maybe I shouldn't have done it," Barney went on, "but they offered to rent the Arena if I'd promise to have you as the speaker—"

"Speaker?"

"Don't get upset. Just a few words. I'll write them for you."

David regretted having indicated his distaste at the idea of speechmaking. Doing so had allowed Barney to make the issue on that, less important, point, rather than on the whole fantastic idea of the trip itself.

"You can get the midnight plane out of San Juno," Barney said. "That'll put you in New York about four tomorrow afternoon. Get a plane back after the meeting and be back on the Coast by two o'clock Sunday afternoon."

"That," David said bitterly, "leaves me all of Sunday to kill."

"You'll do it then," Barney said, not asking a question.

"I didn't say that," David pointed out.

"Well, say it now."

"I've got to think about it."

"Think about it then," Barney said, without emphasis. "But think fast. If the answer is 'no,' this call is costing you about one-half a per cent of your defense fund every minute."

David knew this was quite literally true. He knew, too, that another hundred jurors would be called on Monday, and that the cost of investigating these jurors, which investigation he had already ordered, would, if further funds were not forthcoming, leave the defense penniless. It was, he suddenly knew, his weekend (for which he had a great need) against Angel's chance for life; and he weighed the two momentarily, and resolved them, and was ashamed of having weighed them.

"All right," David said, adding cautiously: "If it's that important."

"It is," Barney said, and Barney spoke to David about the details of the trip, what clothes he should bring with him, what he should say (nothing) if, through some mischance, reporters were to confront him at the airport, what arrangements he should make against the possibility that, through bad weather, he should be delayed beyond the opening of court on Monday, and then to Abbe about the mechanics of obtaining the airline ticket, and of how Barney was to be advised of David's time of arrival. But all this was detail, and David scarcely listened to it. The weekend was gone. David found himself remembering the time—he was eleven, he thought—when his father had promised (or David had thought he had promised; it didn't matter which) to take him to a football game. Who was playing he no longer remembered, but it was called the Big Game. And on that Saturday morning it had rained, and by eleven o'clock David knew that his father was not going to keep his promise (if, indeed, there had ever been a promise). But then there had been his father to blame for the unkept promise; and this weekend was something he had promised himself, and there was no one, not even himself, to blame for its loss.

When the phone call was done, Abbe finished typing the letter, and David signed it, and they took it with them and mailed it on their way to the shack. The trip was a hasty one, as David had planned it would be, but not for the reason he had planned, namely his own (and Abbe's, he thought) haste to be bedded, but because the plane left at eleven, and he had to shower and change his clothes and eat a dreary meal, composed of the same elements that might have made a feast, and pack. And then, because Abbe did not drive, and David was uncertain about leaving his car in the open at the airport for the forty hours he would be away, they had called a cab.

At the doorway of the shack, with his bag under one arm and his brief case under the other—for there were the reports on the new jurymen to peruse and make extracts and cryptic pencil marks from—with the cab waiting across the street, David realized he had forgotten his journal, and asked Abbe to bring it to him.

"Do you write everything that happens down in the book, David?" she asked him.

"No," he said. "But I try to get what's important. Maybe a page a day."

"Write a lot down, David," she said with sudden inexplicable emphasis. "You'll need it all." And then, as if she had not said something rather bewildering, she smiled and kissed him. "I'd like to read it someday, David," she said. "I might know you better."

"You'll read it someday," he said. "But you'll never know me better."

They kissed again, and David found it hard to believe that he would travel seven thousand miles before he saw her again. Juggling his three burdens, he crossed the street to the cab.

"Airport?" the driver asked.

"That's right." David got in and seated himself, looking out the window, across the street, to Abbe framed in the yellow light of the house door. Her image jumped to the other window as the cab turned around, then grew large as it passed close to the house, then grew suddenly narrow and disappeared.

As he waited by the desk at the airport for his luggage to be weighed, David was suddenly aware that the man next to him, an elderly man, with watery blue eyes and white hair, was staring at him curiously. "Can I do something for you?" David asked.

"I doubt it." The man smiled. "You're Blake, aren't you? David Blake?"

For a moment David was surprised. Then he told himself that he was, locally at least, and perhaps elsewhere, a celebrity. "That's right." He tried to make the admission politely and yet in such a way that it could not be taken for an invitation to further conversation.

"I'm Charles White," the man said. "I'm the publisher of the *State Record*."

David looked at the man with interest. The *Record* was the oldest paper in the State, with a history of continuous publication that went back to territorial days. Published in Capitol City, it had a considerable statewide circulation. It was the only paper, aside from the *University Telegraph* and the *New York Times*, that circulated widely on the campus of State University.

"I'm pleased to meet you," David said, shaking White's outstretched hand.

"It's none of my business," White admitted, "but how come you're at the airport? I should think you'd be too busy to be going anywhere?"

David considered making up a story about meeting someone, but the baggage he was in the process of checking made it unlikely that such a story could be believed. Moreover, if White waited, he would see David board the midnight plane for New York. "I'm going to New York," David said; and then, for no reason at all, he added: "Just for the weekend."

"Good." White smiled pleasantly. "I'll have somebody to talk to."

God forbid, David thought. But later, as the plane droned through the night, David found himself not merely talking with Charles White but actually doing so with keen pleasure.

White, he soon discovered, had spent the first forty years of his adult life in the practice of law, in and out of the State. Much of that practice had been trial work, and he had some firm and interesting opinions about juries, judges, and other aspects of what Dean Paley would have called "the law *in vitro*."

"Juries," White was saying, about an hour after the take-off, "develop a sort of corporate personality. Their likes, their dislikes, their opinions, tend to crystallize into a single attitude, as it were, especially in a long trial."

"I don't think I understand you," David said.

"You haven't practiced much. Before juries, I mean. Have you?"

"This is my first case." David realized he should not have said the words the instant it was too late for that realization to have any practical application. He glanced quickly at White, who seemed not to react at all to what should have been a rather startling piece of intelligence.

"You'll see it in a long case," White said. "You start out by arguing to the jurors as individuals, watching first one and then the other. And then, without your ever being conscious of it, you stop thinking of them as individuals and direct yourself to the twelve of them in the mass. And the wonder of it is that they respond in the same way."

"It's hard to believe," David said.

"But true. Especially in a long case. You'll see. This'll be a long one. The Chavez case, I mean. Won't it?"

"That's up to the State, isn't it?" David replied.

White nodded his agreement. He reached above his head and turned the cuplike device on his overhead light so that the light was covered. David, taking this as a sign that his companion felt the hour for sleep had come, was surprised to realize that it was White who was ending, temporarily, at least, the conversation and David himself who would have preferred to talk at greater length.

He turned off his own light, tipped his seat back, and stared at the dark interior of the plane, the odd shapes that were the seated passengers now clearly outlined in the moonlight, now dim as the plane passed through a cloud bank, finally merging together and becoming somehow confused with the drone of the motors.

When he awoke, it was morning, and the faint blueness of the air outside his window, and the wispiness of the clouds that crept by from time to time, told him they were flying quite high.

White was already awake. He greeted David and signaled to a stewardess, who brought them coffee.

With the coming of the coffee, the talk began again. David listened through all that morning to White's views on judges, juries, and the law, speaking himself only in answer to the older man's questions. The questions came in pairs, one general, relating to the subject on which White had been discoursing, and the second, highly specific, dealing with the subject in terms of the Chavez case.

Thinking it over, in the airport restaurant in Chicago, as he waited for White to return from the men's room, David decided that he had, in response to these questions, disclosed to White a great deal of information about the Chavez case, information he would not have thought of disclosing to a close friend, much less to a stranger who was also a newspaper publisher. He stared at White when he came back from the men's room, and wondered if White had been pumping him. But there was a frank openness about White's face that made him ashamed to have wondered.

He became, however, more cautious in his answers. "I really don't know," he said, when White, after a recountal of the vagaries and prejudices of certain judges before whom he had practiced, pointed out that a judge's prejudices become plain to the attorney against whom they are directed from the jurist's manner of ruling on points of law more quickly than from the rulings themselves, and asked: "Haven't you found it that way? With Motley, I mean?"

David started to justify his uncertain answer by pointing out that he hadn't had sufficient time to reach any conclusion about Judge Motley, but White, ignoring him, plunged into another dissertation, eventually ending it with another specific question. This time David fenced without attempting an apology.

Later, White fell silent, and David felt ashamed again at having suspected anything beyond genuine interest in his views in White's occasional interrogation, and wondered, hoping it was not so, if White had guessed what was in his mind and taken offense at it.

Hours later, David saw Manhattan pass below him, and then a river; then the suburban houses, in rows, tipping up in his view, and the suddenly mounting pressure in his ears, told him they were landing. In obedience to the illuminated sign ahead of him, David fastened his seat belt.

"Mr. Blake." There was an urgency in White's salutation, David thought, but turning, seeing the other's smiling, composed face, he would have decided he was wrong had not White, seeing him turn, said: "Have you sent your answer to Mr. Battle yet?"

For an instant, David doubted that he had heard correctly. The pressure on his ears, the roar of the motor, the fear which every air traveler must know, subconsciously, in knowing that the difficult transition from airborne to landborne is about to be attempted, all these, perhaps, had conspired to make him think he had heard—

"You don't have to tell me," White said, and David knew he had not imagined the question. "But let me tell you something: if you haven't answered his invitation, do it right away."

He paused as if to permit David to speak, and then, when David was silent, went on. "Send him a telegram from the airport if you have to. Capitol City will be address enough. But send it. That way, you'll postpone the trouble."

The plane shuddered as its wheels found the earth, then slowed as its flaps took hold. "Postpone the trouble?" David repeated stupidly.

"Young man," White said firmly, "don't bother trying to figure out how I know what I know. That's not important to you. What is important is that you are heading for bad trouble. Very, very bad trouble. Just about the worst trouble a man, in this day and age, can get into. Even though," he added significantly, "you're getting plenty of help."

"I really don't understand what you're talking about," David said.

"I don't mean by that last," White went on, "that anybody's helping you out of trouble. Into it, is what I mean. You have plenty of help getting into it."

The plane was turning at the end of the runway, starting back toward the point at which it would be unloaded. David undid his safety belt and stood up.

"I'm sorry," he said, "but I'm afraid I just don't have the time to—"

"Don't apologize." White, who occupied the seat between David and the aisle, made no move to get up. "I might have known you wouldn't have any idea what I was driving at."

"I—"

"Don't interrupt," White commanded, in the sharp tones of one who is accustomed to having his commands obeyed. "It wastes time, and you say you're busy. Waste of my time and yours, my explaining. Waste of time now because you won't believe me. Waste of time later, because you won't need explanations then."

The plane jarred to a stop. "You'll have to excuse me," David said.

Still White did not move. "I'm a newspaperman now," he said. "I deal in facts. Collecting them, and using them. Some day you're going to find you've collected a lot of facts, but you won't know how to use them. When you do, let me know." He handed David a card. David, glancing down, read *White's House, Highway 40, Sparks, Nevada.* "Just east of Reno," White explained. "I'm almost always there. If I'm out when you arrive, somebody'll know where to get me."

Suddenly David felt sorry for this old man, and grateful for his offer to defend him from harm, even if the harm existed only in the old man's confused mind. It was as if a child had come to him and offered to defend him against a bogeyman. David tried not to smile. "Thank you," he said, tucking the card away in his jacket pocket.

White moved out into the aisle, and David followed him. Other passengers came between them, and by the time David reached the door to the ramp, White was gone.

"David!" It was Barney's voice. David blinked in the afternoon sunlight. Barney was standing with another man near the passenger gate. David walked quickly down the ramp toward them.

"Good trip?" Barney asked after shaking David's hand.

David nodded.

Barney gestured toward the brief case in David's hand. "You got a lot of work done, I suppose," he said, his tone making it clear that he supposed no such thing.

"Not much," David admitted.

Barney announced that, in his opinion, no one could work on an airplane, it being, in his view, sufficiently unreasonable that a man should allow himself to sit ten thousand feet in the air with only an inch of metal between himself and eternity, without requiring him to work at the same time, and introduced the other man as "Lewis Cheever, of Free World Communications." Mr. Cheever said "Pleased to meet you," and he seemed about to say more, but Barney interrupted to ask David for his baggage check; and, when David had produced it, Barney gave the check to Cheever and commanded him to get the bag, and Cheever trotted off toward the baggage desk.

"Who's he?" David asked, when Cheever was out of sight.

"Cheever," Barney said. "Lewis Cheever. They call him rabbit because when he gets excited his nose twitches."

"I heard his name," David said. "I meant where does he fit in?"

"David," Barney said, putting his hand on David's shoulder, "in the next few hours, you are going to meet so many people, and hear about so many organizations, it'll have you as dizzy as it's got me. I'll try to explain what I can, but you'll just have to take my word for the rest."

"Your word on what?"

"My word that everything that's done is done with Angel in mind." Barney glanced around warily. "Cheever's outfit," he went on, "is devoted to giving a voice to those who speak for peace, and who are denied access to the normal channels of communication." His voice made it clear that he was quoting from something he did not entirely believe.

"That what Cheever says?"

"That's what's in his pamphlets," Barney said. "My idea is that his outfit is primarily a fund-raising device for his own private benefit. But that doesn't matter. He's helping us, so we're helping him."

"How does he help us?"

Barney looked around again. Cheever was nowhere in sight. "Free World Communications has mailing lists," he said, "and we're canvassing those lists for contributions. Also, the Furriers' Political Action Group had the Arena for tonight, and we're subletting it from them."

"That's his outfit too?" David asked. "He doesn't look like a furrier."

"It's his brother's outfit," Barney said. "And the brother doesn't look like a furrier either. But by being nice to Cheever, I got his brother to let us have the place for twenty per cent of the gross. A third is more usual. In return—" Barney's eyes had been searching nervously for Cheever while he talked. Now he saw him and called his name. Cheever came over, carrying the bag. David started to take it from him.

"Let him keep it," Barney said firmly. "Come on, Lew. Let's get going."

David thought he saw a look of hatred in Cheever's face as he took back the bag. Then Cheever turned and led the way out of the building and put the suitcase in the back seat of a moderately old black sedan. At Barney's suggestion, he and David got into the back seat.

They rode for some time in silence. David found himself thinking about Charles White, wondering whether there was any theory that could explain his peculiar conduct, or whether the whole episode had to be written off as incomprehensible. If he knew of Battle's letter—which he did; that much was certain—then perhaps he had known of David's trip in advance. But he could not have known of David's trip. On the other hand—

They slowed down for the tollgate on the bridge leading to Manhattan. Barney produced a quarter and handed it forward to Cheever. Cheever handed it to the collector, and turned his head slightly as they pulled away from the gate.

"Thanks," he said. And then, to David, he added: "Are you the one who broke up that jury tampering business?"

David said that he was. "You did it all wrong," Cheever said. "You should—"

"You a lawyer, Lew?" Barney cut in. "I didn't know that."

"No," Cheever admitted. "I'm not."

"Then shut up," Barney snapped. "And watch the road."

David could see the back of Cheever's neck growing red as he complied with Barney's order. They traveled on in silence down the east side of Manhattan, and across the island to the hotel. Cheever handed the keys to a doorman, took David's bag, and tagged along at the rear as Barney led David through the lobby to the elevator; the elevator took them up, and Barney led the way down a hall to a room, and, after producing a key, into the room, and commanded Cheever to put the bag on the bed. This Cheever did with unnecessary violence.

"Careful, Lew," Barney warned. "I may not give you a tip." He did not speak lightly, nor did he smile as he spoke. "Come on," he added. "Let's go down to my room."

Barney's room was slightly larger than David's and contained, in addition to the bed, a divan, in front of which a wire recorder had been placed. Consuela, who had been sitting on the couch with a tall, handsome man in his forties, got up as Barney and David (followed at a respectful distance by Cheever) entered. She embraced Barney, greeted David, and introduced the man on the divan as Mr. Hopper.

"Just call me Max," Hopper said, extending his hand but not rising for David's handshake. David noticed a pair of crutches balanced against the end of the divan, and realized that this was *the* Max Hopper, a man for whom David had, in his boyhood days, an almost fanatical admiration. This was the man who, as a foreign correspondent, had narrowly missed winning the Pulitzer Prize for his report on the Riff rebellion. Later he had gone to Spain to cover the battle of Guadalajara, and had remained to lead first a platoon, and later a company, and finally a regiment of Loyalist infantry. Even after the Ebro line had been breached, and Madrid had fallen, and the Loyalist government had fled in defeat across the border into the Pyrenees, Max Hopper had remained and fought, until, while he was blowing up a German tank during a Falangist parade in the streets of Cadiz, the tank's treads had passed over both his knees. The story of these exploits, and of his subsequent escape from a top-security prison (carried on a litter, David recalled, by three fellow prisoners, two of them women) had formed the basis of *I Fight for Man*, a controversial best-seller of David's college days. On his return from Spain, Hopper, a life-long Democrat, had broken with the Administration over what he called "the sale of Spain to Hitler and Mussolini," and had then helped found the New York People's Party, of which, after half a dozen "splits" and "splinterings," he remained the titular leader. In 1946, he ran for Congress; though he was beaten, it was necessary for the Republicans and Democrats to join in support of a single candidate to defeat him, and even then the margin of defeat had been thin.

"Are you undressing me politically?" Hopper asked mildly.

"No." David did not realize he was staring. "It's just that meeting you, after all I've heard— I remember—"

"That's what people do when they meet me," Hopper said regretfully. "They remember. I'm like an old song people like to hear. The song isn't any good, but hearing it takes them back to when they were younger. I am," he concluded, "a living souvenir."

Cheever threw a switch on the wire recorder and a green light on top of the machine went on. "We're all set," he announced. "Let's get going."

"Get going with what?" David asked.

"Mrs. Chavez is going to cut a tape for me," Cheever said, talking to David, but looking at Barney as he spoke.

"Not until we straighten a few things out," Barney said. "I never did get to see that script."

"All right," Cheever agreed unhappily. He produced, from his wallet pocket, two typed pages and handed them to Barney. The others watched as Barney, his expression darkening, read quickly through the pages.

"This is pure crap," Barney announced at last. "I don't object to party-line stuff, but this business about—" he read scornfully— " 'to kill my boy is but a way my country make war on her dark-skin peoples' is plain nonsense, and everybody that hears it is going to know it's nonsense."

"It's been cleared," Cheever said.

"Not by me." Barney's eyes roamed the page he was holding, and then he read again: " 'Even if my boy die, he no die for nothing.' Why the mammy dialect? Consuela's English is all right."

"My speech is awkward," Consuela said diffidently. "But not that bad."

"I was trying," Cheever explained, "to give it the Sacco touch."

Barney's laugh was loud and ugly. "Christ Almighty!" he shouted. "You guys throw some soap-opera dialogue on top of some used up *Worker* editorials and talk about Sacco. David, you think you can fix this up?"

"I don't know—"

"Of course you can. Just have her say who she is and where she lives, and that she has a boy seventeen years old. The boy's accused of a terrible crime, and he didn't do it, but he won't get a fair trial because he's a Mexican. And wind up with something about how every man's fate is a little involved with Angel's. You know. No man is an island, and all."

"It really isn't necessary," Cheever argued. "We'll use it mostly abroad. People'll hear Mrs. Chavez's voice, but the words will be translated as she goes on."

"Well," Barney said, "I'm sure you'll screw up the translations, but at least let's have the original make sense." He handed the script to David, who sat down on the divan, borrowed a pencil from Max Hopper, and began to write, on the back of one of the pages, a version along the lines Barney had proposed.

"You got the contract?" Barney asked.

"For the tape?"

"I already signed that," Barney said. "For the hall?"

Hopper produced a contract and handed it to Barney for his inspection. Barney skimmed part way through it and then stopped short. "Hold it, David," he said. "We're not going to need any script."

David, who had written three words, stopped. "What's the matter?" Max Hopper asked.

"The matter is that this contract calls for twenty-five per cent of the gross for the god damn furriers. Lew told me twenty."

"My brother Artie," Cheever said nervously. "He's a hard man to deal with. He usually gets thirty-three and a third."

"I don't usually spend defense money on whipping up enthusiasm for my client in Prague or New Delhi," Barney pointed out. "You promised twenty. No more."

"Twenty-five's the best I can do."

Barney flipped the various switches of the tape recorder until the green light blinked and went out. "Then take this gadget out of here," he commanded.

"I've got a contract," Cheever protested.

Barney told him in some detail what he could do with his contract.

"Give me a break, Barney," Cheever pleaded. "I can't go back to Artie now, after I told him you agreed to—"

"I'm doing you a favor letting Consuela cut the tape," Barney said. "We're paying you twenty-five hundred dollars for the job. That money comes right out of the funds we've got to use to defend a boy's life. If you think that, in addition to that, your brother's two-bit pressure gang is going to get one dollar out of every four we collect tonight, just forget the whole thing."

"Barney's right." Hopper's voice had a judicial ring to it. "Twenty's enough for the furriers."

"That's all I'll have to pay?" Barney asked cautiously.

"I'll talk to Artie," Hopper said. "I'm the party chairman. I don't think he'll risk an outright break with me over it."

"Go ahead then, David," Barney said. David worked quickly, following the outline Barney had suggested to him, finishing as Barney had suggested, with a paraphrase of Donne's lines. When he was finished, he handed the sheets to Consuela, who read them through and said she thought she could read them. Cheever turned on the green light on his machine, then handed Consuela a microphone, and threw another switch that started the tape running from reel to reel. Consuela read David's words into the microphone, and, when she was done, Cheever stopped the machine, removed the reel, and put it in a box.

"Now," Barney said, "will you please get yourself and your equipment the hell out of here."

"I haven't been paid yet," Cheever objected.

"You will be," Barney assured him. "Now blow."

Making a show of his haste, Cheever dismantled his recorder, put it in his carrying case, and blew.

"He's afraid of you, Barney," Hopper said, when Cheever was gone.

Barney lit a cigarette and blew the smoke up toward the ceiling. "That's right."

"I thought you told me last night you'd never met him."

"I didn't remember the name," Barney said. "He may have changed it."

"But you recognized him."

"He recognized me the second we met this morning," Barney said. "And that made his nose twitch, and then I recognized him. It goes back a long ways." Barney paused, but Hopper was silent. Apparently, David thought, he wanted Barney to go on. "I was about twenty," Barney went on. "Cheever, I guess, was about sixteen. I came East for a Mooney rally, and I got a job with a labor defense outfit and stayed on. The committee was a part of some youth action group. Cheever was a member of the group, an officer of it, I think. They used to hire a Hudson Day Liner all for themselves and cruise up the river on warm summer nights. It combined business with pleasure. They'd bring their girls, get two speakers to have a debate on the way up, and then screw on the way home. One night, the outfit didn't have the money to hire speakers, so Cheever and I put on the debate. The question was: Resolved: that the worker's state will be achieved in the United States within the framework of existing law. I had the affirmative. I read from a book pointing out that the people of the so-called liberal bourgeois democracies had an aversion to violent revolution and would stop it with a violent counter-revolution. But that their liberal traditions would permit the widest use of an electoral majority, even its use to remodel basic institutions. Cheever really let me have it. He called me a deviationist, a factionalist, and a sentimentalist. My beliefs, according to him, were typical of decadent socialism and the reason why the socialists would never accomplish their aims while the Russians were well on the way to making theirs a reality. When the time for rebuttal came, I held up the book. Everybody on the boat recognized it. They all had it, but very few of them had even glanced inside it. None of them had read it. It was by Lenin. I stood on the steps of the ballroom and shouted down at Cheever. "I stand with Marx and Lenin," I said, and I made it impressive, because I had him dead to rights. "Where do you stand, Comrade?"

"Where did he stand?" Hopper asked.

"We never found out," Barney said. "The son of a bitch got off the boat at Poughkeepsie and never came back."

Hopper laughed uproariously and David found himself joining. This was not entirely politeness; the idea that Cheever was still afraid of Barney because Barney had publicly embarrassed him a quarter-century before was, in part at least, comic.

"I suppose," Barney said, "I've got to give him that twenty-five hundred dollars."

"That's right," Hopper said. "In this fund-raising business, the strong have to carry the weak. You know that. And you're going to have to do something for the Philadelphia Five, too."

"I turned them down cold," Barney said.

"I know. They came to me."

"What have you got to do with it?"

"Who," David asked, injecting himself into the conversation, "are the Philadelphia Five?"

David saw—or thought he saw—Hopper turn almost imperceptibly toward Barney for an instant before replying. "They're schoolteachers," he said. "Party members. Communist Party, that is, not People's Party. And they're up for tenure in a suburb of Philadelphia. The school board turned them down, and they're suing the board. The People's Party," Hopper continued, "is underwriting their suit. It's costing more than we figured on. Now every dime that committee raises on its own is a dime less for us to pony up. That's why I had—"

"I didn't know there was a People's Party angle to it," Barney admitted. "It makes a difference."

"You'll do it?"

Barney shook his head. "Not the way they laid it out."

"What was that?"

"They want Consuela and me at their rally Tuesday night."

"For free?"

"Worse than that," Barney said. "Their idea of a payoff is to send one of their teachers to *our* rally tonight. You get the setup. Consuela's got name value. She'll bring 'em in for the Five. Then they send us some dame we never heard of, whose name won't mean a quarter in the till, who takes up our time, and maybe even gets our people to take their eye off the ball, and they call it even."

"What proposition did you make?"

"I didn't make any," Barney said. "Just turned theirs down cold. But I'll make one for you." Barney took a pencil and pad from his pocket and made some quick calculations. "Suppose we go to their rally. Consuela will be the main speaker. I make the money pitch. They take the first five hundred dollars, we take the next five. Beyond that, fifty-fifty."

"And your rally?"

"Let them send one of the teachers. When I ask for fifty-dollar contributions, she stands up and introduces herself and hands over a bill. I'll give her the bill before the meeting. That's all."

"You fancy yourself as a fund-raiser, don't you, Barney?" Max Hopper asked.

"I've been at it a while, Max."

"You know those little outfits like the Philly Five don't usually raise more than a couple of hundred at a meeting?"

"I know."

"And you're taking the *second* five?"

"That's right."

"Suit yourself." Max Hopper reached for his crutches, and began to place them in front of him. David started to help him get to his feet, but Barney, with a quick gesture, warned him not to.

"I'll see you at the rally then," Hopper said, propelling himself up onto the crutches. "Nice to have met you, Mr. Blake, Mrs. Chavez." He maneuvered himself laboriously to the door, leaned on one crutch while he used the other arm to open it, and went through, out into the hall. An instant later, the door closed behind him. David assumed he had gone through the same intricate procedure to close it.

For a moment after the door slammed, there was silence. Then, as David was about to ask Barney to explain exactly what he was to do at the rally, Consuela spoke. "May I ask you a favor, Mr. Castle?"

"Sure," Barney said. "But I wish you'd make it Barney. What's the matter? You getting tired of meetings and rallies?"

"Not tired exactly," Consuela said almost apologetically. "But I do not feel well."

"I'll get a doctor," Barney said quickly. "And you won't go tonight."

"I want to go," Consuela said. "I must go. But will there first be a dinner?"

"Yes," Barney said. "You and me and the rally committee. But I'll get you out of it. It's customary, that's all."

"They work for Angel," Consuela replied. "If they wish to see me, I am honored. But I wonder—would it be too much to ask—"

"Go ahead. If it's possible—"

"I'm ashamed." Consuela turned to David. "You will think I am ungrateful." Beneath her dark skin, David realized with surprise, Consuela Chavez was blushing.

"Name it," Barney urged. "You've done all I asked you for."

"Not frijoles," Consuela blurted out. "Not the corn that comes from cans that they call Mexican corn. I never in my life saw it before I came here. No tamales. No enchiladas. One does not eat these for dinner."

"They're only trying to be helpful," Barney said. "Still—"

"When we went to—was it Kew Gardens?—to the Citizens for Peaceful Means, to the fund-raising breakfast, you ate ham and eggs?"

"Didn't you?" Barney asked.

"Chile con carne," Consuela reported sadly. "One cannot live on this sort of food alone. At home we eat meat—beef, pork, sometimes veal—and potatoes and vegetables, and sometimes canned pork and beans. But my diet here would give ulcers to a peon."

Barney laughed. "You hungry now?" Consuela nodded. "How about a steak?"

"Now?"

"Right now." Barney picked up the phone, called room service and ordered, pausing after each item to be assured by Consuela's nod that he was choosing well, a shrimp cocktail, filet mignon, medium rare, baked potato, apple pie, and coffee. When he was done, he asked Consuela for her room number, and then ordered the meal sent there.

"But I will not be able to eat tonight, with the committee," Consuela protested.

"Take a little of whatever they serve," Barney advised. "No one will criticize. You can't be expected to eat normally. Your boy is on trial for his life."

Consuela trembled and seemed, to David, to be suddenly near the breaking point. "I will have a bad conscience," she said. "I will feel wicked. To be eating steak while Angel is—" She stopped quickly, seemed to pull herself together by a visible effort, got up, and walked toward the door. "Thank you, Barney," she said, before she went out. "Thank you very much."

"Well, David, what do you think of all this?" Barney asked, when Consuela had gone.

"I don't know," David replied. "I—"

"It's not what you expected?"

"No," David said thoughtfully. "Not at all."

"What did you expect?" It was not a challenging question; plainly, Barney was genuinely interested in David's opinion.

"Less commotion," David said. "All these people—Cheever, Hopper, the schoolteachers in Philadelphia—all the committees. I just don't see where they fit in?"

"You figured I'd just find some rich people who were interested in a kid in Angel's predicament and con them into chipping in. That it?"

"Something like that," David admitted.

"I could do it too," Barney said. "There happen to be three people who meet that description. I could hit each one of them for five hundred dollars. That's all. How long would that last?"

"Not long." David winced at the thought of attempting the Chavez defense on that kind of money."

"Well, this is the other way." Barney eased himself onto the couch and leaned back. "You get in touch with Cheever and Hopper and dozens more like them. I hope you won't have to meet them all, by the way. They do things for you. They form committees and run rallies, but that's only the beginning. They've got the mailing lists to canvass by direct mail. They run ads in magazines. Send A Buck For Decency. Did you know Hopper's got two hundred girls out on the streets collecting with tin cans?"

"No," David said. "I didn't know."

"It's a fact," Barney said. "Justice For All. That's what it says on the cans. There are people who never pass a tin can without putting money in it."

"But all these people," David protested. "What do they get out of it?"

"Don't you know?"

"Money?"

"That's right," Barney declared. "Money. David, they cut you at every turn. Two per cent for this guy, five hundred dollars for that one. Twenty-five hundred for Cheever alone. You run a rally, and suddenly you find you've got a co-sponsor. Then somebody else runs a rally for you, and you never see what they take in, only what they give you. Five guys come up here for a conference; they order ten Scotches. It goes on the bill. Nobody drinks beer in this business. Not on me, anyhow. And then you get printing bills. If you think Max Hopper hasn't thrown in some People's Party printing bills with what he's given me to pay, all I can say is you don't think he's as smart as I do."

"Why let them get away with it?" David asked.

"Because the minute you stop, the whole thing stops. And you're left with a hundred per cent of oh. The point is, David, I came here to raise the money you'll need for the case. And I'm doing it. You're going to have enough for investigations, witnesses expenses, secretarial service, office rent, everything. And you'll have enough left over for the expense of an appeal."

"If we lose," David put in.

Barney accepted the amendment. "If we lose. And the other way—well, we're on a shoestring. So a lot of people cut in on it. So what? Putting it crudely, we're getting ours."

David, who felt there was a flaw somewhere in what Barney was saying, thought the matter over in silence, could not find the flaw, and decided there was none. "Where," he asked, the question putting a stamp of *finished*, and hence *approved*, to the previous discussion, "do I come in?"

"You're a big man," Barney assured him. "The papers are full of you. You foiled the big plot to strong-arm the jury."

"Besides being a big man."

"Because you're what you are," Barney went on, "you're going to be the main speaker at the rally tonight. You'll drag them in. I'll get the money out of their pockets."

"I can't make much of a speech," David pointed out. "I've got the possibility of contempt of court to think about."

"I don't want you to comment on the facts of the case," Barney said. "Or the law either. You'll just thank the people for being there, and for contributing. Tell them an innocent boy is counting on them. Assure them that you'll do your best whatever happens, but the more they contribute, the better your best will be."

"It doesn't sound like much," David said. "I don't see why I had to come all this way—"

"Not strong enough for you?" Barney demanded. "A minute ago you didn't want to say anything. Now you want to stir up the animals."

"No, I don't," David argued. "I just can't believe people are going to lay out money to hear that kind of a speech."

"They don't give a damn what you say," Barney declared. "They want to see you. They want to be able to say they heard Angel Chavez's lawyer. And I want to give them what they want, so they'll give me what I want." Barney stood up and walked to the dresser. "Let Uncle Barney decide, David," he urged, rummaging through some papers on the bureau top. "I'm like the quack that cured dropsy with high colonics. My methods may not make sense, but they work." He found the paper he was looking for and handed it to David. "I've got your speech typed out for you. My idea is you take this back to your room, read it through for a couple of times, change the wording if it seems awkward for you, and then relax." He paused and glanced at his watch. "It's ten of six," he said. "We'll need you at the Arena around nine. That ought to give you time to run through your speech, grab a shower, have a meal sent up, and maybe even get a little nap. You look like you can use one."

David became aware that he had not slept in a bed for a day and a half. "Sounds good," he said.

Barney gave him the key to his room, and a card inscribed

PRESS which, Barney said, would admit him to the rally, and led him down the corridor to his room. An hour later, David, having showered, shaved, and committed his speech to memory, decided he was not hungry, called the desk and asked to be called back at eight, crawled into bed, and fell gratefully into an uneasy sleep.

At eight, he awoke, acknowledged the clerk's greeting, splashed cold water on his face, and put on the blue suit, blue-gray tie, black socks, and shoes Abbe had packed for him. "Good thing you'll only have to change once," Abbe had said. "I'd hate to give you any choices." Remembering Abbe's words caused him to think that when he took these clothes off it would be in the bedroom of the beach house, and that the moment when that would happen was then less than a day away, and he smiled, and stuffed the clothes he had worn for the trip east into the suitcase, picked up the suitcase and the brief case, and went out.

"The Arena?" the cab driver's voice went up in perplexity when David gave his destination. "What the hell's going on there on a Saturday night?"

The driver's name, David noticed, was A. C. Eubank. "It's a rally," he said.

A. C. Eubank flipped the flag down, drove abreast of the red traffic signal at the corner, and stopped. "Ah read about that rally," he said, half turning to face David. "Some nigger raped a white gal, and a bunch of yids are trying to get him off." He remained facing David for an instant after he had finished speaking, as if daring his passenger to make a reply. Then he turned to face the road.

David said nothing, but his impulse was to thank Eubank for what he had said. David had been so long in the company of Cheever and of Hopper, had become so aware of their imperfections, that it was with pleasure that he experienced this reminder that there were imperfections in the other side as well, that he was making common cause with the Cheevers and Hoppers be-

152

cause not to do so would be to make common cause with the Eubanks.

Eubank did not turn around again. Ten minutes later, outside the Arena, David gave him the precise amount shown on the meter, received an elaborate "Thank *you*," and got out.

It was then eight-forty. At first glance, David had the impression that the rally was a tremendous success. Then he saw that the people who walked slowly back and forth by the main entrance were not potential ticket buyers but pickets. There were three separate groups of them, each with its own marching orbit, each restricted to that orbit by two policemen. One group, predominantly male, carried signs describing the rally as a "Red Stink." The second group, likewise male, described the first as "advance agents of Fascism." The third group was the smallest, being composed of five elderly women in peasant dress, whose signs called for the freeing of a Middle European prelate.

David walked past the pickets, showed his pass to the gatekeeper, and identified himself. The gatekeeper enlisted the services of a shapely young lady who sported a blue and white badge lettered: FAR(PC). The lady took him through a tunnel and up a flight of wooden stairs. The door at the top of the stairs was closed.

"Right through there, Mr. Blake," she said.

"Thank you."

David opened the door and stepped through. He found himself standing at the top of a three-tiered platform. Below him, seated on canvas chairs, were perhaps fifty people, whom he took to be the speakers and the honored guests. Beyond them was the arena floor itself, and above the floor, at the edges, the balconies and mezzanines, mounting opera-house style to the high cantilevered roof. Somewhere a band was playing "El Capitan."

The band stopped in mid-measure, and played a fanfare. David blinked in the glare of a baby spot directed at him from above. "Here he is, ladies and gentlemen," Max Hopper's voice, heavily amplified, thundered. "Let's give a real welcome to the man who'll represent you and me and justice and Angel Chavez in court—David Blake." The crowd roared its approval. David stood immobile, not knowing what was expected of him. Then he saw Barney coming back from a front-row seat toward him. As Barney thrust out his hand in a broadly theatrical gesture and David grabbed it, the band struck up "The Battle Hymn of the Republic." David smiled narrowly remembering that it was to this tune that the would-be lynchers had sung their obscene doggerel.

"Come on." Barney led David down the three steps and across the front row to where Hopper stood with a microphone. Hopper shook David's hand, and this time flashbulbs went off. Barney led David past Hopper to a pair of empty seats in the first row.

"Ladies and gentlemen," Hopper said, "I declare this meeting open. We will hear first from an old friend who is always welcome here, Dr. Abraham LeFebre." A white-haired Negro came forward and stood by the microphone waiting for the applause to diminish.

"Is he a doctor?" David asked, under his breath.

"Of philosophy," Barney replied. "A distinguished scholar, a credit to his race, and totally senile."

The applause ended. Dr. LeFebre began his talk. He began by describing the operations of seventeenth-century slavers on the African Gold Coast, and, as he continued, David was amazed to realize that he proposed, beginning at that point and continuing in some detail, to give a complete account of the history of the Negro in America.

"Don't worry about him," Barney said. "He's like a preliminary fighter. Just something to kill the time until the rest of the crowd shows up."

"Why have him at all?" David asked. Other people were openly conversing while the doctor droned on, and David did not trouble, this time, to murmur.

"He's going to run for something," Barney said. "Maybe Governor."

At the microphone, Dr. LeFebre was up to the birth of Crispus Attucks.

"It's a nice crowd," Barney said. "Run close to fourteen thousand."

David looked out in front of him. There were some empty chairs on the main floor, but these might well represent late arrivals. The balcony was solidly filled on the end and on the right side of the horseshoe as it curved toward them. The left side was nearly empty.

"We've got Hopper to thank for that," Barney said, when David asked him about it. "You ever hear of U.A.L.?"

David confessed he had not.

"United American Liberals," Barney explained. "A new outfit. Factionalist, sentimentalist, maybe Trotskyite. That's what I told Hopper. But he knew better. So he sent four thousand tickets over to the chairman of U.A.L. in the city. Guy named Burns. Thoroughly unreliable. Burns does just what that kind of guy always does. He called a membership meeting. We sent somebody to the meeting, under cover, of course. You should see our guy's report. They wanted FAR (PC) to agree to a full accounting, in public."

"What's the matter with that?" David demanded.

Dr. LeFebre was pointing out the injustice of the Three-fifths Rule.

"The matter," Barney said, "is that we can't make our books public without naming our contributors. Some of them don't want to be named. Why should they? Anyhow, U.A.L. didn't sell the tickets, and they didn't return them. They just debated what to do. For all I know, they're still debating. Costing us about seventy-five hundred dollars."

"Four thousand tickets?" David hadn't realized tickets were that expensive. "That costs us—"

"The tickets were a dollar each. Some of them would have been given away. So that's, say, three thousand dollars lost right there. The other forty-five hundred—well, when I do the fundraising at an affair like this, I figure on just over a dollar a head."

Dr. LeFebre, whose pace had apparently picked up, was past the Missouri Compromise and nearly up to Harper's Ferry. A thin, stooped man came by, and Barney introduced him to David as Gene Epstein, treasurer of the Free Angel Rally, Provisional Committee. David shook his hand. It was the first time he had known exactly what FAR (PC) (the letters were everywhere around the hall) stood for. "Everybody's here," Epstein said to Barney. "We've passed the word to LeFebre to wind it up."

"Good," Barney said. "The next time that guy talks, get me a softer chair."

Epstein laughed. "Give 'em hell, Barney," he said, and walked on.

As they were speaking, Dr. LeFebre, now moving at breakneck pace, had gone, almost in one jump, from Reconstruction to Harry Wills, and from Wills to the Scottsboro Boys, and on to the present.

"Prejudice and bias, race hate and race war," he said, and David could sense that he was into his peroration, "these have always been with us, but they need not always remain to poison our national life. How well we stand up to them, how courageously we fight against them, with what perseverance we resist the efforts of those who seek to fan the bitter flames—these will determine how long this hideous evil will dwell in our land. We have here tonight a charming and gracious lady, who has conducted herself admirably in the face of the most cruel assault the forces of hate and the disciples of bias could mount against any living person. She is a mother, and they sought to strike at her through her son, and she is here tonight because *she* knows what decency is, and she means to fight for it. Ladies and gentlemen, Mrs. Consuela Chavez!"

For an instant there was handclapping, and then the clapping was drowned in a sea of cheers, frantic cheers as if each person in the crowd were under some desperate compulsion to outshout his neighbor. Incredibly, the torrent mounted as Consuela came from the far side of the dais to the microphone, and shook Dr. LeFebre's hand. Then the cheers died down, and from all over the hall came the shouted cry: "Freedom for Angel" merging into a chant. "Free-ee-DOM for A-a-n-GEL, Free-ee-DOM for A-a-n-GEL."

Consuela raised her hands and the chant stopped. "My very good friends," she said, and David noted with pleasure—for there was a natural coarseness in Consuela's voice—that she was standing close to the microphone and speaking softly, letting the amplifier supply the added volume needed without increasing the coarseness, "I want you to know that never will I forget this night. I am fortunate—" she paused and the crowd whispered, apparently commenting on the fantastic courage of this woman who called herself fortunate when her boy—"I say fortunate, because I will carry to my grave the memory that, this night, twenty thousand people, from the goodness in their hearts, came to help me in my trouble, and only because of my trouble. You must remember—all of you—that you gave hope tonight to one who needed hope. That will be your only reward, that memory." Without pausing, she gestured toward Barney. "Now I want you to meet the man who has been a savior to me. This is the man who has given to me hope. Barney Castle."

Barney stood up as the crowd applauded. "It looks pretty good," he said to David. "Watch me at the beginning. If my hands go over my head, you'll really see something. That's the signal."

Barney turned and made his way quickly to the microphone, arriving just before the applause died away.

"You're all my friends," Barney said, dispensing with any salutation. "So I can talk to you. Max Hopper told me, if people aren't your friends, don't talk to them." The crowd laughed. David was momentarily baffled. Then he remembered that Hopper had, the year before, appeared before a committee of the House of Representatives, where his entire testimony consisted of "I do not believe that a proper question, and I refuse to answer it on the ground that it is irrelevant," which refusal would, but for the fortunate absence of a quorum of the committee, have been punishable by a year's imprisonment. "Because you're my friends, I trust you," Barney went on. "But the question is: do you trust me?"

There was a roar of "yes" in response, but Barney, cupping one hand over his ear, affected to be dissatisfied with it. He asked the question again, and this time the response was louder. Suddenly he threw both hands over his head, as if the microphone were a highwayman's pistol. David saw people moving rapidly at the back and sides of the crowd, and remembered that Barney had said something about raising his hands over his head being the signal.

"Will you prove you trust me?" Barney asked.

This time the yes was even louder than before.

"All right," Barney said, "I'll give you a chance to do it. Now of course you trust your neighbors. You know they wouldn't rob you. So I want everybody here to take out a dollar bill and hold it in the air. That's it. Way up." Around the Arena floor, and in the balconies, starting at the edges and along the aisles, bills began going up. "Just a moment, sir!" Barney called. "You there—in the nineteenth row. No ostentation, please. I said a *one*, not a *five*." The crowd laughed. About eighty per cent of the hands, David estimated, were now up. "Look around you," Barney said. "The people with the baskets are still in their seats. You're not taking any risk. Now," he commanded with urgency, "I want everybody in this place who's not an undercover agent to hold up a bill. *Everybody*. I want to see a sea of green. What about you, sir?" Barney pointed down to a fat man in the first row. "You the F.B.I. man?" he asked. The man gestured broadly with his hands. "No dollar?" Barney asked. The man nodded. "Get it from the pretty girl next to you," Barney suggested. The man grinned and complied. Now nearly everyone was holding up a dollar bill.

"Wave 'em," Barney ordered. "That's beautiful. No, don't stop to look. I tell you it's beautiful, and you trust me. Now," he lowered his voice dramatically, "I want you to do one more thing, and when you've done that, then we're all blood brothers, and the clambake can proceed. I want you to keep that hand, with the bill in it, up in the air, and close your eyes for two minutes, *and keep them closed*. And, just to resolve any lingering doubts you might have, I give you my solemn oath, on my sainted mother's grave, that it will still be there when I tell you to open your eyes."

Barney paused and peered out at the audience. As far as David could see, his order was being complied with. Suddenly Barney raised his right hand and pumped it up and down. The house lights went on, and the basket gang sprang to their feet and went into action, going up and down the aisles and spreading out between the rows like so many locusts. A minute and a half later, David could no longer see any dollar bills. "All right," Barney said. "Open up, brethern and sistern."

The crowd murmured in mild resentment at this apparent betrayal of its trust. Barney, David decided, would have to explain this betrayal of his oath—even though he had made the oath in burlesqued fashion—if he hoped to do any more collecting that night.

"Do you think you've been had?" Barney asked. The response, while not angry, was not entirely good-natured, either. "Did I lie to you?" This time the response was a shouted "Yes!"

"I did not," Barney said. "I promised you it'd still be there when you opened your eyes. I meant your hand. *That* was still there, wasn't it?" Barney paused. The crowd groaned derisively. "All right," he admitted. "I deceived you. I misled you. I didn't actually lie, but I led you to believe something that wasn't true. Well, you've learned two things. The first is, when anyone swears on his mother's grave, watch out! It just so happens that my mother is a healthy Republican in Cook County, Illinois."

The crowd laughed. Gene Epstein, with an armful of small wicker baskets, walked across the platform smiling broadly. As he passed David, he winked.

"Moral Number Two!" Barney shouted, crowding the microphone so that the amplifier turned his voice rough and nasty. "Don't trust anybody!"

The crowd roared. "I tell you," Barney declared, "the time for trusting is long past. We've trusted, and we've turned the other cheek for far too long. Blessed are the poor—yes, if they've got the guts to take their blessings with their own hands. The meek will inherit the earth—you're damn well told they will, when they forget meekness and begin to act like the inheritors of the earth." The crowd cheered wildly. David saw the collectors reappear, spacing themselves down the long aisles.

"I'm not asking you to perform an act of charity." Barney spoke with excessive softness. "I'm asking you to contribute to a fighting fund. You don't have to do it. No one will know if you do or if you don't. But remember this: nobody's going to make your fight for you. Nobody else is going to take up the slack. Other people don't care. As a matter of fact, other people are going to make it as tough for you as they can. For example, I'll tell you right now, your contribution is not a tax deduction, so don't try and take it off next March." There were a few boos in protest, David assumed, of the government's unwillingness, already well publicized, to recognize FAR(PC) as an organized charity for income-tax purposes. "If you need a tax deduction," Barney said, speaking a little louder, "give it to the Red Cross." This time the boos were louder, and David remembered that the

New York Red Cross had once practiced the segregation of blood donated by Negroes from that donated by whites.

"We're not just fighting City Hall," Barney proclaimed. "We're fighting a whole State, and a big one. I'm not going to tell you how important it is that you contribute or how disastrous it will be if you don't. I am simply going to ask if there is anyone here who will donate the sum of five thousand dollars to save Angel Chavez from what the race haters plan for him." He paused and let his eyes search the hall. "Five thousand dollars," he repeated. "The State spends that much every day to put a rope around a seventeen-year-old boy's neck. We can make it last quite a while, but we've got to have it. And remember, that rope isn't just for Angel. This is your fight, because *they* never stop. Let them railroad one Mexican boy in San Juno, and the next Chavez case may happen anywhere. And, sooner or later, the terror will be right here with you. Five thousand dollars? Who'll give it?"

Barney paused again. From the back of the hall came a delighted squeal. The crowd cheered lustily as a girl ran down the main aisle and handed Barney a card.

"Local One," Barney read from the card, "Western Seamen and Dock Laborers, an *independent* union, pledges—" The applause that began at the word *independent* caused him to stop and smile. "Pledges quarterly," he resumed, "the sum of twenty-five hundred dollars, for a total of ten thousand dollars!" The crowd cheered. "Signed: Ray Kelso, President." More cheers. "Mr. Kelso also pledges, personally one thousand dollars for each of the next four quarters. Thank you, Ray." The cheers grew louder.

"All right," Barney said, "we've got fourteen thousand dollars in the till. It's a good beginning, but that's all it is. We need a lot more than that. You people in the balcony"—Barney gestured toward them and waited for a moment—"go to sleep. Shoot craps.

Neck. Go out for a short beer. I'm not talking to you now. This is for the people downstairs." He waved his hand in a semicircle toward the raised perimeter of the main floor. "Fifty mezzanine boxes," he said. "Ten seats to a box. If you haven't got ten bucks, you shouldn't sit in such expensive seats. All right, the tax is one hundred dollars a box. The man sitting in the rear seat, on the aisle, is the revenue agent for that box. Now, I want the collectors to go down the long aisle behind those boxes and pick up a hundred dollars from every revenue agent. You collectors, if you run into anybody that doesn't give, sing out and we'll put a spotlight on him. That's not to intimidate anyone; I'm just curious to see what a guy who won't give a tenspot for his own neck looks like."

David watched the nearest collector start out down the aisle behind the boxes. The first "revenue agent" he encountered shook his head, and the collector smiled and moved on. Apparently, Barney's threat was pure bluff. "Meanwhile," Barney was saying, "we ought to have at least five thousand dollars in one-hundred-dollar pledges and contributions, and another five thousand dollars in fifty-dollar contributions. No pledges less than a hundred dollars. If you're going to pledge, pledge a lot. We don't care if you're broke. We know you'll have better luck before the pledge comes due."

The collectors on the main floor began coming down with pledges and contributions, and Barney began reading off names and amounts. Most of the names were unfamiliar to David, Lewis and Arthur Cheever were down for $100 each. In addition, they had apparently done some spadework with their organizations, for Free World Communications gave $250, the Furriers' Political Action Group, $100, the Fur Processors' and Tanners' League, $100, and the board of Governors of the Furriers' Political Action Group, $200, in addition to the group's own contribution.

"Miss Ruthie Dill," Barney sang out. "Fifty dollars." There was some applause. "Miss Dill," Barney explained, "is one of the Philadelphia Five." The applause was louder. Barney went on reading names. The collectors began coming back, their baskets filled with cash, filing past David onto the platform, and up the steps to the wooden door through which he had entered.

"Now everybody!" Barney shouted. "Leave yourself carfare. We don't want you walking. But you don't have to take any cabs. Everything else you've got, we want it. And if you've got more than one coin, jingle them together before you drop them. I like to hear that jingle noise."

The crowd responded favorably. Nearly everyone seemed to be putting something in the baskets that went from hand to hand across the long rows on the main floor, and around the balcony, and the jingle noise was everywhere.

"Bless you all!" Barney shouted. "I believe we could keep this up all night. But we've got a wonderful show coming up, and it's getting late. Pass those baskets quick, but don't drop them. And thank you, ladies and gentlemen. Thank you very much." Barney made as if to begin a shallow bow. Then, suddenly, he straightened up. "Uh oh," he said, banging his hand against his forehead, "I nearly forgot."

He abandoned the microphone, dropped from the platform to the stone floor of the Arena, and ran to the nearest basket. He dropped a bill into the basket and kissed the attractive Negro girl who was holding it. The crowd cheered as he jumped back onto the platform, signaled to the electrician to kill the house light, and, in the darkness, sat down next to David.

The cheering went on. A spot picked out Max Hopper standing at the microphone. He smiled, but made no move to quiet the cheering. Then he gestured toward Barney, and the spot came round as Barney arose, and gave the light a mock-military salute. The spot went back to Hopper, who raised his hands for silence, and introduced a dark young lady who proceeded to execute what David took to be a habanera.

"When do I go on?" David asked.

"You were going to follow me," Barney said, "but this girl

has to make a club date in Jersey. You follow her. When you're done, meet me up in back."

David nodded. The habanera was nearing its climax. The young lady launched herself into a series of frenzied whirls which displayed red garters surmounting legs well worth displaying. As her final twirl ended, she stamped one foot, raised her skirt, extracted from one of the garters a small silver dagger, and flung the dagger on the floor so that it stuck there, quivering. As the applause began to mount, she sauntered past the dagger, placed her hands at the back of her neck, and leaned backward, picked the dagger up in her teeth, and went off (David assumed) toward New Jersey.

"A young man is here tonight," Max Hopper said when the applause finally died down, "who has come a long way to be with us. Ladies and gentlemen, here's a fighting young attorney, a credit to the bar and to his State, David Blake!" The crowd screamed ecstatically. The band struck up "Pomp and Circumstance" as David, trying hard not to give the impression that he was marching in time to the music, made his way to the microphone.

Facing the microphone, David suddenly realized that the speech Barney had written for him, the speech he had committed more or less to memory, being concerned with the urgency of contributing to the defense fund, was inappropriate now that the collection was over. And yet, Barney had known that the collection would be made before David spoke. Or had he? Hadn't he said something about a change in the program? In any event, he could not exhort these people to contribute when the time for contributions was past.

"Ladies and gentlemen," David said, "I want to thank you all, on my own behalf, and on behalf of my client, who is unavoidably detained elsewhere." There was a little applause and mild laughter, and David waited for it to die away. "With your help," he said, "we are going to carry on, and with your help we are going to win." This time there was more applause. "We are going to win," David went on, "because our cause is just. There are those—and I am not among them—who say that the verdict in this case will be arrived at without regard for the evidence. If that were true, neither my work, nor your help which makes that work possible, would be of the slightest use." He paused. There was a dead, oppressive silence in the hall. "But it is not true," David said, trying to raise his voice suddenly, dramatically, as Barney had done. "The armies of bigotry and the disciples of hate overreach themselves when they seek to intrude into the orderly functioning of justice. We—you and I—are going to turn back that intrusion. And, when the evidence in *State v. Chavez* is in, and the verdict arrived at, Angel Chavez, who has committed no crime, will leave the courthouse a free man. His vindication will not be entirely his own. It will belong to you and me and to every man who believes this country still adheres to the fundamental principles on which it was founded." He waited for an instant, but there seemed to be no applause. "Thank you for your help," he said, speaking even louder. "I give you—all of you and each of you—my solemn word that that help will not be given in vain."

The applause as he turned away was perfunctory, and David was sorry he had departed from Barney's prepared text. Then, as the band struck up "The Battle Hymn of the Republic," the applause swelled and continued to swell until David reached his seat and the spotlight that had followed him swung back to pick up Max Hopper at the microphone. David reached under his chair for his suitcase and, carrying it, picked his way along the darkened platform to the center aisle, and up the aisle to the door by which he had entered, and out.

In the hallway outside the door, tables had been set up, and at these tables men and women were at work, counting the money in the baskets and transferring it to cloth bags. David looked around for Barney and saw him in conversation with a man at the end of the row of tables. Barney turned and came toward him, and David saw that the man to whom he had been talking was the treasurer of FAR (PC) Mr. Epstein.

"How come you threw my speech away, David?" Barney asked, when David reached him.

"It didn't make sense," David said, "asking people for a contribution. You'd already—"

"O.K.," Barney said pleasantly. "It was a mistake, but I don't blame you."

"I don't see where—"

"Look, David," Barney said, with an elaborate show of patience, "I've been in this business for a long time. Right?"

"Right. But—"

"Forget it," Barney commanded. "What you did wrong wasn't important, and for me to make you understand why it was wrong I'd have to synthesize my whole experience for you. And even if it was important, I don't have the six weeks that would take. How are you fixed for money?"

David considered ignoring Barney's question in order to take up the matter of his speech. Then he decided this would be unrealistic. Barney was right as to one point, at any rate. It was unimportant. "Personally, you mean? Or the defense fund?"

"Both," Barney said.

"I got about fifty dollars in my pocket," David said. "The defense fund hasn't got enough to take care of the bills it'll get in the next few days."

"Gene?" Barney called. Mr. Epstein, who had been talking to one of the money counters, turned and came over. "Let me have five hundred, Gene," Barney asked, "and a blank check."

Epstein dug in his pocket and produced a roll of bills from which he extracted five one-hundred-dollar bills. Then, silently, from another pocket, he produced a checkbook, tore off a check, and handed it to Barney.

Barney crossed out the name of Epstein's bank, substituted

another, and wrote a check payable to David for $5,000. He handed it to him along with the money. "That's an advance to the defense fund," Barney explained. "I'll try to send you some more when we get these accounts straightened out." He consulted his watch. "You ought to get going, David," he said. "There's a plane out at midnight."

It was the best news David had heard all day.

from the Journal of David Blake
Sunday, July 13, 1947

. . . It might, I think, have been just as easily $1,000 in cash and a $10,000 check, which makes me (unreasonably, perhaps) uneasy. Barney (if I spoke of this uneasiness to him) would remind me that the State has the taxing power to raise its money; that everyone in the State, myself, even Consuela, included, must contribute to that fund; and that the defense, which has an equal need for money, must raise it any way it can. The test of whether the Cheevers and the Epsteins and the other organizations, like the Philly Five, and the Furriers' Political Action Group, should be allowed to participate in the process, as well as to share in the rewards, has to be a simple one: do they bring in—as a group— more than they take out?

That is Barney's argument, and it is unanswerable. The need for money for Angel's defense is great, and it cannot be met except in the way it is being met. At least I could not meet it, and Barney can and is meeting it. Yet why must I constantly remind myself that this is true, that I do not need to make common cause with Hopper, Cheever, et al., but merely to accept their money, that money has no morals, that . . .

7

David paused in his questioning of Juror George Kiley to glance at the clock on the wall opposite the jury box. It was ten minutes to five. In ten minutes, court would recess until the beginning of the evening session at eight.

"It is not quite the hour of adjournment, Mr. Blake," Judge Motley remarked acidly. "I may say," he added, "that the court is somewhat fatigued and looks forward to the dinner hour with some feeling of pleasure. Meanwhile, however, please proceed."

"I'm sorry, your honor," David said, turning to direct his gaze toward Mr. Kiley. "You're a druggist, Mr. Kiley?"

"I am." David knew this, of course. The question was designed to give him an entering wedge into his examination.

"I take it your drugstore includes a soda fountain?"

"It includes," Kiley said, "everything. Flashlight batteries, rubber pants, shoelaces, even drugs."

On the first day of the trial, even this weak sally would have provoked laughter. Now it drew only silence.

"And a soda fountain?"

"The best in town," Kiley replied.

"Your pride in your establishment is understandable," Judge Motley put in. "But please confine yourself to answering the questions of counsel."

Kiley bobbed his bald head in acknowledgment of the rebuke.

"Has it always been your policy," David asked, "to give fountain service to anyone who enters your establishment and asks for it?"

"I have to," Kiley replied. "It's the law."

"I know that," David said. "I'm not asking you about the law. You were in business during the war, weren't you?"

"Twenty-two years in one location," Kiley replied. He looked up at Motley in some alarm, but the Judge remained silent.

"During the time that Camp Stuart was operating, did you display in your window a sign reading—"

"Your honor," District Attorney Armstrong asked, "is it absolutely necessary that we go through this all over again?"

"We do seem," the Judge observed to David, "to be traveling over somewhat familiar ground."

"I assure the court that I find this as tedious as I'm sure you do. But I think the defendant is entitled to be tried by jurymen who will not be prejudiced against him on account of his race. And I know of no other way to find out whether a prospective juror has such a prejudice than to inquire about possible manifestations of such prejudice in the past," David said quietly.

"Well, I suppose you might as well go ahead then," Judge Motley said regretfully. "Though you are aware, I am sure, that the fact that a juror may have displayed such a sign does not, in my view, render him ineligible."

"I assume," David said, "that the court will judge each challenge on its merits, taking into account all evidences of prejudice or bias as they are revealed." The Judge waved his hand as a signal for David to proceed. David turned to face Kiley. "I was asking you about a sign reading: We do not solicit the patronage of servicemen. Did you display such a sign?"

"Yes, I did," Kiley said. "I've got nothing against soldiers, but there were such a lot of them—"

"I thought," David said, "that retail stores welcomed customers. The more the merrier."

"Let him finish his answer," Armstrong suggested.

"I'm sorry," David said. "You were telling us why you displayed such a sign."

"A lot of the stores did," Kiley argued. "The Chamber of Commerce—"

"I know where the signs came from," David said. "I want to know why you displayed one."

"Because there were too many of them, and they cluttered up the store, and they caused trouble, and they didn't buy."

"You didn't put the sign in your *window*, did you?"

Kiley thought for a moment. "No sir," he said. "I didn't."

"Where did you put it?"

"On the soda fountain."

"All right, Mr. Kiley," David said with a show of impatience. "Now let's stop beating around the bush. Stuart was a quartermaster post, wasn't it?"

"Yes."

"And the men stationed there were almost all Negroes?"

"Yes."

"And isn't it true that you put that sign on your soda fountain because you didn't want Negroes eating and drinking there?"

"Objected to," Armstrong declared. "What possible—"

"It is surely immaterial as far as the court is concerned," Judge Motley observed. "However, counselor has a single peremptory challenge remaining, and he may use it on any basis he wishes. Overruled."

At Kiley's request, the question was reread. "My regular customers," he said, "didn't like it with the fountain all jammed up with servicemen. I had to think of after the war."

"That would be the war," David observed, "that these men were training to fight in."

"Highly improper," Armstrong said loudly. "Prejudicial. Not a question at all."

"I'll withdraw the question," David said.

"Mr. Blake," Judge Motley declared. "I'm glad you withdrew your remark, which was indeed improper and most insulting to the juror. That does not alter the fact that the remark ought never to have been made."

"I apologize, your honor." David returned to his questioning. "You had no prejudice against these Negro soldiers?"

"None," Kiley said flatly.

"And you would give the same answer under oath?"

"Yes sir."

David paused. "Your drugstore is near the City Hall, isn't it?"

"Right across the street."

"I imagine you see some city officials from time to time."

"All of them," Kiley said proudly.

"And you must know them all pretty well."

"That's right."

"Then you know A. A. Sanders?"

"That's right," Kiley replied. "Fats Sanders."

"The gentleman sitting over there?" David pointed toward the jailer, who occupied his usual seat in the press section.

"Yes."

"Do you consider him a good friend?"

"I certainly do."

"How good a friend?"

Kiley hemmed, and David was about to rephrase the question when Armstrong interposed an objection.

"I don't see just where you're going, Mr. Blake," Judge Motley said. "What if he and the jailer swore an oath of eternal fealty, and signed it in blood?"

"I think the importance of this line of questioning will be apparent after one or two more questions," David said mildly.

Motley shrugged. "Then we'll admit it, subject to connection."

Once again Kiley had David's question reread. "I don't know what you mean about 'how good a friend?' " He seemed distressed, as if he were genuinely anxious to help David find out something, but was unable to do so.

"Is he," David asked, "the sort of friend you do favors for?"

"Oh yes."

"And you wouldn't do anything to harm him?"

"I wouldn't harm anyone."

"But you have a special regard for Mr. Sanders' interests. Isn't that true? Isn't that what a friend is?"

"I suppose so," Kiley said doubtfully.

"And if Mr. Sanders' political future depended on—"

"I object," Armstrong shouted. "This is highly prejudicial."

"Now I'm going to ask to have Sanders sworn and to have him testify," David shouted, "unless you will stipulate, for the purpose of this question, that his interest is precisely as I will state it! I'm sick and tired—"

Judge Motley brought his gavel down sharply. "That will do, Mr. Blake," he snapped. "Mr. Armstrong, you will please be seated. Now I want no more of these outbreaks." He glanced quickly at the clock. "It is somewhat past the time for the evening recess, and I think we might all benefit from a rest now. I wonder if I might see Mr. Blake and Mr. Armstrong briefly before they leave. Court is adjourned until eight o'clock."

In the Judge's chambers, David sipped ice water from the newly installed refrigerator while he and John Armstrong, at Motley's urging, told the Judge the story of the near lynching, and recounted the pledge Sanders had made to the mob. When they had finished, the Judge mopped his brow with his handkerchief and cursed idly at the heat before replying.

"Now look, David," he said earnestly, as if it were of the utmost importance to him that David be convinced by what he was about to say, "I really don't think you ought to go into the prejudices and motives of the *friends* of the jurors. There are plenty of people here in town, I think, who want your client found guilty and have said so. Of course they can't serve. If they haven't said so, but you can show me how they feel, I'll excuse them. But, my God, if we're going to excuse every juror with a prejudiced *friend*—"

"It's more than a prejudice in Sanders' case, I think," David said. "His whole future—"

"But it's not Sanders we're discussing."

"It's his friend," David argued. "He's not going to do anything to harm his friend."

"Don't snow me, boy," Judge Motley said, not unpleasantly. "You're my friend, David. If anybody asked me if I'd do anything to hurt you, I'd say 'no.' But that doesn't mean I'd vote to please you if I were on a jury."

"In a capital case—"

"Please, David," Judge Motley said. "I know it's a capital case. I've given you the widest latitude. I've allowed challenges for cause whenever, in my opinion, there was the slightest color of justification. But I am not going to disqualify for cause on the basis of the alleged prejudice of a juror's friend, and I am not going to allow you to question jurors along those lines. I don't know about you fellows," he went on without stopping, "but I'm hungry."

David mumbled an acknowledgment that he understood the Judge's position, rose, and went back through the door that led to the courtroom. As he closed the door behind him and looked for (and found) Abbe seated at the defense table, he became aware that there was something unusual about the room. The reporters still sat patiently at the press table, and they had been joined, now, by photographers, whose presence had been forbidden by Judge Motley during actual sessions of the court. Surely they did not think that either Armstrong or himself would reveal what had taken place in the Judge's chambers.

A man in a gray suit arose in the press section and came forward toward him. Out of the corner of his eye, David saw the cameras in the hands of the photographers go up.

"Mr. Blake?" the man said. A flashbulb went off. David nodded. The man smiled. Another flashbulb went off, and David saw another photographer go by to take a station behind him. "I have something for you," the man said, handing David an envelope. As David took the envelope, the flashbulbs went off almost in unison.

Before he had carried the envelope to the table, before he had opened it, before he and Abbe had read it together, David knew that it had to contain a subpoena from the Assembly Committee on Subversion and Disloyalty. Standing next to Abbe's chair he skimmed through, saw that it commanded his presence at an executive session of the committee the following Saturday at 10 A.M. in the State Office Building, that he was instructed to bring with him "all papers, documents, books of account, journals, records, memoranda, and other material pertinent to the subject of the inquiry," and that the subpoena had been issued by Carl Baron Battle. "Christ Almighty!" he muttered. Abbe, seated beside him as he stood, nudged him, and David, suddenly aware that the photographers were still awake, tried to assume a less dejected expression.

The reporters, about a dozen of them, crowded around. "You have anything to say, Mr. Blake?" one of them asked. David recognized him as Pete Wells, the man he had seen parked outside Gail Wiltse's house the afternoon before the funeral. He glanced quickly at Abbe, who nodded almost imperceptibly.

"I don't know," David said. "What do you want to know?"

"Are you going to respond to the subpoena?" another reporter asked. "Will you go down there?" A third added.

David held up his hands. "One at a time," he begged. "Yes, I will respond to the subpoena. I will send Mr. Battle a telegram tonight explaining that I am engaged in trying an important case, and—"

"Then you won't go?" Pete Wells asked.

"Just a minute," David said a trifle sharply. "Let me put it

174

my own way. My telegram will explain to Mr. Battle that I will be unable to appear."

"On Saturday?" Wells asked.

"On Saturday."

"I didn't know," Wells said with elaborate innocence, "that there would be a session of the trial on Saturday."

David remained calm with an effort. "You may not believe this, Mr. Wells," he said, "but there is a certain amount of work done in connection with a law case that is not done in the court-room."

"You work all the time you're not in court?" Wells asked. "Is that it?"

"I need some time to sleep and eat," David said.

"You couldn't even give Battle Saturday morning?"

"No."

A tall reporter who wore shell-rimmed glasses pushed Wells aside. "Will your telegram ask him to withdraw the subpoena?" he asked.

"That's right," David said.

"What if he won't?"

"I'm sure he will."

"If he doesn't, will you comply with the subpoena?"

"If he should persist with his subpoena," David said, "I would go before the State Supreme Court and ask that it be vacated. As defense attorney, I am, as you probably know, an officer of this court. For a legislative committee to seek to interfere with me in the conduct of my duties would be an invasion of the State's judicial system by the legislature."

"Do you think that's his motive?"

"I didn't say that. But that's what the result of answering the subpoena would be."

"What do you think his motive is?" Pete Wells asked.

"I haven't the slightest idea," David replied.

"Do you have any information for the committee?"

"I don't think so."

"If you answered the subpoena," the tall reporter asked, "what papers would you bring with you?"

"I don't know."

"You don't know? Or you won't say?"

"You heard my answer," David said belligerently.

"You really work on Saturdays?" Pete Wells asked.

"That's what I said."

"I heard you made a trip East."

"In connection with the case," David added. "That was a week ago Friday night. I was back a week ago yesterday."

"Where do you work?" Wells asked. "Weekends, I mean."

"I've got a place down at the beach."

"And you worked there last weekend?"

"That's right."

"At ten o'clock Saturday morning?"

David smiled. "This is ridiculous," Abbe said suddenly. "You're not asking him for information. You're cross-examining him."

"Sorry, lady," the tall reporter said. "It's the way we work."

"I don't think there's any point in going on with this," David said. "If you'll excuse me."

The flashbulbs were exploding again as he and Abbe left the courtroom. The cameramen followed them to the telegraph office, and David began to think they would be with him for the entire evening recess, but, after pictures had been taken of David dictating the telegram to Abbe, and of David filing the telegram with the clerk, and after the name, age, and address of the clerk had been ascertained, the photographers left.

The restaurant across the street from the courthouse was crowded by the time they reached it, and the crowd waiting for tables spilled out onto the street. It was Abbe's idea that they get the car and drive to the beach, stopping along the way to buy hamburgers.

And a good idea, David thought. They were parked not far

from State Beach, on a paved parking area along the seaward side of the highway. Below them, the sea splashed against the rocks, dampening and cooling the breeze that ruffled Abbe's hair and blew a bit of it against David's face as she leaned against him. From a neighboring car's radio a tenor inquired about conditions in Gloccamora.

"I wish," said David slowly, "that Angel Chavez had met some other girl that night."

"Who would have slapped his face and walked away," Abbe added.

"Or necked with him, petted, fornicated, anything but drop dead on him."

"And where," Abbe asked, "would you be now? Up in Capitol City talking law with some character, class of nought-nine, I'd think."

"I hadn't thought of that." David leaned over and kissed Abbe gently. When he was done, he left his hand at her throat. In the silence that followed, he could feel her quickened pulse. "It's a terrible thing to say," David said, "but I don't really wish anything of the kind. I couldn't wish for anything that would put me anywhere but here. Unless you were there with me."

David found himself resentful of and bewildered by Abbe's silence. His statement, a difficult one for him to make since it was a confession that he valued Abbe's love above the life of a human being, deserved some reply.

"Is anything wrong, Abbe?" he asked. "Have I offended you?"

"No," Abbe replied, in the tone women reserve for answering such questions, the tone implying that what is wrong is so obvious that to ask the question is to compound the wrong.

"You've been preoccupied lately, almost distant," David complained. "If I've done anything, I wish you'd tell me."

"It's nothing, David," she said, almost unpleasantly. "I'm a little tired. If I've seemed distant, I'm sorry. There." She leaned toward him and kissed him forcefully but without passion.

"There. There's nothing wrong, and I love you, and what are you going to tell Carl Baron Battle?"

"I don't want to talk about him," David protested. "Anyhow, the telegram—"

"He'll get you sooner or later, David," Abbe said. "Maybe not till the trial is over, maybe not till after the appeal—"

"I'm not figuring on an appeal," David said firmly. "We're going to win it right here."

"Of course, dear." There was in Abbe's voice, David thought, just a hint of the tone used by mothers in assuring their children that dentists never cause pain.

"We're going to win," he said, more loudly than before.

"I know," Abbe said. "But when it's over—when you've won—you'll have Battle to deal with. You can't stall him off forever."

"I'm not afraid of him," David said. "It'll be an inconvenience going down there, especially that business about bringing all my records. But that's all. As a matter of fact," he went on, "when all this is over, I think I'll go down to Capitol City and see him. It ought to be easy to make him see that he's made some sort of mistake. I haven't got any information he'd be interested in. Some other David Blake, I guess—"

"By God you mean that, don't you!" Abbe sounded as if she had suddenly reached a quite astonishing conclusion.

"About going down there and—"

Abbe broke away from his encircling arm and sat bolt upright in the seat. The radio in the other car was off now, and from its interior came a playful squeal, plainly part of an amatory scuffle. "About not knowing what Battle wants to question you about."

"I swear to you, Abbe," David said earnestly, "I haven't the remotest idea. Do you?"

"Don't they even put windows in those ivory towers these days?" Abbe asked. "Don't you know anything about anything that isn't reported in some Law Review or somebody's Cases on Something?"

"I'm familiar with Battle's career," David said. "You might not believe this, but I sent some money to his opponent once."

"Because of the thing with the oath," Abbe said. "And that affected you personally. You had to take the damn oath yourself, and you felt insulted. So you went into action. What about the rest of what he's done? The things you weren't involved in? Do you know anything about that?"

"Not much," David said. "I know his investigations seem to have gone somewhat far afield, and that serious constitutional—"

"I mean," Abbe said impatiently, "things that don't get talked about at Law School Faculty teas. You ever hear of O. B. Fairfax?"

"I don't think so," David said. "But—"

"O. B. Fairfax owned a building supply company. He dealt mostly in traprock. Traprock is used mainly in making road beds, so obviously his biggest customer was the State. Fairfax had a brother, Willis. Willis was the owner of a small daily paper in the western part of the State. Well, it seemed that Willis's paper once used some comic strips supplied by the same syndicate that employed Max Hopper in its Paris office. Well, Baron hauled O. B. up before himself—he sits as a one-man subcommittee, you know—and questioned him about his brother's 'subversive connections.' That was in executive session, of course. Afterward, he spoon-fed the reporters the story that he had questioned O. B. Fairfax about the possibility that the money paid him by the State for traprock was being used for disloyal and subversive purposes. In the next six months—"

"That's absolutely ridiculous," David said. "They ought to laugh the son of a bitch right out of office."

"It's a funny story," Abbe said, "But wait till you hear the punch line. Over the next six months, O. B. didn't sell a dime's worth of traprock. Then his brother, and some employees of the traprock company, and some of O. B.'s friends, got up a committee to see if something couldn't be done to clear his name.

The committee met one evening, and elected Willis chairman. Two days later, Willis got a subpoena from Battle. He went over to his brother's house to talk it over, and there was O. B. swinging from a rafter in the attic. *His* subpoena was in his pocket."

David made a wordless exclamation of shock.

"And you," Abbe went on, "travel seven thousand miles to appear at a meeting at which Max Hopper serves as Master of Ceremonies, and you wonder why Carl Baron Battle wants to talk to you. David, naïveté is no crime; it's all right in its place, even charming in a way, but you mustn't build your whole life around it."

"All right, I'm naïve then," David admitted, not meaning the admission seriously. "But I still don't see what he can ask me. Or what's wrong with knowing Max Hopper, for that matter."

"Max Hopper," Abbe said, "was one of the prime names on the government's P.A.F. list. He—"

"P.A.F.?"

"Now that," Abbe said firmly, "is something you once knew and forgot. You were in the Army, weren't you?"

"Oh yes." David was remembering.

"Premature Anti-Fascist," Abbe said. "The P.A.F. list was about the worst-kept secret in Washington. A list of people—mostly who'd fought in Spain—who weren't to receive commissions, have access to secret material, work in certain war plants, or do a few other things I've forgotten. Passports," she added. "If you were a P.A.F., you couldn't get a passport."

"But to destroy a man just because his brother—"

"That's how those lists are made up," Abbe said. "You take one list. Then you get all the people who know the people on that list and they go on another list. Then the people who know *them*. After a while, people get so frantic to prove they were never associated with the people on the other lists that everybody forgets that it doesn't really matter if they were."

"But why? Battle must know—"

"It isn't just Battle," Abbe said. "There are list makers everywhere. Some of them are just plain garden-variety blackmailers, out to make a buck by destroying a few reputations just to scare a few people into paying up to protect their own. Others, like Battle, see it as the coming thing, politically, and I think they're right. You start out by scaring a few people, and maybe it's hard to do, but it gets easier every time you do it. Because people know you can. And they're afraid to stop you from doing it to somebody else, because as long as you're after somebody else, you're not after them. We're in the year of the list makers. And you're on the list." She paused and held her watch in front of her face, cupping it and squinting to see the illuminated hands. "It's a hell of a thing to tell the defense attorney," she said, "twenty-five minutes before court convenes."

David backed the car out of the parking space, ground the gears as he started toward town, and drove in silence through the streets of San Juno and into the parking lot next to the courthouse. As he walked from the car, he remembered something. "You've miscalculated somewhere, Abbe," he said. "I got Battle's first invitation to appear *before* I went East for the meeting."

"I'll explain it to you," Abbe said, "later tonight. After court adjourns."

John Armstrong met them just inside the entrance to the courtroom itself. He looked tired and drawn as David suspected he must look himself. "You think we can wind up this jury business tonight, David?" the District Attorney asked almost plaintively.

"I hope so," David said. "I'm getting pretty tired of it."

"If it runs much longer," Armstrong said sadly, "it's going to cost me my vacation."

"Why don't you take it later on?" David asked.

"Because the people of the State, in their infinite wisdom, see fit to hold their elections in odd-numbered years," Armstrong replied. "You ever hear of a District Attorney taking a vacation—"

The bailiff's "all rise" and Judge Motley's entrance cut short the exchange. Armstrong scuttled back to his own table.

"Before we proceed," Judge Motley said, "I'd like to ask whether, in the event that the jury is completed quickly, the State will be ready to begin."

"If it please the court," Armstrong rose. "It would be extremely inconvenient and embarrassing to us to keep our first witness continually available when there is no certainty that he will be heard."

"But we could surely hear your opening remarks, and those of the defense," Judge Motley suggested, "And then we might recess and begin taking testimony tomorrow."

"My opening remarks," Armstrong pointed out, "will be extremely brief."

"And mine also," David added, rising.

"Then I must ask the State to make its first witness available." Armstrong cleared his throat, but the Judge continued his discourse. "Against the embarrassment and inconvenience alluded to, we must offset the expense of this trial, which mounts with each day's delay, and the defendant's right to as speedy a trial as may be compatible with fairness." Armstrong sat down without speaking, and David approached the jury box.

"Mr. Kiley, I believe you said you considered Mr. Sanders a good friend." Kiley nodded, and, when Judge Motley pointed out to him rather acidly that his nod was rather difficult for the court stenographer to record, expanded the nod to "Yes, sir." "Do you think," David asked, "that that friendship would influence your vote as a juror, in view of the fact that Mr. Sanders—"

Judge Motley cut David off with a sharp rap of the gavel. "I think," he said firmly, "that the question of whether his friendship would, in his view, influence his vote, can be answered without going any further."

"If I might be permitted to finish my question, your honor, then—"

Again Motley rapped his gavel. "We went all through that in chambers," he said with asperity. "If you persist in asking the question, I will have the jury removed. You may then ask it in full, and I will rule on it. I think you know what that ruling must be."

"Could I have an answer to the question, then, as far as I'm allowed to go with it, Mr. Kiley? Would your friendship for Mr. Sanders influence your vote, do you think?"

"No sir," Kiley said flatly. "It certainly would not!"

For David, whose mind was balanced nicely on the question of whether or not to expend his last precious peremptory challenge on Kiley, the druggist's now apparent anxiety to serve was the deciding factor. The challenge made, Kiley left the stand. The juror who replaced him was Mary Ackerman, a birdlike woman with bright blue eyes. Next to that name, on David's abstract of the Pine & Pine reports, was the circle indicating that, since she was certain to be challenged by the State, she should under no circumstances be challenged by the defense.

David returned to the defense table and rummaged through the papers piled in front of his seat to find out why he had put the circle next to Mrs. Ackerman's name. It was important to know, since he had to decide immediately whether to question her, or, by not doing so, to run the risk of calling Armstrong's attention to his willingness to accept her. "She led a block committee against racial zoning," Abbe whispered, and David was once again conscious of how essential Abbe was to him, not merely outside the courtroom, but inside it as well. To question Mrs. Ackerman, he decided, would be a mistake; it would give Armstrong time, which would increase the chance that Armstrong would discover—he certainly had the information somewhere on his table—the very fact David wished to go unnoticed. "No questions," he said, trying to make the words hopeless.

There was a long pause. John Armstrong leafed through his papers, looked questioningly at one of the young ladies sitting across the table from him, and received a blank stare in reply.

"Has the State questions for this juror?" Judge Motley asked, hiding and at the same time revealing an impatience at this delay.

"No questions," Armstrong said uncertainly.

There was a stirring in the press section as some of the reporters tiptoed out of the room to telephone to their offices the information that the jury was complete. On a previous occasion, Judge Motley had warned the press, following a helter-skelter dash to the rear when a defense challenge for cause was allowed, against such conduct. This time he merely stared at the departers with a sort of mild regret.

"May I proceed?" Armstrong asked.

"You may."

The District Attorney rose and walked to the jury box. David watched, not so much interested in Armstrong's opening remarks, which would be purely routine, as in the jury's reaction to them, especially the reaction of Juror Twelve, Mary Ackerman.

Armstrong put one hand on the rail of the box and spoke calmly but entirely without emphasis. "The State will prove to you, ladies and gentlemen," he said, "that Marie Wiltse met her death while defending herself against the loathsome attack of the defendant. We will show that that attack was a felony, and, when we have done that, the court will instruct you that any death resulting from such an attack must constitute murder. For this we ask—and the law compels us to ask—the extreme penalty. This is an extremely simple case, and I am confident of your ability to reach a correct decision on the evidence, disregarding the emotional factors with which I am confident the defense will attempt to becloud the issue."

No juror gave visible sign of pleasure or displeasure at Armstrong's words. David rose. "My friend Mr. Armstrong has put the issue quite well," he said, ambling toward the box. Mary Ackerman, he thought, was smiling vaguely at him. "If, when all the evidence is in, you are convinced that Marie Wiltse met her death as a result of resisting a felonious attack by this boy, you must find as Mr. Armstrong asks. But I doubt very much that Mr. Armstrong will be able to prove any such thing to your satisfaction. You see, it *simply did not happen that way.*"

The spectators murmured in appreciation of the brevity of the opening arguments. Armstrong called his first witness, Johannes Schacter, M.D., who had signed Marie Wiltse's death certificate. Under Armstrong's gentle questioning, he identified himself, gave his pedigree, and said that he had seen Marie Wiltse's body at the morgue and had signed her death certificate, stating the cause of death to be "heart failure due to violent exertion." Armstrong thanked him for his testimony, and David began his cross-examination.

"I take it, Doctor," he began, "that you were convinced, at the time you signed the death certificate, that the cause of death stated on it was correct."

"I was," Doctor Schacter said calmly, "and I am." From the gentleness of his tone, and from the fact that his answer cut the ground from under David's next question, David would have guessed, had he not already known it, that this doctor was no stranger to the witness stand. He was, in fact, as David knew, what lawyers call "an insurance company doctor."

"Well, that's what I was going to ask next." David smiled. "You do still believe the girl died from 'heart failure due to violent exertion'?"

"Yes, sir."

"Well, without being too technical about it, do you think you could explain to us just how you decided that?"

"Certainly." Schacter leaned forward on the witness chair. "The functioning of the heart—"

"I'm sorry," David said. "I guess I didn't make that clear. I don't mean how you knew the heart had failed. I mean how you knew that the failure was the result of violent exertion."

"I didn't know that at all."

"You didn't?"

"Oh no. The law merely requires me to state what I *believe* the cause of death to be." There was a ripple of appreciation of this exchange. Courtroom spectators always like to see a lawyer beaten by a witness in a word haggle.

David was unperturbed. "What made you *believe* that was the cause?"

"I was informed that the girl had undergone violent exercise. When the heart fails after violent exercise, one is justified in attributing the failure to the exercise."

"There was, then, no real evidence—apart from what you were told—that the girl's last few minutes were in any way violent?"

"There was some physical evidence, but I did not base my conclusion on it. It supported that conclusion, though."

"What was the evidence?"

Dr. Schacter hesitated, and when he spoke, his voice was so low that only David heard him.

"Would you repeat that?"

"Her—her pants were pulled part way down."

"And from that you deduce your violence?"

"No, sir," the doctor said firmly. "That merely supported what I was told."

"I don't quite see that," David said mildly. "How does it support your theory of violence?"

"I believe that's obvious."

"Not to me," David snapped.

"Do you think a girl would permit her underpants to be pulled down without resisting?"

"I wouldn't know," David said. "Does your medical experience give you the answer?"

"I knew the girl," Dr. Schacter said, almost belligerently.

"Mightn't they have been taken down after she was dead?"

"There wouldn't have been any reason—"

"Mightn't they?"

"Perhaps, but—"

"Mightn't she have taken them down herself?"

"I doubt—"

"Isn't it a fact, Doctor, that all you know about this girl is that her heart failed her? Isn't everything else just supposition, theory, and hearsay?"

"I based my finding on—"

"That's not what I asked."

John Armstrong was on his feet. "That is what he asked, your honor," he declared. "And he's not letting the witness answer."

"Mr. Blake," the Judge said, "please permit the witness to finish his answers."

David acknowledged Motley's remark and fell silent.

"Am I excused?" Dr. Schacter asked.

"No," David said. "I was waiting for you to finish your answer. I think you were telling us how you arrived at your finding."

The doctor took a deep breath. "If I find a man at the scene of a train wreck," he said, "and the man is dead of a concussion, I am justified in concluding that it was the train wreck that gave him the concussion."

"Are you through?"

"Yes."

"But you wouldn't be absolutely certain about that concussion, would you? I mean, the man might have received it before the wreck? Or after it?"

"He might," Doctor Schacter admitted.

"And in this case, you didn't find your corpse at the scene of any wreck. You were only told about it."

"I stand on what I wrote on the certificate."

"Very well." David could hear the jurors whispering among themselves. If he had not won his point, he had at least put the issue in doubt. "I think you said, Doctor, that you knew this girl."

"That's right."

"How well did you know her?"

Armstrong interposed an objection. Judge Motley turned to David. "This line of questioning will go to the question of whether a crime has been committed," David explained, and the Judge indicated that he might continue.

"I knew her as a patient," Doctor Schacter said.

"When?"

"Many years ago. She was about three."

"And have you treated her more recently?"

"Yes. Last year."

"Now will you tell the court the nature of her illness and of your treatment, and of your conclusion as to her condition on the night of the accident."

"Can he answer that?" John Armstrong asked. "Doesn't that last call for a conclusion quite remote from his own knowledge?"

"This man is an expert," David argued. "He has stated his qualifications, and the defense has not challenged them. I'm asking him, as an expert, for an opinion."

Judge Motley did not speak, and Armstrong subsided.

"She suffered as a child from rheumatic fever," Dr. Schacter said. "The only treatment is prolonged bed rest and complete avoidance of all excitement. That was the treatment when she was three."

"Did she make a satisfactory recovery?"

"She seemed to."

"But she suffered a recurrence of the disease about a year ago, didn't she?"

"That's right."

"And what happened then?"

"The same as before. Bed rest."

"And the result?"

"That too was the same as before."

"A satisfactory recovery?"

"Yes."

"Now she had had a satisfactory recovery before—the first time, is that right?"

"Yes."

"Followed by a recurrence of the disease?"

"A dozen years later. That is correct."

"There was no reason to suppose at the time of the first recovery that, if there was a recurrence, it would happen many years later, was there?"

"None."

"Was there the second time?"

The doctor smiled. "I see what you're getting at," he said. "No, rheumatic fever, so far as we know, can always recur."

"In that sense, there is never a complete recovery."

"Very rarely."

"What else can you say about someone who has suffered from that disease?"

"I don't think I understand."

"I'll put it another way. About ten months ago you examined Marie Wiltse. Is that correct?"

"Yes. Prior to the opening of the school year."

"And you recommended that she resume her schooling."

"Yes."

"To whom did you make that recommendation?"

"To Mrs. Wiltse. The girl's mother."

"Do you remember where you were when you made that recommendation?"

"I'm not sure. In the garden of the Wiltse house, I think."

"If it is Mrs. Wiltse's recollection that it *was* the garden, you would agree."

"By all means."

"Now, Doctor, I want you to think back to that day, last September 7, as a matter of fact, when you examined Marie Wiltse and then went into the rose garden with her mother to make your report. Now, this is very important, so take as long as you wish to think it over. As nearly as you can remember, what else did you tell Mrs. Wiltse at that time?"

The doctor threw back his head and appeared to be counting the holes in the air-conditioning grid over his head. "I really can't remember," he said. "I see many people—"

"Please, Doctor," David said, "think some more. A man's life may depend on your answer."

"I object to that characterization of the answer," John Armstrong said. "He doesn't know what the answer will be."

"I withdraw the observation," David said.

"I'm sorry," Dr. Schacter sounded quite regretful. "I really can't—"

"If I told you that Gail Wiltse had told me that you said—"

"Objection!" Armstrong shouted. "This is fantastic. Let him call Mrs. Wiltse if he wants to establish what *she* said."

"I'm interested in what he said," David replied. "I'm trying to refresh his memory."

"What answer can he possibly give? He doesn't remember, but he's not going to call Mrs. Wiltse a liar?"

"Let me ask the question," David suggested. "Then we won't have to guess what he might answer."

Judge Motley beckoned David and John Armstrong to the bench. "Has Mrs. Wiltse told you what Dr. Schacter told her?" he asked.

"Yes," David replied.

"And what was that?"

"In substance," David said, "it was that Mrs. Wiltse should let Marie have whatever she wanted, within reason, as it was quite possible that she wouldn't live long."

Judge Motley pitched his voice louder. "Dr. Schacter," he said, "what counsel is driving at is: did you give Mrs. Wiltse any advice as to how she should conduct herself in regard to any demands her daughter might make?"

"I might have."

"Did you?" David asked.

"Objection."

"Overruled," Judge Motley said flatly. "Answer the question, please."

"Yes."

David was glad that, being at the bench, he could raise his voice, drawing the jury's attention to what was being said, without appearing to browbeat the witness, "Didn't you say," he roared, "substantially that Mrs. Wiltse's attitude toward her daughter should be extra-kind, extra-indulgent, because—" he raised his voice to a full shout— "the girl might not be with her mother long?"

"Yes," the doctor said apologetically, "I guess I said that."

"You don't give that sort of advice every day, do you?"

"No."

"As a matter of fact, you know now that that was more or less what you said?"

"Yes. I'd really forgotten, you see—"

"No one's accusing you of anything, Doctor. Now, what did you mean when you said: 'Your daughter might not be with you long'?"

"That she might die at any moment."

"Now didn't you also say, at that time, that her heart was extremely weak as a result of her two illnesses?"

"That's right. It was."

" 'It might go at any moment.' Did you say that?"

"I don't believe I said that."

"But you believed that, didn't you? That's why you said what you said?"

"Yes."

"So that in September, it was your opinion that Marie Wiltse's heart might stop beating at any moment, and without warning."

"I suppose so."

"Whether or not it was subjected to any unusual strain?"

"That depends," the doctor said, trying to regain his composure, "on what you mean by an unusual strain."

"I mean that every time that girl got out of bed, every time she stood up, or sat down, or walked around, her weakened heart might give out. Isn't that, in effect, what you told her mother?"

"Yes."

"You wouldn't have told her mother anything you didn't believe?"

"No."

"So in September you believe that this girl may die if she stands up or walks around, you believe that her heart may not prove strong enough to stand the ordinary strains of everyday living, peaceful though her life may be. In June this girl is found dead, and you describe her heart failure as 'due to violence,' in spite of the fact that you know she was found on a staircase landing?"

"Walking down that staircase could hardly have—"

"Who said she walked *down?*"

There was a gasp from the spectators, and David realized he had captured the imagination of every person in that room.

"I was told—"

"We're not interested in what you were told. You're asked to testify to what you know, out of your own knowledge."

"Just a moment." Judge Motley's voice broke the excited mood of the moment. John Armstrong was on his feet. "Mr. Armstrong?"

"It's nearly ten o'clock, your honor," Armstrong pointed out. And I have a witness to interview tonight. I can hardly ask him to wait in my office much longer."

Judge Motley nodded. "I think we might adjourn now," he said, "and resume with this witness tomorrow."

"My cross-examination is nearly finished," David protested.

"You can finish it in the morning, when we'll all be better able to appreciate it. The jury is cautioned against discussing the case with anyone. Court is adjourned."

"Your honor," David shouted desperately.

"Court is adjourned," the Judge repeated.

That was how they got you, David thought bitterly as he turned away. Not with the objections and the motions, not even with the questioning of prospective jurors. They gave you all the rope you could use there, because all that showed in the record, and all of it could be used as the basis for a retrial. But in the little things, like adjourning or not adjourning— Who would grant an application for a new trial on the grounds that, by permitting a witness to rest in the middle of cross-examination, the court had prejudiced the right of the defendant to a fair trial? He tried to return Dr. Schacter's smile as the witness came down from the stand, and, conscious that his rage and disappointment were mirrored in his expression, returned to his table and gathered up his papers.

"Mr. Blake?" David looked up. Pete Wells was leaning negligently on a corner of the table.

"I really have nothing to say." David tried to make the words firm but pleasant, and succeeded only in the former.

"Come on," Wells cajoled. "What's the defense theory? The girl just died? How about that staircase? You got any evidence that she—"

"The defense never has a theory," David snapped. "We leave that for the prosecution. And," he added bitterly, "the reporters."

David stuffed the last of his papers into his brief case, snapped the lock, and walked out, leaving it to the people in his way to step aside, and ignoring a "Good evening, Mr. Blake," from the guard on duty at the main door.

"Calm down," Abbe said, as they neared the car. "You did fine."

"I did like hell!" David opened the car door for Abbe, slammed it shut after her, went around to his own side and got in. He clashed the gears and maneuvered jerkily out of the lot. "I needed five more minutes," he said. "Five more minutes to have that doctor contradicting himself and winding up by admitting he *guessed* at the cause of death. By morning he'll have thought about it, and talked to Armstrong."

"Sure he will," Abbe agreed. "The adjournment'll get him off the hook. Don't you think the jury knows that? And don't drive like Barney!"

David eased his foot off the accelerator, permitting the interval between his car and the car ahead to increase somewhat. "It's going to be this way all through the trial," Abbe went on. "Armstrong'll get every break. You've just got to keep the pressure on. You've got to force Motley to come to Armstrong's defense as often as you can."

"Why?" David asked hopelessly. "What's the use?"

"To begin with," Abbe said, "every time you make Motley move, you increase the chance that he'll commit some error."

"I don't think so," David said. "He's a very intelligent fellow. He knows exactly where judicial discretion ends and reversible error begins. He'll never—"

"I didn't say he would. I said making him move increases the chance. But it does more than that. Tomorrow, after Schacter wriggles off, some of the jurors'll wonder—maybe even without knowing they're wondering—just what he would have said if there hadn't been an adjournment."

The traffic had thinned out. David increased the car's speed as he headed down the incline leading to the beach highway. "They're not going to acquit on the basis of what they wonder," he said.

"And they wouldn't acquit on the basis of anything you could get out of Schacter tonight," Abbe added. "But it's going to happen over and over and over. You're going to have every doubtful objection overruled, and Armstrong's going to have his sustained. Sure, Motley can see to it that Armstrong gets what he wants into the record and you don't. But, in order to do that, he's going to have to make his own prejudice clear. Just how clear depends on how well you work. If you work it right, you'll be able to make the whole dirty arrangement plain. You'll be able to rub the jury's nose in it. They're not going to like it. And there's only one way they can show their dislike."

There was, David knew, something less than a full measure of reason in what Abbe was saying. But, by the same token, her argument, while plainly intended to inspire confidence regardless of whether any was merited, had some validity. The hopeless dejection which had flowed over him as the Judge adjourned court began to ebb, even if no flow of confidence came to replace it. David began to believe that the research that had preceded his cross-examination of the doctor, and the care that had gone into the questioning itself, were not entirely wasted.

The parking area between the road and the ocean, where they had been during the intermission before the evening session, came into view. Now it was devoid of cars.

"Turn in there," Abbe said.

David did. "What for?" he asked.

"Because I'm still a girl." Abbe's words, to David at least, had no coy aspect. "I'm incurably romantic. I like to park on the way home."

"Even when you're going home with the man?" David asked.

"I'm *incurably* romantic," Abbe repeated.

David allowed the car to coast to a stop at the edge of the parking area, facing the ocean. He turned off the headlights, and turned on the radio, pulled Abbe to him and kissed her, not lightly as he had before, but almost fiercely.

"Very nice," Abbe murmured. "Do it again."

David did it again.

The radio gave forth suddenly and too loudly the tones of a string quartet. David reached around Abbe to turn it down. He put his lips to her throat and held her close and the quartet played on. The music stopped, and a man's voice read the 12:30 headlines. In Paris, Czechoslovakian representatives, at Russian insistence, were boycotting the organizing conference of the Marshall Plan. In California, the Black Dahlia killer was still at large, but an arrest was expected momentarily. In San Juno, the jury had been completed for the Chavez trial, and the taking of early, routine testimony had begun. There were, the announcer said, no fireworks, and the high point of the day's session had actually been reached during the evening recess when Defense Attorney Blake had been given a subpoena to appear before the Battle Committee. The Yankees had won a night game from Cleveland.

David turned the radio off. "How come Battle was interested in me before I went East?" he asked.

"You're so romantic." Abbe tipped her head back.

"Let's have it," David said firmly.

Abbe disengaged herself and moved as far away from David as the limited area of the front seat permitted. "One of the most delightful things about you, David," she said, "is the way you take people on absolute faith. I hate to be the one to spoil it for you, but you'll have to learn the facts of life anyhow."

"Meaning?"

"Meaning I only used Hopper for an example. Meaning Battle is interested in anyone who associates with Barney. Or me."

A cloud that had hidden the moon drifted away, and in the sudden silver light David looked at Abbe. Her face was entirely devoid of expression.

"Does he have any reason to?" David asked. "You don't have to tell me if you don't want to."

"Why not?" Abbe asked. "Because a man's politics is his own affair? Since when? If I ask you whether you're a Democrat, you don't get insulted."

"It isn't the same thing."

"It is if they're both political parties. Barney," she went on, without any change in tone, "has been a Party member all his adult life."

"And you?" David made his tone gentle.

Another cloud covered the moon, and David could barely see the outlines of Abbe's face as she said: "I was for a while. A short while. When we were leading the workers of the world in the fight against fascism. Then came the Hitler-Stalin pact, and the fight against fascism became an imperialist war. It was tough for me, but I made it. Then Hitler broke the pact, and the imperialist war became a holy crusade, and that was one switch too many."

"You got out."

"Out of the Party," Abbe said slowly.

For a while there was silence. Then David asked: "Is this what's been bothering you? Why you've been so distant?"

"I've been worried about you," Abbe said. "I knew you were going into this with your eyes wide open, writing everything you saw in your book, and seeing nothing. I knew you were going to get hurt, chopped to pieces for a principle you didn't know existed, a principle you wouldn't believe in in any case."

"But you believed in it."

"Once," Abbe said. "Once I believed, and because I believed I did terrible things. You wouldn't have liked me then."

"Nonsense," David declared. "Don't fool yourself. My feeling for you is not an intellectual thing. I don't have any urge to put my hands on your beliefs."

"Don't," Abbe protested. "This is serious. I want you to understand. It's important to me."

"I'm sorry. Go ahead."

"My father," Abbe began, "was a deeply religious man. He was also extremely ethical. His ethics ran directly contrary to his religion. He solved this conflict by a sort of translation which he called 'bringing the teaching of the prophets up to date.' By this he meant: where the prophet has written *white*, the ethical man must read *black*, but he never admitted, not even to himself that this is what he meant."

"And this is why you joined the Party?"

"I'm trying to tell you," Abbe protested. "Where the Bible says: 'If a man shall put out the eye of another, he shall suffer his own eye to be put out,' my father interpreted it to mean that an evildoer ought not to be too harshly punished for he will suffer eternal punishment at the hands of his conscience. In other words: *an eye for an eye*, in my father's translation, meant *temper justice with mercy*."

"I don't see—"

" 'Vengeance is mine, saith the Lord.' Do you know what that means? According to my father, it means there shall be no vengeance on earth, because the Lord reserves it to himself, and, of course, He will never exercise it. Every year my father made a solemn promise, in front of the congregation, to sacrifice a fine spring lamb on the altar of the Lord. He never did it. It's hard for an ethical man to promise to do something he has no intention of doing. Not for my father, it wasn't hard. He just translated his promise to mean that he would be charitable, and sent a hundred dollars to the Community Chest!"

"I still—"

"He was a fraud!" For the first time, Abbe's disquiet was showing in her tone. "He had a code of ethics, but he didn't have the guts to admit that he lived by his own code, so he related it to a printed book, but to do it he had to alter the book so that it made sense to an ethical man. When I was sixteen, he died, secure in the belief that, not because he was an honorable decent man, but because he was a religious man, he was safe in the afterworld. God, how I wanted the kind of security he had! And I couldn't find it in religion, because I wasn't capable of the sophistry you have to commit to find it there."

Where the highway curved, beyond Abbe's head, David could see a truck coming by, the chain hanging from the truck's rear axle shedding a train of sparks like a comet's tail. "I was sixteen, and I went away to college, David, looking for a faith, a code, something I could believe in, something that would stand up to real tests, and not fall apart the first time a strain was put on it."

"Everybody wants something like that, Abbe," David pointed out. "A code. A way of life. Some assurance that what you're doing is right."

"But not everybody turns to the Party? Is that what you're getting at?" Abbe did not wait for David to reply. "David, I saw my father die. I saw him go peacefully, confidently, not just reconciled to going but glad to go, because he had a code of conduct and he'd lived by it. He made it up out of his own head, out of his own understanding of right and wrong, and he attributed it to priests and prophets and writers whose own ideas were exactly opposite to his own, but that didn't matter. He had a code, and he lived by it, and he found peace, and I wanted that. I wanted it badly, the way kids that age want to get rid of pimples, get a bid to the prom, be popular. And in the years that I looked for it, that wanting grew bigger and bigger until it dominated me. And then," Abbe said, "I found the Party. They gave me a written code, and an end that I didn't have to wait for the next world to gain. They gave me companions, co-religionists, as it were, who were working toward that same end. And a card. The card was important. It was proof that I was a true believer, because carrying that card was a risk an infidel would never assume."

"But didn't you think—"

"That's just it, David. I didn't. I didn't want to. I wanted to have something I could believe in without thinking. Something I could take on faith. It's usually the other way around. I mean, first they try the Party, and, when that fails them, they turn to religion. Mother Russia to Father God. But always take on faith. Never think for yourself, because thinking is lonely, and these are lonely people who want to lose their loneliness. To lose that, you need a code, and the Party gave me that. Not just a code of political conduct. It gave you a whole way of life, and you had to take it all, and that's what made it easy for me to take. Did you ever wonder why lady comrades are such frumps?"

"I'd never noticed," David said.

"If you're writing a play," Abbe said, "and you write a Party woman into it, you get a woman with stringy hair, bad skin, thick glasses, and uneven hems. That's cartoon thinking, but it's sometimes accurate."

"Not if you were one," David said. The moon, freed from its cloud blanket, was dropping quickly into the Pacific, its glare forming a silvery road leading away from them into the ocean and on to the horizon. "It's getting late," David said. "Maybe—"

"In a few minutes," Abbe replied. "There's a reason for this. In the Party, ill-fitting clothes, sloppy make-up, these are proof that you accept that part of the code that says that sex is of no special importance and that romantic attachments are bourgeois impediments. Sex is like a drink of water. Do you get dressed up to go to the drinking fountain?"

"I believe all this in general," David said. "But I don't believe it of you. I can't quite see you as a frump."

"I could show you pictures," Abbe said. "On Fourteenth Street, they used to say that before Comrade Klein went out on the street, she stood in front of a mirror and looked back over her shoulder to make sure her seams were crooked."

David laughed. "And when," he asked, "did all this change?"

"No one time," Abbe said. "Gradually. I began to read Party literature. Not the current literature, but old stuff that was out of date. It wasn't that the interpretation had changed; a party is like a man; it can change its point of view. But the facts. They should have been permanent, fixed points of reference like the words in the books my father read. But they weren't, and I couldn't accept the Party explanations of why this was necessary. I began to drift, to deviate in other ways. I made myself more attractive, but I told myself this was for my own satisfaction only. Now that I look back on it, I can see that it had to be gradual, because I was growing up, and growth is never anything but gradual. That's why I don't think meeting you was responsible for the final break. It only speeded it along."

"Now *that*," David said, "I don't understand at all."

Abbe moved along the front seat toward him, reached out for him, and laced her fingers behind his head. "I could never feel about a drink of water," she said, "the way I do about you." David's head went down to hers, as if to write a period to the conversation.

"Let's go," said Abbe, a few minutes later. "I want to get out to the shack. Even if it's so late we'll have to go right to sleep. We have to be up early."

"Not that early," David said.

8

With the selection of the jury completed, the trial of *People v. Chavez* moved along with such dispatch that, on the third day of testimony, Judge Motley announced that the evening session would be dispensed with, and, thereafter, the court observed more normal hours. On that same day, David received a letter from Assemblyman Carl Baron Battle only a few hours after it had been made public by the press. In it he informed David that the subpoena for him had been withdrawn. "I was certainly unaware," Battle wrote, "that for you to take a few hours on a Saturday morning to appear before my committee would interfere with your work on behalf of your client. It was certainly not my intention to do so, and we shall dispense with your testimony until such time as your presence may be more readily available."

"Meaning," Abbe said, "that the trial can't last forever, and he'll get you when it's over."

But David had no time to give to thoughts of what might happen when the trial was over. He was fully occupied in the day-to-day routine of cross-examining the witnesses Armstrong called. In this he was developing a considerable proficiency, aided greatly by the fact that there had been no witness to Angel's presence on the stair landing prior to the death of Marie Wiltse. What Armstrong was drawing from the witnesses he called was a series of inferences and deductions based on their observation of Angel *after* the event, and nothing Armstrong, or even Judge Motley could do, could prevent David from driving this point home to the jury.

On Thursday of the third week of the trial and the second week of the actual taking of testimony, Barney and Consuela returned from the East. David was glad of this. He was anxious to have Barney's help in the preparation of his summation, and he felt it politic that the defendant's mother appear in court before the end of the trial. The end of the trial, in David's view, was then close at hand. The case for the State was plainly near its conclusion, and he did not intend to make a case for defense, proposing instead to argue that the State had failed to prove (a) that a crime had been committed, or (b) that if a crime had been committed, Angel was the guilty party.

Consuela and Barney made a dramatic entrance that day, coming down the center aisle just a few minutes before the opening of the afternoon session of the court. When the flashbulbs stopped popping and the bailiffs had shooed the reporters away from the defense table, there was barely time for David to accept Barney's handshake and Consuela's whispered thanks before the Judge entered the courtroom.

The witness whose direct examination John Armstrong had concluded at the close of the morning session was recalled to the stand and informed by the Judge that his oath was still in effect. He was Harold Butteridge, a lanky Texan who had been one of the first on the scene following the discovery of Marie Wiltse's body.

David walked to a point from which he could observe both witness and jury. "Mr. Butteridge," he said gently, "I wonder if you'd mind telling me what you told the District Attorney yesterday, about the events just preceding your discovery of the body. I believe you said you heard something."

"Yes," Butteridge drawled. "It's like I said then. I heard the sounds of a scuffle-like, and then I heard this girl crying."

"*A* girl crying," David suggested. "Since it was dark, you could hardly say it was any particular girl."

"*A* girl crying," Butteridge conceded.

"And before that, you heard the sound of 'a scuffle-like.' "

"Yes. And then I went up the stairs and found—"

"Just a moment," David put in. "I'm not interested in that. I don't think there's any dispute in what you found. I'm interested in what you heard."

John Armstrong, who had arisen during the latter part of David's speech, remained silent until David had finished. "I don't think he should argue with the witness," he said.

"The point is well taken," Judge Motley said, leaning toward David. "I think you might confine yourself to the asking of questions. If you are not satisfied with the answers you get, ask more."

"But I think," David said, "that I'm entitled to responsive answers to the questions I ask."

"Quite so," the Judge agreed. "Mr. Butteridge, please merely answer the questions."

"Yes, sir."

"Can you describe these sounds—which you call 'the sounds of a scuffle-like'—in other words?"

"I don't think I can," Butteridge said. "That's just how it sounded to me. Like a scuffle."

"Your honor," David said, "I move that the entire testimony of this witness, insofar as it relates to what he heard, be stricken as representing his conclusion."

"I think not," Judge Motley said quietly. "I think he is describing what he heard as best he can."

"He's characterizing what he heard," David argued.

"The motion is denied."

"Exception," David said, without heat. "Now, Mr. Butteridge, let me see if I can help you describe these noises more exactly. Would you say they were in the nature of grunts?"

"Sort of."

"Well, were they or weren't they?"

"Objection," Armstrong snapped. "He can't ask for a yes-or-no answer to that sort of question."

"Overruled," Motley said. "The witness may answer yes or no, and if he cannot answer yes or no he need only say so."

"They were like grunts," Butteridge said.

"Now according to the diagram the District Attorney introduced, you were about a hundred feet away. And yet you heard grunts? Is that right?"

"Not grunts exactly. Gasping. Groans maybe. And bumping. You know."

"I don't know," David pointed out. "Bumping?"

"Yes. That's what I said."

"What sort of bumping? Flesh on flesh?"

Butteridge smiled. "Don't reckon you could hear flesh on flesh that far away, sir."

"Then, if it wasn't flesh on flesh, what was it?"

"Now who's asking him to characterize a sound?" Armstrong asked.

"If you're making an objection," Judge Motley said reprovingly, "you might make it a little less uh—colloquially."

"Objected to as calling for a conclusion of the witness."

"Overruled."

During the exchange between the Judge and the District Attorney, David watched the jurors switch their gaze alternately between the sweating Texan and Angel, who sat impassively at the defense table. This, David knew, was a good sign. It is elementary that, in a capital case, a jury that looks fixedly at the defendant is seeing him with a rope around his neck. A jury that studies a witness has, somewhere, a lingering doubt as to the truth of his testimony and is seeking to resolve that doubt by observing the witness's demeanor.

"What sort of sound was the bumping?" David asked.

"Like if somebody was pushed against a wall."

"Or fell."

"No. I don't reckon—"

"You aren't going to tell us you could tell by listening that someone had been pushed?" David raised his voice. "The most you could have heard would have been the body hitting the stone. If you could hear that. Isn't that true?"

"I objected before to his arguing with the witness," Armstrong said angrily. "And I object now to his bullying him."

"I'm cross-examining," David snapped.

"Then please do so more quietly," Judge Motley suggested. "I think we could all hear you before."

"Could the sound you heard—by the way, was there more than one bump?"

"No, sir," Butteridge said. "Only one bump."

"Could it have been made by someone falling?"

"Yes," the witness drawled. "I suppose it could. But," he added too quickly to be interrupted, "I don't think it was."

"Now that's his own conclusion, your honor. I ask that that last part be stricken."

"Why?" Armstrong asked. "You asked him."

"I asked him could it have been caused by a fall. I don't care whether he thinks it was."

"I think the answer was responsive and may stand," Judge Motley ruled. "If there was fault, it was in the question."

David considered taking another exception, and decided against it. He turned back to the witness. "You don't think the sound you heard was the Wiltse girl falling, then?"

"I don't."

"You think you heard her hitting the wall as a result of being pushed?"

"That's right."

"Tell me, Mr. Butteridge, are you an expert in distinguishing between sounds?"

The witness's bewildered "Sir?" and John Armstrong's angry "Objection" came simultaneously.

"Yes, yes," Judge Motley said. "You seem to be wandering a bit afield, Mr. Blake. Just what is it you are trying to bring out?"

"I want the jury to see that when this witness tries to interpret what he heard, he is merely guessing."

"The State conceded that the witness is not an expert," John Armstrong stated. "He is merely—" Judge Motley silenced him with a reproachful glance. "Sorry," he said, "I thought you were done."

"The distinction between a guess as to what caused a sound and a reasoned evaluation of the sound is a fine one," the Judge said. "I think the jury will regard this as testimony of what the witness heard, and will regard his estimate as to the source of what he heard as merely descriptive of the sound itself."

"Were you alone on the beach at this time, Mr. Butteridge?" David snapped, when Judge Motley had finished.

"No. I wasn't."

"Would you tell us who you were with?"

"No."

David turned wearily to the bench. "May he be instructed to reply?" he asked.

"He must answer all relevant questions," Judge Motley said. "I am not convinced that this is relevant."

"It relates to the sounds he says he heard," David argued. "I would like an opportunity to find out if his companion or companions heard those same sounds."

"He doesn't care about the sounds," John Armstrong blurted out. "He wants to embarrass the witness. He's trying to intimidate future witnesses. He's done it before."

"Now I object to that," David shouted. "Especially to the last four words."

"Yes, Mr. Armstrong," Judge Motley declared. "That is a serious charge."

"I withdraw the remark."

"May I ask again that the witness be instructed to answer my question?" David asked.

"Mr. Butteridge," Judge Motley asked, "was anyone standing next to you at the time that you heard what you heard?"

"No, sir."

"Where were your companions at that time?"

"They were about a hundred feet away, down by the water, watching for grunion."

"They could not have heard the sounds?"

"No, I don't think so. They were further away, and the surf—"

"That will do." The Judge turned to David. "I don't think he has to answer your other question, at least if you have given your correct motive for asking it."

David flushed at the faint touch of sarcasm in the Judge's final remarks. "Do you infer that I have misled the court?" he asked angrily.

"I infer nothing," Judge Motley said. "You are making the inference."

David held his anger within him. "Of course you know you are under oath," he said to Butteridge.

"I know that, sir."

"You respect that oath?"

"I do."

"You swore to tell the truth, and of course that is exactly what you are doing?"

"Yes."

"Have you taken many oaths?"

"A few, I reckon."

"And you've kept them all?"

"Yes."

"Tell us about some of them."

"Must we go into this?" Armstrong demanded. "What possible bearing—"

"The testimony goes to the credibility of the witness," David said. "His understanding of the nature of the oath is, of course, always a subject for questioning."

"Proceed," Judge Motley said.

"What other oaths can you recall taking?"

"I was a witness in a traffic case, once," Butteridge recalled.

"And your testimony was truthful?"

"The man I testified for," Butteridge said proudly, "won his suit."

"I didn't ask you whether the jury believed you," David said mildly. "I asked you whether your testimony was the truth?"

"Of course it was the truth!" Butteridge shouted.

"Very well." David lowered his tone to increase the contrast between his own calm manner of speech and Butteridge's excited ranting. "What other oaths have you taken?"

Butteridge thought for a moment. "My primary oath," he said. "You have to take an oath that you belong to the party that you vote in the primary of."

"And you kept that oath?"

"You bet I did," Butteridge said. "I'm a Democrat," he explained.

"Yes," David said. "Is that all? Isn't there another oath you've taken?"

"I don't believe so."

"Are you married?"

"Yes, sir."

"Were you married in church?"

"Yes."

"Did the ceremony include a vow on your part to be faithful to your wife?"

"Yes, sir."

"Most of them do," David said. "My own church requires an oath quote in the presence of God and this company close quote. That's pretty strong stuff."

"I think that's what the preacher said at my wedding," Butteridge said.

"Have you been true to that oath?"

"I have."

"And true to your wife? That's the same thing."

"Certainly."

"Now I ask you again," David said, letting his voice come up in intensity, "who was with you on that beach party the night of the grunion run? It wasn't your—"

"Objection!" John Armstrong shouted, coming to his feet. Judge Motley brought his gavel down, and the rest of David's remark were lost in the turmoil.

"Mr. Blake," the Judge said, when things quieted down. "Your question was one on which I had already ruled. Asking it again, and especially in the context in which you asked it, was highly improper, and unquestionably contemptuous."

"I withdraw the question," David said, "and I apologize to the court."

"Very well," Judge Motley said. "The jury will disregard that last question. Have you any further questions for this witness?"

"No, your honor."

"And no redirect," Armstrong added.

"Very well," Judge Motley said. "Call your next witness."

"He will be my final witness," Armstrong said. At his request the bailiff called "Captain McAndrews," and a young man arose from a seat at the rear of the courtroom and made his way toward the stand.

"I must warn you, Mr. Blake," the Judge said sternly while this was going on, "that any future conduct of the sort you have just displayed will be regarded as contempt and treated accordingly. I may add," he went on significantly, "that I do not *fine* attorneys guilty of contempt."

"I understand, your honor." David tried to make his words contrite. Motley obviously meant business, and a judge's power to punish for contempt is almost absolute, no proof being required save what the judge demands, the judge imposing any sentence he deems reasonable.

Captain McAndrews was a typical outdoorsman who seemed somewhat out of place in long trousers. His title, it rapidly appeared, was not military but referred to his rank in the Fish and Game Division of the State's Department of Conservation. Under Armstrong's questioning, he explained that, on the night of Marie Wiltse's death, he had been detailed to patrol Village Beach and enforce that section of the law restricting grunion hunters to "bare hands and buckets." His tour of duty, he said, was nearly through, when he became aware of a disturbance on a landing of the stairway leading up the cliff.

"And what did you do then?" Armstrong asked.

"I went up the staircase to the landing, where I found a Mexican boy surrounded by a number of white men and women. There was a young girl lying near the edge of the landing. I gathered—"

"I object to his telling what he gathered," David said. "It is—"

"Quite so." Judge Motley cut the objection short. "Mr. McAndrews, please just tell us what you did and what you saw."

McAndrews nodded. "Do you see the Mexican in court?" Armstrong asked.

"Yes." McAndrews pointed to Angel, who looked at him unflinchingly. "There he is."

"Go ahead, then," Armstrong said. "You arrived at the landing. What happened next?"

"The people there seemed very angry at the boy. I thought—"

"Same objection," David said casually.

"Sustained. The jury will disregard the answer."

Armstrong seemed unperturbed. "Well, just what did you do, then, as a result of what you saw and heard?"

"I object to the qualifying phrase 'as a result of what he saw and heard,'" David said.

"I think we may assume that whatever act he took was in response to what he saw and heard," Judge Motley observed. "So perhaps the phrase might be omitted."

"*After* what you saw and heard," Armstrong said, with a side-long glance of triumph at David, "what did you do?"

"I drew my pistol and ordered the crowd to stand back. They did so. I then ordered the defendant to lie down on his face, on the steps where I could watch him, while I examined the girl. When I found that she was dead, I placed the defendant under arrest and took him in my car to the police station."

"On what charge did you arrest him?"

"When I picked him up? None. I just told him 'You're under arrest.' Later, at the police station, I told the desk sergeant what had happened, and he said—"

"Objection," David interposed. "If we need to know what the sergeant said, we can have his testimony."

"Sustained."

"In any event," Armstrong went on, "you know, of your own knowledge, that he was charged with murder?"

"Yes, sir."

"And that was after you had told the desk sergeant what had happened."

"Yes, sir."

"Now I take it that what you told him had to do largely with what you had been told by the people on the landing?"

"That's right."

"Well," Armstrong said, "I can't ask you about that, then. But I can ask you whether, looking back on it now, you think your act in preferring a murder charge against the defendant was justified."

"Objection," David said, his voice rising in intensity. "He's asking the witness for an opinion as to the defendant's guilt or innocence."

"Not at all," Armstrong replied. "I'm asking him to judge his own motives for his own acts."

"Overruled."

"Exception," David said, feeling a triumph that stemmed from his certainty that Judge Motley had erred, and feeling, a moment later, shame at the triumph because a judge's errors are of value only in the event of an appeal from an adverse verdict.

At McAndrews' request, the clerk reread Armstrong's question.

"No, sir," McAndrews said forcefully. "It was the only thing I could do. You see—"

"That will do," Judge Motley said before David could protest.

"That's all," Armstrong said. "You may cross-examine."

For a moment, David weighed the idea of refraining from cross-examination. McAndrews' testimony was hardly damaging. And yet, since this was Armstrong's final witness, and since the defense did not propose to call witnesses, to discredit or minimize McAndrews' testimony would be to wind up the actual taking of testimony on a point favorable to the defense.

"Mr. McAndrews," David said, advancing toward the witness stand, "I just want to make one thing clear. When you say you were justified in what you did on the night in question, you mean you were justified on the basis of what you were told. Is that right?"

"Partly, sir," McAndrews seemed to be following the question with some difficulty. "I saw things too."

"You've told us about that. But what you saw wouldn't have justified your making an arrest, would it?"

"Added to what I was told," McAndrews said.

"Exactly. So it was on the basis of what you were told that you made your charge."

"Yes," McAndrews said.

"Told by whom?"

"By the people on the landing."

"Do you know their names?"

"No, sir."

David continued the questioning evenly. "Do you think you would recognize them if you saw them again?"

"I might," McAndrews said.

"You're not sure?"

"It was pretty dark."

"Of course. Now you never made any effort to find out if what you had been told was the truth, did you?"

Armstrong was on his feet. "Objection. It's immaterial, and he's asking for an opinion."

"No," David argued. "We've already had the opinion. Now I'm trying to show how the opinion was arrived at and what weight the jury might give it."

"I think you're wandering somewhat away from the case," Judge Motley said. "But the witness may answer."

"No, sir," McAndrews said earnestly. "It wasn't my business to check."

"It certainly was not," David agreed. "And I certainly didn't mean to imply that it was." He paused for a moment, and worked the next question over in his mind, regretting as he did so that the practice of beginning a question "I put it to you that . . ." is limited to British courts. "Now would this be a fair statement of your testimony? That you arrested the boy on the basis of what you were told by people whose names you don't know and whom you might not recognize if you saw them again. That the facts they stated formed the basis of your arrest, but that you, of your own knowledge, had no reason then to believe the boy guilty, and have none now?"

"Objected to," Armstrong said. "His present opinion—"

"Sustained."

"Let me put it this way: you don't know anything at all, of

your own knowledge, of what went on on that landing before you got there. Is that right?"

"Only what I was told."

"By anonymous informants. And you've made no effort to find out if what they told you was true or false?"

"I couldn't—"

"Of course you couldn't," David said. "And when you say: 'I couldn't,' it follows that you didn't. Doesn't it?"

"I don't think I understand." McAndrews looked around help- lessly.

"That's all right," David said. "I have no more questions."

McAndrews sat motionless in the witness chair, as if unable to believe his good fortune. Then, in sudden quick motions, he arose and departed.

"That is the case for the people," John Armstrong announced.

"Is the defense ready to proceed with its case now?" Judge Motley asked.

David got to his feet to announce that the defense proposed to call no witnesses, but before he could speak, he heard Barney's deep voice say: "Your honor."

For a moment, David stood flabbergasted. "Your honor," he said at last, in bewilderment, "may I present my associate, Mr. Castle?"

"Proceed, Mr. Castle."

David sat down and smiled at Abbe, who stared back at him as if she didn't see him. "If it please the court," Barney said, "I have been detained until today on business connected with this trial. I am constrained to ask if the court will not grant us a recess now, until tomorrow morning, in order that I may confer with my associate before we proceed further."

"I have no objection to that," Judge Motley said. "But I'm very anxious that there be no undue delay. May I ask if the defense plans to call witnesses?"

"That," Barney said, "will be one of the matters to be covered at the conference between Mr. Blake and myself. I may say, however, that we are concerned with only a single witness, whose testimony, in the event that we decide to introduce it, should easily be disposed of in a day."

"Very well," Judge Motley agreed. "We will begin to hear your witness, if you decide to call one, tomorrow morning. Immediately thereafter—or on convening, if the defense decides against calling its witness—we will hear motions, if any, and proceed immediately to summations. Court is adjourned."

David turned to Barney, who was talking to the attendant charged with escorting Angel to and from the courtroom. "I want him in the conference room at nine in the morning," Barney was saying. "That O.K.?"

"Sure thing," the guard said. "Let's go, Angel."

Angel, who had been embracing his mother, dutifully released her and followed the guard to the side door.

"How about that, Barney?" The questioner was Pete Wells, who had plainly heard Barney's request of the guard. "Is that your witness? You going to put the kid on the stand?"

"Maybe," Barney said.

"Sounds like more than 'maybe' to me," Wells said. "Why the conference unless he's going on the stand?"

"Do you want me to write your story for you?" Barney asked, not unpleasantly. He punched Pete Wells on the arm hard and winked as he pushed him away.

"You want to go home?" Barney directed the question to Consuela.

"Why?" Consuela replied. "What is there for me there? My husband is dead, and my son—" Her inability to go on, while understandable, seemed to David almost forced.

"O.K.," Barney said. "We'll get you a hotel room."

When this had been done, the three returned and ate in silence in the back booth of the restaurant across the street from the courtroom. When the meal was finished, the restaurant was empty except for the owner, who served as waiter and cashier as well, and whose principal qualification for operating a restaurant so located was his discretion, which caused him to station himself ostentatiously in the front of the room when his guests seemed to be conducting important conversations in the rear.

"Who the hell is our big mystery witness?" David asked. "And why do we need a conference with Angel before court tomorrow?"

"And why," Abbe asked, "did you lead that poor rum-pot reporter down the path?"

"I didn't lead him down any path," Barney said, answering all three questions at once.

For a moment, David did not believe that he had heard correctly.

"Jesus Christ!" Abbe gasped.

"You keep out of this," Barney said, not especially gently. "Unless," he added more softly, "you went and got a law degree while I was East."

"Barney," David said urgently, "we can't put Angel on the stand. Everything we've done has been on the theory—"

"That the duty of the defense is to create doubt."

"That's right."

"And I gather—now this is based on what the papers carried, and on what you wrote—that you've pretty well prevented the State from proving the facts it needs for its case."

"We've made it tough for them," David said. "Their case is built on inference, supposition, guesswork, and hearsay. They haven't proved that any rape took place—or any attempted rape, either, not even under the terms of the statute—and they haven't proved cause of death, or connected Angel with what happened except through the longest of inference. They—"

"Save it," Barney said. "You aren't summing up. What you

mean is, the jury doesn't really know—from the evidence—just what did happen that night on that landing."

"That's right," David said. "And what they don't know—"

"What do you think happened?"

"That's not my concern."

"Come off it," Barney commanded. "Talk to me. Don't give me legal hanky-panky."

"You could put me on the stand and swear me," David declared, "and I still couldn't—"

"Of course not. But you're not on the stand. Tell me what happened. What really happened. You know what it was, even if you can't be legally held to know."

"The way Angel tells it," David said, "he met this girl, and she kind of led him on, and he kissed her, and, the next thing he knew, she was dead."

"You believe that?"

"Of course I do."

"Why?"

"Because I only have to hear the boy tell that story and I know it's the truth. You can look at him and see that."

"What makes you think a jury can't do that?"

"Why take the chance? I think we're better off this way."

"I don't," Barney said, signaling for fresh coffee. There was silence while the cups were filled. David looked quickly at Abbe, who smiled nervously. "What conclusion do you think the jury will draw if Angel doesn't testify?" Barney asked when the waiter was gone.

"They can't draw any conclusion. The law—"

"The law can't go in the jury room with them," Barney declared. "Just because this is the first case you've tried doesn't mean you have to act as if it was the first one you've ever heard of. God, you must know that every jury, if the defendant doesn't testify, figures he's afraid to take the stand."

"Motley'll charge them—" David began.

"Sure he will," Barney said. "He'll charge them not to draw any conclusion from the failure of the defendant to take the stand. And you know what effect that'll have? It'll remind them that he didn't take the stand. That's all."

"Barney, I know I've got 'em—some of 'em, at least. Why rock the boat?"

"What good is having some of them going to do us?"

"Let them hold firm in the jury room, and the worst we've got is a hung jury."

"The worst we've got?" Barney shouted. "How bad can we get? Send that boy out of court with a hung jury on a rape-murder charge, and what do you think becomes of him?"

"We can't be choosy—"

"Don't talk nonsense," Barney snapped. "How many jurors do you think you have? Four? Five?"

"That's about it," David admitted.

"And they're going to hold out? The hell they are. They'll knuckle under. They're afraid of what'll happen to them. And even if they hold out, they'll never bring the others around. Turn loose a dirty Mex who didn't have the guts to take the stand?"

"Barney—"

"Shut up!" Abbe gasped at Barney's words, and Barney carefully lowered his voice. "I'm sorry I said that," he said. "But not letting Angel testify is a terrible gamble, and you lose even if you win. Because Armstrong won't move for a dismissal, even if the jury is hung eleven to one for acquittal. They'll try him again, and this time they won't miss."

"Why?" David asked. "Why will it be any easier the second time?"

"Because we're flat broke," Barney said. "We've got contributions coming in, sure. But a hung jury is proof that the boy is getting a fair trial, and once that happens the contributions stop like you turned off a tap, and we go into the second trial with no money."

"I don't know—"

Barney leaped on David's admission of doubt. "I know," he said, more gently than he had spoken before, but somehow with more power. "What happened on that beach was an accident," he said. "It could have happened to anyone. To a juror. To his kid. You've got to make them see that."

Abbe entered the argument for the first time. "I don't see it," she said. "David's conducted the classic defense of simply blocking the prosecution off from proving its case. And they haven't made a case. Tomorrow, he moves for dismissal. If that's denied, he asks for a directed verdict. If that's denied—and I think there's an outside chance Motley might have the guts to grant it—there's your appeal. There isn't enough of a case to go to the jury, and the conviction will be set aside."

"Sure," David agreed. "We've brought off just what we tried to do. Right or wrong, we're stuck with this theory for the case. We can't back off now."

"We're going to back off, though." For the first time, it was clear that Barney wasn't arguing. He was saying how things were going to be. David started to resume the argument but Barney cut him off with a raised hand, the gesture being, somehow, almost menacing. "I hate to do this," he said, "but the time has come when I have to take charge."

"Take charge?" Abbe blurted. "By whose—"

"I've got the authority, all right," Barney said. "Don't make me use it."

"You're putting this on a very unpleasant basis," David said. "I'm afraid you'll have to show me where you get the authority to tell me—I'm the attorney of record—how I've got to run my case."

"The boy is under age," Barney said too gently. "His mother is his guardian. She engages the attorney."

"She already—"

"And discharges him," Barney went on. "She trusts me," he

said, "and I'd be betraying that trust if I didn't advise her that the defense was being mishandled. If it was, that is."

"She'd never believe you. Angel—"

"Angel's a kid. Sure he likes you. I like you. But if I say you're doing it wrong, Consuela will go down and see Motley tonight and explain the situation to him."

"He doesn't have to let her change."

"The law isn't clear on that. On the other hand, he won't let a capital case go to the jury if the defense is dissatisfied with its own counsel. Will he?"

"I don't know," David lied.

"You're bluffing," Abbe said, a little shrilly. "It would kill whatever case you might make—for the defense to stall that way."

"Perhaps," Barney admitted. "I'd have to ask for a continuance to read the transcript and prepare the case for the defense. That might prejudice the jury. But I'll do that before I see you let the case go by default."

"Default?"

"I'm not bluffing," Barney said coldly. "You put him on the stand, or I will. It's up to you which way it is."

Barney got up from the table. "I can't sleep on those plane trips," he said casually, as if this were a casual conversation to be ended with small talk. "I'm going to get my car out of the garage and go down to the shack. Don't wake me when you two come in." On his way out, Barney paused and chatted with the proprietor and signed something, and David knew he was charging all three meals to the office account.

"Well, darling," David said after a while, "what do I do now?"

"What do you want to do?" Abbe asked.

"Spit in the crazy bastard's eye," David said, without heat.

Abbe laughed. "That's good," she said. "For a while I was afraid he had you."

"He has got me," David said tonelessly.

"The hell he has. He's got the case. He's got Consuela. He's got Angel. But he doesn't have you at all."

"I've got an obligation—"

"To yourself," Abbe said, speaking too loudly for the quiet room. "Forget about Angel. It sounds brutal, but you've got to do it. The State wants Angel found guilty. So does Barney. Barney wants him to commit a sort of legal hara-kiri, and he wants you to help. Only you don't have to help."

"I don't know—"

"You've got to know," Abbe said angrily. "Angel Chavez is going to die; you've got to know that. He's going to die because Fats Sanders promised a mob he would, and because John Armstrong promised Sanders he wouldn't get off. For a while it looked like you might get him off, but now Barney's back, and it suits his purposes to have that boy convicted, and what chance has the poor little Mex got with both sides working for a conviction?"

"If he gets through cross-examination—"

"He won't," Abbe declared. "Armstrong's tough. You haven't let him show how tough he can be, because you haven't called a witness. As a matter of fact, it's partly the other way around. You haven't called witnesses because you're afraid to let Armstrong get at them. And you're right. He'll tear Angel apart."

"Look—"

The proprietor came to the table and set drinks down, two double Scotches, water on the side. David knew the discussion had reached a point where the drinks were almost necessary, and he hated Barney for knowing this would happen.

"I'll tell you something else." Abbe paused and gulped down half the drink. "If, by some miracle, Armstrong screws up and doesn't make a monkey out of Angel, Barney'll think up some other way to blow the case."

"Why, Abbe?" David asked. "Why do you say that? All right, maybe Barney's got other interests; maybe he doesn't care if

Angel lives or dies. But why do you say he wants him found guilty? It's bad enough to say he doesn't care."

Abbe stood up, and David could tell that the double Scotch, plus the excitement, were having an effect on her. "He does care," she said. "He cares terribly. He wants to see Angel hang."

"But why? I can't believe—"

"Because Barney's new world's a coming. A world where a man's color won't make any difference. A world—oh, hell, you've heard about it. And, to bring that world about, there have to be sacrifices. And Angel has to make his sacrifice, just the same as Barney would make it, if their places were reversed. Get Angel off, and what have you proved? That there's no prejudice in San Juno. In the whole State, for that matter. But that's not true. There is prejudice. The kind that'll railroad a Mex to his death on a charge that wouldn't take a white man past a coroner. That's the truth. And to bring that truth into focus, to prove it, the prejudice has to be permitted to do its work, to do its murder right out in public, where it will drive the truth home to the people who have to be brought together and united, to fight the prejudice, so that it won't be here any more and the new world will be here. Only—" she was crying now, and David suddenly noticed that his glass was empty—"only of course Angel won't be here to enjoy that wonderful stinking day."

David shook his head and signaled for more drinks. "You're wrong about Barney," he said.

"I couldn't be, David," Abbe replied, smiling as the tears ran down her flushed cheeks. More drinks were brought to the table, and the empties were taken away. "I know him, and I know his beliefs, because I went to bed with both of them. You understand me?"

"Yes," David said. "You—"

"Good," Abbe said. Her speech was becoming a trifle thick. "Because I know you, David. You couldn't kill an innocent man to advance an idea of your own, and you think no one could. And you'll think it even after you see the killing. You're a cheek-turning, reconstructed liberal. 'I will defend to the death your right to be heard.' That's sacred to you. 'I disagree with what you say.' That you forget. Free speech—"

"How," David asked mildly, "did we get around to free speech?"

"It's all part of the same thing. Some guy wants to sterilize me and put me to work in the salt mines in Utah, and somebody else says he's got no right to be heard, and you get so excited defending the son of a bitch's right to be heard you wind up defending what he stands for." She paused and downed another drink. "Free speech comes into this because it's like justice, and Barney's for both—when they help him. But where was Barney and his dirty crowd—and I was one of them, so I have a right to ask—where were they when—" Her voice trailed off.

"Well?"

"I forget." Abbe shook her head violently. "I remember now. Where were they when they put Fritz Kuhn in the clink?"

"For stealing," David pointed out.

"Yes," Abbe agreed. "They caught him with his little jam-covered hand in the till. But they prosecuted him because he was a Nazi."

"I don't see—"

"And Barney stood on the sidelines and cheered. The dirty Nazi was getting what was coming to him."

"Calm down, Abbe. None of this—"

"But when they caught Browder on a phony-passport rap, and they prosecuted him because he was a dirty Communist, Barney bled like he was stabbed. You should have heard him. Everybody commits crimes. A man shouldn't be prosecuted when others are let off."

"This has nothing to do—"

"Yes it does," Abbe shrieked. "It shows you what Barney is, and what he'll do for what he calls his principles."

"And you're arguing that because those principles are wrong, I should walk away and let Barney handle the case on his theory, when Angel's life—"

"No, no, no!" Abbe stood up and upset the water glass, and the water soaked across the table, around the lumps of ice. "Angel is gone, dead. He was dead the minute Barney decided—oh, quite regretfully, I'm sure—he might even have cried over it—the minute he decided that Angel's death would serve a higher purpose. It's your life I'm talking about. You've got to get out now, while you can. Get clear of all the quibbling, and all the evasion, and all the god damn double standards. They're going to kill Angel, David. Don't let them destroy you!"

In the front of the restaurant, the proprietor was making a show of turning out lights. "We're not getting anywhere," David said. "Let's get my car and go out to the shack."

"I'm never going there again," Abbe said. "Never. Never, never, never."

"All right." David welcomed the idea of spending the night elsewhere. "We'll drive up the coast a ways, find a motel—"

"You will," Abbe said. "Not me. I'm going to a hotel. Desk clerk's a friend of mine. He'll give me a room. Tomorrow," she went on, "I'll go out to the shack and pick up my stuff. While you two are in court."

"At least let me take you to the hotel," David pleaded. "You're going to be sick."

"I'm going to puke," she corrected, straightening up. "I'm going to throw my guts up, and I'm going to do it alone. And then I'll be rid of Barney's food and his liquor. You won't, because you haven't got your bellyache yet, but when you do, you'll never get rid of it by vomiting."

"Abbe, please," David argued. "You're asking me to let Angel die. That's the price you're making for—well, for yourself. And I can't do it. I can't let him die. And I can't go on without you. You know that."

"You're wrong, David." Abbe stood up, swayed, almost falling, and then regained her balance. "You'll find out as you go along," she said, "that I never meant any more to you than—" she paused for a moment and then resumed—"than a drink of water."

Abbe walked away, past the cashier's desk, and out the front door, swaying as she went, moving drunkenly, sickly and despairingly, but with a dreadful, purposeful dignity nonetheless.

David ordered black coffee. He had no desire to think, but he had to do it. A man's life—of this he was painfully aware—would depend on what he could tell him the following morning, and on what he would ask him afterward.

9

The sun came over the edge of the window behind the jury box and fell on David's eyes as he warily led Angel through his direct examination. David moved slightly to the side, never taking his gaze from Angel's face, and ran his hand across his forehead.

The hand was damp when he returned it to his side. David knew that this was only in part due to the extreme heat of the morning, that it was, in large measure, due to his own nervousness.

This nervousness was the result of many factors: that David had arrived at the shack after three that morning, that he had risen at six-thirty, to make what he knew would be a vain appeal to Barney to abandon his insistence on Angel's testimony, that the hours from three to six-thirty had been spent in fitful lonely sleep; all this contributed to his nervousness, as did his unease that only Barney sat at the counsel table, where Abbe had sat so often. And above and beyond all this there was the terrible possibility that, at any moment, in response to any question, Angel might make the answer that would send him to his death.

"Your first impulse, then," David said, "was to conceal yourself, to hide?"

"That's right."

"And why did you want to hide?"

"Because I knew I shouldn't be there." Angel's answers were

coming calmly, almost mechanically; in the same manner he had replied to the earlier questions David had asked him, both on the stand and during the hour in the conference room before court convened.

"Did you consider yourself a trespasser?" David asked.

"That means I shouldn't be there?"

"That's right."

"Yes."

David permitted himself a narrow smile. Angel plainly was remembering what David had told him when the morning's conference ended. "Answer all my questions," David had said. "But don't give more of an answer than you have. And answer all Armstrong's questions the same way. But be a little slow answering his questions. Got it?" And Angel had nodded and assured David that he understood. So far, it appeared that he had understood, and David was glad that this was so, and hopeful that it would continue to be so, especially insofar as his final admonition was concerned. Some of Armstrong's questions, David knew, were sure to be objectionable, just as he knew that many a defendant has been convicted as a result of a damning response to a question later ruled improper, despite the judge's painstaking instruction, invariably given in such case, that the jury is to disregard both the question and the answer.

"What did you think would happen if you were caught there?" David asked. "On the beach, or on the stairway leading to it."

"I—"

"Your honor," John Armstrong said. "I see no relevance here."

"I'm trying to show just what this boy's state of mind was that night," David said. "I consider that extremely relevant."

"I don't quite see how," Judge Motley said. "But you may continue. If you don't tie it in, I think the jury can disregard the whole line of questioning without prejudicing the interest of either party."

"If his state of mind—" David argued.

"The point is moot," Judge Motley stated. "The objection is overruled. Please proceed."

"What did you think would happen if you were caught?" David repeated.

"I didn't know. I heard—"

"Now what he heard," Armstrong said with some heat, "is surely inadmissible."

"Yes," Judge Motley said coldly. "Please, Mr. Blake, do not abuse the wide latitude the court gives you. You know better than to ask what this boy thinks some anonymous person told him about a matter that, as far as I can see, is not at issue."

"Very well." David nodded his head in acknowledgment of the Judge's rebuke. "Angel, had you any idea what might happen to you if you were caught?"

"I heard—"

"No," David corrected, "just tell us what you thought, not why you thought it."

"That they might roast me over a bonfire."

There was nervous laughter all over the courtroom.

"I ask that that be stricken," John Armstrong said angrily.

"Your honor," David said quickly. "Everything in this case turns on intent. If this girl died as a result of the defendant's criminal intent, we are within the purview of the felony-murder statute. But if, as we contend, her death was accidental, and the defendant had no criminal intent whatsoever, then no case can lie against him."

"But this fantastic belief—you don't maintain, by the way, that he had any justification for it?"

"No, your honor."

"Then what has it to do with the case?"

"We cannot go into the boy's head and backward in time in order to find what his state of mind was," David said. "We judge his state of mind from his actions. His actions, the State may argue, were those of a man about to commit a crime. My question is designed to show that they were the actions of a boy in fear for his safety, whether those fears were real or fanciful."

"He's having it both ways," Armstrong argued. "First he says the boy's actions will explain his state of mind, and then he asks him questions about what he was thinking to explain what he did."

"It is a little tangled," Judge Motley said, "but I think we'll let it go in. Proceed."

"Why did you think they would do that?"

"Because I am a Mexican, and Mexicans are not allowed on that beach."

"So you sat in the darkness and said nothing."

"Yes."

"Now did the girl, Marie Wiltse, speak to you?"

"Yes."

"What did she say?"

"I don't remember. Hello, how are you, something like that."

"Did she say anything else?"

"I don't remember exactly, whether it was at first, or later; but she said I shouldn't be afraid; she said she shouldn't be there either."

"And what did you think she meant by that?"

"Objection."

"Sustained. That calls for a conclusion of the witness."

David continued undisturbed. "What did you do then?"

"I told her my name."

"In English?"

"Objection. He's leading his own—"

"Sustained."

"In what language did you speak to her?"

"In Spanish."

"Why?"

"I thought she was Mexican."

The jury chuckled.

"What happened then?"

"She told me her name—Marie Wiltse. And she said she knew who I was."

"Were you surprised that she knew you?"

"Only a little. I knew her brother."

"Stretch?"

"Yes."

"Now tell us exactly what happened after she said she knew who you were."

"I wanted to leave, to get away. I was frightened. I was afraid she would tell someone I had been there. So I said good-by and started to leave. But she said don't go, and she held my hand."

"You're absolutely sure of that—that she held your hand?"

"Oh, yes. I wanted to leave, you see, but she—"

"Yes. I just wanted to be sure. Now go on."

Angel spoke very slowly when he resumed, seeming to pause and think before every word, and David was hopeful that the jury would see what was quite obvious to him, that Angel was telling the truth as he remembered it, and, at the same time, was making a sincere effort to be sure what he remembered was true.

"She pulled me down beside her, and she put my hand on her knee. She said her brother told her never to let a boy do that. I said nothing. Then she said her brother wasn't there. Then I kissed her, and I put my hand on her neck. Then I put my hand under the top of her dress, and she screamed and scratched my face and stood up and started up the steps. Then she fell, and the people came and found her."

"Now—this is very important—if she hadn't screamed and stood up, what would you have done? What were you trying to do when you put your hand on her neck?"

"I wanted to kiss her again. I thought it would be better that way."

"Now, Angel," David said quietly, "you know what sexual intercourse is?"

"Yes," Angel said. "You explained it."

There were titters from the spectators but, David was pleased to note, none from the jury.

"Did it at any time enter into your head to have sexual intercourse with Marie Wiltse?"

"No, it didn't."

"Did you do anything, in the time you spent with her on the landing, against her will?"

"No."

"You say she scratched you. What did you do then?"

"I jumped back."

"Did you strike her?"

"No."

"Or push her?"

"No."

"Molest her in any way?"

"No, sir. I did not."

"Did you do anything except kiss her?"

"No."

"As a matter of fact, you didn't even hold her hand, did you?"

"No," Angel said. "I didn't. She held my hand."

"You may cross-examine."

Barney was smiling as David returned to the table. David nodded in acknowledgment that Barney had, so far at least, been proved right. Far from weakening the position of the defense, Angel's testimony had immeasurably strengthened it. Now the tenuous nature of the charge against Angel was even more apparent than it had been when, at the beginning of the day's session, David had moved for a dismissal of the charge on the ground that the State had failed to make a *prima facie* case, and this motion had been denied. The jury could only gather from Angel's testimony that he was confused and frightened, that he had been confused and frightened that night on the landing, and, because he had testified, his existence as a person, his

232

reality as a boy, would be impressed on the jury, to make a conviction on supposition and theory more distasteful to them than
if he had remained a silent and impassive figure at the defense
table, who existed for them only in the words of others.

There remained, however, Armstrong's cross-examination, the
final hurdle, and by far the highest.

He began it mildly enough, and David shivered to see this,
because Armstrong, like David, was only mild when he was sure
of his ground, only began at a low pitch when he was certain
that his emphasis would be better reserved for the telling points,
the damaging admissions, that he would bring forth as he proceeded.

"You've told us the whole truth, haven't you, Angel?" Armstrong asked.

"Yes, sir."

"You don't mind my calling you 'Angel,' do you?"

"No, sir."

Armstrong looked down at a note he held in his hand. David
shifted forward in his seat nervously. "Now it was still light when
you went down the staircase toward the beach, Angel? Isn't that
right?"

"Yes, sir."

"Could you read the sign at the top of the stairs?"

"Yes, sir."

"Did you read it?"

"I don't remember for sure. I think so."

"But you read it before. You know what it says."

"Yes, sir."

"But you still went down those stairs?"

Angel shot a quick glance at David, who nodded reassuringly.
"Yes," Angel said. "I went down."

"Now," Armstrong's voice went up almost imperceptibly.
"What does that sign say?"

"I don't know, exactly."

"If I told you that it reads: 'No Admittance. Reserved for Residents, Village of San Juno,' would you say I was wrong?"

"I—"

David arose. "If it please the court," he said, "the defense will be happy to stipulate that Mr. Armstrong is correct."

"Thank you," Armstrong said without a trace of expression. "What did it mean to you," he asked, turning toward Angel, "that afternoon?"

"It meant keep out," Angel said.

"And you knew that sign had the force of law?"

"Yes, sir."

"But you went in anyhow?"

"Yes, sir."

"And broke the law."

"I guess so."

"You did, didn't you?"

"Yes, sir."

"Why?"

"I don't know." There was a buzzing in the courtroom.

Armstrong put a hand on the arm of the witness chair and leaned toward Angel. "I believe you," he said, his tone implying that his belief grew out of friendship for Angel and out of his own naïveté, not out of the incredible thing Angel had said. "I believe you when you say you don't know why you broke that law. But I want to help you find out. Will you help me?"

"Yes, sir," Angel said uncertainly.

"Many times, Angel," Armstrong went on, "boys do things that are against the law just because they *are* against the law. I remember I used to play in a railroad yard, *only because* there was a sign that said: 'Keep Out. Railroad personnel only.' Now some people might not understand that, but you do, don't you?"

"I think so," Angel replied.

"Good. Now, Angel." Armstrong let his voice go up a little

234

further. "Didn't something like that cross your mind when you went past that sign?"

"I don't think so," Angel said quietly.

Armstrong scratched his head. "Weren't there other beaches, just as nice, that you could have gone to?"

"Yes, sir. I suppose so."

"You went to the one that was forbidden. And I'm asking you if you didn't go there *because* it was forbidden."

David took advantage of Angel's careful pause to speak up. "I object to this line of questioning," he said. "The defense will concede that the boy was guilty of trespassing. That," he added, "is all he was guilty of."

"Overruled," Judge Motley said, without explanation.

"And I ask that the latter part of the objection be stricken," Armstrong said. "The defense is summing up a little early."

"Exactly," Judge Motley agreed. "Mr. Blake, I hope I won't have to remind you again to abide by the rules."

"Will you answer the question, please?" John Armstrong asked. Angel stared blankly at him. "Didn't you pick that particular staircase because you wanted to break the law?"

"No," Angel said. "I don't think so."

"There are thousands of reasons why you might have gone down those steps, aren't there?" Armstrong asked.

"I suppose so," Angel admitted.

"But you don't know which one of them was in your mind?"

"No, sir, I don't."

"Might it have been a desire to break the law?"

"No, it wasn't that."

"And is that the only reason you're sure it could not have been?"

"I object," David said wearily. "I can't quite see what that question calls for."

"It's a hard thought to convey," Judge Motley observed. He

turned to Angel. "Do you understand Mr. Armstrong's question?"

"I don't think so," Angel said.

"He wants to know why you went down those stairs," the Judge said patiently. "And you don't seem able to tell him. So he's trying to find out what *didn't* make you go down."

"I didn't want to break the law," Angel said. "It wasn't that."

"But you might have gone down to look at the ocean?"

"Yes, sir."

"Or because you wanted to sit on the landing?"

"Yes, sir."

"Or for any other reason under the sun?"

"Yes, sir."

"But not because you wanted to break a law?"

"No, sir."

"I'm afraid," the Judge told Armstrong, "that this is as far as this line of questioning can be carried."

"Thank you." Armstrong glanced at the jury, shrugged his shoulders, and returned his gaze to the witness stand. "You went down the staircase, then, for some unknown reason, and you hid there. Then you met Marie Wiltse?"

"That's right."

"You had a conversation with her?"

"I told her my name. She told me hers. Not a conversation, really."

"That was all that was said."

"I think so."

"I thought you said before that she told you she shouldn't be there."

"That's right. I forgot."

David sensed that this was a trial-wise jury, that too many witnesses had already told the same story twice with minor variations for them to be impressed by this discrepancy in Angel's testimony.

"Then she took your hand and you tried to run away?"

"Yes."

"Why didn't you?"

"Because she was holding my hand."

"And you couldn't break that grip?"

"No, I—"

"As a matter of fact, you're an athlete, aren't you?"

"I play baseball."

"Hardball?"

"Yes."

"Shortstop?"

"That's right."

"What do you bat?"

"I don't know. We don't keep averages."

"But you'd say it's over .300, wouldn't you?"

"Yes, I think so."

"Well, if you play shortstop and bat .300, I guess you're an athlete, all right." There was mild laughter in which, David noted, the jurors joined.

"She was a sick girl?"

"Objection," David snapped. "That calls for another conclusion."

"She was a girl, wasn't she?" Armstrong asked. "You can draw that conclusion."

"Yes."

"Would you say she was a particularly strong girl?"

"I don't know," Angel said. "I don't think so."

"Now, as an athlete, you could certainly have broken away from this girl's grip, couldn't you?"

"Yes, I suppose so."

"But you didn't?"

"No."

"Why not?"

"I was afraid."

"Of what?"

"That she might be frightened. Or scream."

"You didn't want to frighten her?"

"No, sir."

"As a matter of fact, she wasn't frightened by the kiss, was she?"

"I don't think so. Not at first."

"So you put your hand on her knee."

"No. She put my hand on her knee."

"Oh, yes." Armstrong's irony was light. "I forgot. You put your hand down the top of her dress."

"No." Angel, David noted fearfully, was becoming visibly upset and failing to pause before his answers. "I put my hand on her neck."

"Your other hand. The hand that wasn't on her knee."

The laugh was louder than before. "Yes," Angel said. "That's right."

"Why did you put your hand on her neck?"

"I don't know," Angel said unhappily. "I thought it went with the kissing and all."

"What made you think that?"

"That's what I'd heard."

"From whom?"

"From the guys I went around with."

"They'd talk about the girls they'd been out with, is that it?"

"Yes, sir."

"And you listened?"

"Yes, sir."

"But you never talked yourself, about those things?"

"No, sir."

"Because you'd never been out with a girl."

"That's right."

Armstrong paused. No one could argue that the pause, in which he remained motionless and devoid of expression, signified disbelief, and because this was true, it was the most devastating gesture of skepticism that could be made.

"Now you did move your hand—not the one that was on her knee—down from her throat, didn't you?"

"Yes, I—"

"You popped the buttons that held her dress closed, didn't you?"

"Yes."

"Why?"

"That wasn't part of the kissing, was it?"

"No."

"Then why did you do it? What were you trying to do?"

"I don't know."

"You weren't trying to catch grunion?"

The roar of laughter following the question rolled over David like cold sea water, sending a fear-inspired paralysis through him. Angel's story was laughable, but his life depended on the jury's belief in it. Armstrong was directing them toward the ridiculous aspects of the story, as if nothing ridiculous could ever be true. The laughter that was the measure of Armstrong's success covered Angel's answer before it died away as the Judge rapped heavily with his gavel.

"You don't know why you did it."

"He's answered that," David pointed out, more to break the rhythm of Armstrong's interrogation than to prevent the question from being answered.

"So I did," Armstrong admitted. "I'm giving him a chance to change that answer. You don't know why you did it?" he repeated, stepping back from the witness stand and raising his voice.

"I don't understand," Angel said.

"Why you put your hand under her dress?"

"Not exactly. I just wanted to."

"But you didn't want to rape her?"

"Objection!" David shouted. "This is preposterous. There's

been no evidence of any resistance by the girl to his fumbling advances. I ask that the District Attorney's extraneous ad lib about rape go out."

"The girl was under age," Armstrong said mildly. "If he planned intercourse with her, he was planning rape."

"Only," David pointed out, "if he was a lawyer."

"The point is well taken, I think," Judge Motley declared. "In asking him whether he planned to commit rape, you seem to refer to statutory rape, which presupposes that the witness knew the girl's age and the provisions of the statute. We have no reason to believe that he had such knowledge."

"Thank you, your honor." David sat down.

"Did you plan to sleep with the girl?" Armstrong asked mildly.

"Sleep?"

"Were you planning to have sexual intercourse with her?" Armstrong roared in exasperation. David knew that Armstrong's impatience was not real, that it was an actor's trick, that Armstrong was using it to identify his own feelings with those of the jurors, who must, David felt, have been irritated at the long line of unproductive questions and answers.

"No." Angel waited for a few seconds and then added: "I didn't even know what that was."

Again the laughter, and again the fear that was like a salty wave immersing David and pommeling him about. Now it was more than fear; it was dreadful certainty that the initiative had passed. This day's testimony had begun before a jury that, despite its background and prejudices, had a tendency toward sympathy for the defendant caught in a legal trap not of his own making, or perhaps not caught, for it was within the jury's power to release the trap's main spring. It would conclude before an angry jury which found humor in what it plainly took to be the clumsy attempts of the felon before it to evade responsibility for his own acts.

"I assume from your answer," Armstrong went on, "that you now know what sexual intercourse is. Is that right?"

"Yes," Angel said. "I know now."

"How did you find out?"

"He told me." Angel pointed at David.

"I object to all this," David said. "It is clearly irrelevant."

"If the court please," Armstrong said, "its importance will soon become clear."

"The importance of who taught him the facts of life—after the so-called crime had already occurred?" David demanded.

"I'm trying to make it very clear that he is claiming not to have known those facts at the time of the crime."

"He's already claimed that," David pointed out. "You don't need to go way around in left field—"

"I think I agree with you," Judge Motley said. "However, there doesn't seem any harm in the State bringing out the evidence in a roundabout way, if it chooses."

"I have objected," David said icily, "on the grounds that the question is irrelevant. Do I understand it to be the court's ruling that relevancy is not required of the State?"

"I will not hear argument on this objection," Judge Motley said with some heat.

"Might I have a ruling on it?" David fought to control himself.

"I have ruled on it," Judge Motley said. "The objection is overruled."

"Exception."

"All you know of sexual intercourse, then," Armstrong went on, "is what your attorney told you?"

"No," Angel said carefully. "I'd heard—"

"But he taught you what the sexual act is?"

"Yes, sir."

"After he entered the case."

"That's right."

"So on the night Marie Wiltse died, you wouldn't have known how to go about having intercourse with her if you had wanted to."

"I didn't want to."

"Please answer the question."

"No. I didn't know."

Armstrong nodded, and went to his table, and returned with a long piece of paper in his hand. "What class are you in, Angel?" he asked.

"A-eleven," Angel replied.

"That would be the class of summer, 1948?"

"Yes, sir."

Armstrong faced the bench. "I have here," he explained, "the Certificate of Completion of the State Lecturers on Hygiene and Care of the Body for the Class of Summer, 1948, San Juno High School," he explained. "The course is required by the State. It consists of eight lectures, one during each high-school term. At the end of each lecture, the instructor is required to fill out a part of this form. There is a copy available for the defense."

David waved his hand to signify that he would not require his copy. The District Attorney returned his attention to Angel. "You have completed the first six terms of high school," he said, "and so I assume you have attended six of these lectures. Is that right?"

"Yes, sir."

"As a matter of fact, those lectures are required by law. Had you been absent, you would have been required to attend at some other time. So you must have attended them."

"Is that a question?" David asked.

"I think not," Judge Motley said.

"I'm sorry." Armstrong came close to the stand again. "The attendance rolls show you attended all six lectures, and you did attend them. Is that correct?"

"Yes, sir."

"No one else would have answered to your name, so as to make it appear you were present when you were not?"

"No, sir."

Armstrong held the sheet of paper up. "I want to read you the form which the lecturer fills in after each session. 'I'—then there's a blank for the lecturer's name—'certify that on such and such date at such and such place I delivered lecture number blank of the Personal Hygiene Series to the class named above. I further certify that my lecture was in clear language geared to the understanding of the class and covering all the material in the syllabus, with special emphasis on the section entitled: Procreation; The Sexual Act: Its Use and Abuse. I certify that at the conclusion of the lecture I stated that if any member of the class did not understand anything in the lecture, he was required by law to notify me of this so that an appointment might be made for further instruction. The number of students applying for such instruction was blank, and the names of such students are appended hereto.' Now you've attended these lectures six times. Is that right?"

"Yes, sir."

"In your opinion, was the language simple and geared to the understanding of the class?"

"Objection."

"Sustained."

"Well, did you understand it?"

"Most of it," Angel said. "They used some long words sometimes."

"Was sexual intercourse—as your attorney has described it to you—explained in those lectures?"

The crowd tittered at the reference to David having explained sexual intercourse to Angel. "I don't think so," Angel said. "There were some parts I didn't understand."

"So it might have been explained in those parts, and you wouldn't have known what the man was talking about?"

"Yes, sir."

Armstrong handed the paper to Angel. "I'd like you to look at the bottom part of that paper. Down where the lecturer certifies that he notified the class that anyone who did not understand any part of the lecture—*any part of it*—was to see him after class. What do you think was meant by that?"

"Objection," David said. "Not the best evidence."

"I'm not trying to show what it means," Armstrong explained. "I want to know what he thinks it means. It is the best evidence as to that."

"Overruled."

"It means," Angel said, "that if you didn't understand, you were to go up afterward and make an appointment to have what you didn't understand explained to you."

"Good. Did the lecturers actually say that at the end of each lecture?"

"I think so."

"Wasn't there a lecture the last day that you attended school? The day Marie Wiltse was killed?"

"Yes, sir."

"Did that lecture end that way?"

"Yes, sir."

"All right. Now I want you to look at the last of the forms that is filled in. That would be form number six. Have you found it?"

Angel squinted at the paper and announced that he had found it.

"Do you see the very last portion, where the lecturer states the number of pupils who came forward after the lecture to say they had not understood and to arrange for further instruction?"

"Yes."

"What is that number?"

"Zero."

"And the space below, where the names of those coming forward are to be put down. Is that space blank?"

"Yes, sir."

"Now," Armstrong roared. "I want to ask you again—and I'm speaking now only of this one lecture, the one given the afternoon before Marie Wiltse's death—did you understand that lecture?"

"Not all of it."

"Did you understand that part of it relating to the sexual act?"

"I—I don't remember anything about that."

"So it must have been in the part you didn't understand?"

"I suppose so."

"But you understood the very last part of the lecture, the part where the instructor explained that the State law required anyone who did not understand the lecture to come forward and give his name after class?"

"Yes, sir."

"And you did not come forward?"

"No, sir."

"In spite of the fact that you knew the law required you to?"

"I—well, you never understand all that a teacher says, and I didn't want to come forward."

"You just didn't want to," Armstrong echoed.

"That's right."

"You didn't care about the law."

"I didn't see what difference it would make. I didn't see how they would know whether I understood."

Armstrong paused and stared at Angel before resuming. "In other words, you broke the law because you thought you could get away with it?"

"It didn't seem so serious."

"Or did you really understand the entire lecture, including the parts that you now say you didn't understand."

"No."

"I take it that you thought that law was a sort of formality, something that had no real meaning?"

"Yes."

"Like the oath you took to tell the truth before you testified today."

"Objection," David shouted. "There's nothing here to show that the witness hasn't been telling the truth. This is an attempt to prejudice the jury, without any legitimate foundation in the questioning."

"The objection is sustained. Mr. Armstrong, I think you know better than to ask that kind of a question."

"I ask leave to withdraw the objection without prejudice," David said, realizing he was doing this all wrong.

"I take it," the Judge said, "that you wish to move for a mistrial."

"Yes, your honor."

"Leave to withdraw the objection is denied. You have two remedies when a wrongful and prejudicial question is asked, but your choice, once made, cannot be remade."

"Under the circumstances, with a man's life—"

"All the more reason for me to insist on an orderly procedure. Leave is denied."

David sat down, disgusted with himself. The motion for a mistrial, of course, would have been denied, but he could have taken an exception, and, on appeal, that might well have been the one sound ground for granting a new trial. But no judge can err in not granting leave to withdraw an objection, for that is an extraordinary request, and the laws of the State made it clear that the granting or denial of such leave was wholly discretionary with the judge and not a fit subject for review by another court.

"I have no further questions," Armstrong said.

"And no redirect," David tried, without success, he feared, to match the District Attorney's obvious self-confidence. He remained standing and smiled at Angel as the boy left the witness stand and took his usual seat at the defense table. David turned to face the court.

"Your honor," he said firmly, "the defense now moves for a directed verdict of acquittal, on the grounds—"

"Just a moment," Judge Motley said, raising his hand. He glanced at the clock which, David noted, showed ten minutes to twelve. "May I ask how much time you think you will need to argue your motion?"

"Very little," David said. "Perhaps five minutes."

"In that case," the Judge said, "we'll hear your argument now, following which we will take the noon recess, or have our final adjournment as the case may be."

The reference to a final adjournment following his argument was, David knew, a scrupulous allusion to the possibility that his motion might be granted, just as Motley's presumably inadvertent omission of any reference to time for argument by the State was conclusive evidence that it would not.

There was whispering in the courtroom as David came forward, and David knew that the more sophisticated spectators were explaining that this was an automatic motion, made as a matter of course by every defense attorney, so that he could, by taking an exception to the equally automatic denial of the motion, undertake to get a ruling from a higher court on the question of whether the evidence produced in court *could*, legally, support a conviction.

"Your honor," David said, "it is the position of the defense that a directed verdict of acquittal is now mandatory, because to permit the case to go to an undirected jury would be seriously to compromise the defendant's constitutional rights. I suggest—and I submit that the record of the testimony will bear me out—that two theories bearing on the death of Marie Wiltse have been introduced in this case. As to the defense theory—that her death was an unfortunate accident, probably resulting at least in part from her physical weakness—we have introduced some evidence this morning. I am not entirely satisfied that we have proved the truth of our theory, though I submit that we have introduced powerful evidence to that end. But we are exempted, of course, by the constitutional presumption of innocence, from any such requirement of proof. The State, on the other hand, is required to prove, not that its theory is possible, or even likely, but that it is *true*. When we examine the evidence which the State has adduced to support their theory, we find that it has brought forth witness after witness, whose testimony, if we accept it as entirely true, can only be described, if we take a viewpoint favorable to the State, as *not in conflict* with that theory.

"In order for a case properly to go to a jury," David went on, "it is necessary that the State introduce evidence supporting its theory. If a case is permitted to go to the jury when the State has, as I submit is the present situation, merely produced a theory and then brought in evidence which failed to rebut that theory, such a submission to a jury would fly in the face of all known Anglo-Saxon precedents. To hold that to introduce evidence not in conflict with a theory is to prove the theory in the sense that the law requires proof in a criminal case would destroy utterly the presumption of innocence, and would permit the bringing of convictions on pure supposition, providing the supposition were not disproved, and thus throw on this defendant, and on all defendants, the impossible task of bringing in positive proof of their innocence." David remained standing waiting for Judge Motley to rule.

"You have advanced a most ingenious theory," the Judge said, smiling at David. "It is, perhaps, not without merit. But I am not persuaded that the question of whether evidence supports a theory or merely fails to rebut it is a question of law. I think it a question of fact and therefore properly a matter for the jury. The motion is denied."

"Exception."

"Noted." Judge Motley announced that court would reconvene at two for closing argument, and adjourned court.

When David turned after the Judge had gone, he saw Consuela

standing next to Barney. "What do you think of it?" he heard Barney ask.

"They seem very fair," Consuela replied. "The Judge and th jury, they listen when your Mr. Blake speaks. It is very orderly. I think it would not be so orderly unless they really wanted the truth. And this pleases me. Mr. Blake?"

David came closer. "Yes."

"It will take long this afternoon?"

"It's hard to say," David replied. "I will give my closing argument. Mr. Armstrong will give his. And then the Judge will explain the law to the jury."

"And then will be the verdict?"

"Yes."

"Do you think all that will happen this afternoon?"

"It's possible," David said. "I will speak for perhaps fifteen minutes, Armstrong, I should think, for about an hour. The Judge might take another hour."

"And the jury?"

"Frankly, there's no way to tell. Some juries are out for days. Others decide without leaving the box."

"But they might decide today?" Consuela asked urgently.

"I suppose so," David replied. "Why?"

Consuela blushed. "It is so foolish of me. I am ashamed."

"Of what?"

"Angel will be eighteen tomorrow," Consuela said apologetically. "I know in my heart that it does not matter, but I hope he may spend his birthday at home."

"I hope so too," David blurted quickly. He turned away so that Consuela could not see his distress. He felt within him an almost intolerable urge to talk to someone, but, because Barney sat where Abbe had sat before, that was impossible.

He had intended to eat, perhaps with Barney, but now he had no appetite. Instead, he walked into the little park behind the City Hall, and sat on a bench there, and went over in his mind the general outline of what he would say to the jury, trying to fix it clearly without thinking of the actual words he would use; because not to have it fixed clearly would be to run the risk that his remarks might be disorganized, while to think now of the words he would use then might result in giving his address the appearance of having been memorized, which might, in turn, cause the jury to regard it as insincere, for juries somehow tend to suspect that a man only means what he makes up as he goes along.

This, David knew, would be an important speech, and a difficult one. The summing-up of the defense always is, because the State's final address will follow, and no sur-rebuttal is allowed. So that whatever the defense attorney wishes to be left with the jury must be implanted in that final address, and implanted so strongly that it will resist the District Attorney's subsequent efforts to uproot it.

David had no time, in the hour he spent in that park, to think of Consuela's faith that Angel would be freed, nor to speculate on whether he would have been in a stronger position if, by closing his case the previous evening, he had lost the benefits of Angel's direct examination and the detriments of his cross-examination. And, except in the sense that to put something out of your mind is to think of it, David did not think of these things.

Barney and Consuela sat with Angel at the defense table when David returned, and David, realizing he had not spoken to Angel except in the formal dialogue of his examination, slapped him on the back and told him he had done well, meaning it when he said it, because Angel had done remarkably well. And then he was facing the bench as the Judge came in, and a moment later he was advancing to face the Chavez jury for the last time.

"Ladies and gentlemen," David said, standing squarely in front of the box and letting his eyes run over the jury as he spoke, "I will be extremely brief, because the case before you is, I think, quite a simple one."

The jurors were attentive; their eyes were fixed on his, and David was thankful that, at this time at least, they were not looking at Angel. "Each of you must now decide," he went on, "whether you are convinced, utterly and firmly convinced, that Angel Chavez murdered Marie Wiltse. If you are convinced of that, you must vote him guilty. If not, you must acquit him. I want to emphasize that there is no possible middle ground, no possible shadow area in which you might find yourself wavering, half tempted to vote one way, and half another. Because if you do feel that way, then you are not convinced, and you must, as a matter of law, and as a matter of good conscience as well, find for the defendant.

"Ordinarily, murder is distinguished from other crimes in which death is caused, by the intent of the accused. In other words, if I accidentally cause death, I may be guilty of crime, but that crime is not murder. In this case, however, we are faced with the single exception to that rule, the so-called felony-murder rule. Stated in simple terms, that rule states that when someone, in the course of a felony, kills, that act is murder. Now the State, I am sure, will concede that Angel Chavez did not plan the death of Marie Wiltse. He had no motive to do so; he bore her no malice; he did not—of this we are all agreed—commit any act intentionally designed to cause her death. No, the only possible way in which it can be argued that what this boy did can be called murder is by the felony-murder rule.

"To this point," David went on, moving closer to the box and lowering his voice, "the State and the defense are, I think, in agreement. But here the agreement ends. The State maintains, and the defense denies, that Angel Chavez caused the death of Marie Wiltse in the course of a felony, and the felony charged is, of course, rape. Rape is the act of sexual intercourse without the consent of the other party. The defense concedes that Marie Wiltse, because of her age, was incapable of giving consent.

"Ladies and gentlemen," David said very slowly, "no rape was committed. You know that; I know that; the State knows it; and a medical examination of the girl's body proved it without any possibility of error. The bald, incredible fact is that, in this case, the State is asking for a boy's life because, in effect, he raped a girl who died a virgin. And here, in my judgment, the State's case collapses of its own weight."

David began to walk slowly back and forth as he spoke, and he was pleased that the jurors followed him with their heads, like spectators at a tennis match. "There remains one possible ground on which the State, relying on a fantastic chain of inference, supposition, hypothesis, and plain guesswork, demands that the life of Angel Chavez be forfeited."

He stopped walking and put both hands on the jury box rail. "Here is the reasoning. Angel Chavez contemplated rape. There is no evidence that he did; but the State asks you to assume it. Of course, he must have decided to commit this crime—this is the State's theory, you understand—on the spur of the moment, after he met Marie Wiltse on that landing; he couldn't have known she would be there. And then, the State speculates, he attempted to rape her, and, in that attempt, he caused her death before the crime could be committed. In other words, her death, admittedly accidental, becomes murder in the State's eyes because it occurred as a result of Angel Chavez's intention—never proved —to commit a crime which we know was never committed.

"What," David demanded, stepping back from the rail and raising his voice, "could be more fantastic than that? On what thinner thread could you be asked to reason your way down the line to the point at which you are to take away a human life? I could stop right here," he went on. "I've shown you a reasonable doubt as to the defendant's guilt, and as a matter of fact, I'm sure that, as reasonable people, you were troubled by those doubts before I pointed them out to you. And one such doubt, of course, requires that you find the boy innocent. But I'm going to go further. I know that, while a reasonable doubt as to guilt compels a verdict of not guilty, it is pleasanter to find such a verdict when you have a real belief in the accused's innocence."

David started pacing again, and still the jurors followed him. "I'm going to tell you what I think happened. And, while it's of no special importance that you accept this theory, so long as the State does not convince you of the validity of its own, I think this theory is so ordinary, so reasonable, so thoroughly in accord with the evidence, that you will certainly be inclined to believe in it, rather than in the far-fetched suppositions offered by the State.

"Let us suppose that this defendant is not the depraved sex criminal the State's case requires." David was careful to restrict his irony to the words themselves, speaking them evenly and seriously. "Let's assume, instead, that he is just what he seems—an ordinary teen-ager, who plays ball, and pals around with the other boys of his class. He's a little shy, perhaps, terribly proud, as boys sometimes are, and afraid to commit any act which will stamp him as an outsider, not one of the gang. For instance, he doesn't quite understand the cold impersonal lectures on sex that the State requires him to hear. But he doesn't come forward and admit he's confused, because that would set him apart from his classmates. That's not entirely logical, but an adolescent is not always—as I'm sure you all know—a completely logical being.

"Now, still just supposing," David went on. "On the night of the grunion run, this boy is wandering along the road that runs at the top of the palisade above San Juno Beach. He goes down the stairs not knowing exactly why; it's an adventure the same as climbing around a building under construction on Sunday is an adventure. Sure it's trespassing, but boys don't have as high a regard for the niceties of the law as they might. He sits on the landing while it gets dark, and watches the people on the beach making campfires and getting set for the grunion run. Then, suddenly, it is dark, and he's scared. He remembers all the wild stories he's heard about what happens to a kid caught trespassing on that beach, and they don't seem so wild in the dark with only the lights from the campfires blinking down below and the long narrow flight of steps between himself and where he's got a right to be. Maybe he even scares himself a little on purpose to make it more of an adventure.

"Now, suddenly this boy, sitting there in the darkness, realizes that he's not alone. There's someone else on the landing. His fear rises inside of him. Then someone speaks to him, and he knows it's a girl. He still isn't safe; certainly this girl couldn't harm him, couldn't hold him there against his will, but she could scream, and that would bring the men from the beach, and what would they do to him? But this girl doesn't scream. She talks to him, calls him by name, holds his hand, and when he tries to take the hand away—because he's still scared—she hangs on to it. Now this person in the darkness, who could have been his enemy, turns out to be his friend, and an extremely pretty girl, too. He's not in danger any more; he's alone in the moonlight with a pretty girl who seems to like him.

"He's happy," David went on. "He's relieved. He's grateful to this girl for being what she is. And he expresses that feeling—all those feelings—in a single, fumbling kiss, because he's heard that this is how a boy shows his affection for a girl.

"So far, there is nothing unusual about this story. Many of you, I suspect, have something of the sort stored away in your memories. A pretty girl, a chance meeting in the moonlight, the roar of the surf, the lonely spot, all the standard ingredients for a romantic episode. But this one had a tragic ending almost as soon as it began. A few moments after that first kiss, the girl lay dead at the edge of that landing. Why? Why was that girl dead and this boy's life permanently scarred by what happened that night? That is the question you must answer, and on your answer a human life depends."

David walked back to the defense table, picked up a bound portion of the transcript and opened to a page he had marked with a paper clip. "To help you answer that question," he said, leaning back against the table, "we have the testimony of Dr. Schacter. Frankly, I thought he was rather long on conclusions and rather short on facts. But I would like to read you a short passage from his cross-examination." David looked down and found the portion he had previously marked against this moment. " 'Question:' " he read. " 'In September, it was your opinion that Marie Wiltse's heart might stop beating at any moment, and without warning. Answer: I suppose so. Question: I mean that every time that girl got out of bed, every time she stood up, or sat down, or walked around, her weakened heart might give out. Isn't that, in effect, what you told her mother? Answer: Yes.' "

David put down the transcript and turned back to the jury. "Isn't that the answer?" he demanded. "The girl was excited. Of course she was. She was being kissed by a boy she scarcely knew. Perhaps she struggled, as girls will in such an embrace. Perhaps she felt pain as her weakened heart tried to meet the sudden demand she was putting on it. We may surmise that the pain made her panicky, and her panic increased the strain. And so she died. Is there anything incredible in that explanation? Is there one bit of evidence before you to indicate that this is not what happened? Or, on the other hand, doesn't that theory fit the evidence not merely as well as, but infinitely better than the strained, tortured reasoning of the State, which, you must now know, is trying to make a murder out of what was plainly a regrettable accident."

David nodded his thanks for the jury's courtesy in hearing him and sat down. He glanced at the clock and noted that his address had lasted some twelve minutes, two minutes longer than he had planned. Angel murmured his thanks, and David smiled in return. Judge Motley rapped sternly with his gavel to silence the buzz in the courtroom, and John Armstrong arose.

The District Attorney spoke without coming out from behind his table, and he spoke casually, referring to notes when he wished to, reading at length, from time to time, from the transcript, rarely raising or lowering his voice as if he needed no tricks to make the points he was urging. His method was to cite a point of testimony and from it to draw a conclusion, never arguing that the conclusion he drew was the only one possible, but always pointing out that it was the most likely.

"The girl is dead," he said at last. "That is the cold hard fact with which we must deal. We cannot ignore it; we cannot evade it, nor explain it away. She was alone with the defendant on that landing; that is beyond dispute. He kissed her; that is beyond dispute. He ripped her clothes in putting his hand under the top of her dress; that is beyond dispute. And she screamed, and a few minutes later, as I've said, she lay there dead. These are the facts, and from these facts you may draw—you *must* draw—a reasonable conclusion."

Armstrong raised the volume of his speaking just a trifle, and David surmised that he was nearing the end of his discourse. "I say you *must* draw a reasonable conclusion," he went on, "because the law requires that of you as jurors. You must find that a man who is seen drinking a quart of whiskey, whose breath stinks of alcohol, and who staggers as he walks, is drunk. You must find that a bottle of milk in which a trout is swimming has been watered. And you must find that a girl who is found dead after screaming in an embrace in which her clothes are torn died in resisting an attempted rape, which the people of this State, by their laws, have quite rightly called murder."

Armstrong leaned forward over the table in a gesture rather like a bow, and David thought he was done, but he straightened up quickly and continued, now using the lower tones with which he had begun his closing remarks. "As to the testimony of the defendant," he went on, "I do not think you need be confused by it. It is contradictory, and we must say that if he told the truth in this passage, he lied in that. I merely suggest to you that it is well known that a criminal brought within the shadow of the gallows will say exactly what he pleases, exactly what he thinks, as he goes along, will help him evade the penalty for his act. There is doubtless some fact and some fancy in his story; but I strongly doubt that anyone, even the defendant himself, could possibly separate the one from the other now. But, of course, it is not necessary for anyone to do this. It is only necessary for you to render a verdict on the facts, on the evidence as it is presented to you, and I am confident that you will discharge that responsibility seriously, and in accordance with the law, however unpleasant that may be."

Abruptly, John Armstrong stopped speaking and sat down. The jurors watched him for a few seconds and then, one by one, as the horror mounted in David's stomach and it seemed to him possible that the case might go to the jury while the defense attorney was vomiting on the courtroom floor, they turned and fixed their gaze on Angel.

Judge Motley produced three typewritten sheets and, from them, proceeded to charge the jury, looking up at them occasionally when he reached for other material. He made it clear that any reasonable doubt was to be resolved in favor of the defendant, but he drew quite sharply the distinction between reasonable and unreasonable doubt. He read from the State Criminal Code the definition of statutory rape, which was as David had given it, and that of felony-murder, on which last he spoke at some length, pointing out that, while motive might be a part of the felony portion, neither motive nor malice was needed as to the murder. "You are to cast your votes as individuals, according to your individual consciences. No one among you may yield to any other the right to cast his vote, nor be guided exclusively by the opinion of another in casting his vote. But, in the event that you do not immediately agree, you are, under the direction of your foreman, required to confer, to consider each other's points of view, to reason with one another, to the end that those differences may, if possible, be composed and a verdict arrived at."

"The possible verdicts," Judge Motley concluded, "are three. If you find that Marie Wiltse met her death as the result of some act on the part of the defendant while he was committing or preparing to commit a felony, you must find a verdict of guilty of murder. If you find that Marie Wiltse died as a result of a wrongful act on the part of the defendant, but that the act was not a felony, and that death did not result from any malice on the part of the defendant, then you must find a verdict of guilty of manslaughter. If you are not convinced, beyond a reasonable doubt, that either of these correctly describes the way in which Marie Wiltse met her death, then you must find a verdict of not guilty. A room in this building has been prepared for your deliberations. The bailiff will take you there now. You are to inform him when you have reached a verdict, or if, before such time, you wish further advice from me, or if you wish to have any portion of the testimony read over to you by the clerk."

He tapped his gavel to signify that court was, pending the return of the jury, adjourned. As the bailiff led the jurors from the room, the reporters bolted for the main door.

"You want to go back, Angel?" David asked. "It might be more comfortable for you."

"It is not yet five," Consuela pointed out. "Let him stay for an hour."

David turned his head and explained to the guard that Angel would remain for an hour. "It's O.K. with me," the guard said. "For his sake, I only hope they're out that long."

David glanced quickly at Consuela, but apparently she had not heard the guard's remark. Had she heard it, David told himself, she might not have understood its significance. But he understood and agreed. A quick verdict is always the obvious one, and the obvious one in this case was "guilty of murder." If the jury returned within fifteen minutes, it could only mean that there was no minority, and it was on the minority, if any, that Angel's chance for a favorable verdict depended. If they stayed out an hour, then there was a definite minority, one or two or more who were convinced that the obvious verdict was not the correct one, and who were willing to adhere to that position in the face of strong pressure from their fellow jurors. Then, as the hours—even the days—might wear on, the chances for a hung jury, a manslaughter verdict, even an acquittal would mount, until, on the third or fourth day, it would be clear that the minority would not yield, and then only the hung jury and the acquittal would remain as possibilities.

David stared at the clock on the wall. The jury had retired at 4:47. Angel was to remain in court until 5:47. The time seemed a sort of target to David; if the jury remained out of court until the time set for Angel's leaving, then he would allow himself to hope.

Five-twenty.

Five-twenty-five.

The reporters, having phoned in the fact that the case was in the hands of the jury, began drifting back into the courtroom. Pete Wells came to the defense table and was told by David and then by Barney that neither had anything to say. Wells told, rather badly, the story of an apocryphal jury foreman who, at dinnertime, had asked the bailiff to bring in "eleven T-bone steaks and a bale of hay."

The crowd outside the courtroom, in the corridor leading to the jury room, shouted suddenly. Pete Wells went back to investigate. Two minutes later he came back to report that the crowd's excitement had been occasioned by the bailiff being called to the jury room, but had petered out when it became known that the jury had not reached a verdict but required some more paper and a pitcher of ice water.

Five-thirty.

Five-forty.

David watched the clock now; 5:47 had suddenly become very important. The clock had no second hand, and David wished that it had, or that, at any rate, its minute hand moved evenly instead of remaining in one position for a full minute, and then snapping up to the next minute mark.

Five-forty-three. The crowd in the corridor cheered again, and this time the cheers were sustained, and there was no mistaking their meaning. Led by the bailiff, the jurors entered and took their places in the box. The bailiff mounted the little steps behind the bench and knocked on the door that led to Judge Motley's chambers.

"Have they decided?" Consuela asked.

"Maybe," David said. "Maybe they just want to ask the Judge a question." But he knew this was not true. Mary Ackerman, Juror Twelve, had been crying. The long tear stains ran down her cheeks, and her eyes and nose were red. And from this David knew that this jury had returned to give its verdict, and he knew what that verdict would be, and how inconsequential had been the minority which favored a different verdict.

The bailiff failed to make his usual announcement, but the people in the courtroom stood up out of long habit, and remained standing until Judge Motley had seated himself.

"Has the jury reached a verdict?" Judge Motley asked. In the press section, cameras were coming up from under chairs and turning toward Angel.

"We have," the foreman said, rising.

"What is that verdict?" David, who did not believe in God, suddenly realized he was praying.

"We find the defendant, Angel Chavez, guilty of murder."

There was a gasp in the courtroom, and then the empty searching silence resumed.

"That is the verdict of all of you?"

"It is."

David dug his hand into Angel's shoulder. The flesh beneath the gray jacket did not flinch. David let go of Angel and stood up. "I ask," he said gently, "that the jury be polled."

This was done, the bailiff stopping before each juror long

enough for the fatal word to be spoken. When he came to Mary Ackerman, she was crying again, but after a moment she sniffed and became the twelfth and last to speak.

"I will pronounce sentence tomorrow morning." Judge Motley arose and tapped his gavel, and the reporters, freed by that tap from all restraint, raced for the phones while the photographers came forward and began taking pictures almost at random, of the jurors as they left court, of the spectators, of Armstrong and the girls at his table, of Angel, with the guard holding his arm, and of David.

Then the horror that made David know that what had gone before was not horror at all began. From the defense table, dodging across the aisle, Consuela Chavez ran, her black hair unkempt, falling across her face. Through the crowd she came, screaming her boy's name as she ran. Judge Motley, who had been about to enter his chambers, turned. She saw him and ran to the space before the bench and looked up at him and shook her fists.

"You kill my boy!" she screamed. "Santa Maria! You kill my boy, my Angel!"

The photographers swarmed around her, some climbing on the witness stand, pushing the witness chair down in order to get better angles, and their flashbulbs popped as Consuela continued her disorderly harangue. What made the moment uniquely horrible was that David could see that, even as she gestured toward the Judge, she turned her body so that the corner of the Judge's bench did not hide her from the lenses, and that her gestures became more pronounced and her face more distorted whenever a flashbulb popped.

10

Above the throughway was the white-on-black sign: BEACH
POINTS, KEEP RIGHT, and David, seeing the sign, was tempted to
swing right and follow the coast highway as it ran south from
Capitol City. San Juno lay along that road, and there was something in him that made him want to drive past the shack, past State
Beach, past the parking area where he had been so often with
Abbe. But this was irrational. Abbe belonged to June, and this
was September, and, while David did not know exactly what he
was going to do, he knew that, whatever it was, he would have
no time for sentimental pilgrimages, no time to visit with ghosts,
no time for detours to the places where he had been happy and
where he had made the mistakes that had ended that happiness.

The throughway turned inland, lost its street lights, picked up
billboards, and became, thereby, an ordinary highway. Then the
billboards became rarer and David, knowing that he had four
hundred miles to go, and wanting, somehow, to arrive where he
was going before dawn, which was then ten hours away, and
knowing, too, that the flat straight road would not take him all
the way there, that the last two hundred miles would be on the
twisting Sierra Road, tramped heavily on his accelerator, and
watched the speedometer needle go up past 60, to 70, to 75, and
stay there.

A lighted billboard came toward him in the darkness, snapped into his view, then whipped past. David made out the name of a gambling house, a picture of a fisherman, and the words—above: You'll LIKE Reno! and, below: 397 miles.

Would Angel have liked Reno? David shivered not at the thought, but at the conditional tense which it was now necessary to use in speaking of Angel in relation to the present or the future, which David did very rarely, or in thinking about him in such a way, which David did often.

David began to think of Angel, and especially of how Angel had died and of what he had said the night before he died, and then, quite deliberately, he decided that he would not think about that, because it was irrational for him so to torture himself to no purpose. And then, because his mind refused to think of anything else, David, who was, to that extent at least, the master of his mind, caused his mind to become a blank, to think of nothing except the mechanical problem of driving the car over the straight black pavement, to stare into the darkness watching for the lights of approaching cars, to concentrate on divining when, and in which direction, the road would eventually curve.

But even this limited mastery David could not long maintain. Had the weather been other than clear, had the road been other than straight, had there been some mechanical defect of the car on which he could have permitted his mind to dwell, he might have been able to avoid thinking of Angel all that long lonely night. But the road was straight and the visibility excellent, and David's mind freed itself easily from the restraint he sought to put upon it and fixed itself on Angel, on the late Angel Chavez, on the trust he had placed in David, and the way in which David had—if not betrayed that trust—at least been a party to its betrayal by others.

The guard had admitted him to Angel's cell, in death row of the State's maximum security prison near Capitol City.

"Ten minutes," the guard said, closing the door and remaining outside.

Angel was sitting on the bed. He got up and looked hopefully at David's face. But he saw there what David had hoped to conceal, and the hope drained away.

Still, Angel managed to smile. "How are you, Mr. Blake?" he asked.

"I'm O.K.," David said. "How about you?"

"I'll live," Angel said, laughing at his own joke.

"I left a package for you at the main gate." (It was strange; in these matters which David wanted most badly to forget, he seemed to possess an involuntary total recall. In other matters, which he wanted badly to remember in detail, he was forced to refer to his journal, and from that to project the detail.) "A few pieces of fruit, some candy bars, and this week's *Sporting News*."

"Thanks," Angel said. "Thanks a lot. They give us a prison newspaper every night at dinnertime. That has the scores in it. But the *Sporting News* has a lot more. Fielding averages, earned runs, all that."

"Good," David said. "I hope they get it in to you soon." He regretted the words, but it was too late to recall them.

"I've got plenty of time," Angel said. "They're not coming for me until seven in the morning."

Would Angel be asleep when seven in the morning came, David wondered. It was possible. Angel was strong, self-reliant, self-contained, and somehow this only made it worse. Had he been hysterical, or badly frightened, calming him would have been something to do, and, had David succeeded in calming him, he would have been able to say to himself that at least he had made Angel's last few hours pleasanter.

"The Governor said no?" Angel asked.

David nodded. "I didn't even get to see him," he said. "His secretary saw me. There's no chance there, Angel." How do you make it clear to a healthy eighteen-year-old that he is spending his very last evening on earth? "There's no chance anywhere, Angel," David went on. "I don't want you to have any false hopes."

"I've known for a long time," Angel said. "I didn't have any false hopes."

"I'm sorry," David said. "Looking back on it, I think it might have worked out better if we'd done it a different way."

"Only you couldn't look back on it when it was happening," Angel pointed out. "You had to make your move then. Like in a ball game—when it's over, you figure, back there in the fourth inning, if we hit away instead of playing for the one run—but that's crazy. You did what seemed best at the time, and, if it didn't work, it didn't work. That's all. My mother didn't get to see the President?"

"No," David said. "I didn't think she would."

Consuela was, he knew, at that very moment seated in a camp chair across the street from the point at which tourists enter the White House, where she had declared it her intention to remain until the President saw her, or until her boy was, as she put it in her statement to the press, "lynched by the law."

"One minute," the guard said, through the bars.

"Do you want me to stay until—until morning?" David asked. "I don't think you'll be able to see me. They have one-way glass, I think, between you and the spectators. But if it would make you feel better to have someone out there who was a friend—"

"No," Angel said. "Don't bother. The priest will be with me. That will be enough. You should go home and go to sleep. You have worked very hard for me. I don't know how to thank you."

David turned his head and faced the wall behind the bed. It would not do, he realized, to permit this boy who, facing the abrupt and calculated end of his life, expressed gratitude to the attorney who had, putting the best possible light on the matter, failed him, to see that he was near tears. "It means a great deal to me," David mumbled, "that you don't blame me."

"I blame myself," Angel said. "I knew what I did was wrong, though I did not know how wrong. I could not blame you. You did all you could."

He put out his hand, and David shook it. The guard let him out of the cell. In spite of what Angel had said, David waited in the warden's office until morning, and then went with the warden to the courtyard, and saw what happened there, saw Angel walk with the priest to the gallows, and, leaving the priest behind, mount the steps, saw Angel shake his head when the warden asked if he had anything to say, saw the noose lowered over Angel's hooded head, saw the three convicts swing their knives at the three cords, one of which, when cut, released the trap, saw—

David suddenly became aware that an oncoming pair of headlights was blinking at him and that a horn was being sounded in frantic, irregular blasts. He swung the steering wheel to the right, abandoning the crown, felt the hot air of the truck's motor as the two vehicles passed at a combined speed of perhaps 120 miles an hour, felt the softness of the road's shoulder pull him one way, and the vacuum behind the truck the other. Then, accelerating, he straightened out the car, and the road ahead was clear again.

When—at what instant in time—had the fact that Angel was to die been determined beyond any possibility of redetermination? Obviously not at the instant that the knives fell across the cords, David reasoned, for, had anything gone wrong then, had the trap failed to operate, Angel's death would have been delayed by only a few minutes.

Perhaps the instant the appeal was read—perhaps that had been the determining instant. David saw himself in the courtroom, sitting alone at the table reserved for the appellant. The courtroom was air-conditioned, and more luxurious than the one in

San Juno, for this was the Supreme Court of the State; and David sat alone because he had refused Barney's offer to help with the appeal, and he had made the refusal stick, because it was now to Barney's interest to keep David on the case at all costs, and it didn't matter to Barney who argued the appeal.

"Oyez, oyez," the bailiff said. "The Supreme Court of this State is now in session. Let all who have business with this honorable court draw near, and ye shall be heard."

"Chavez versus State." David saw again the long face of the Chief Justice as he read the opinion of the court, heard his voice again, the long sonorous phrases, evenly read, like a classroom lecture, into a microphone which fed an amplifying system that only slightly increased the volume of the words, so that they fell gently, and yet audibly, in the somber room. "Appellant seeks the reversal of a conviction for felony-murder in the Superior Court of Junipero County. He relies, in his application, on three main lines of argument, which we must consider separately, since any one might, if found meritorious, justify the relief asked for.

"First, appellant maintains that his motions for dismissal following the completion of the case for the people, and for a directed verdict following the completion of his own case, were improperly denied. As to both of these motions, his argument is in essence the same, namely that the evidence adduced by the State was, as a matter of law, insufficient to support a conviction. His argument here is that only *negative proof* was brought to bear by the State, that is, that the State established a theory covering the events in question, and then introduced evidence which, though it did not contradict such a theory, did not actually support it. A reading of the record supports this argument only to the extent that the evidence might reasonably be so regarded. But it might also be regarded as proving, affirmatively, the validity of the State's theory. Where two possible interpretations may be put on the evidence, it is, of course, for the jury to choose between them, unless the trial Judge, on a motion for a dismissal or a directed verdict, shall hold that the weight of the evidence so clearly inclines toward the interpretation favorable to the defense that the case may not go to the jury. The Judge refused to do so, and the jury, following his refusal, chose the theory of the State as valid, and so found in its verdict. It would be manifestly unreasonable for us, acting on the printed record alone, to find that, in choosing between two possible courses, they chose wrongly, in view of the fact that both Judge and jury, of course, were able to act not merely on the basis of the words attributed to the witnesses in the printed record, but in response, as well, to the way the words were said."

And so the Chief Justice had closed the first of the three doors David had opened in his appeal. Before proceeding to the other two, however, he paused to double-lock this one. "In connection with this point," he said, "we note that the defense did not content itself with rebutting the evidence and theories advanced by the State, but offered a theory of its own, and apparently introduced evidence in support of that theory. It is in precisely this situation—when two theories have been introduced and evidence in support of each brought forward—that the jury performs its classic and most valuable function, that of indicating which of the two theories it believes to be correct.

"For his second argument, appellant relies on numerous exceptions made to the rulings of the trial Judge during the taking of testimony. In all of these cases, it would appear that the trial Judge was within the area where he might use his discretion, that is, that existing law did not mandate on him a particular ruling on a particular objection. For example, a defense motion to strike out the words 'scuffle-like' from a description by a witness of certain sounds he had heard was denied, and appellant takes exception to this denial, arguing that the words were not descriptive but represented an opinion as to the source of the sound. Plainly either interpretation might have been placed on the words, and we cannot hold that the Judge erred in interpreting them as descriptive; nor in any event can it be held that, if the Judge here erred, the error was of such importance as to prejudice seriously the rights of the defendant and warrant a new trial."

The Chief Justice droned on, disposing of several of David's exceptions in similar fashion—that is, by demonstrating that, while Motley may not have been correct, he was surely not entirely wrong and that, in any event, the errors complained of, if errors, were not sufficiently important to require a retrial. Then he announced that the remaining exceptions were similar to those he had discussed.

"Appellant's third argument," the Chief Justice continued, and David shivered as he heard the words, for his third argument had been, when he wrote his brief, the one in which he placed the greatest reliance, and now it was the only one left to him, "is that the atmosphere in which the trial was conducted was such as to preclude his receiving a fair trial. In support of this argument, appellant has submitted an affidavit relating to certain incidents alleged to have taken place prior to the trial. On this point, he asks leave to introduce evidence. The introduction of evidence before this, an appellate court, is, of course, highly unusual, but, providing only that a single requirement is met, it is possible. That requirement, of course, is that, since the introduction of evidence is only appropriate to the trying of facts, opportunity did not exist to try these same facts below. It is elementary that where there is a wrong there is a remedy, and for that reason unusual procedures may be permitted where the usual ones fail to meet the standards of justice. In this case, however," the Chief Justice went on, and with the word *however* David saw the last door begin to swing shut, "there existed a normal procedure of which the defendant did not avail himself below. We have no choice but to regard his failure to do so as deliberate. There is no showing here that the facts complained of came to the attention of appellant after the trial; it is, in fact, clear on the face of the affidavit that these facts were known to him before the taking of testimony commenced. Had he asked, at that time, either before the beginning of the jury selection, or at the point where that selection was interrupted due to what the Judge calls 'the excessive zeal of the State,' for a change of venue, he might have introduced then, in order to prove that the atmosphere in which the trial was to be conducted was adverse to the defendant, precisely the same evidence which he now seeks leave to bring to us. He is, in short, asking that an unusual procedure be followed because he failed to avail himself of the usual procedure. We need not speculate on why the defense failed to move for a change of venue at the appropriate time. It is enough that no such motion was made. To permit litigants to choose between normal and extraordinary procedure would be to invite legal chaos. The law wisely holds that he who fails to make timely application for relief may not use that failure as the basis for an appeal."

The Chief Justice continued to read for some time, but David scarcely listened as he read off the cases David had cited as precedents in support of his three arguments and distinguished between them and the case at hand. It was all over. The last door was closed.

"Appeal denied. The stay of execution granted appellant pending a decision in this matter is hereby vacated."

And locked.

The road was beginning to curve gently now as it mounted the foothills that lay between the Sierras and the coastal plain. Ahead of him, David could see the lights of an all-night gas station. Drawing up to it, he could see that the station was a part of a chain at which the credit card in the glove compartment of his car permitted him to buy gasoline on the strength of his signature. He braked hard, and eased the car to the side of the pump, wondering as he did so where the money was going to come from to pay for the gasoline when the parent company got around to rendering its bill.

The attendant cleaned his windshield, added water to the radiator, and checked the oil and the battery level, and from all this David guessed he was in California, where such service is a matter of course. He was somehow pleased that he had crossed the State line, and had, temporarily at least, put the State behind him, including the State courts, the State University, with its School of Law, and the State Legislative Committee on Disloyalty and Subversion. The attendant came over and handed David the delivery slip, David signed it and returned the credit card to the glove compartment.

"How far is it to Reno?" David asked.

"Two hundred and ten miles," the attendant replied. "Just keep on this road till you get to Tahoe. Then pick up U.S. Seven. And take it easy on those curves," he cautioned. "I'd like to sell you gas on your way back."

"It'll be a pleasure."

David gunned the car forward, out of the station, into the darkness, broken only by the cone of light his own headlights made.

It was now the Battle Committee, which had begun by being, for David, just a minor annoyance, that was now his main concern. It was because of the committee—because of Carl Baron Battle, really; the others didn't count—that David was now under suspension at the University, and that it seemed unlikely that he would ever be reinstated.

Strangely enough, it was not of Battle that David was thinking as the road began to wind and climb in the darkness ahead of him, but of the round, fat, bald Mr. Finn, who was the committee's process server. (Perhaps, David corrected, he was one of their process servers, but he was the one who had served David on four occasions.)

Finn introduced himself by name the second time David saw him. That was in the courtroom in San Juno, as it had been the first time, but this time there were no reporters crowding around with pencils and questions after the subpoena was served. The reporters were busy elsewhere, reporting the dread sentence Judge Motley had just finished passing upon Angel Chavez: "You shall be taken hence to the State Prison, there to be confined until the week of August eighteenth, during which week, at a time to be named by the warden, you shall be put to death in the manner prescribed by law."

David could not remember what he had said to Angel before the guards—there were three of them then—had taken him away, but he was sure he had said something. And, having said it, he had turned, and Finn had been there, to introduce himself ("The name's Finn, Mr. Blake") and smile, and make his little joke ("The business we're doing, I may give you a rate") and hand David the subpoena, and turn and go.

Except for necessary differences in dates, the subpoena was identical with the one David had received from Finn previously. David went again to the telegraph office and sent a wire to Assemblyman Battle pointing out that though a verdict had been given and a sentence pronounced, there remained—or would as soon as David could set the machinery in motion—the appeal to be heard, and until that, and other matters connected with the case had been disposed of, "I regret that I will not be able to appear before your committee."

The next morning, David received in return a telegram signed by Battle informing him that the subpoena had been withdrawn, and that a letter of explanation followed. The letter itself arrived the following day, but David had been able to read its full text in the morning papers before the mail was delivered. "As a practicing attorney," Battle's letter read in part, "I am of the opinion that your excuses for failing to honor the subpoenas that have been served on you are just that: excuses, rather than legitimate reasons. However, I am always willing to give a witness the benefit of any possible doubt, so we will not persevere with our subpoena until the Chavez matter is disposed of. But rest assured, Mr.

Blake, you will eventually come before this committee, with the records and documents named in the subpoena, and you will then answer the questions of this committee or be found in contempt of the legislature of our great State. Incidentally," the letter concluded, "I am pleased that your recent wire does not contain the claim, which you asserted in your first communication to us, that you have no idea why we should want to question you. Frankly, I am sick and tired of people who do what you have done—namely, associate with, and give aid and comfort to, members of a diabolical godless conspiracy against this State and Nation—and then claim that they 'have no idea why their testimony might be of interest to a Committee on Subversion and Disloyalty.' "

David's first thought on reading the letter was that, in charging him with giving aid and comfort to a conspiracy against the nation, Battle had come painfully close to the exact language of the statutory definition of treason and might, therefore, be wide open for a libel suit. But a sobering second thought reminded him that this letter was part of the official business of the legislature and that, in writing it, Battle was protected by legislative immunity against suits of that kind.

He therefore wrote, and sent to Battle and to the newspapers, a letter suggesting that if Battle would be kind enough to repeat, in public and without immunity, "the disgusting libel you have made against me in the last sentence of your letter," David would be happy to file suit against him, and would agree to as early a trial as possible once the Chavez matter had been concluded.

The newspapers dutifully carried David's challenge and Battle's reply to it, which was that he would be happy to repeat in a personal letter "or in an affidavit, if you prefer" exactly what he had said in his privileged, official letter, but that he did not propose to "get involved in side issues until after you have testified before the committee" and that he "considered it highly unlikely that David would wish to continue the matter at that time."

It was at the time of this exchange that David first met Will Benson, legislative correspondent for the *State Record*. Benson had called from the lobby of the hotel in which David was staying in San Juno to ask for an interview, and David, partly because of the *Record*'s considerable influence and reputation, and partly because he was curious to know what sort of men Charles White employed, told him to come on up.

Benson turned out to be a sandy-haired young man who wore a jacket even in the late July heat and managed, despite a rumpled, disorderly appearance, to give himself an air of confident purposefulness.

"I don't think so," David said, in answer to Benson's request for a further statement on the Battle controversy. "I'm going to testify before his committee, and I'm going to sue him when he repeats his charges publicly. Isn't that enough?"

Benson laughed. "You don't think he really will repeat them, do you?"

"He said he would," David argued. "He agreed to."

"He agreed to do it after you testified," Benson said. "With Battle, agreeing to do something after something else happens is the same as agreeing not to do it all."

"You mean he won't do it? He'll repudiate his pledge?"

"Repudiate hell," Benson said. "He'll just forget it. You'll never hear another word about it. If you remind him of it—publicly— he'll say he's too busy saving the State from whatever he's saving it from at the moment to get involved in legal shenanigans with a man whose testimony proved he was no better than a—and then he'll put in something that means the same thing to the public as 'traitor' but isn't actionable. Then, if the public still gives a damn about you, if you aren't a dead issue by then, people will say he called you practically what he called you in the letter, so why don't you sue?"

"But he gave his word—" David protested.

"You've got a lot to learn," Benson said, "if you take Carl Baron Battle's word seriously. But," he added, "I have a feeling you're going to learn fast."

Benson had gone then—after asking once more if David would not make a further statement—and David had returned to his work and had finished it, and sent it to the printer who sent it on to the Supreme Court, which found it lacking in merit.

David was suddenly aware that the increasing altitude was bringing with it a biting cold. He pulled his elbow in and rolled up the car window, switched on the heater and felt the warm air rush across his knees. The horseshoe turn ahead banked off to the right. David put his car low down on the bank and accelerated as he went round, feeling centrifugal force lift the car up, continuing to accelerate until it seemed the rear wheels must skid, then easing off as the road straightened out and became a shiny ribbon curving upward in front of him.

The ubiquitous Mr. Finn had waited on the steps outside the Supreme Court Building for David to emerge after his appeal had been denied. He smiled and said: "We meet again," and he handed David, for the third time, a subpoena different only in the dates contained in it from the others. And David accepted the subpoena, and went again to the telegraph office. This time he made the message briefer and less polite than he had before: IMPOSSIBLE FOR ME TO APPEAR PENDING PREPARATION AND DISPOSITION OF MY PETITION FOR EXECUTIVE CLEMENCY IN CHAVEZ CASE. BLAKE.

This telegram Carl Baron Battle did not deign to favor with a personal reply. Instead he called a press conference at which he admitted that "this Blake" might be on firm ground from a technical, legal standpoint, in that so long as his client lived there were, theoretically, things that an attorney might be doing for him, and to require that the attorney take time away from these efforts in order to answer a subpoena might be to do a technical injustice to his client. "However," Battle told the press, "we're going to serve him one more time, and this time it's going to stick. Because, when we serve it, Mr. Blake's rapist friend is going to be twitching from the end of a rope."

The prediction, as it turned out, was not quite literally fulfilled. By the time Mr. Finn next made contact with David, Angel had ceased to twitch and had been pronounced dead by the prison physician, and David, acting on a power of attorney signed by Consuela, had executed the necessary forms required to send Angel's body to San Juno for burial. He was leaving the prison when Finn encountered him, and handed him the fourth subpoena, and said: "I don't suppose I'll be seeing you again."

It was in obedience to that subpoena that David presented himself, "at ten o'clock in the forenoon, of Thursday, September 4, 1948, at the main hearing room of the State Office Building in Capitol City." A uniformed guard took his subpoena from him, and led him into the hearing room. The seats set aside for spectators were about half filled, mostly, David noticed, by sharp-faced women ranging in age from forty on up.

Carl Baron Battle looked somewhat older than David had anticipated, the result, David decided, of the legislator's deep-set, tired-looking eyes. He was tall and thin, and, though his face was hairless, he somehow gave David the impression that the rest of his body was covered with the same wiry black hair that fell across his eyes when he spoke.

"I'm a little sorry you finally decided to show up, Mr. Blake," he said. "I had rather looked forward to swearing out a warrant for you."

"I'm sure you did." David tried to return Battle's empty smile but had the feeling he was failing.

"There's been a slight change in plans," Battle said. "We may not get to you today. We have a surprise witness. But I think you'll be interested in his testimony. Anyhow, I have the idea you're in no special hurry to testify."

David was about to protest that he was most anxious to testify, that he had no desire to wait in Capitol City indefinitely while Battle questioned other witnessess, but Battle had suddenly turned away to engage in a whispered conference with another man. The guard showed David to a small table at the front of the room, and David sat down there.

Carl Baron Battle rapped for order and, when the spectators had quieted down, called the roll of the committee. The four other members answered to their names. It was the last time that day any one of them was to speak.

Battle arose behind the long table and faced the audience. "Ladies and gentlemen," he said, "I am delighted to report that the elusive Mr. Blake has deigned to honor us this morning with his presence." There was laughter which Battle made no special effort to quell. "Before we hear from Mr. Blake—and I am sure this will be good news to Mr. Blake—however, we will hear from a witness who, I am frank to say, I never hoped to see in this room, and from whom I believe we may extract much pertinent information." He paused for a moment to let the crowd speculate (David presumed) as to the identity of the surprise witness, and then commanded: "Mr. Epstein, take the stand and be sworn, please."

For a moment, David did not recognize the stooped figure that walked slowly across the room to the witness chair, took the oath from the committee clerk, and sat down. Then he remembered having read or heard somewhere—had it been Barney who had told him?—that the treasurer of FAR (PC) whom he had met at the meeting in the Arena, had left the Party, or had been read out of it (there was a difference of opinion as to which it was) but had, the Party said, lost his mind as a result.

"Mr. Epstein," Battle began. "By the way," he interrupted himself, "is it 'steen' or 'steyn'?"

"Steyn," Epstein replied. "Eugene Epstein."

"Have you a middle name?"

"Yes, sir. Debs."

"I thought so," Battle said. "You were named, then, for an earlier Communist."

"Socialist," Epstein corrected shyly.

"In any event, he was finally sent to jail."

"For pacifism," Epstein pointed out.

"For participating in a draft-dodging conspiracy," Battle said. "I—"

"I beg your pardon," Epstein said. "Eugene Debs never—"

"I'm not going to debate it, Mr. Epsteen—pardon me, Epstein," Battle snapped. The crowd laughed at the error, and David realized suddenly that Battle had made it intentionally.

"But—"

"You just answer the questions, Mr. Eugene Debs Epstein," Battle suggested, "and I'm sure we'll get along fine."

"Yes, sir." Epstein seemed painfully anxious to please.

"We may as well begin with the jackpot question. Are you now, or have you ever been, a member of the Communist Party?"

"Yes, sir," Epstein said. "I joined the Party in 1926. I remained a member until about three weeks ago."

"But you are not a member now?"

"No, sir."

"I am told that you are anxious to make amends for the harm you did your country—your adopted country, that is—during the time you were a party to this conspiracy. Is that right?"

"Yes, sir."

"And that is why you are here?"

"Yes, sir."

"Tell me, Mr. Epstein, does the name 'Minnie Alston' mean anything to you?"

Epstein stared at the floor. The crowd began to whisper. "Yes, sir," he said at last. "She was my wife."

"Is that all you can tell us about her?"

"I don't understand."

"I'll put it very simply. Was she a white woman?"

"She was a Negro," Epstein mumbled.

"I beg your pardon."

Epstein repeated his answer.

"That was in line with the Communist view on intermarriage between the races, was it not?"

"No, sir."

"You mean the Party opposes such marriage?"

"No, sir. The Party has no views on intermarriage."

"But it opposes segregation?"

"Yes, sir."

"And discrimination?"

"Yes, sir."

"And, of course, if you chose a wife on the basis of race, that would be discrimination."

"Well, you see, sir—"

"Would it or wouldn't it?"

"I can't answer it that way," Epstein said miserably.

"Then don't answer it at all," Battle said grandly. "You're here voluntarily. I'm not going to press you on that sort of question. Where is Minnie Alston Epstein now?"

"She's dead," Epstein said.

"How did she die?"

"She killed herself."

"Would you tell us where she killed herself?"

"In—in jail."

"I take it she wasn't just visiting there?"

"No. She was under arrest."

"On what charge?"

"They never brought her to trial," Epstein said frantically. "The charge was never proved."

"Of course not," Battle said. "She killed herself before they could bring her to trial. What was the charge?"

"It was just a formality," Epstein said. "Just a charge that they used, when there was no—"

"What was the charge, Mr. Epstein?"

"Being a public woman," Epstein said.

"A public woman," Battle echoed. "What we would call, in this State, a lewd-vag."

"No," Epstein shouted. "It wasn't like that at all. That was just a made-up charge. They had to use something. The Governor himself—"

"Shut up!" Battle roared. Epstein subsided. "I'm sorry if I was rude," Battle went on more calmly, "but we don't want a lot of detail on this. After all, it's just background."

"But you've got to be fair," Epstein argued.

"I don't 'got to' do anything," Battle retorted. "The Party isn't running this meeting. I am. And I intend to ask questions and get answers, not speeches. You think you can do that?"

"Yes, sir," Epstein said meekly. David suddenly remembered the Minnie Epstein case, and the finding of the commission appointed by the Governor of the southern State where it had occurred, which commission had found that the charge "being a public woman" was used, in the town where the tragedy had taken place, as a formality in placing under arrest all unescorted Negro women found in the white section of the town at night. Battle was inquiring into Epstein's family.

"I have one brother," Epstein said.

"What is his name?"

"Harvey Emmons."

"Emmons?" Battle's eyebrows went up in mock-bewilderment. Then he nodded as if he had figured something out. "Oh," he said. "I guess he got tired of explaining whether it was steen or steyn, so he changed it. That right?"

"Not quite." Epstein was trying to smile too. "He thought the name might handicap him."

"Has it handicapped you?"

"No. It hasn't."

"I shouldn't think it would, in New York." Battle paused and waited for the laughter to die away. "What does your brother do?" he asked.

"He teaches school."

"Where?"

"I'd rather not say."

"I'd rather you did."

Epstein named the city and school at which he worked, and Battle, half jokingly, raised the question of whether, if Epstein were asked the same question the following day, he could truthfully give the same answer.

The questioning continued in this vein throughout the morning session. Battle inquired into collateral branches of Epstein's family and that of his brother's wife, and into Epstein's business associates and friends. When the hour for the noon recess arrived, Battle was discussing with Epstein his life at college before he joined the Party, and trying, without success, to get him to name the teacher or teachers who had subverted him.

As Battle led his legislative colleagues out of the room, David saw a man at the press table get up and come over toward him. When the man came near, he saw that it was Will Benson.

"He's rough, isn't he?" There was no need for Benson to state to whom he referred. "You think you can handle him?"

"I think so," Davis said, trying to make his tone convey a self-confidence he did not feel.

"I hear it'll be more interesting this afternoon," Benson said. "From your point of view, anyhow. He's going to go into the Chavez case."

As the afternoon wore on, it began to appear that Benson had been misinformed. Battle continued to direct his questions to the distant past, trying to get Epstein to recall who had signed this appeal, who had appeared on the dais at that public meeting, who had been present when this or that discussion was held, and who was responsible for the decisions taken. Epstein, at Battle's insistence, was naming names, a great many of them, but Battle's dissatisfaction with the names brought forth was evident. Most of them were associated, even in David's mind, with Party activity.

Three o'clock came, and three-thirty, and Battle's questioning had still only reached the middle thirties. David stirred in his seat. Epstein declared that he could not recall exactly when and how it had been determined that the support for the Spanish loyalists was to be organized on the basis of a "popular front."

"All right," Battle said. "Let's leave that for a moment. You were, until recently, the treasurer of the New York People's Party, were you not?"

"I was."

"Which is the New York arm of the Party. Is that right?"

"Not exactly," Epstein said. "The New York People's Party is an independent—"

"Well, forget about the exactly business. Isn't what I said substantially correct? At any rate, as treasurer of the New York People's Party, you would know the financial details of any fundraising in which the People's Party participated."

"Yes, sir."

"And the Chavez case was such a cause?"

"That's right."

"How much money would you say was raised in the various appeals for the Chavez defense fund?"

"I couldn't say exactly," Epstein said. "It was still coming in when I left."

"Three weeks ago. The case was over then, wasn't it?"

"Yes," Epstein explained. "But we had some pledges outstanding. Some people won't honor a pledge in circumstances like that. Others will. Naturally, it's hard for me to say—"

"Well, give us an approximate figure then. How much was raised—approximately—that you know about?"

"I know about it all," Epstein pointed out. "When the Party takes part in fund raising, it manages to keep a pretty close accounting."

"All right then," Battle said. "As of the time you left, how much, approximately, had been raised for the Chavez case?"

"Approximately," Epstein said, "three hundred and twenty thousand dollars."

David, who had tipped his chair forward, felt it slide from under him as he stiffened in astonishment, and made a quick grab for it to keep from falling. Battle looked over at him in amusement. "How much of that," he asked, "was diverted to other Party purposes?"

"About two hundred thousand," Epstein declared.

"And the remainder—that would be a hundred and twenty thousand?"

"That was sent out to the Chavez defense in San Juno."

"To whom, exactly?"

"To Barney Castle, I should think."

"Was any of it sent directly to David Blake?"

"I don't think so," Epstein said. "Castle was in New York most of the time. It was easier to give it to him and let him take care of his partner."

David counted up, in his mind, the various checks Barney had sent him, and the sums of money Barney had given him in cash. The discrepancy, if Epstein was telling the truth, was nearly a hundred thousand dollars.

"Before we get done," Battle said, "we're going to account for every quarter of that money. In New York *and* in San Juno.

How," he asked, "did you happen to get interested in the case in the first place?"

"We'd been on the lookout for such a case for a long time," Epstein said. "The Party had never made much headway among the Mexicans. Also, we needed money badly. We'd let it be known that we were prepared to enter a case if it met our requirements."

"Which were?"

"That the defendant be a Mexican. That he be charged with something that would make for wide publicity coverage. That the case against him be something less than airtight."

"Wasn't there one other requirement?"

"I don't think so." Epstein scratched his head. "Oh yes," he said suddenly. "We didn't want a case that would end with an acquittal."

"In other words, it had to be a hopeless case?"

"Yes. In a way."

"What do you mean, in a way? You didn't want a case that would end in an acquittal. That means you wanted a hopeless case."

"Yes."

"Or did it mean one that would become hopeless after you people got in it?"

Epstein flared. "I resent that," he said. "I resent it most—"

"Forget it," Battle commanded. "Don't get upset. I'll withdraw the question. Now, exactly how did this Chavez case come to your attention?"

"I received a telephone call from Barney Castle. He wanted to know—"

"Just a minute." Battle raised his hand to cut Epstein off. "When was this?"

"On June sixth," Epstein replied.

"That would be the morning after the murder."

"After the incident," Epstein corrected.

"After the incident," Battle agreed, "which the jury called murder. All right. Go ahead."

"He said he'd heard of a case that might interest us, and he wanted to know if he should intervene."

"Just go ahead and give us the conversation as you remember it," Battle instructed.

"Well, he told me about the case. Said it met all our requirements. The Mexican boy, the sex angle. It was ideal for us, he said. He even said there was a continuing interest."

"Hold it," Battle commanded. "What did he mean by that?"

"He meant that we'd have something left after the case was over. Something that would justify all the expense and trouble we'd have to go to to handle the case."

"Did he tell you what the continuing interest was?"

"Yes. He said the boy's mother could be used as a rallying point for years after her son was executed."

David's stomach turned over twice, once at the thought of Consuela, who was, if Epstein was to be believed, to be deliberately remade in the roll of a martyr, and again at the thought that Epstein was attributing to Barney the making of plans to be implemented "after her son was executed" on the morning after Marie Wiltse's death.

At Battle's urging, Epstein went on with his report of the conversation. He had, he reported, been lukewarm to Barney's proposal. "I told him he couldn't handle it himself. I said he was too well known among the non-Party people we'd have to canvass for money. I said we'd consider it, if he got a local man to do the actual courtroom work, someone who hadn't been associated with this sort of thing before."

"In other words," Battle suggested, "a front."

"I wouldn't call it that," Epstein said.

"What would you call it?"

"Just what I said," Epstein said testily. "Someone to do the actual courtroom work."

"While you and Barney Castle pulled the strings. But not a front." Battle threw up his hands. "Let's not quibble," he said. "Go on. What did he say to that?"

"He said that that was all right with him, and he'd undertake to find somebody. But he said he wanted a commitment from me before he did anything else. I told him I'd rather wait until he found his man, and in the meantime I'd investigate the case further myself. He said if we did that, we'd run the risk of missing out on the case entirely. Miss the bus, that was the way he put it. I said if we missed this bus, we could always catch the next one. He asked me what made me sure there would be a next one. He said this might be the last bus, and did I want to take the responsibility for letting it go by. He seemed pretty sure of himself, so I told him to go ahead."

Battle said something in reply, and then turned and spoke to the spectators, but David did not hear him. Epstein's recountal of the exchange about missing the bus had a familiar ring to it, and, an instant after he heard Epstein's account of it, he knew where he had heard the phrase used, and when, and that he had recorded it in his journal after he had heard it while he waited in Barney's outer office. "Jesus Christ! What makes you think there'll be another bus?" Those had been the first words he had ever heard Barney Castle say. And then there had been a pause, and then Barney had said: "I'll take the responsibility," and the conversation had ended. David was filled with rage at Barney, but greater than the rage was the shame at the thought of his having walked into that office a few minutes after Barney had been informed of the need for a cat's-paw and offering, in effect, to serve as such. It must have seemed almost too pat to Barney, and David wondered if Barney had suspected him of being a plant.

David forced himself to concentrate on what Battle was saying. He heard the words: ". . . will stand in recess, then, until a week from Monday at ten o'clock," and saw the gavel fall, and saw

Battle lead his colleagues away, as the spectators began to push toward the exits.

Will Benson came over to him. "I missed that last," David said. "How come the long recess?"

"They want a long weekend," Benson explained. "And Monday's Labor Day. That only gives them four days to work next week, and the committee members are all up for re-election. They'd like to get home for a week. Also, Battle has some speaking engagements, though he didn't mention that."

"I'm not going to stick around here all that time," David said angrily, though he was aware that he was wrong to direct his anger at Benson, who had nothing to do with the long recess, nothing to do with David's being in Capitol City at all.

"You are going to go to San Juno for the rally?" Benson asked.

"Rally?"

Benson produced a newspaper and passed it to David. David read the item to which Benson's thumb directed him.

LABOR DAY MEMORIAL
PLANNED FOR ANGEL

San Juno Municipal Park on Monday afternoon will be the scene of the first of a series of rallies honoring the memory of Angel Chavez, who died three weeks ago as a victim of what local progressive leaders termed a "legal lynching." The principal speaker will be Consuela Chavez, who announced this morning that she will attend "because Angel would have wanted me to." Tickets may be obtained at any Labor Bookstore, or at the law office of Barney Castle, rally chairman. Castle announced that box lunches, containing authentic Mexican frijoles and tamales, will be available on the grounds.

"No," David said, trying to keep from shouting. "I'm not going to any god damn rally."

"Look," Benson said. "I want to talk to you. Why don't you go up to my hotel room, and I'll meet you there in a little while? You look like you could use a little rest anyhow."

Why not, David thought. What could he lose? He had nowhere else to go in any case, and it would be better to talk to Benson than to sit somewhere alone, with only his self-reproach for company. He took the key Benson proffered him, and listened to Benson's directions for reaching the hotel.

The moon, which had been only occasionally visible as David drove up the long ascent, came into full view as, reaching the summit of the pass, David could look down into the valley below, see the road down which he would drive twisting its way in looping zigzags along the mountainside. A car, David suddenly thought, if driven through one of those zigzags too quickly, would plunge through the narrow guard rail and onto the boulders which marked the eastern face of the mountain. Another gambling house billboard showed tow skiers and the words: RENO Just For FUN, and below it the legend: 44 Mi. David felt the car accelerate as the road turned down below him, and he made no effort to diminish his speed, holding the accelerator where it had been during the ascent, fighting to hold the car on the road, but doing nothing to make that fight needless.

It was dark by the time Benson came to the hotel room, bringing with him sandwiches and coffee. They ate and drank in silence, and then Benson said: "You figure when you get on that stand, you're just going to tell the truth?"

David nodded. "The whole story," he said. "Just the way it happened. The way I thought things were at the time, and the way I came to find out what they really were. I made mistakes, and I'm going to make people understand that that's just what they were."

Benson smiled. "What's Battle going to be doing while you're telling your story?" he asked.

David stared at him blankly.

"Don't you realize," Benson demanded, "that if I'd asked Epstein last night what I just asked you, he'd have given me the same answer? And he'd have meant it just as sincerely as you do. You can't tell the whole truth with a guy like Battle badgering you, picking up little points, making you answer impossible yes-or-no questions."

"Epstein had something to hide," David argued. "I don't."

"What Epstein had to hide," Benson declared, "he hid. Battle got him to tell the lies Battle wanted told just by asking the right questions and getting truthful answers."

"That doesn't make sense," David protested.

"Maybe not. But what about Epstein? What does the public know about him that it didn't know yesterday? I'll tell you," Benson went on. "That he married a Negress in order to carry out a Party policy of miscegenation. That his wife killed herself when they caught her whoring. And neither one of those things happens to be true."

"But—"

"But nothing. It doesn't make any difference what you decide to testify to. When Battle questions a witness, that witness tells the lies that Battle wants him to tell. Exactly those lies. No others, and never the truth."

"Epstein was scared," David said. "That's why—"

"He was," Benson admitted. "But scared or bold, the result would have been the same. Here. I'll show you what I mean. You're not scared of me, are you?"

"No."

"Then I'll show you how Battle does it. Remember, you're under oath. During the trial, you made a trip to New York, didn't you?"

"Yes."

"Although you were so busy you couldn't appear before this committee."

"The trip was in connection with the trial."

"How? Were you looking for a missing witness?"

"No. I—"

"Doing research on some rare point of law that couldn't have been done elsewhere?"

"No."

"As a matter of fact, didn't you go merely to speak at a fund-raising rally?"

"That's right."

"You consider that 'in connection with the trial.' "

"We needed the money. You can't run a case without money."

"How much money had been raised up to that time?"

"I don't know," David said, suddenly seeing what Benson was getting at.

"Do you know now?"

"No."

"But you knew you needed more?"

"I knew how much—"

"You can answer yes or no, can't you?" Benson asked.

"No," David protested. "I can't."

"Nonsense. The question is: You know you needed more? Either you did know, or you didn't?"

"I knew I needed more," David said, "because—"

"Shut up!" Benson shouted, capturing in his shout all of the savagery with which Battle had interrupted Epstein. He smiled suddenly. "You get the idea?" he asked. "Here. Let's go a little further with this. You say you didn't know—when you went to New York—how much had been raised, but you knew more was needed. Right?"

"I knew we were running dry in San Juno," David blurted quickly.

"But you didn't know how much had been raised in New York?"

"No."

"And you didn't ask?"

"No."

290

"Why not?"

"I assumed they'd sent me all they had."

"Do you still assume that?"

"No."

"Good. As a matter of fact, if I tell you that, at that time, over $100,000 had been raised, nearly five times what the entire case cost the defense, would you believe me?"

"I think so," David said.

"You wouldn't regard it as absolutely incredible, at any rate?"

"No."

"But rather than inquire if money had already been raised that should have been available to you, you went East to help these people—who, it now turns out, were holding out on you—to raise more money which, according to you, you never got?"

"I never got?"

"All right," Benson conceded. "Most of which you never got."

"I can't answer it that way," David protested.

"Of course you can," Benson snapped. "There were two things you could have done. One: write or phone or whatever it was and ask if there wasn't money available to you. Two: go East and help raise more without asking if it was needed. I'm asking you which course you chose."

"You know which course I chose," David said. "I went East."

"And I'm asking you now if you didn't choose that course in preference to the other. You can answer that, can't you?"

"No, sir."

"Mr. Blake." Benson's tone became cold and a little threatening. "Please answer yes or no. Did you go East to raise money rather than ask whether there was already money available?"

"I can't answer."

"You are directed to answer. And you are warned that failure to answer may result in a contempt citation being issued against you."

David was silent.

"Go ahead," Benson said. He smiled and spoke in his own voice. "Or can't you?"

"I can't," David admitted.

"Well," Benson said. "You'll have to. And while you're doing it, that's when you're going to get the truth across. That's your theory. But let me tell you something: when you step down from that stand, you're going to be the guy who sold out his client, stole (or at least can't account for) $100,000, took part in a conspiracy to stir up racial hatred in the State. And that's only the beginning. Everybody who knew you, before or after you entered the Chavez case, is going to have to start explaining just *how* he knew you, and what his excuse for knowing you was, and that he didn't really know you very well, and those explanations are going to have to be made over and over, and in many cases they won't work. Don't talk about telling the whole story on the stand, because that's just whistling in the dark. And too many people are going to get hurt for you to be spending your time doing that. Do you believe me?"

David thought carefully before he answered. It was incredible that a man who was, as he was, substantially innocent of any charge, against whom the most devastating possible accusation was one of naïveté, could be destroyed simply by a public examination under oath at the hands of a man like Carl Baron Battle. He weighed the incredibility of it on the one hand, and on the other the ease with which Benson, who had access only to information that was public knowledge or semipublic knowledge, had done the very thing he maintained—and David now believed—Battle would try to do. David closed his eyes and saw Battle questioning him on other matters. Q: Do you know now that you should have asked for a change of venue? A: Yes. Q: Didn't you know it then? A: No. Q: What is your occupation? A: I am an assistant professor of law. Q: What sort of law? A: Criminal law. Q: Do you wish to leave your answer as it is—that you did not know what the Supreme Court called quote an elementary principle of law close quote that where the defendant's rights are impaired by local prejudice, he must ask for a change of venue? A: Yes. Q: Did you ever suggest to your associates that a change of venue be asked for? A: Yes. Q: Why did you do that, if you didn't know the law on the point. A: —

"Yes," David said. "I believe you."

"Then you must believe," Benson said, "that you are in trouble, deep trouble, just about as deep as a man, in this day and age, can get into." Benson said the words slowly, heavily, syllable by syllable, as if what he was saying were some sort of code, a password. "Did anybody ever tell you that before?" David stared at him.

"A man told you that," Benson continued, "and you didn't believe him, and he said when you did you should come and talk to him. Well, you believe it now, don't you?"

David nodded.

"Don't you think you ought to let him help you?" Benson asked.

David hesitated only momentarily. "What can I lose?" he asked.

"Exactly," Benson replied. "What can you lose?"

Suddenly the telephone on the table between them rang.

The moon had passed overhead and dropped behind the mountain at David's back. The hairpin curves were behind him now, and ahead of him the road slanted down as it cut through the foothills toward the floor of the Truckee Valley. At the end of the long straight decline, David knew, there was a sharp turn and a narrow bridge across the Truckee. A highway sign, rushing by, flashed to his consciousness the words: USE LOW GEAR DESCENDING HILL. David tramped hard on the accelerator and watched the speedometer needle as it climbed past 60, past 70. A red warning light, installed by the manufacturer to warn the driver of excessive speed, blinked on. David turned the dashboard lights off, but the red light alone continued to shine.

"Send him up," Will Benson said. Then he put the phone down. "You know anybody named Robinson?" he asked.

"I don't think so," David replied.

"Neither do I," Benson said. "But he's coming up to see me. At least that's what he says. I think maybe he wants to see you."

"Maybe he's from the committee," David said. "They might want to serve me with another subpoena, now that they're having an adjournment."

"The same subpoena holds good," Benson said, and David knew that this was right. "Anyhow, there's nobody with the committee named Robinson."

A knock on the door made further discussion impossible as well as useless. Benson went to answer it. He returned in a moment, followed by another man. "He does want to see you," Benson said.

"I've got to talk to you, David," the man said.

"Terry." He had changed, had Terry Bliss. David might have passed this gaunt, thin, tired man on the street without recognizing him as the man whom he would have described, if asked three months before—whom he would still describe—as his best friend.

"I've got to talk to you," Terry Bliss repeated. He glanced significantly at Will Benson.

David was about to explain that Benson's discretion could be trusted. But Benson spoke first.

"I've got to go," he said. "You know where to find our friend, don't you?"

"He gave me a card," David said. "It's up in San Juno. I remember everything except the name of the—"

"Here." Benson cut him off sharply and handed him a card.

David tucked it in his pocket. "Slam the door when you go," Benson said. "It's a spring lock. I'll be seeing you."

"How's Ethel?" David asked, when Benson had gone. "And Ilene?"

"They're fine," Bliss replied. "But I didn't come here to talk about them."

"Go ahead then," David said. "Talk about whatever you did come to talk about."

Bliss cleared his throat. "First of all," he said. "I've got to fill you in on what I've done. I told Dean Paley that you'd asked for an unpaid leave of absence."

"What? Terry, you had no right—"

"I had every right," Bliss said. "I told him you wanted to be free to testify before Battle without seeming to speak for the University."

"Christ, Terry!" David said. "I'm broke. You know I can't get along without—"

"I'll tell you what I know about you," Terry Bliss said coldly. "I know you've filled your pockets with lead shot and jumped into the ocean. I just want to see that you don't take any of your friends down with you. Me, especially."

"Maybe it would be better if we skipped the metaphors," David said. "What are you getting at?"

"I'll lay it out for you, David," Bliss said. "I still believe you're essentially a decent man."

"Thanks."

Bliss ignored the interruption. "If you don't ask for the leave of absence—without pay—" he explained, "they'll have you up on charges. There'll be a hearing. Your application for employment will be brought up. I signed that application. I brought you to the University."

"Of course you did," David admitted. "And I've always been grateful to you for it."

"This way," Bliss went on, "there won't be any hearing. David, the University's been under attack for a long time. You must know that the Law School will have to get rid of you before Battle closes in."

"I don't see why I should have to give up my right to a hearing," David said. "It would be different if I were guilty of anything."

"A hearing means controversy," Bliss pointed out. "The University'll have to show where it stands in that controversy. There's only one way it can do that. That's by pitching you out, and pitching out everybody who had anything to do with getting you in in the first place."

One month's pay, David decided, really wasn't that important. "All right," he said. "I'll take a suspension then. But I'm going to apply for reinstatement after I testify. I've got to. If I don't—"

"David," Bliss said, keeping his voice low, but speaking with an intensity David had never before heard in a human voice, "if you've got one ounce of decency in you, you won't do either one."

"Either one?"

"Apply for reinstatement," Bliss said, "or testify."

"You're talking nonsense!" David shouted. "How can I not testify?"

"I make eighty-five hundred dollars a year, David," Bliss went on calmly, "and when I make department head, I go up to ten. That'll be in about three years."

"How?" David demanded. "How do I avoid testifying?"

Bliss might not have heard him. "It's taken me a long time to get where I am," he said. "Are you going to destroy me in a day?"

"Talk sense," David blurted.

"I'm forty-seven years old, David," Bliss went on. "It's hard to start over when you're forty-seven. Ilene's a sophomore at Bennington. I want to keep her there."

David stood up and grabbed Terry Bliss by the arm. "How do I avoid testifying?" he demanded.

"You've got to," Bliss said. "If you have any respect for friendship, you've got to."

"How?"

"By refusing to answer," Bliss said.

"By refusing to answer what?"

"Any and all questions. Except," Bliss added, "your name. If they ask you that, you can answer."

"I really think you're carrying friendship a little far," David said. "I'd hate to see you lose your job, Terry, but you're asking me to go to prison for life."

"No I'm not," Bliss said. "You don't have to answer any question. Your constitutional privilege—"

"But I'm not guilty of anything."

"It doesn't matter," Bliss insisted. "You're the sole judge of whether a question might be incriminating."

David laughed. "You're telling me, seriously, that if Battle asks me where I went to school, I refuse to answer because my answer might incriminate me?"

"That's right." Bliss did not smile. "Your Fifth Amendment privilege," he explained, "doesn't only apply to a particular question which might produce an incriminating answer. It applies to all preliminary questions leading up to it. The earlier questions, while innocuous in themselves, may be links in a chain leading to an incriminating one, and, under the law, you don't have to supply any link at all."

"But I'm not guilty of anything," David declared. "So no question could possibly be incriminating."

"It doesn't matter," Bliss insisted. "You're the sole judge of whether a question is incriminating, or whether it might be a link in an incriminating chain. And no court will go behind your judgment. They can't ask you *why* a question would incriminate you, because, if the question would incriminate you, so would your explanation."

"In other words," David said, "you're asking me to lie under oath, but you assure me that I can't be caught at it."

"Don't be so smug and moral!" Bliss shouted. "I don't know where that hundred thousand went, and I don't care. All I know is that you have a perfect right—and an obvious one, in view of the hundred thousand—to refuse to answer. If you choose to destroy me—and everyone else who ever knew you—by answering questions anyhow, I can't stop you. You did what you did—you gave Battle his opening. And now you sit here priggish and self-righteous and bleat about morals and perjury, and I have to beg you for mercy. For God's sake, David! What are you? Are you just a morality calculating machine? Isn't there any man in you?" He stopped abruptly. "I'm sorry," he said. "I shouldn't have said that. We all have to live with our consciences, and if I have to suffer and my family has to suffer because of yours, well, that's just the way it is. But think it over, David."

Suddenly, as the steel guardrail that marked the turn in the road loomed close, David finished thinking it over. What he had been about to do, he knew in an instant, was wrong, and in the same instant that he knew, that he realized that his death would only vindicate Battle and not help Bliss or any of the others, he drove his foot down on the brake pedal. The road swung crazily in front of him, and David eased his foot up and down, trying to come out of the skid, and yet continuing to slow the car down. Finally he felt the bumpy shoulder under his wheels, and then he was over it, slowing rapidly in the sandy soil that lay between the road and the river bank. It was warm by the river bank. David pushed the button that lowered the car's top and felt the warm breeze. He would, he knew, be in Reno shortly before daybreak.

11

Reno came and went quickly in a flash of pastel neon and two sharp turns, and now David was on U.S. 40, running beside the Truckee toward Sparks, watching for the sign that would mark "White's House."

He wanted to think that Charles White could help him, but he could not make himself believe that this was so. He was making this trip because making it was a definite act, because not to make it would have been to sit back and await inevitable destruction, but he had no faith in White's ability to save him, even though his salvation was, as White had predicted it would be, a matter of making use of the facts he knew, and it was in this field that the old man claimed to be expert.

Now David knew, when it was too late for the knowing to do him any good, that he should have gone with Abbe that night and not back to the shack, that he had failed, by going back, to save Angel, and that his failure was inevitable, and that he had, by going back, allowed to slip past his last opportunity to disassociate himself from what had been done to Angel, even though that disassociation might only have been to his satisfaction and might have made no difference so far as Carl Baron Battle was concerned. All this he had known for some time, and he had been tempted to call Abbe and tell her, but, though he had gone so far as to find out where she was staying (in a hotel in San Francisco) and even, on one occasion, to call the hotel on the telephone and ask if she was registered, he had said "No, thank you" when the clerk asked if he wished to be connected, and he had left no message.

The word WHITE glinted back at him in the darkness and David braked, and reversed, and found that it was written on a mailbox. A dirt road ran off the highway beside the mailbox. David drove along it. Ten minutes later he came to the house, and in another five minutes he sat in the living room and drank coffee and talked to Charles White, who had greeted him as casually as if this were not six o'clock in the morning, and as if David were not four hundred miles from where he was supposed to be.

"You bring your journal with you?" White asked.

"It's in here," David said numbly, indicating his brief case.

"Let's see it."

David, who had never shown his journal to anyone, who would have regarded even Abbe's seeing it as a violation of his own individuality, handed it over.

White read rapidly through it, smiling now and then, and occasionally frowning and half whistling as if there were something there he did not entirely understand. When he was done, he handed it back to David.

"It's just what I hoped it would be," White said. "But I was afraid you'd turn out to be a writer."

"I don't understand."

"A writer would have put art into it," White explained. "You didn't. Oh, you tried all right. Some of those descriptive passages. But you failed. This thing is obviously a series of impressions, and a record of events, set down at the time the impressions were made and the events occurred. And completely truthful. Everybody who reads it will know that."

"Everybody who reads it?" David was outraged.

White ignored him. "There's no art in it," he repeated. "That's why everybody'll know it's the truth as you saw it. Art would have suggested that you went back afterward to change things, make the writing even and the opinions consistent. They're not. You like this room?" he asked abruptly.

David looked around him. It occurred to him that he might say of the room what Charles White had said of his journal, that there was no art in it. Only what was needed was there. Two chairs. The desk. Bookshelves. A ceiling fixture that cast a light on the desk and the chair behind it. A lamp on top of the bookcase that illuminated the rest of the room.

"Yes," David said. "I like it."

"Good," White said. "You're going to work here."

"Doing what?" David asked.

Charles White produced a pipe from his pocket, filled it, lit it, and began to talk. At first what he was saying did not make sense to David, but as he went along, David began to understand. The whole thing, White said, turned on the matter of truth. Truth, abstract truth, had, he said, fallen into bad repute, and the world had a tendency to look down on those who regarded it as important. But in their hearts, he said, all people respected the truth, and would choose it over a lie any time, if given the choice.

"Barney and Battle, and the people like them," Charles White said, "deal in lies—their own, each other's, the lies of third parties —these are their stock in trade. You and I deal in truth—absolute truth, as a matter of fact, even if some people say there is no such thing, because we believe what we say when we say it, and that is speaking absolute truth, at least as I understand it."

David, who had learned long ago that what White was describing was not absolute truth at all, but only relative truth, started to speak. But he did not. It suddenly seemed to him that what he had been taught was not itself true.

"Touch Battle—or Barney—with the truth, and he collapses,"

White said. "It's as if they were werewolves, and the truth the silver stake at midnight on the crossroads. You've just got to find some way to hit them with the truth."

"According to Benson, Battle'll use the truth to make me lie, if he gets me on the stand," David pointed out. "And," he added, "I think he's right."

"Of course he's right." White lit a match and applied it to his balky pipe. "The witness stand's no place for truth," he snorted. "Not if there aren't any rules, and Battle's doing the questioning."

"Then—"

"It's no good waiting till you're through testifying," White said. "You'll be a discredited man then, and a discredited man isn't listened to, even when he tells the truth. No, sir. It's got to be now."

"What does?"

"I would have sent for you sooner," White said, "and I suspect you might have come, especially if I'd done some little trick to show you how much I knew. But it wouldn't have worked. I knew you had to come by yourself."

"Benson helped a little," David said.

"But you made the decision," White said. "And you came alone, which is good, because it means the decision is your own. Well, you ready to go to work?"

"Doing what?"

"Haven't you guessed?"

David admitted that he hadn't.

"Writing it all down," White said. "The Chavez case as you know it, from the beginning right up to now. Just the way it happened. How you got into it, what decisions you made, and who helped make them. What you thought of the other people at the beginning, and how those opinions changed, if they did. Everything. And, wherever you can, I want it documented with references from the journal. Word for word, even when you know

302

the words don't make sense. Because they made sense when you wrote them, and you've got to make it clear that they did. Some things you still don't know about, and I'll have to fill you in on them."

"Like what?" David demanded.

"A lot of things." White leafed through the journal. "You've libeled Sam Wiltse, for instance. He didn't tip Wells off about the funeral."

"Who did?" David asked.

White smiled at him. "I won't even give you three guesses," he said. "Just one. And this bit about Jiminez. Didn't you know—no, I guess you didn't."

"Know what?"

"What Barney's got on him. It has to be something, the way he backed out of the case on Barney's say-so. You want to know?"

David nodded.

"It doesn't really matter," White said. "Jiminez just happens to be in the country illegally. But I don't want to tell you too much. Can you do it?"

"Do what?"

"Write what I'm asking you for. A full account of everything."

"I guess so," David said. "But it'll take time."

"It can't take too much time," White said.

"Why?"

"Because we're going to print it in the *Record*," White said impatiently. "We'll have to run it in installments, and we've only got six issues before you're supposed to testify. I hate to run important stuff on Saturday, so I'd like it in five sections, starting Monday. That means I'll need the first section by noon tomorrow, and a section every day until it's finished."

White got up and came over to David's side, and lifted a leaf in front of the desk, and pushed the leaf back so that a typewriter came up to desk level. "There's paper in the drawer," he said. "You better get going."

David sat staring at the machine.

"Get going," White repeated. "The first move is to put paper in it."

Still David did not move.

"What's the matter with you?" White demanded. "Aren't you going to do it?"

"I don't see what good it will do," David said. He ought to have known better than to suspect that any man, even this old man who was, in many ways, quite remarkable, would be able to solve a problem that was patently unsolvable.

"You mean you won't do it on faith?" White asked. "Because I tell you it's the thing to do?"

David shook his head. "I'm tired," he said. "I'm very—"

"Too tired to do the one thing that can get you out of this?" White demanded. "Too tired to save yourself when the means for salvation is at hand?"

"I don't see it," David said. "I don't see what difference it would make."

"Then I'll tell you," White said a little angrily. "Until you write this—until I print it—the truth, as you know it, does not exist, except for you. As far as Battle is concerned, you're a blank slate, and as far as the rest of the world is concerned, they either don't care or they accept whatever Battle writes on you—on the slate—as truth. That's what Battle likes, to put his lies up against nothing, against ignorance. But they won't stand up against the truth."

"What do you think'll happen then, if I write this?" David said.

"If you write it the way I told you to, I know what'll happen," White declared. "There are too many people around that Battle can question starting from scratch, without other people wondering: Why doesn't he ask him this? or: That doesn't answer this. You'll go back there in ten days, and the chief counsel will tell you your testimony's been postponed for a month. And when you get back there in a month, it'll have been postponed indefinitely, and Battle'll be investigating something else—veterans' organizations, the way I hear it—and you'll have beaten him, and everybody'll know it."

"What makes you so sure of this?" David asked.

"I've been around a while," White said, "and I've kept my eyes open. I've seen Battle and people like him operating for years. I never knew one of them that didn't curl up and die if somebody else got in the first lick. Maybe it won't work this time. Maybe you won't get your job back, either. But I think you will."

"Why?" David asked.

"Because Dean Paley doesn't really feel too strongly about you one way or the other. All Brother Paley wants is to be let alone so he can log up a few more years toward his pension. As long as Battle and his crew are hollering for your head, Paley's ready to throw you overboard. The minute they lose interest in you, he becomes reasonable."

Outside, the dawn was breaking. "All right," David said suddenly. "I'll do it."

"Good boy," White said. "But remember, it's all got to be in there. Every decision, even the ones you made wrong. *Especially* the ones you made wrong."

"I understand," David said.

"Even," White said slowly, "the decision not to ask for a change of venue."

David, who had been about to reach into a drawer for some paper, stopped short. "I can't do that," he said. "That's not for me to reveal."

"Not without permission," White said. "But why don't you

ask for permission. You might," he pointed out, "be able to get some stenographic help at the same time."

Suddenly, without a further word, Charles White left the room, closing the door behind him. David sat for a few minutes, motionless, staring at the telephone on the desk. Then he picked it up.

"Operator," he said. "I want to make a long distance call. To San Francisco, California."